Five Nights at Freddy's™

THE SILVER EYES

The Graphic Novel

BY SCOTT CAWTHON AND
KIRA BREED-WRISLEY

ADAPTED AND ILLUSTRATED BY CLAUDIA SCHRÖDER
COLORS BY LAURIE SMITH

ISBN 978-1-338-29848-2 (paperback)
ISBN 978-1-338-62717-6 (hardcover)
ISBN 978-1-4071-9846-0 (UK paperback)

10 9 8 7   21 22 23 24

Printed in China   62

First printing 2020

Edited by Michael Petranek and Chloe Fraboni • Book design by Betsy Peterschmidt

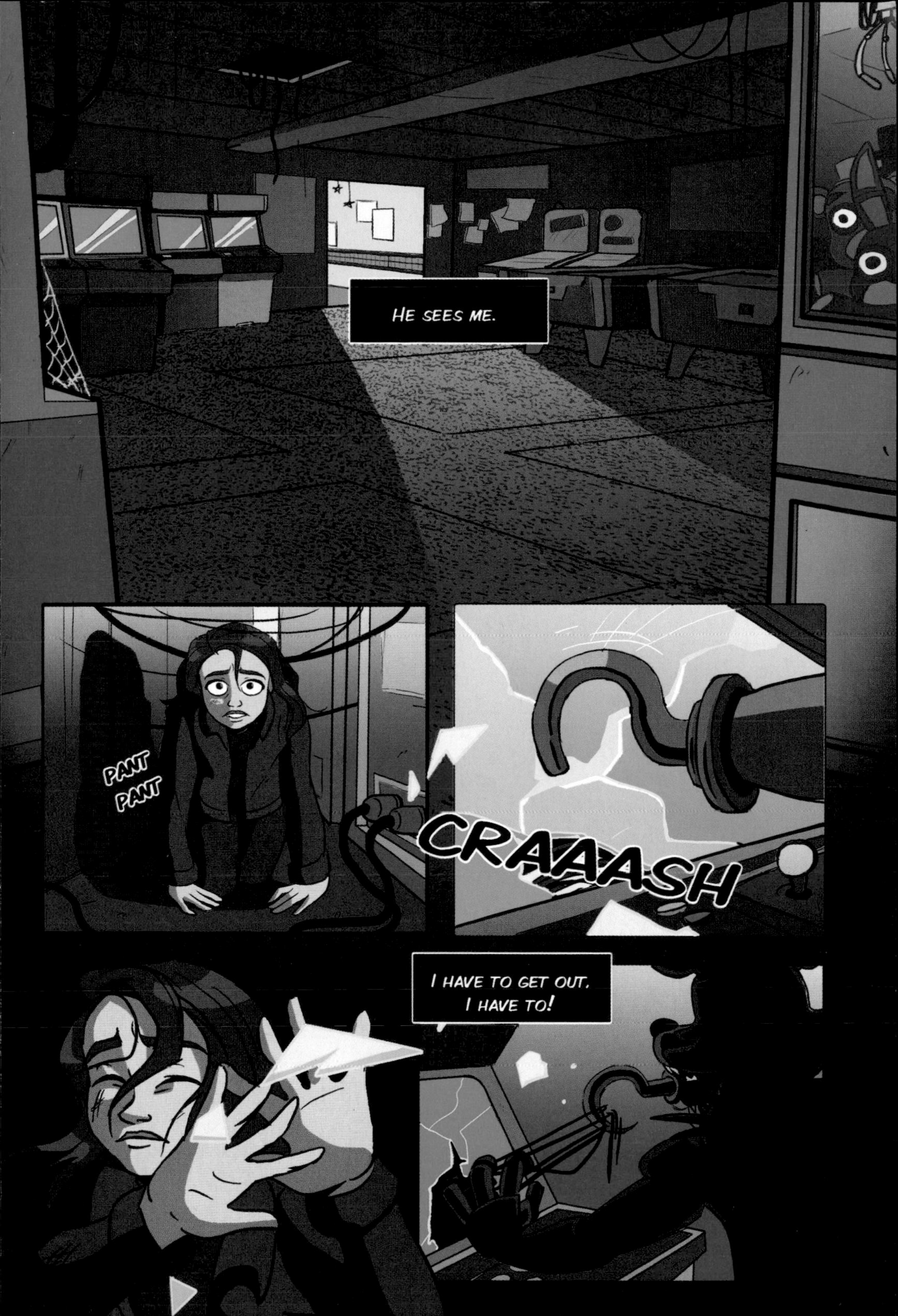
HE SEES ME.
PANT
PANT
CRAAASH
I HAVE TO GET OUT. I HAVE TO!

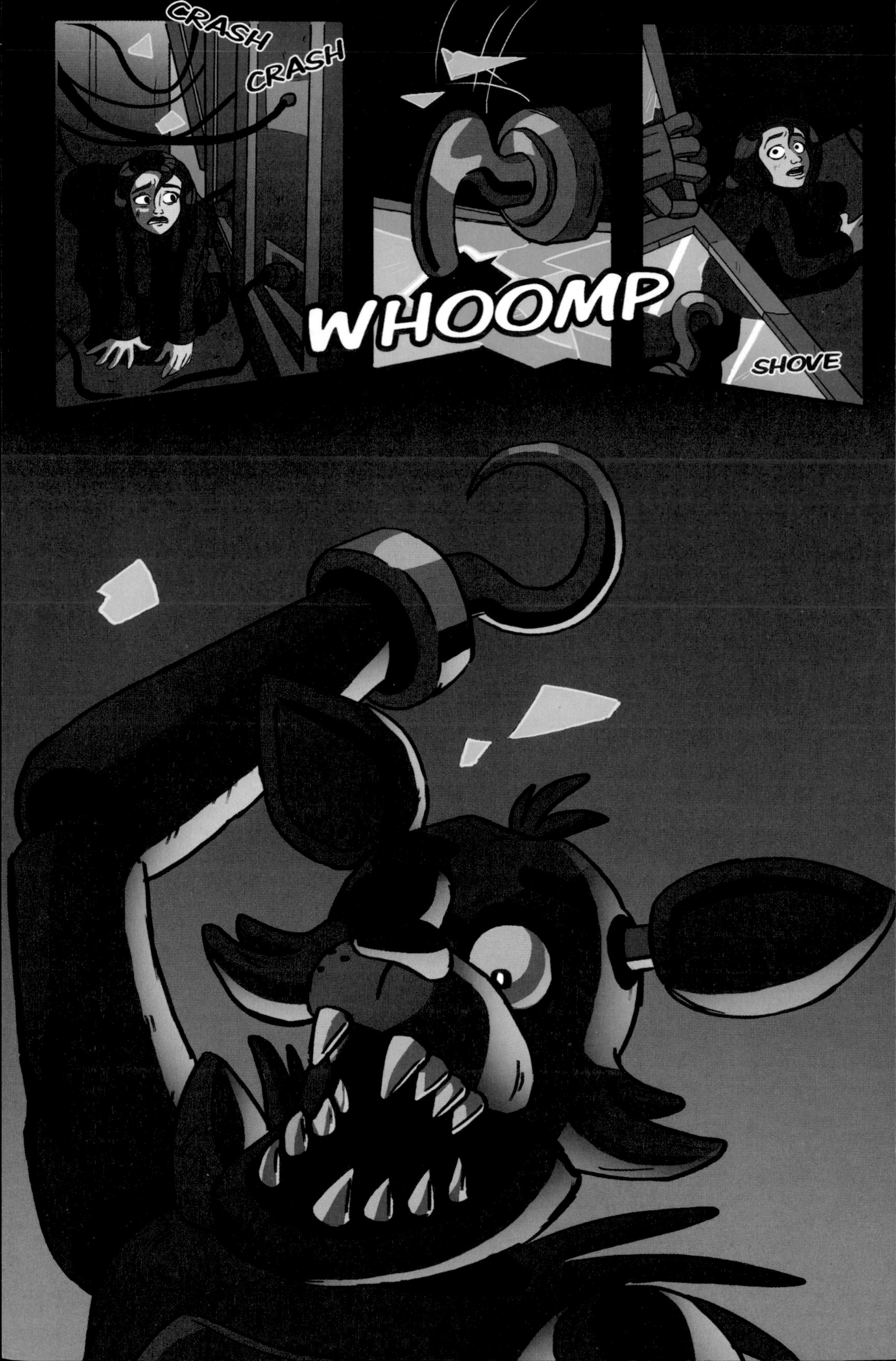
CRASH
CRASH
WHOOMP
SHOVE

CHAPTER 1

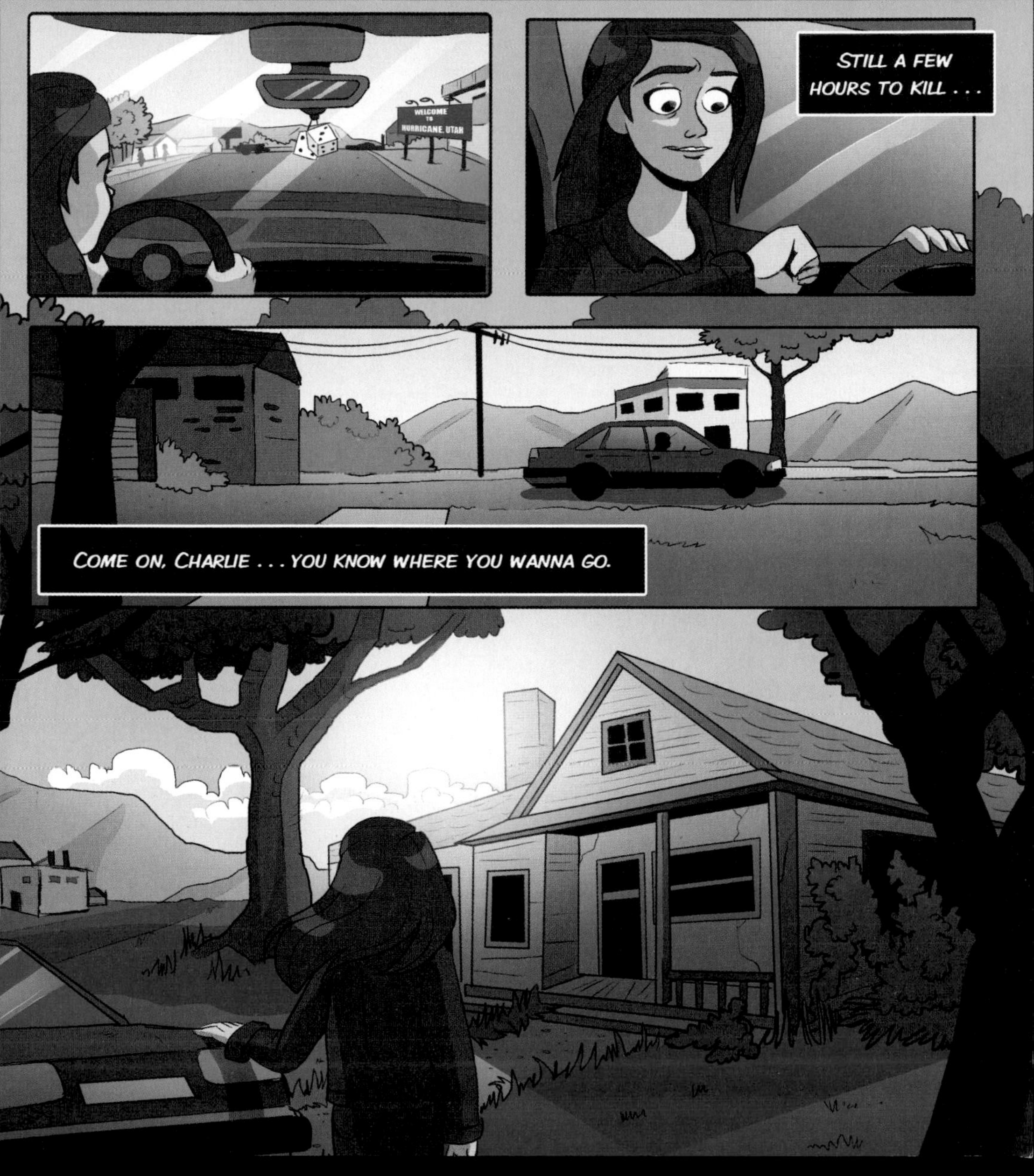
WELCOME TO HURRICANE, UTAH
STILL A FEW HOURS TO KILL . . .
COME ON, CHARLIE . . . YOU KNOW WHERE YOU WANNA GO.

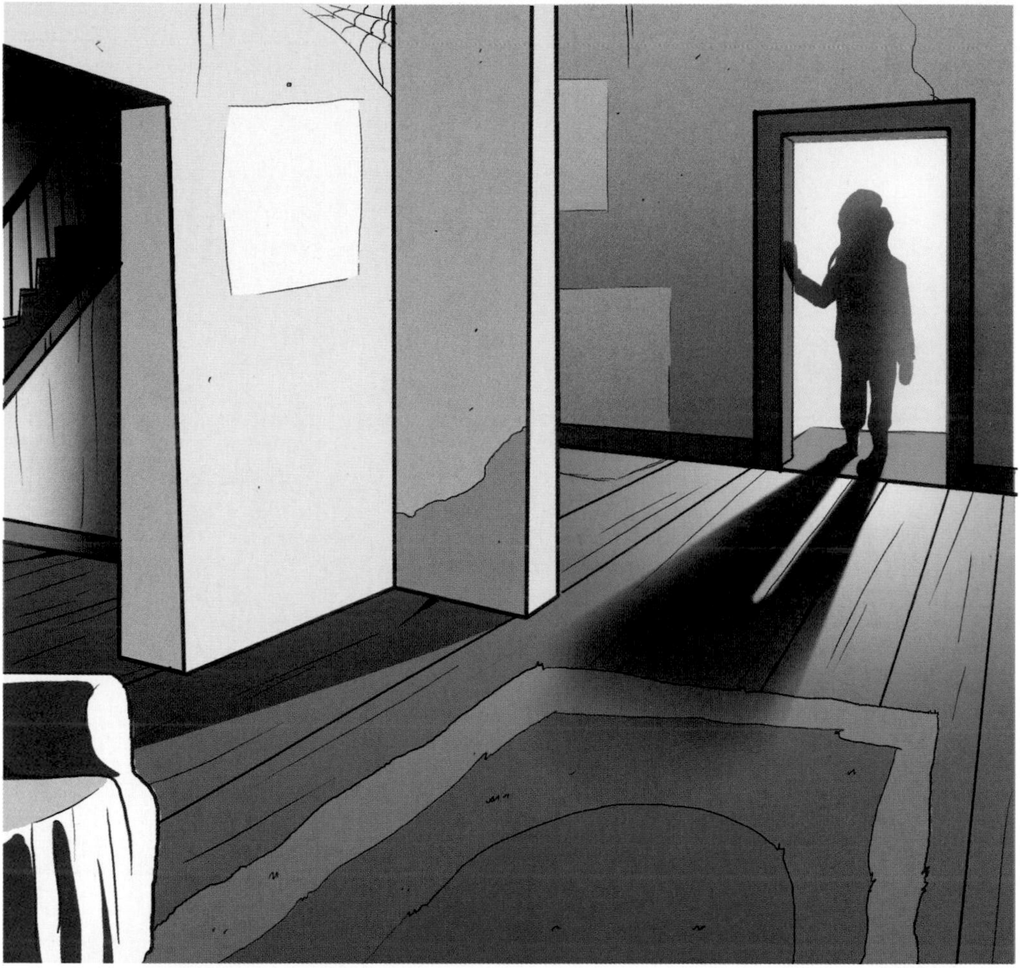

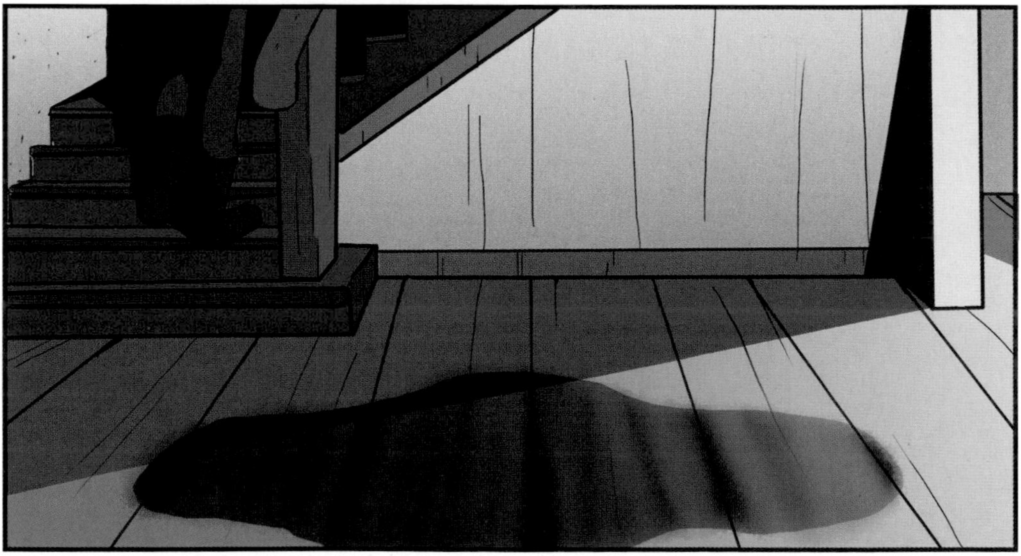

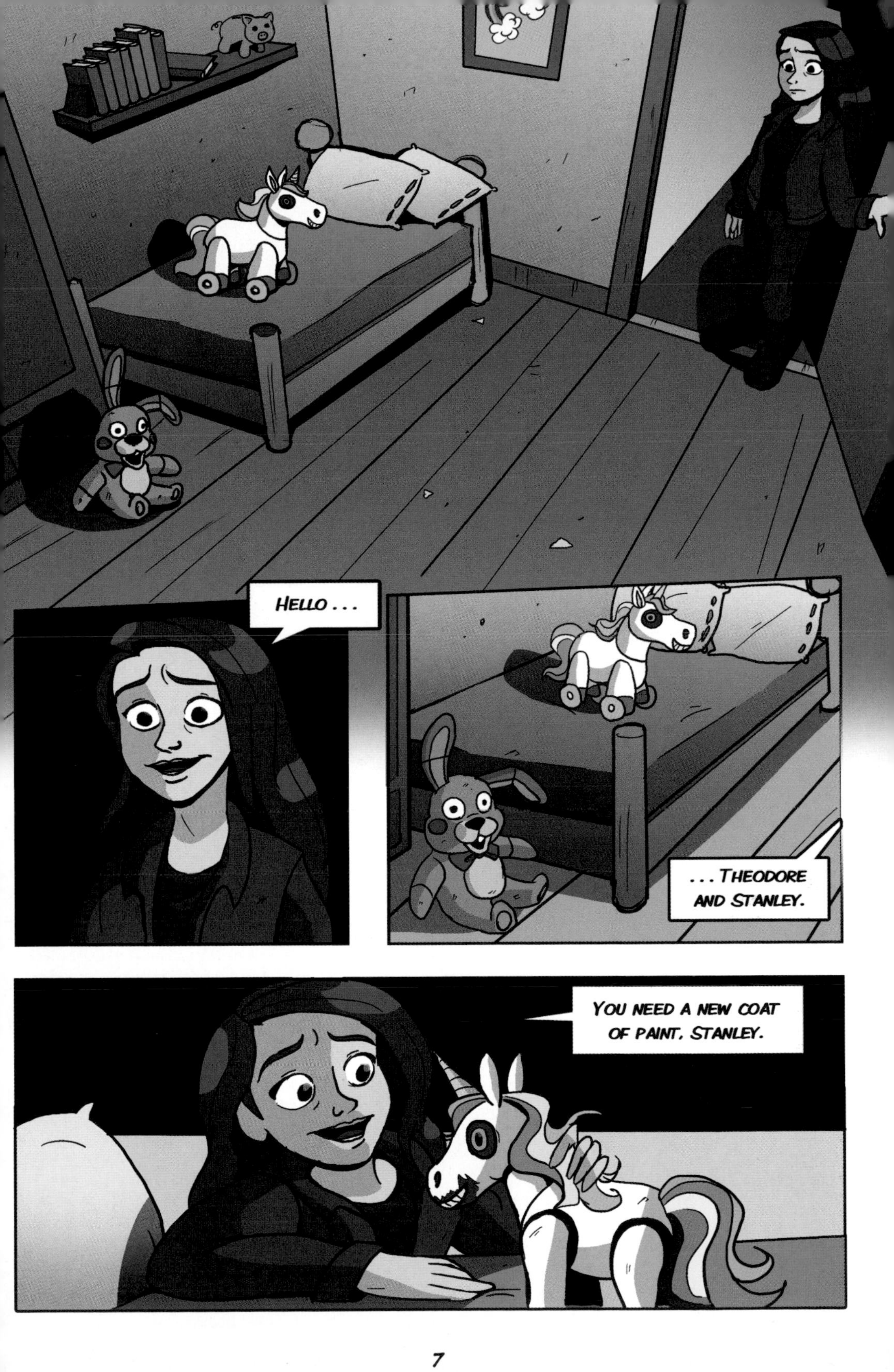
HELLO . . .
. . . THEODORE AND STANLEY.
YOU NEED A NEW COAT OF PAINT, STANLEY.

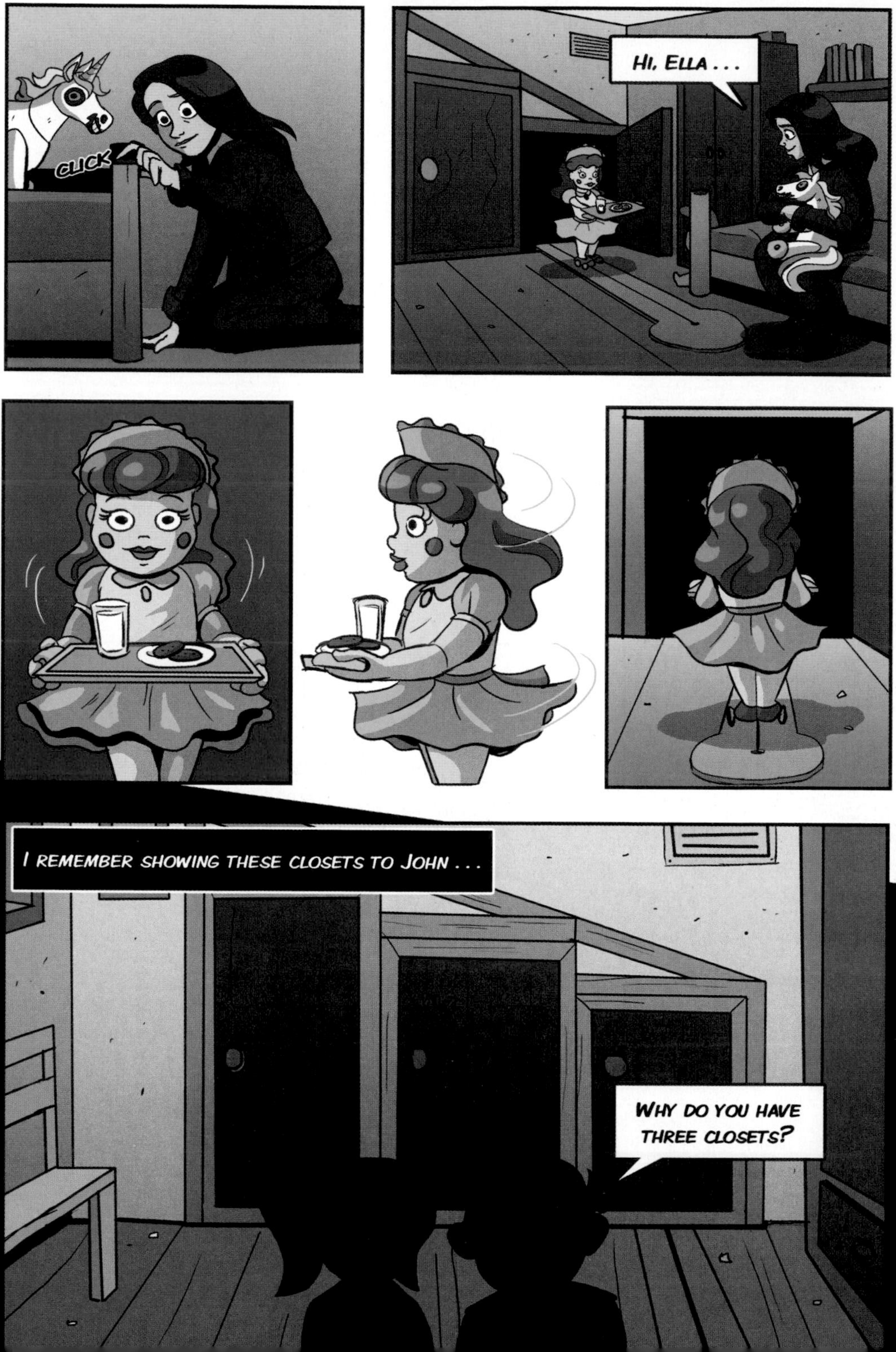
CLICK
HI, ELLA . . .
I REMEMBER SHOWING THESE CLOSETS TO JOHN . . .
WHY DO YOU HAVE THREE CLOSETS?

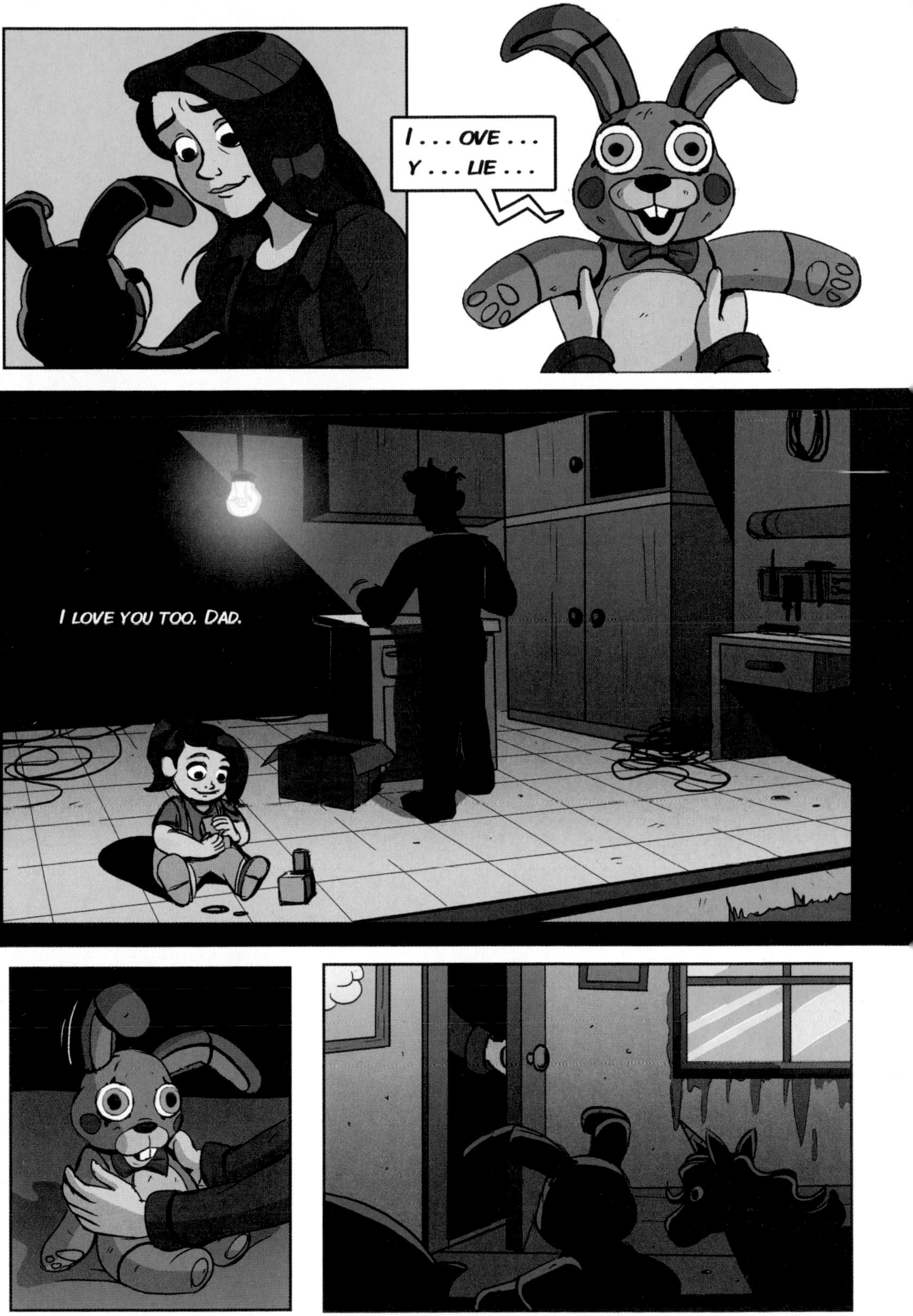
I . . . OVE . . .
Y . . . LIE . . .
I LOVE YOU TOO, DAD.

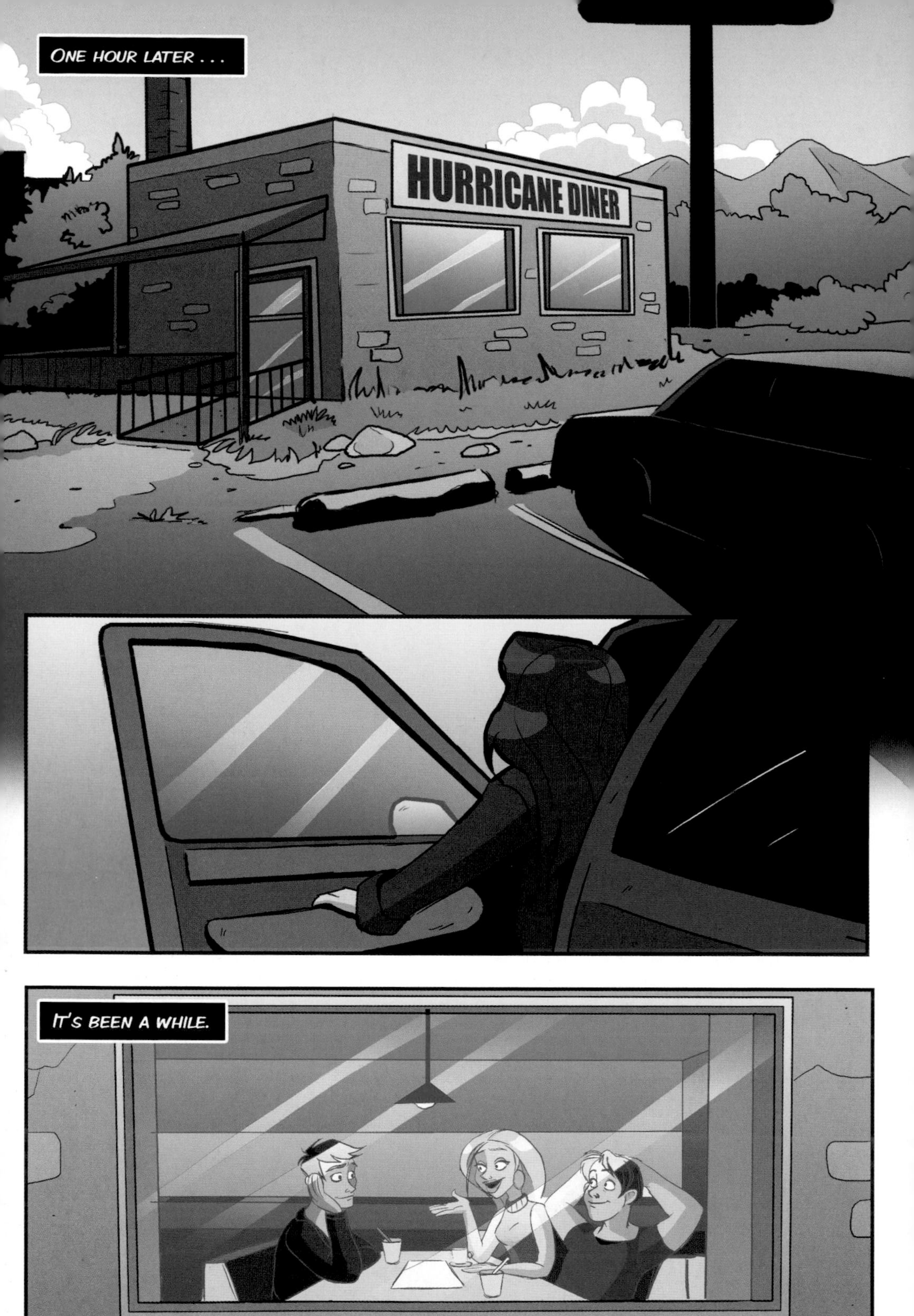
ONE HOUR LATER . . .
HURRICANE DINER
IT'S BEEN A WHILE.

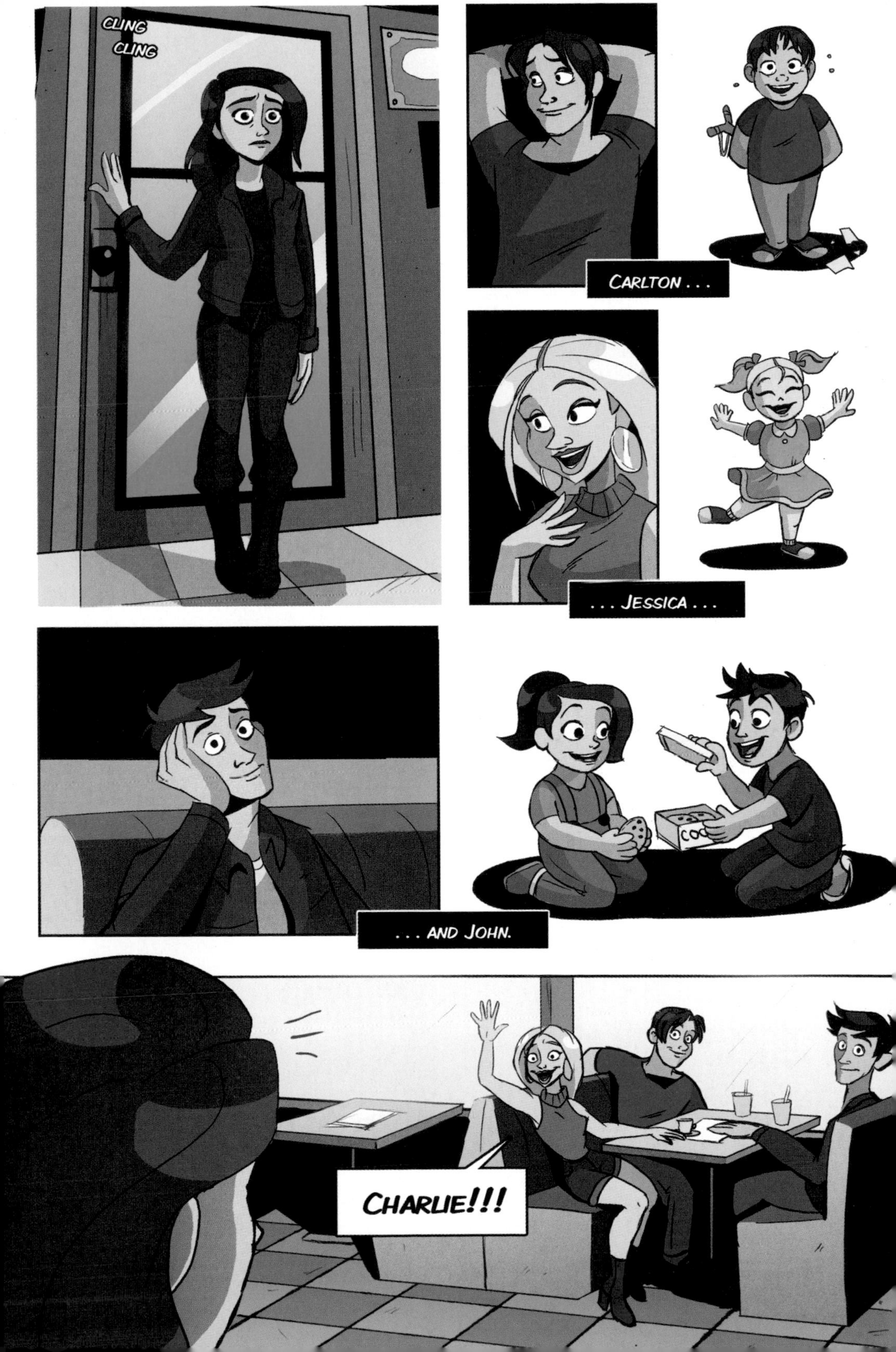
CLING
CLING
CARLTON . . .
. . . JESSICA . . .
. . . AND JOHN.
CHARLIE!!!

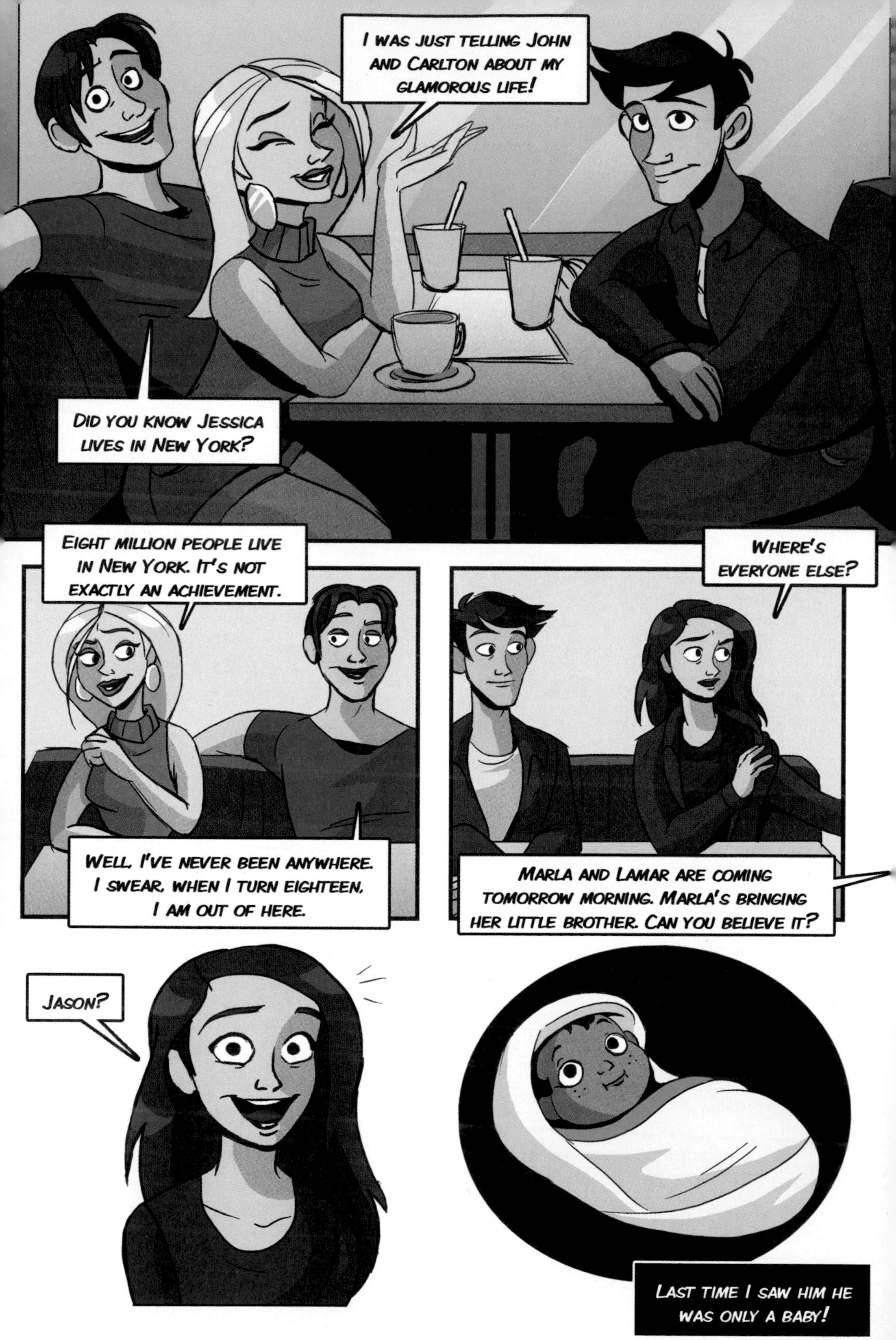
I WAS JUST TELLING JOHN AND CARLTON ABOUT MY GLAMOROUS LIFE!
DID YOU KNOW JESSICA LIVES IN NEW YORK?
EIGHT MILLION PEOPLE LIVE IN NEW YORK. IT'S NOT EXACTLY AN ACHIEVEMENT.
WELL, I'VE NEVER BEEN ANYWHERE. I SWEAR, WHEN I TURN EIGHTEEN, I AM OUT OF HERE.
WHERE'S EVERYONE ELSE?
MARLA AND LAMAR ARE COMING TOMORROW MORNING. MARLA'S BRINGING HER LITTLE BROTHER. CAN YOU BELIEVE IT?
JASON?
LAST TIME I SAW HIM HE WAS ONLY A BABY!

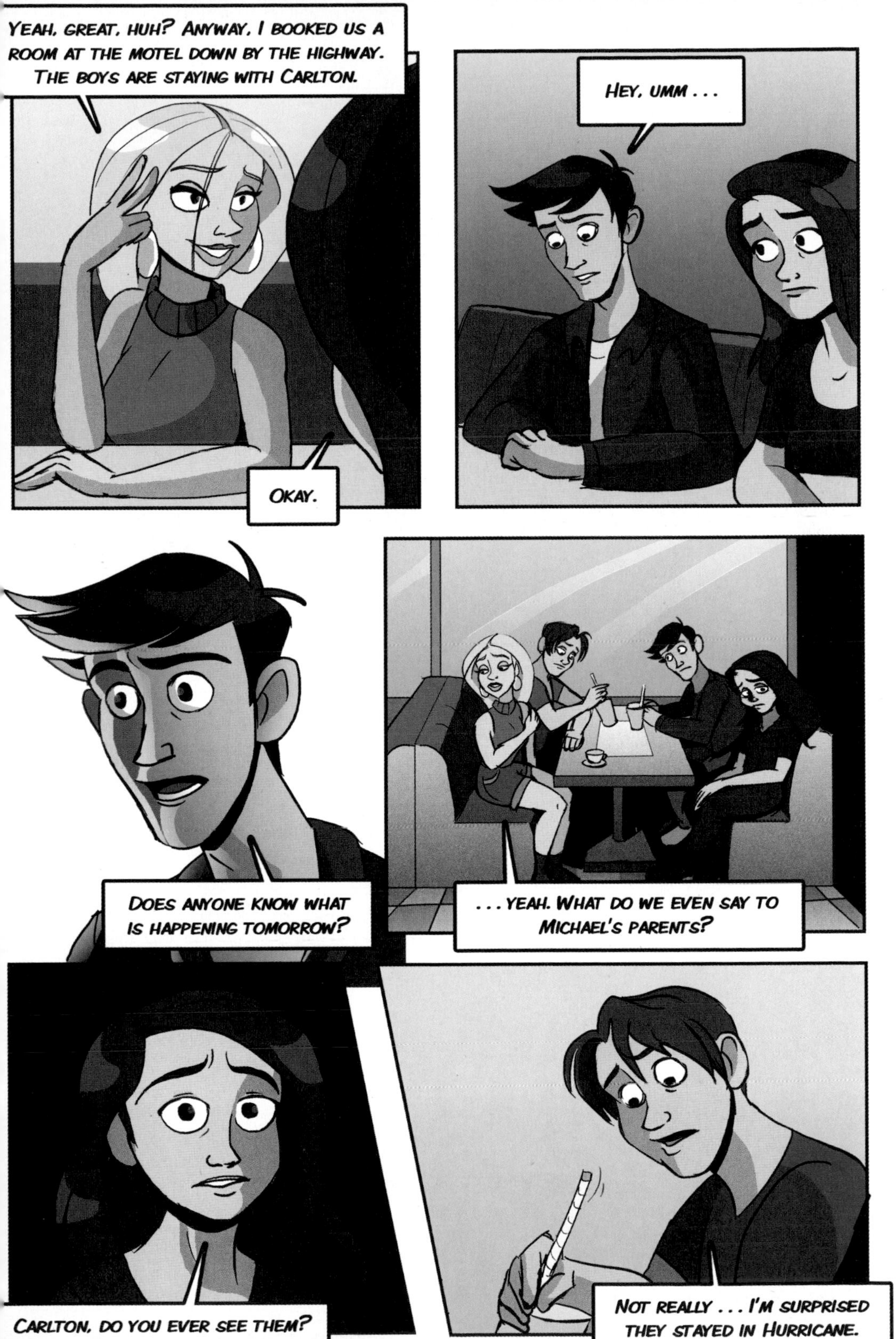
YEAH, GREAT, HUH? ANYWAY, I BOOKED US A ROOM AT THE MOTEL DOWN BY THE HIGHWAY. THE BOYS ARE STAYING WITH CARLTON.
OKAY.
HEY, UMM . . .
DOES ANYONE KNOW WHAT IS HAPPENING TOMORROW?
. . . YEAH. WHAT DO WE EVEN SAY TO MICHAEL'S PARENTS?
CARLTON, DO YOU EVER SEE THEM?
NOT REALLY . . . I'M SURPRISED THEY STAYED IN HURRICANE.

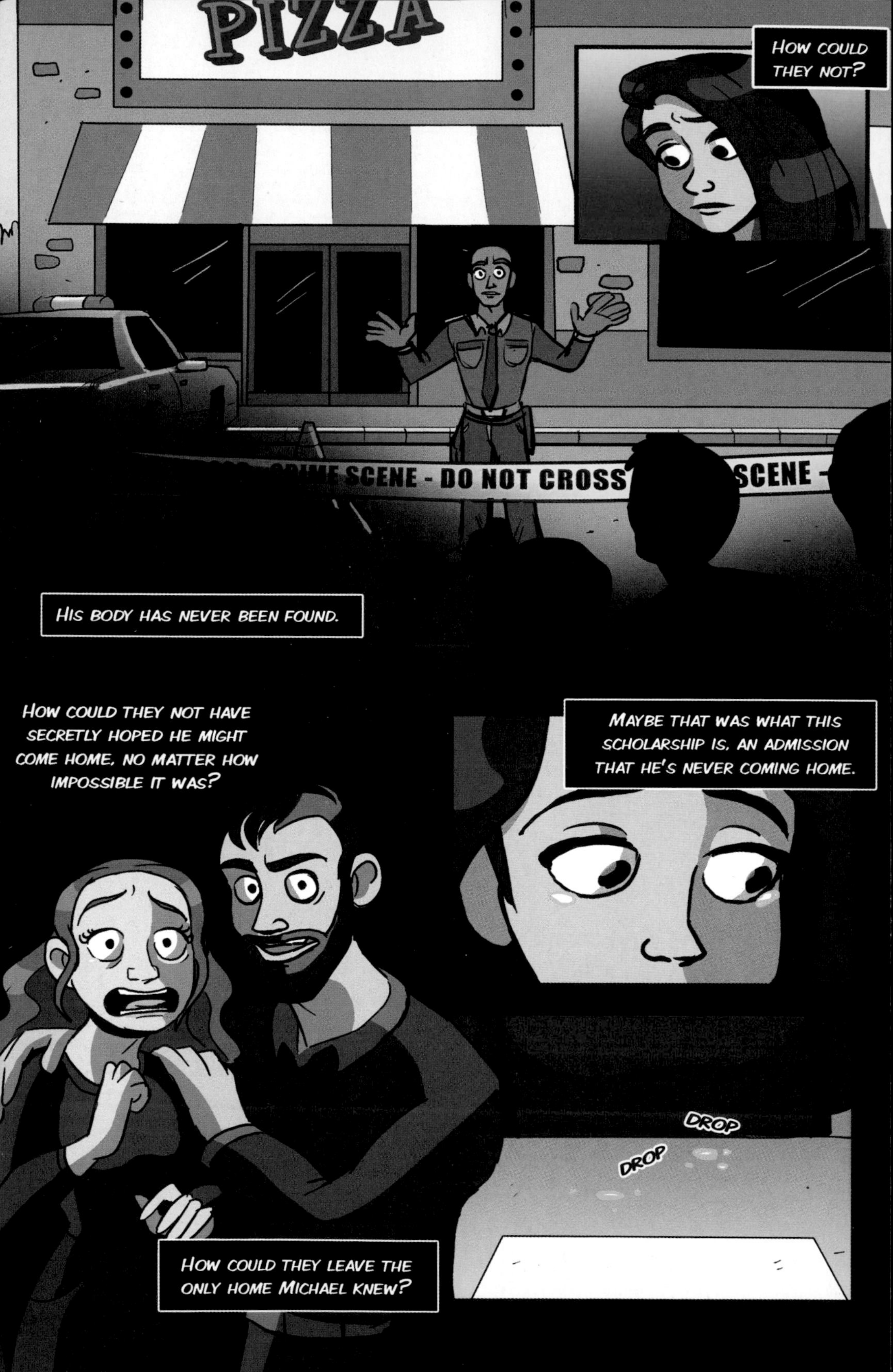
PIZZA
HOW COULD THEY NOT?
CRIME SCENE - DO NOT CROSS
SCENE -
HIS BODY HAS NEVER BEEN FOUND.
HOW COULD THEY NOT HAVE SECRETLY HOPED HE MIGHT COME HOME, NO MATTER HOW IMPOSSIBLE IT WAS?
MAYBE THAT WAS WHAT THIS SCHOLARSHIP IS, AN ADMISSION THAT HE'S NEVER COMING HOME.
DROP
DROP
HOW COULD THEY LEAVE THE ONLY HOME MICHAEL KNEW?

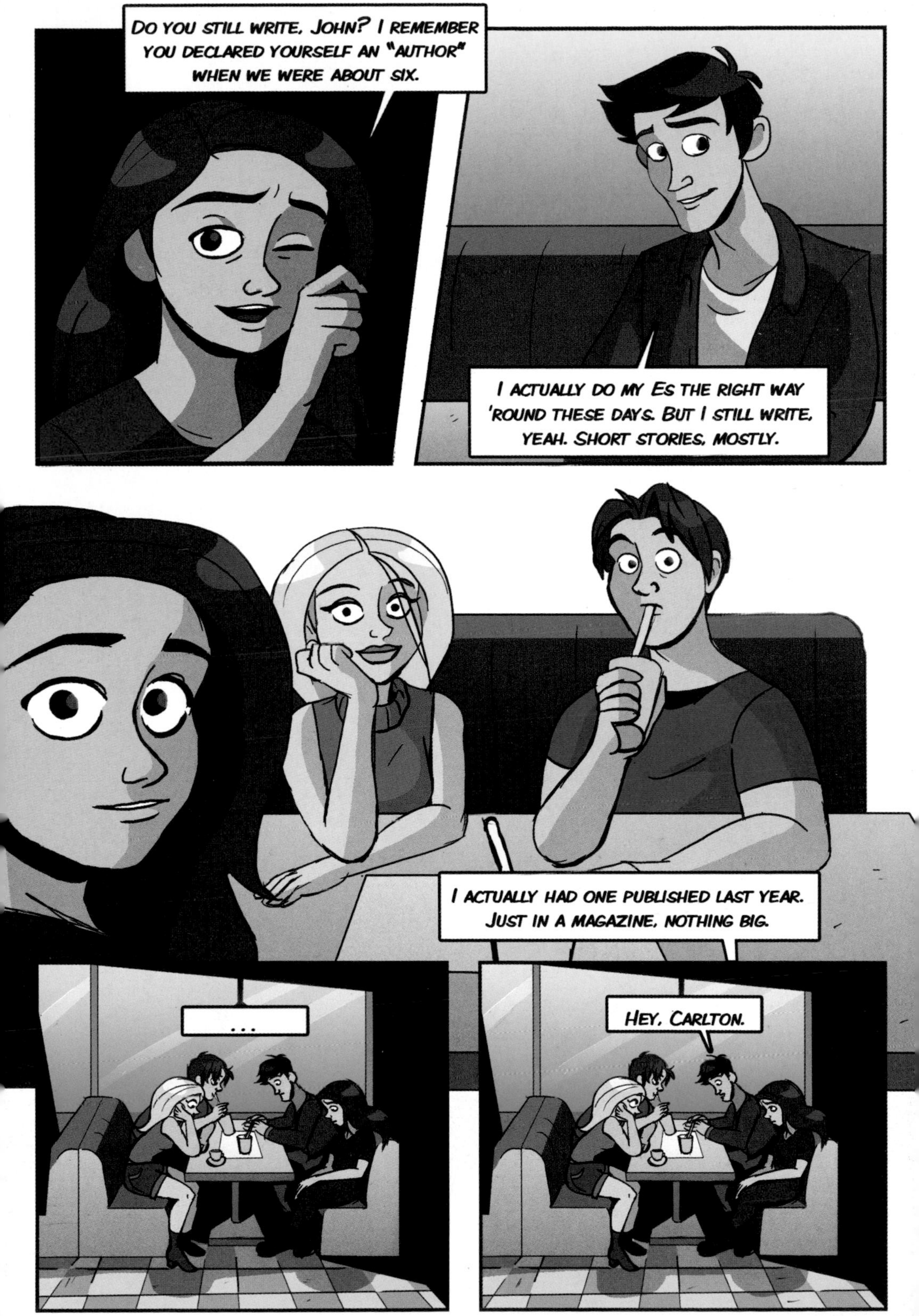
DO YOU STILL WRITE, JOHN? I REMEMBER YOU DECLARED YOURSELF AN "AUTHOR" WHEN WE WERE ABOUT SIX.
I ACTUALLY DO MY Es THE RIGHT WAY 'ROUND THESE DAYS. BUT I STILL WRITE, YEAH. SHORT STORIES, MOSTLY.
I ACTUALLY HAD ONE PUBLISHED LAST YEAR. JUST IN A MAGAZINE, NOTHING BIG.
...
HEY, CARLTON.

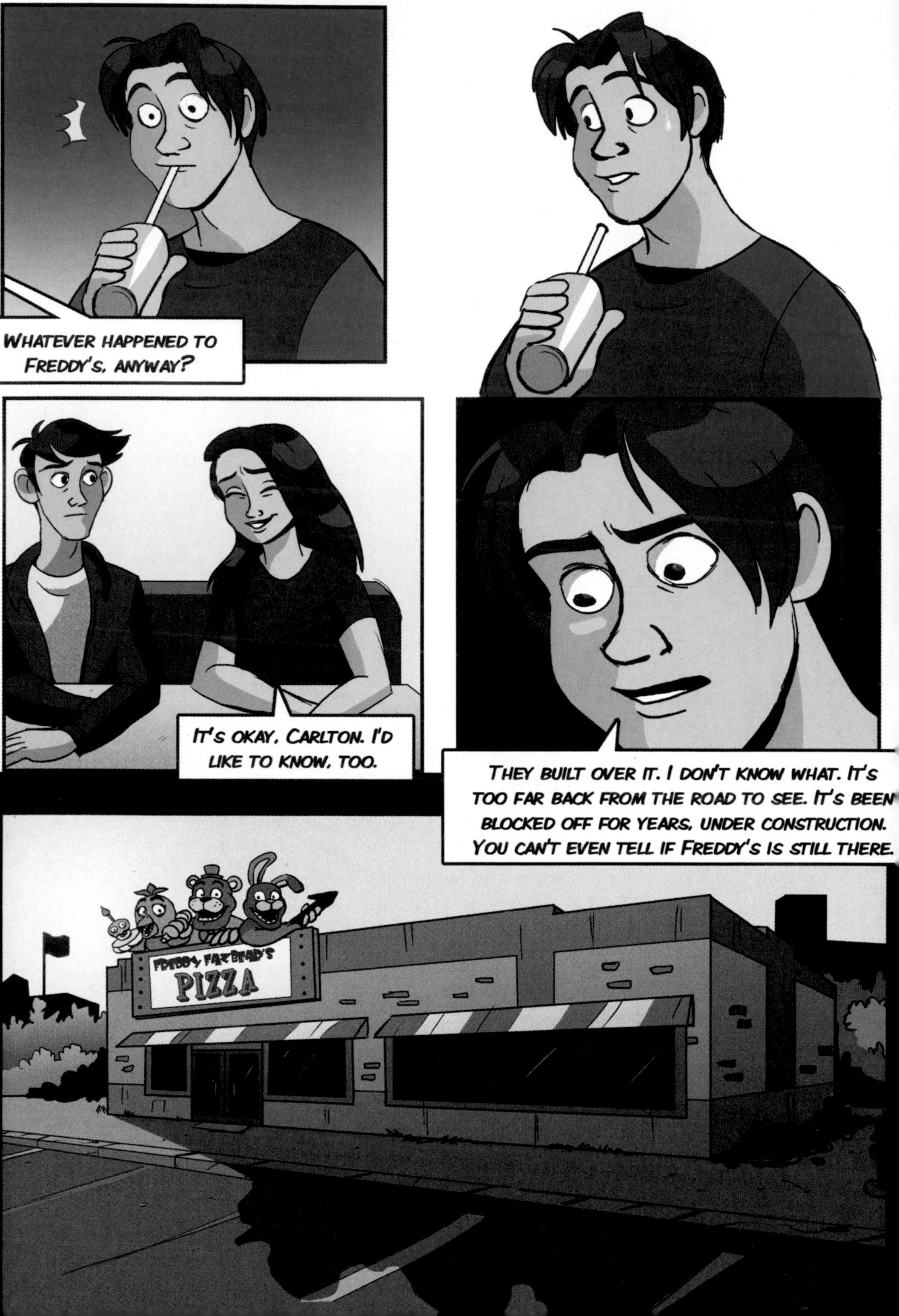
WHATEVER HAPPENED TO FREDDY'S, ANYWAY?
IT'S OKAY, CARLTON. I'D LIKE TO KNOW, TOO.
THEY BUILT OVER IT. I DON'T KNOW WHAT. IT'S TOO FAR BACK FROM THE ROAD TO SEE. IT'S BEEN BLOCKED OFF FOR YEARS, UNDER CONSTRUCTION. YOU CAN'T EVEN TELL IF FREDDY'S IS STILL THERE.
FREDDY FAZBEAR'S
PIZZA

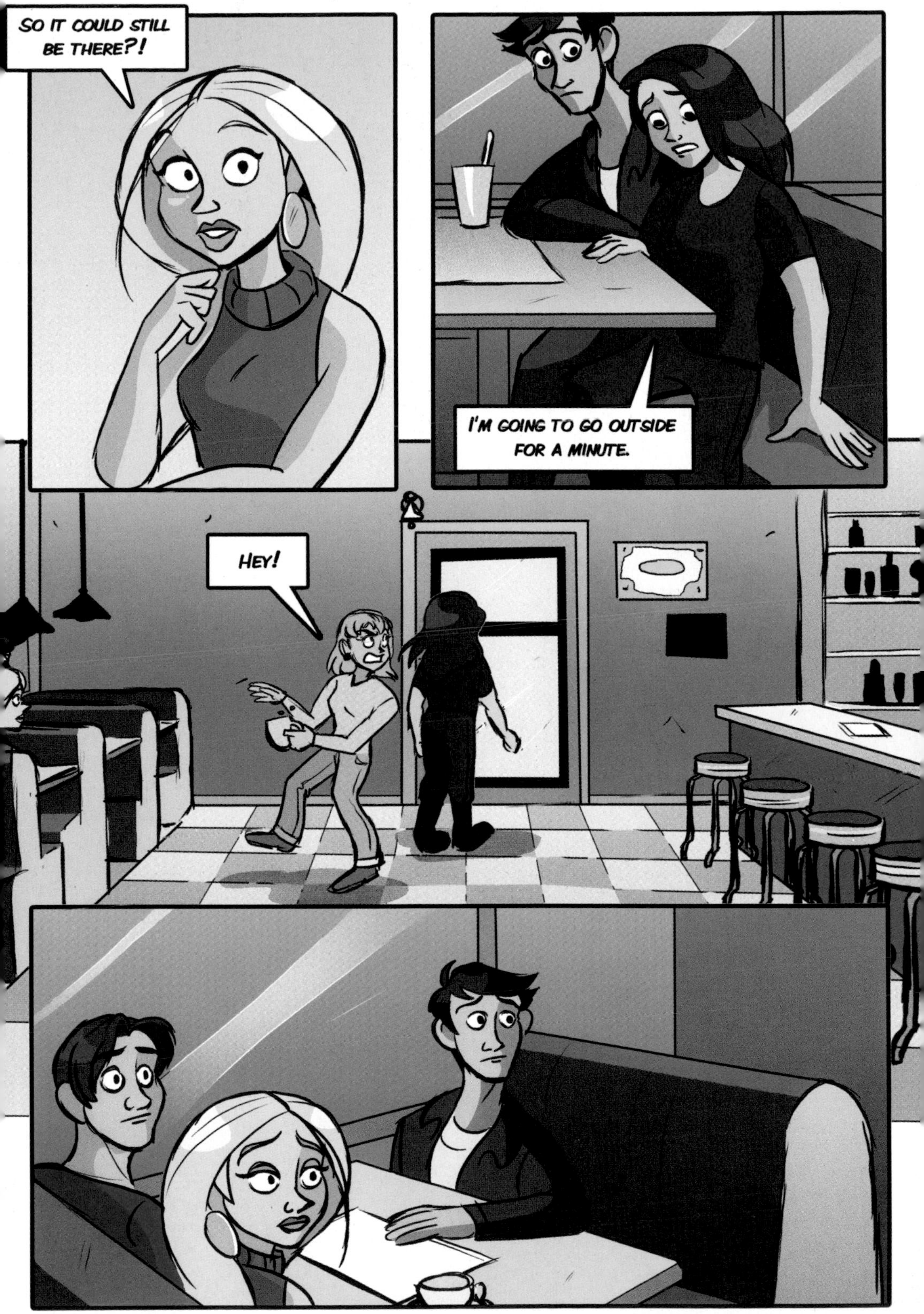
SO IT COULD STILL BE THERE?!
I'M GOING TO GO OUTSIDE FOR A MINUTE.
HEY!

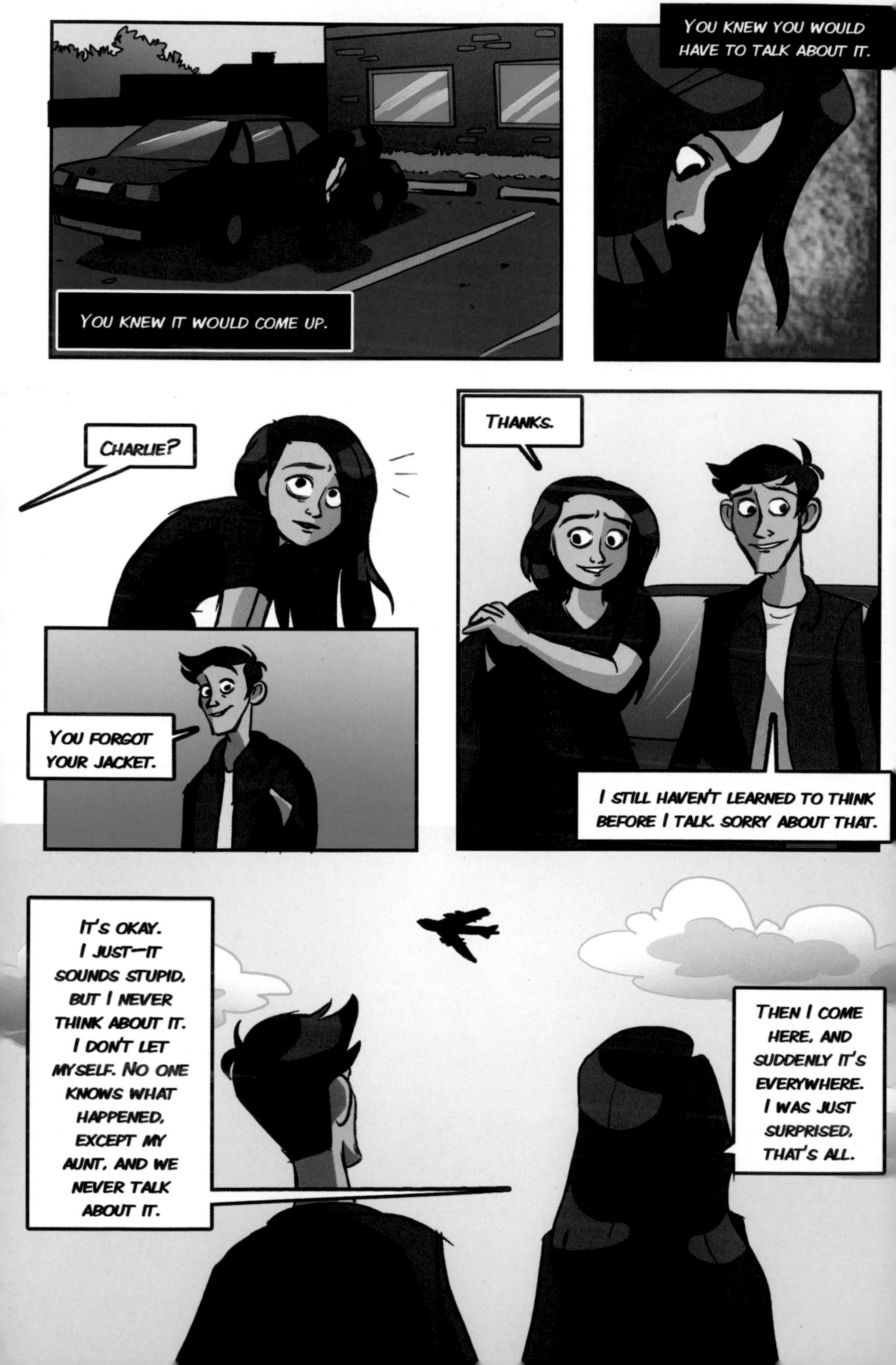

YOU KNEW IT WOULD COME UP.
YOU KNEW YOU WOULD HAVE TO TALK ABOUT IT.
CHARLIE?
YOU FORGOT YOUR JACKET.
THANKS.
I STILL HAVEN'T LEARNED TO THINK BEFORE I TALK. SORRY ABOUT THAT.
IT'S OKAY. I JUST—IT SOUNDS STUPID, BUT I NEVER THINK ABOUT IT. I DON'T LET MYSELF. NO ONE KNOWS WHAT HAPPENED, EXCEPT MY AUNT, AND WE NEVER TALK ABOUT IT.
THEN I COME HERE, AND SUDDENLY IT'S EVERYWHERE. I WAS JUST SURPRISED, THAT'S ALL.

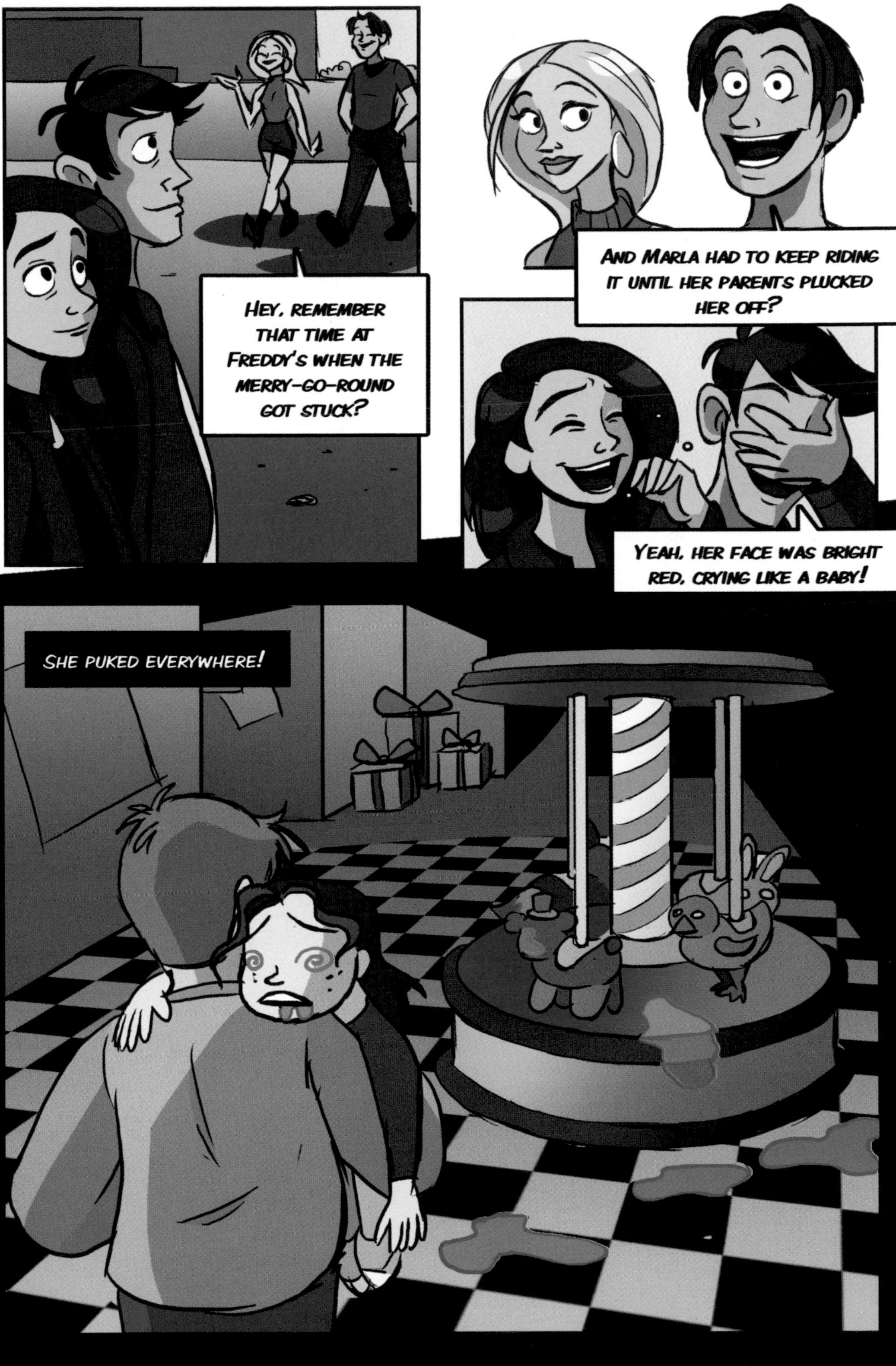
HEY, REMEMBER THAT TIME AT FREDDY'S WHEN THE MERRY-GO-ROUND GOT STUCK?
AND MARLA HAD TO KEEP RIDING IT UNTIL HER PARENTS PLUCKED HER OFF?
YEAH, HER FACE WAS BRIGHT RED, CRYING LIKE A BABY!
SHE PUKED EVERYWHERE!

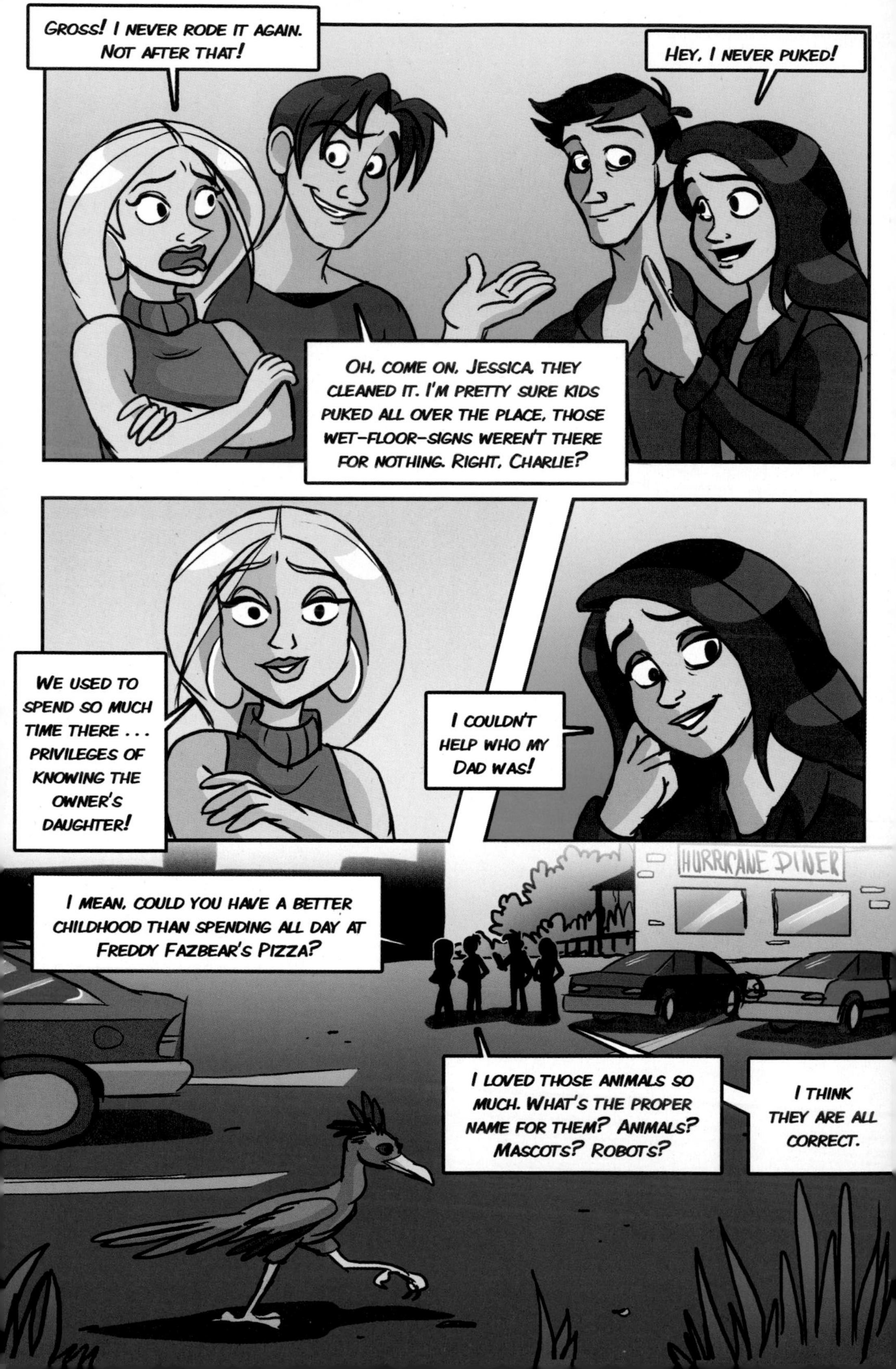
GROSS! I NEVER RODE IT AGAIN. NOT AFTER THAT!
HEY, I NEVER PUKED!
OH, COME ON, JESSICA, THEY CLEANED IT. I'M PRETTY SURE KIDS PUKED ALL OVER THE PLACE, THOSE WET-FLOOR-SIGNS WEREN'T THERE FOR NOTHING. RIGHT, CHARLIE?
WE USED TO SPEND SO MUCH TIME THERE . . . PRIVILEGES OF KNOWING THE OWNER'S DAUGHTER!
I COULDN'T HELP WHO MY DAD WAS!
HURRICANE DINER
I MEAN, COULD YOU HAVE A BETTER CHILDHOOD THAN SPENDING ALL DAY AT FREDDY FAZBEAR'S PIZZA?
I LOVED THOSE ANIMALS SO MUCH. WHAT'S THE PROPER NAME FOR THEM? ANIMALS? MASCOTS? ROBOTS?
I THINK THEY ARE ALL CORRECT.

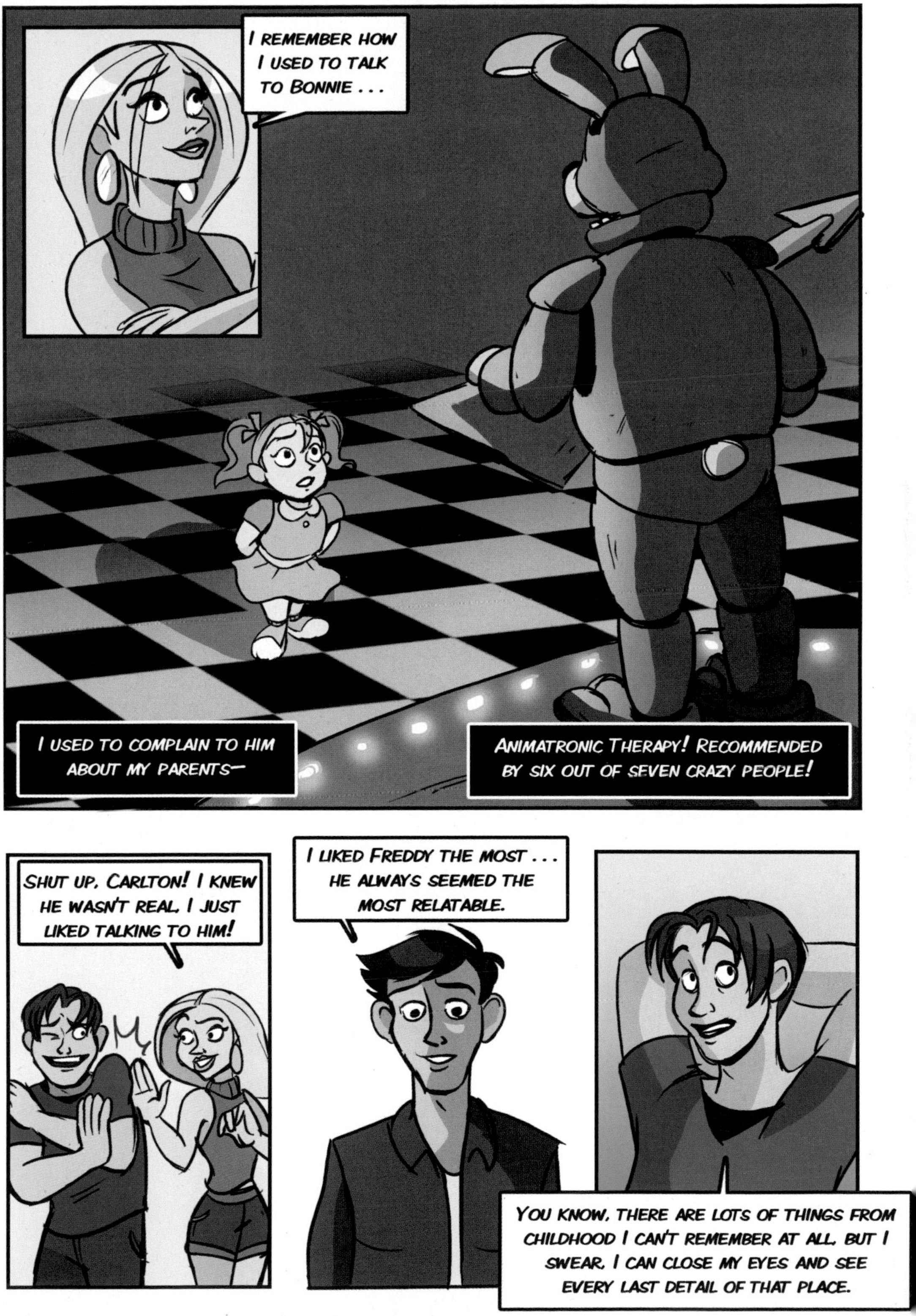
I REMEMBER HOW I USED TO TALK TO BONNIE . . .
I USED TO COMPLAIN TO HIM ABOUT MY PARENTS—
ANIMATRONIC THERAPY! RECOMMENDED BY SIX OUT OF SEVEN CRAZY PEOPLE!
SHUT UP, CARLTON! I KNEW HE WASN'T REAL. I JUST LIKED TALKING TO HIM!
I LIKED FREDDY THE MOST . . . HE ALWAYS SEEMED THE MOST RELATABLE.
YOU KNOW, THERE ARE LOTS OF THINGS FROM CHILDHOOD I CAN'T REMEMBER AT ALL, BUT I SWEAR, I CAN CLOSE MY EYES AND SEE EVERY LAST DETAIL OF THAT PLACE.

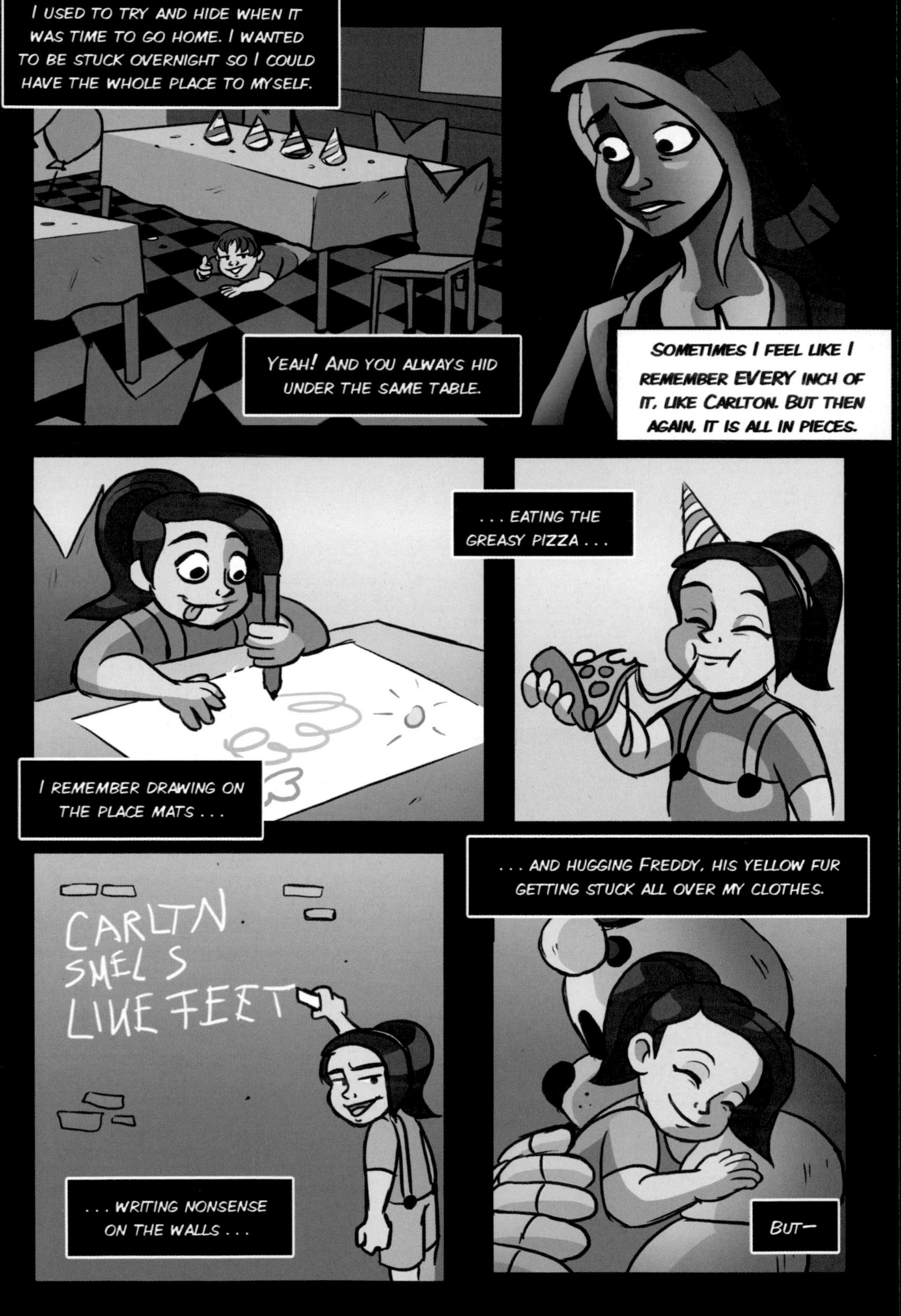
I USED TO TRY AND HIDE WHEN IT WAS TIME TO GO HOME. I WANTED TO BE STUCK OVERNIGHT SO I COULD HAVE THE WHOLE PLACE TO MYSELF.
YEAH! AND YOU ALWAYS HID UNDER THE SAME TABLE.
SOMETIMES I FEEL LIKE I REMEMBER EVERY INCH OF IT, LIKE CARLTON. BUT THEN AGAIN, IT IS ALL IN PIECES.
I REMEMBER DRAWING ON THE PLACE MATS . . .
. . . EATING THE GREASY PIZZA . . .
CARLTN SMEL S LIKE FEET
. . . WRITING NONSENSE ON THE WALLS . . .
. . . AND HUGGING FREDDY, HIS YELLOW FUR GETTING STUCK ALL OVER MY CLOTHES.
BUT—

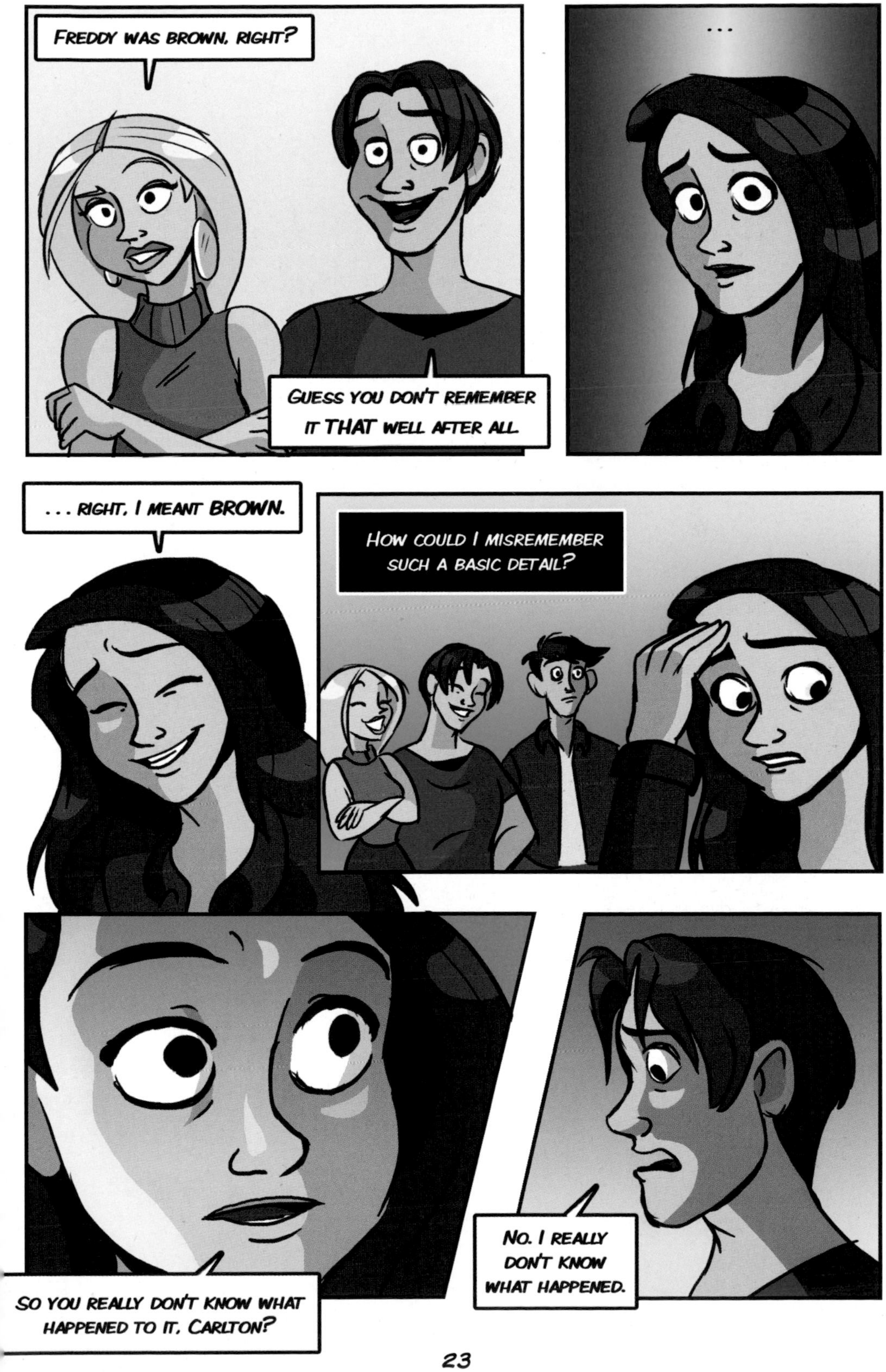
FREDDY WAS BROWN, RIGHT?
GUESS YOU DON'T REMEMBER IT THAT WELL AFTER ALL.
...
...RIGHT, I MEANT BROWN.
HOW COULD I MISREMEMBER SUCH A BASIC DETAIL?
SO YOU REALLY DON'T KNOW WHAT HAPPENED TO IT, CARLTON?
NO. I REALLY DON'T KNOW WHAT HAPPENED.

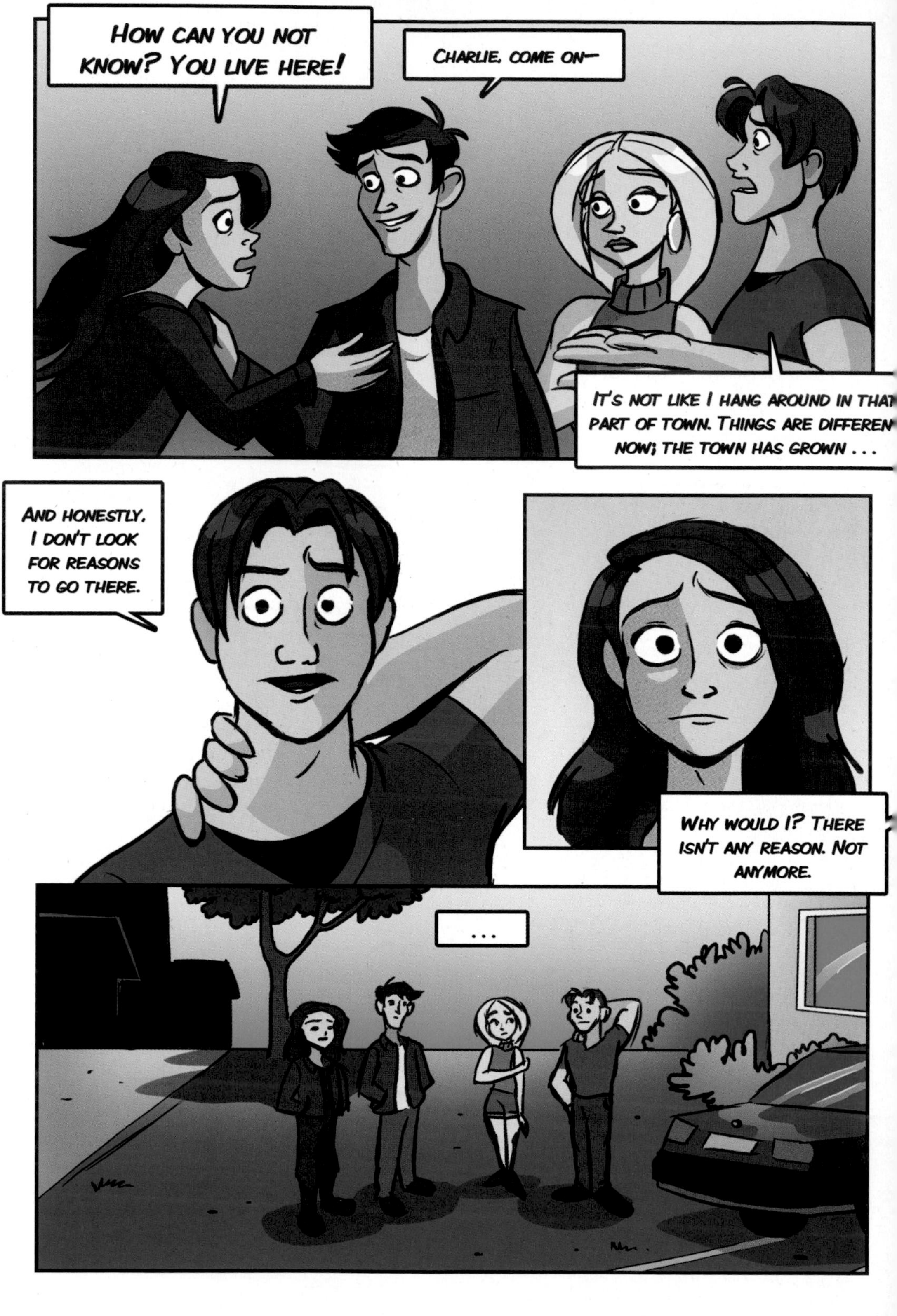
HOW CAN YOU NOT KNOW? YOU LIVE HERE!
CHARLIE, COME ON—
IT'S NOT LIKE I HANG AROUND IN THAT PART OF TOWN. THINGS ARE DIFFERENT NOW; THE TOWN HAS GROWN . . .
AND HONESTLY, I DON'T LOOK FOR REASONS TO GO THERE.
WHY WOULD I? THERE ISN'T ANY REASON. NOT ANYMORE.
. . .

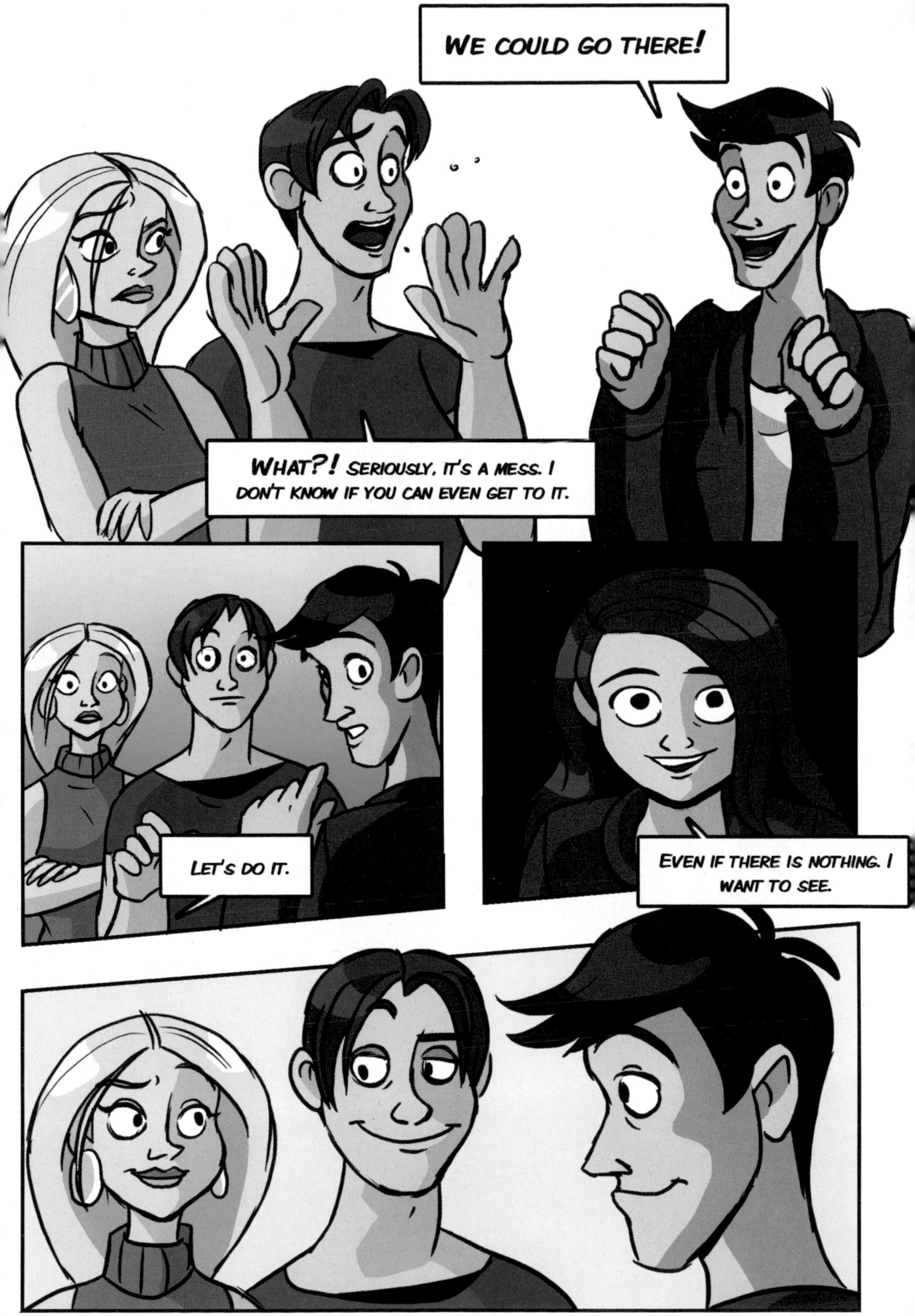
WE COULD GO THERE!
WHAT?! SERIOUSLY, IT'S A MESS. I DON'T KNOW IF YOU CAN EVEN GET TO IT.
LET'S DO IT.
EVEN IF THERE IS NOTHING. I WANT TO SEE.

CHAPTER 2

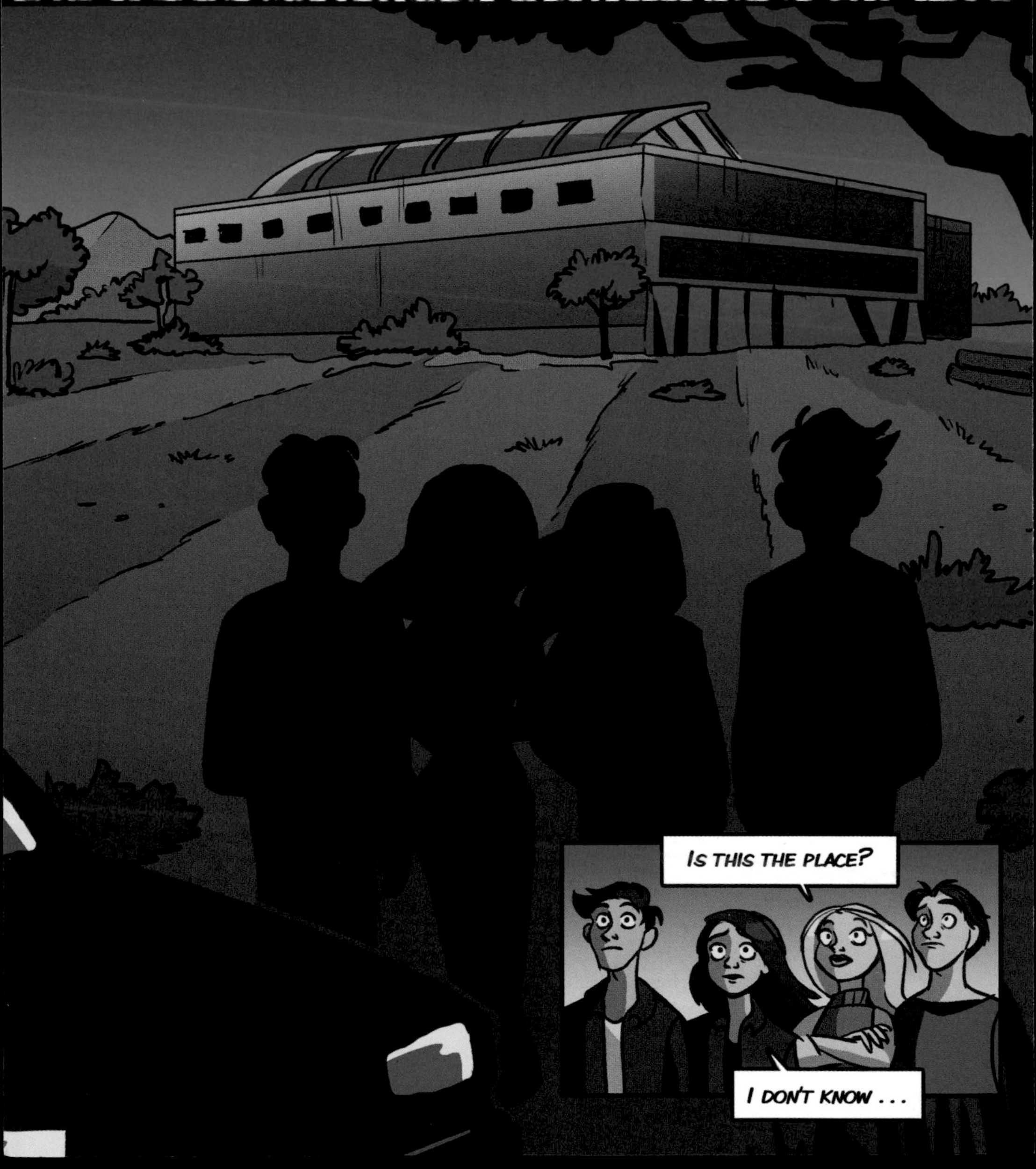
IS THIS THE PLACE?
I DON'T KNOW . . .

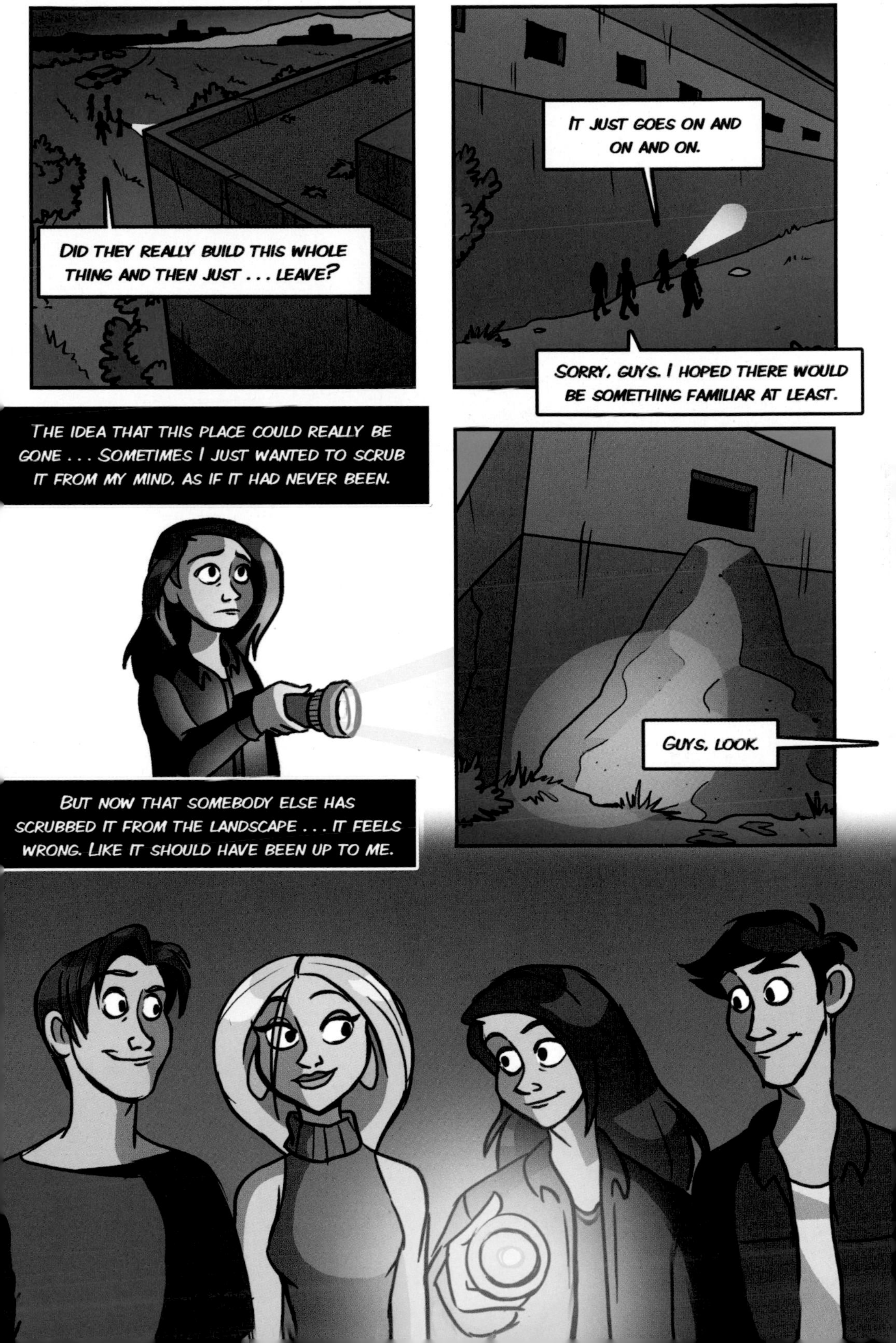
DID THEY REALLY BUILD THIS WHOLE THING AND THEN JUST . . . LEAVE?
IT JUST GOES ON AND ON AND ON.
SORRY, GUYS. I HOPED THERE WOULD BE SOMETHING FAMILIAR AT LEAST.
THE IDEA THAT THIS PLACE COULD REALLY BE GONE . . . SOMETIMES I JUST WANTED TO SCRUB IT FROM MY MIND, AS IF IT HAD NEVER BEEN.
GUYS, LOOK.
BUT NOW THAT SOMEBODY ELSE HAS SCRUBBED IT FROM THE LANDSCAPE . . . IT FEELS WRONG. LIKE IT SHOULD HAVE BEEN UP TO ME.

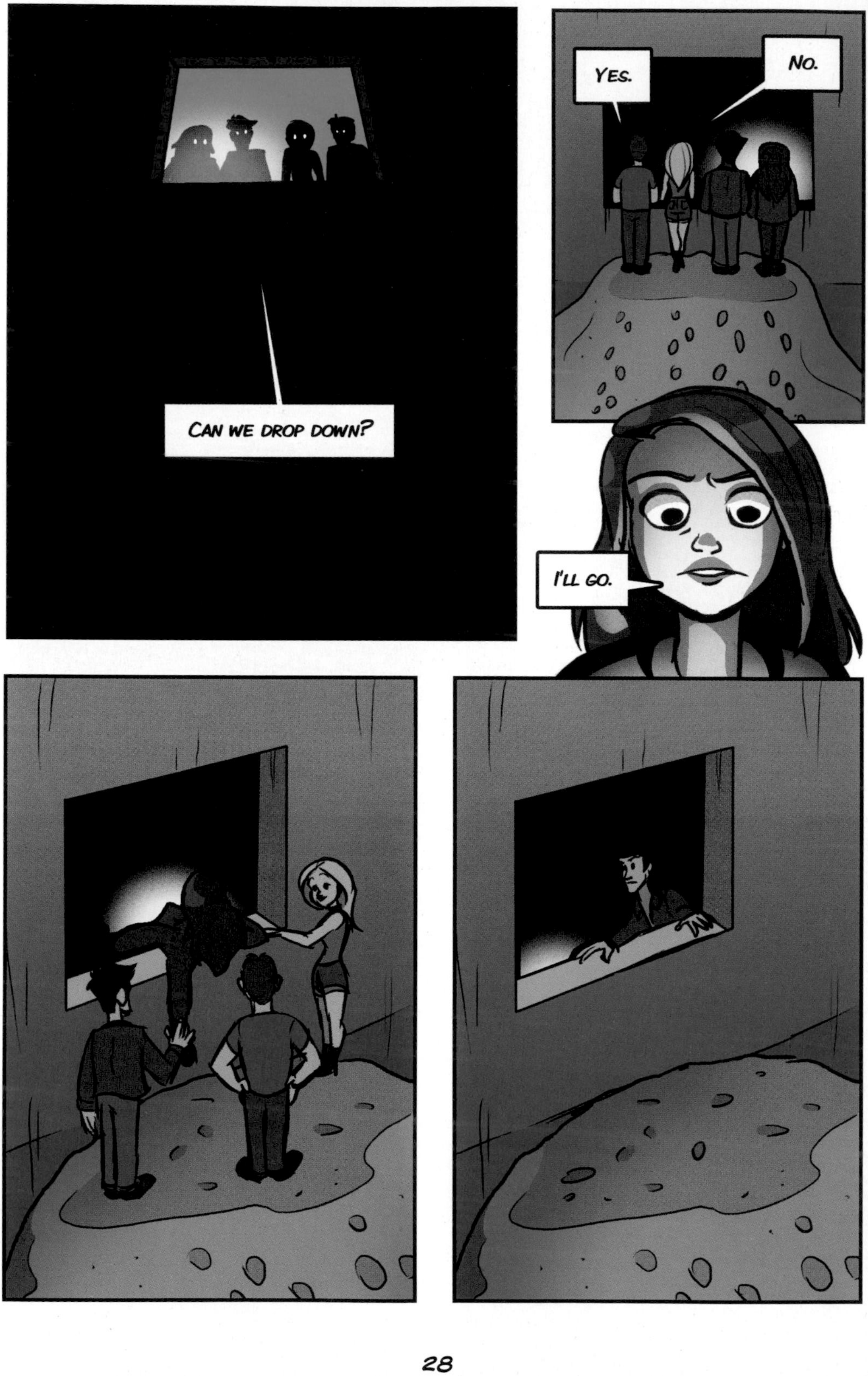
CAN WE DROP DOWN?
YES.
NO.
I'LL GO.

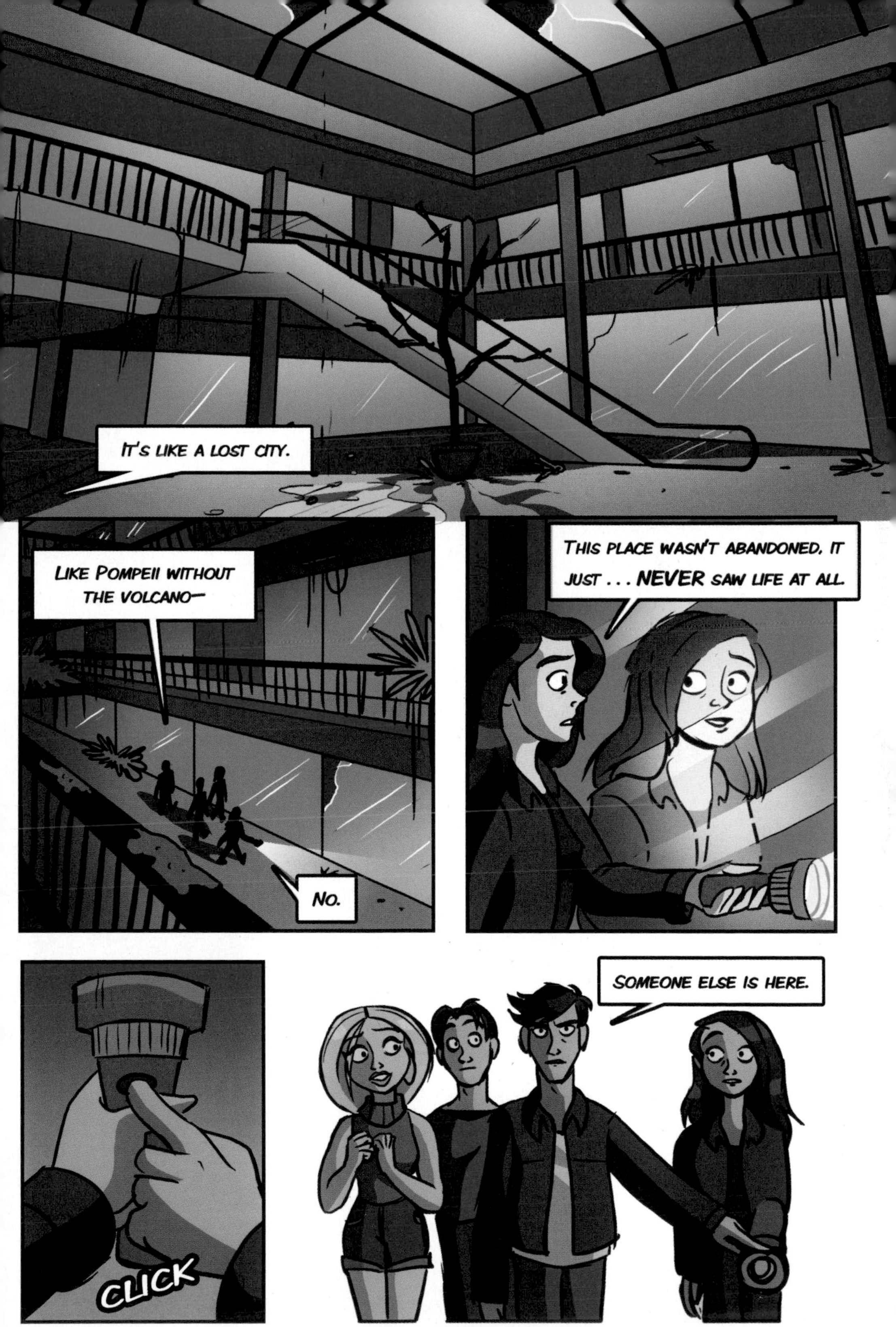
IT'S LIKE A LOST CITY.
LIKE POMPEII WITHOUT THE VOLCANO—
NO.
THIS PLACE WASN'T ABANDONED. IT JUST . . . NEVER SAW LIFE AT ALL.
CLICK
SOMEONE ELSE IS HERE.

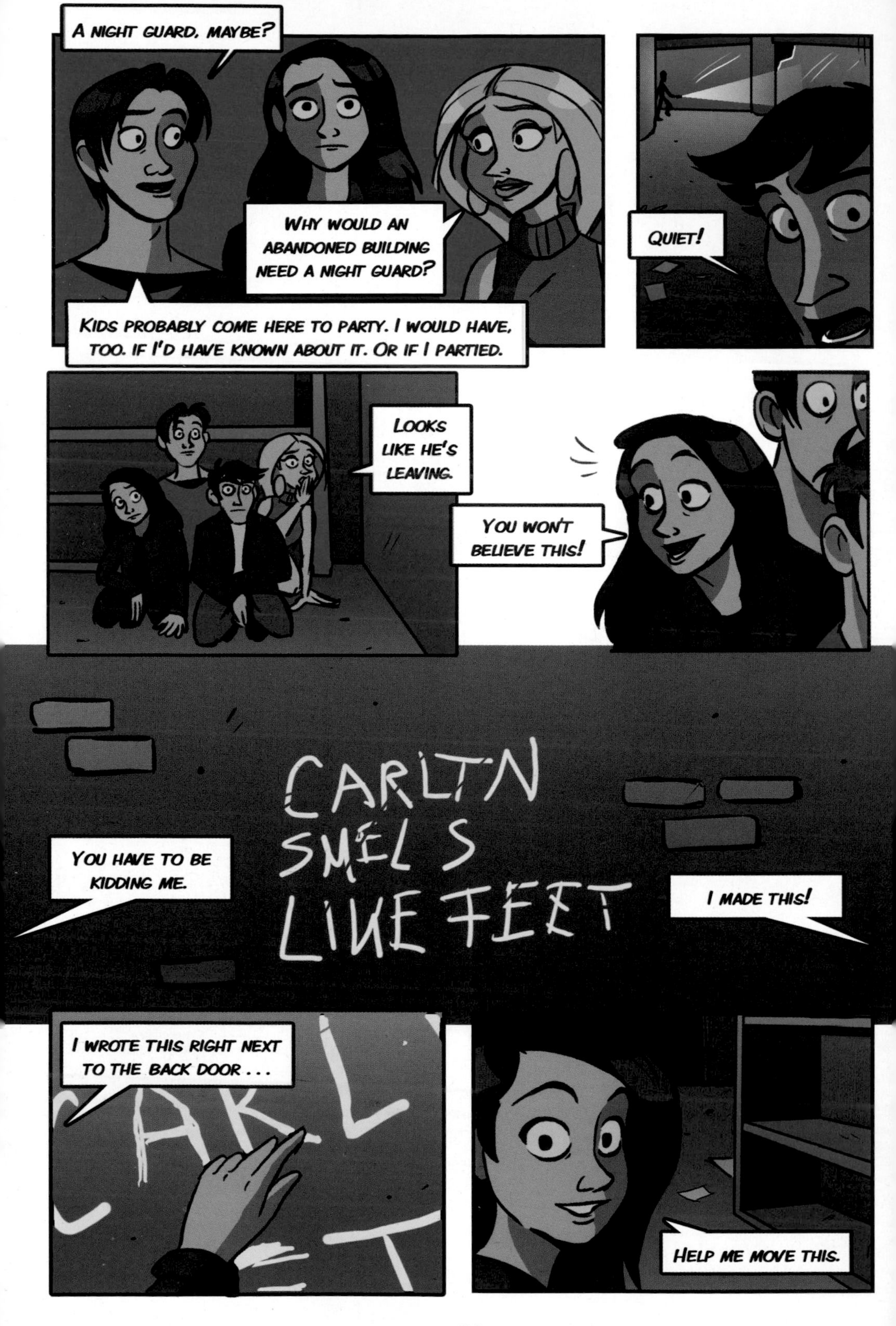
A NIGHT GUARD, MAYBE?
WHY WOULD AN ABANDONED BUILDING NEED A NIGHT GUARD?
KIDS PROBABLY COME HERE TO PARTY. I WOULD HAVE, TOO. IF I'D HAVE KNOWN ABOUT IT. OR IF I PARTIED.
QUIET!
LOOKS LIKE HE'S LEAVING.
YOU WON'T BELIEVE THIS!
YOU HAVE TO BE KIDDING ME.
CARLTN SMELS LIKE FEET
I MADE THIS!
I WROTE THIS RIGHT NEXT TO THE BACK DOOR . . .
HELP ME MOVE THIS.

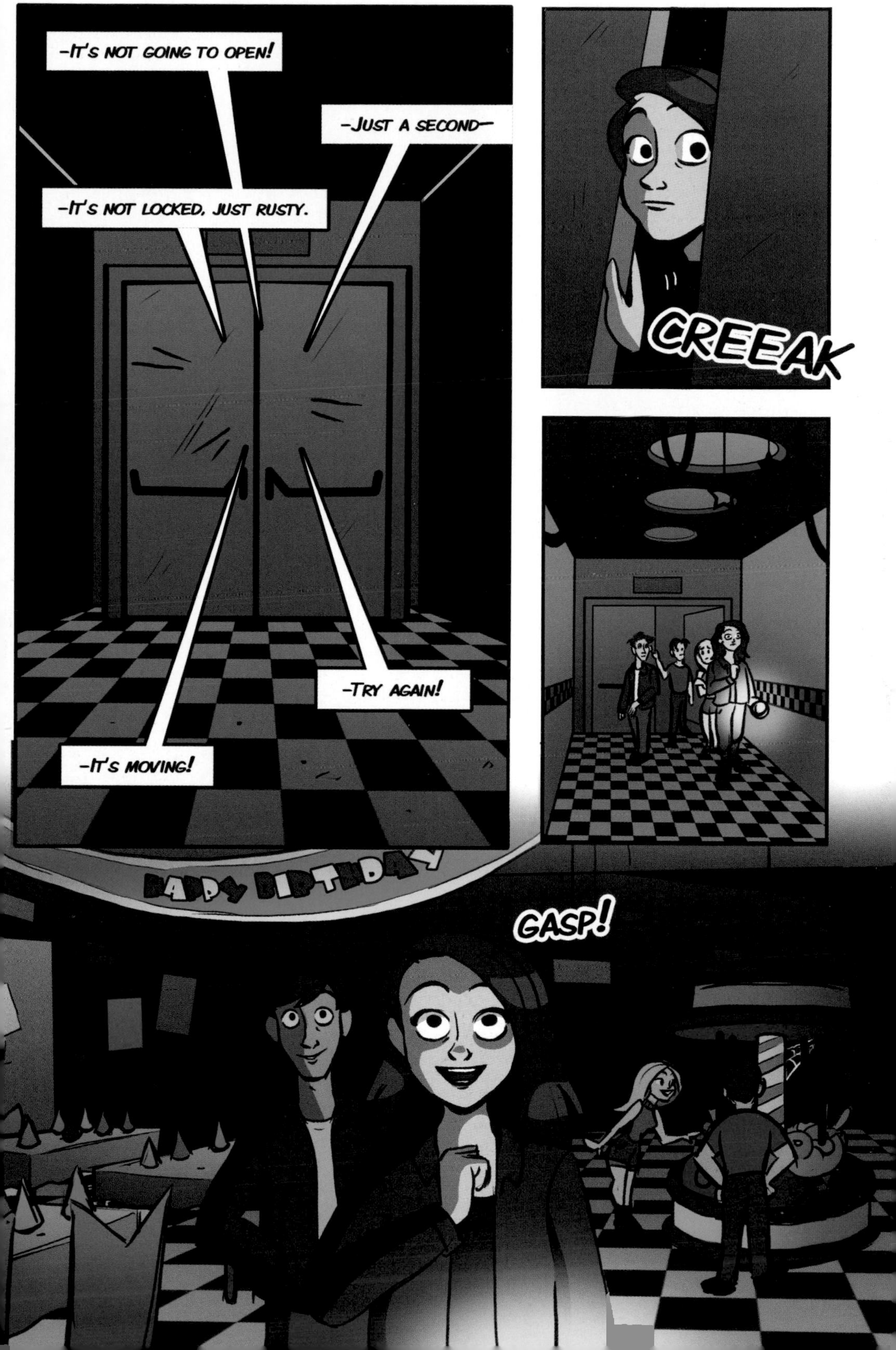
-IT'S NOT GOING TO OPEN!
-JUST A SECOND—
-IT'S NOT LOCKED, JUST RUSTY.
-TRY AGAIN!
-IT'S MOVING!
CREEAK
HAPPY BIRTHDAY
GASP!

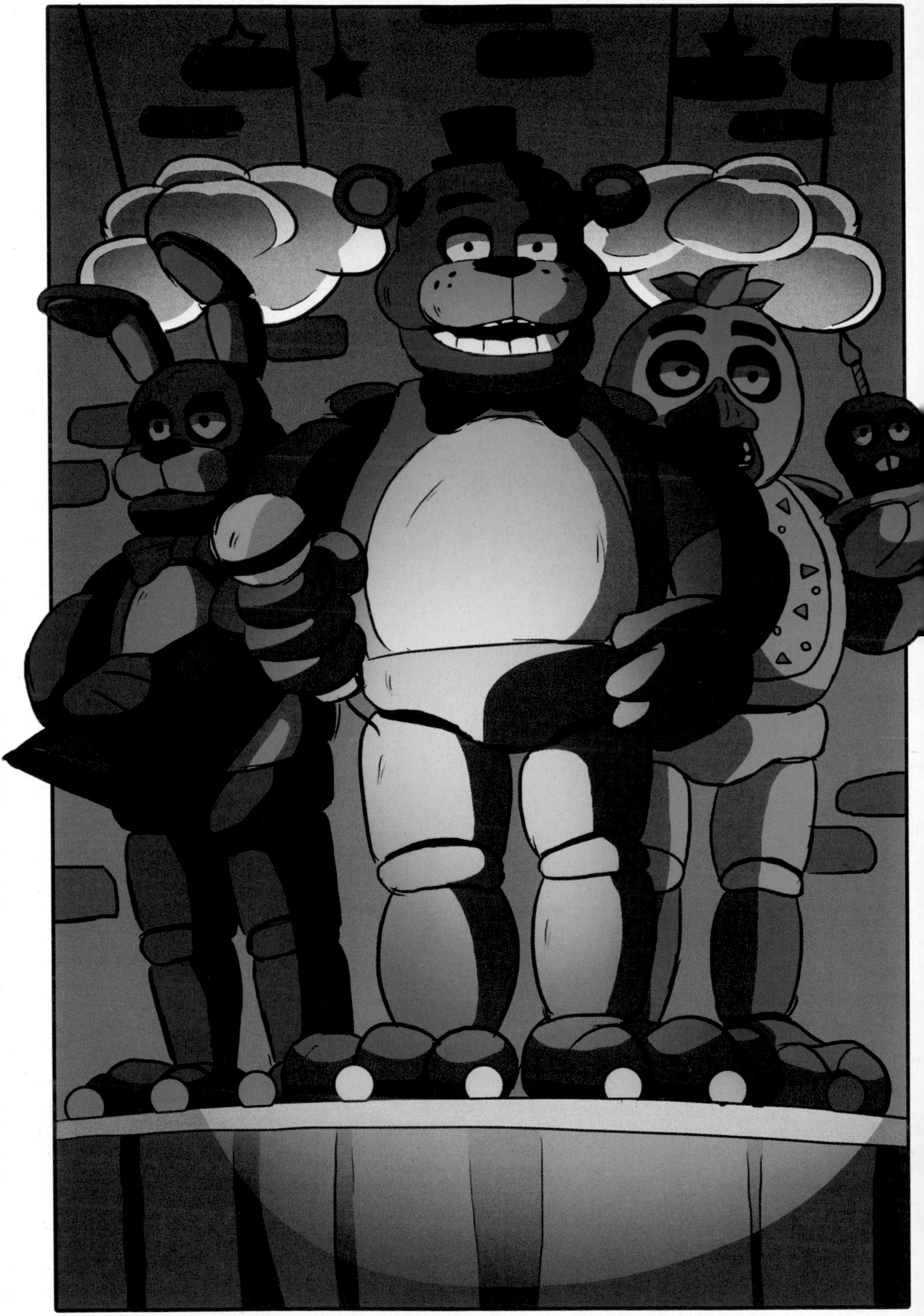

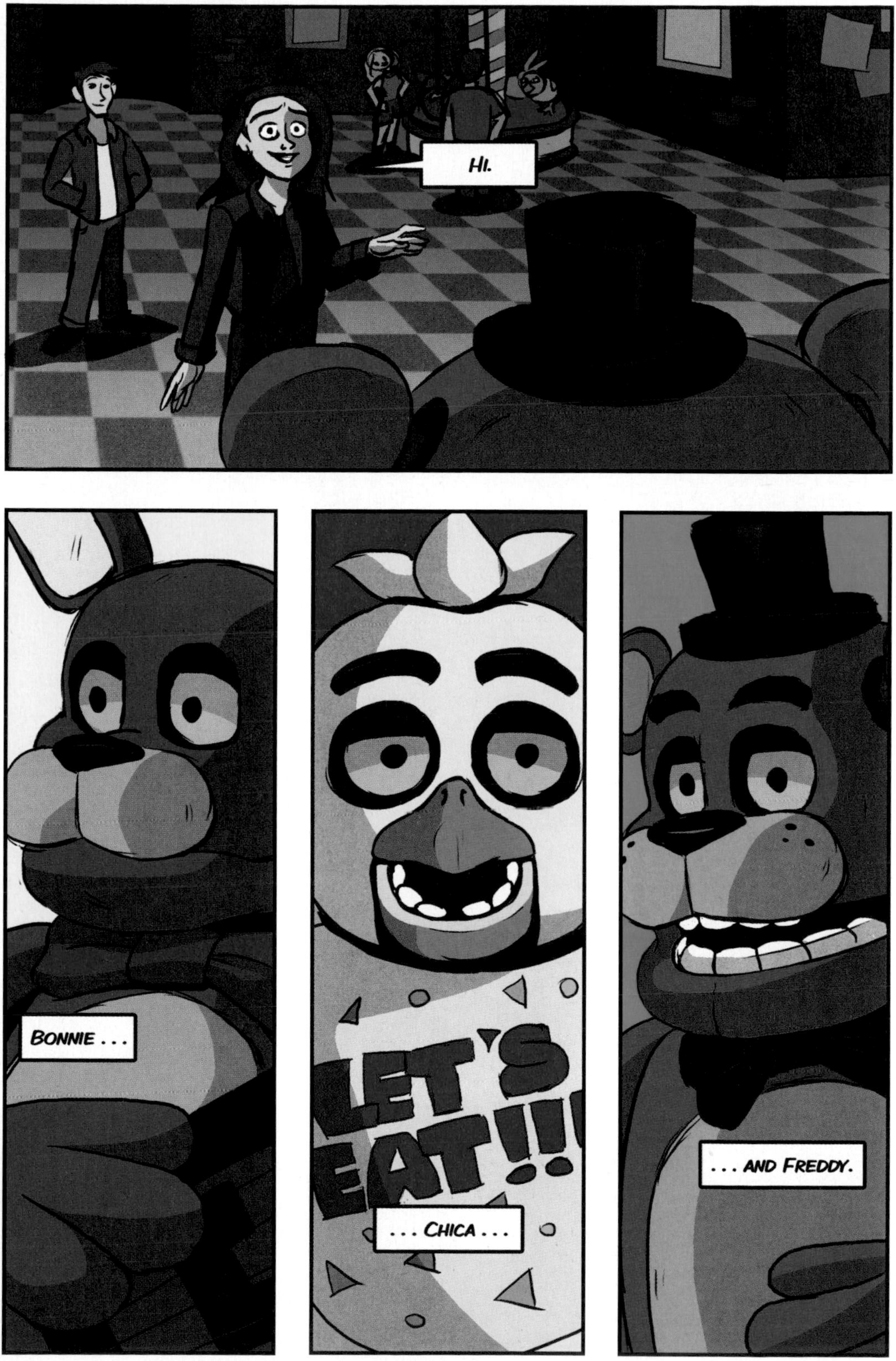
HI.
BONNIE . . .
LET'S EAT!!!
. . . CHICA . . .
. . . AND FREDDY.

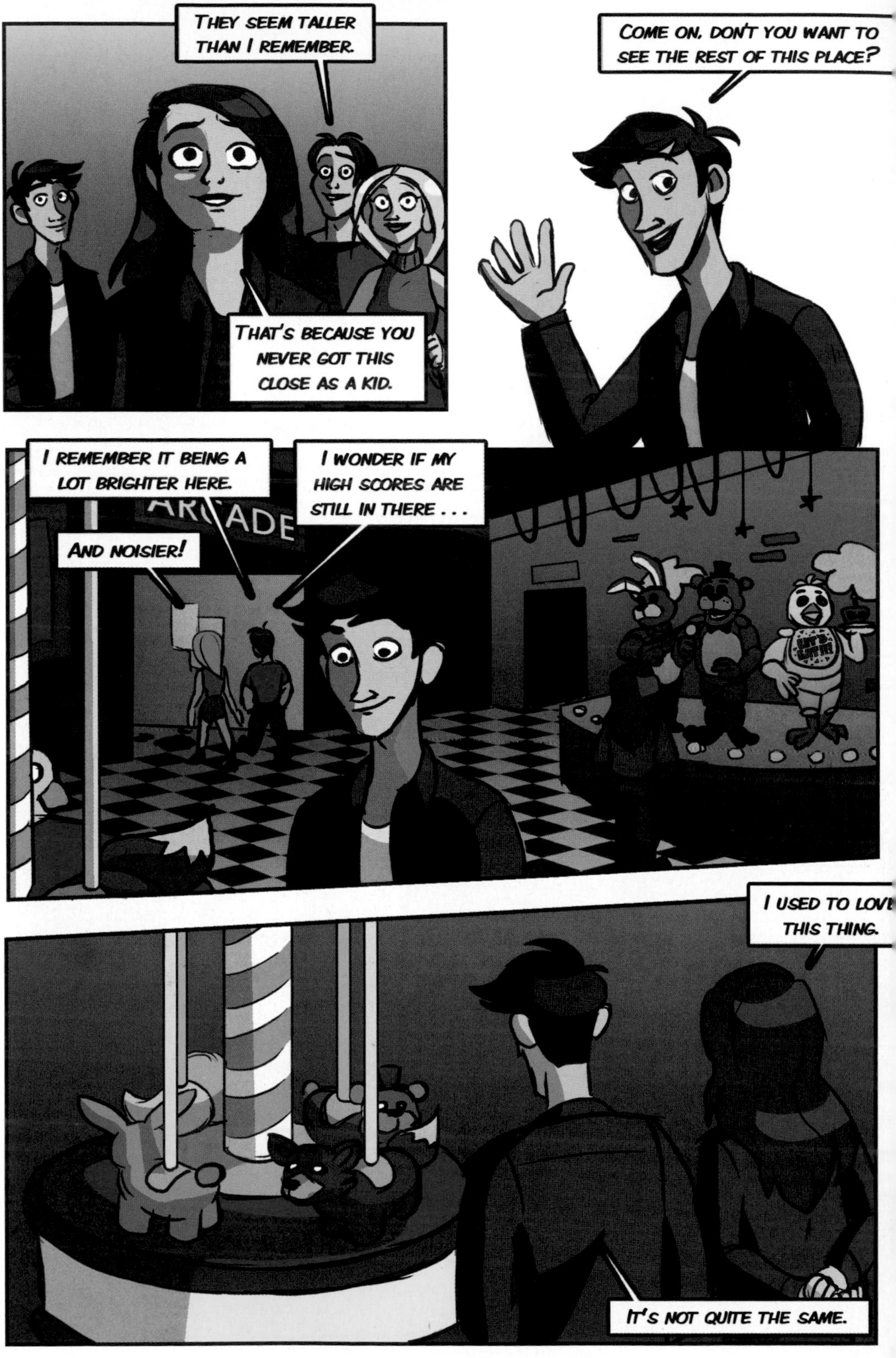
THEY SEEM TALLER THAN I REMEMBER.
THAT'S BECAUSE YOU NEVER GOT THIS CLOSE AS A KID.
COME ON, DON'T YOU WANT TO SEE THE REST OF THIS PLACE?
I REMEMBER IT BEING A LOT BRIGHTER HERE.
AND NOISIER!
I WONDER IF MY HIGH SCORES ARE STILL IN THERE . . .
I USED TO LOVE THIS THING.
IT'S NOT QUITE THE SAME.

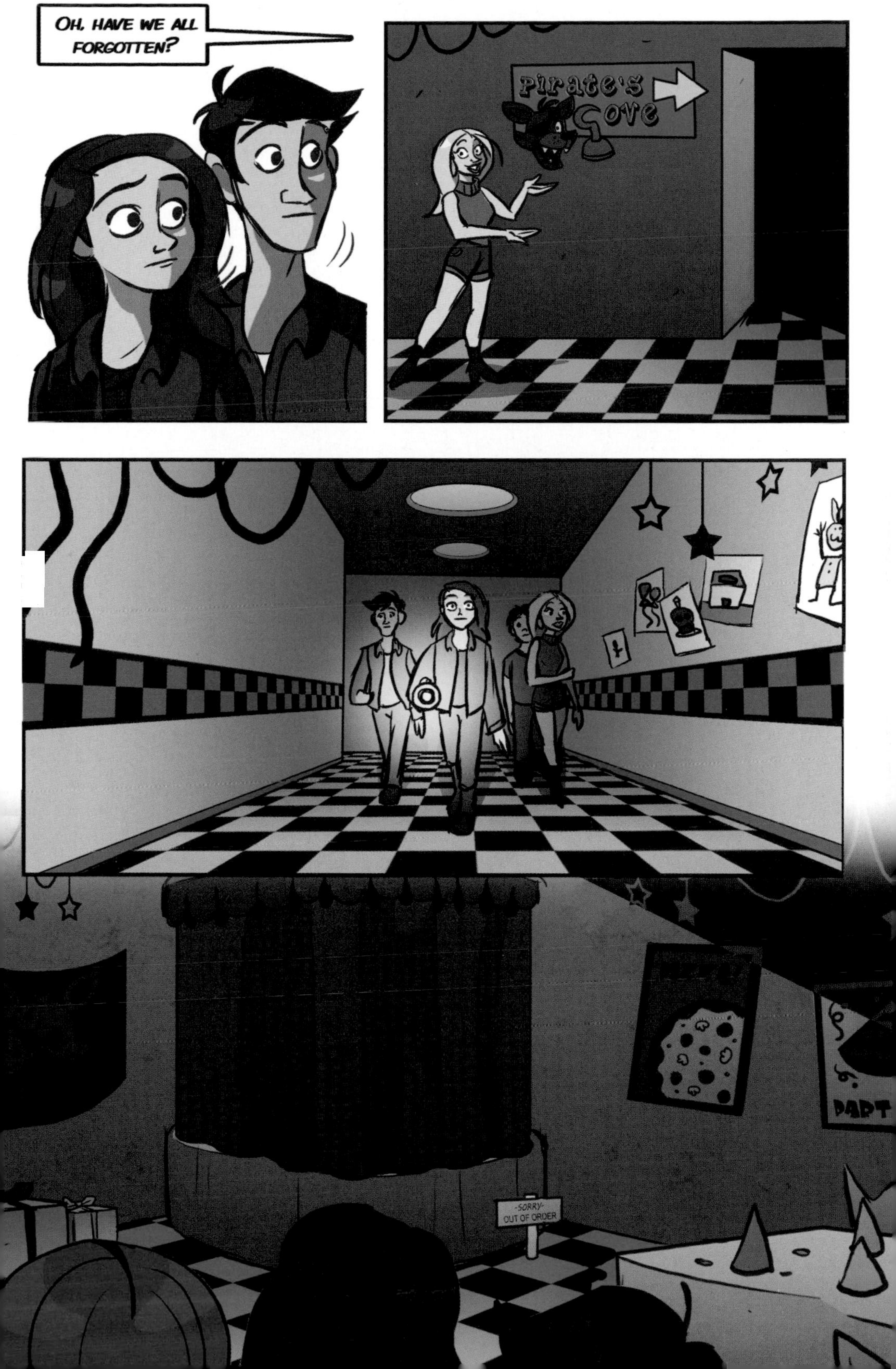

OH, HAVE WE ALL FORGOTTEN?
Pirate's Cove
-SORRY-
OUT OF ORDER
PART

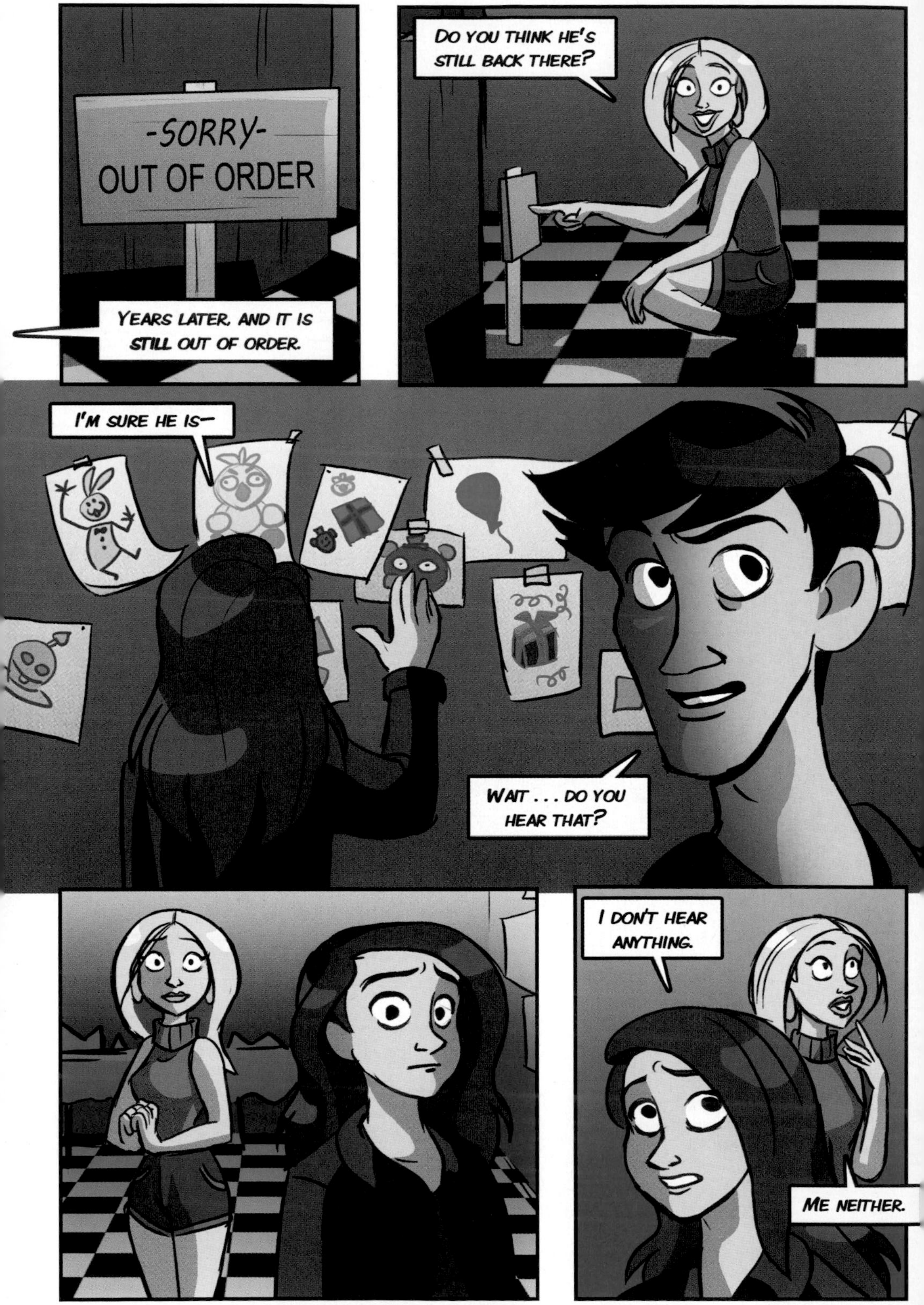
-SORRY-
OUT OF ORDER
YEARS LATER, AND IT IS STILL OUT OF ORDER.
DO YOU THINK HE'S STILL BACK THERE?
I'M SURE HE IS—
WAIT . . . DO YOU HEAR THAT?
I DON'T HEAR ANYTHING.
ME NEITHER.

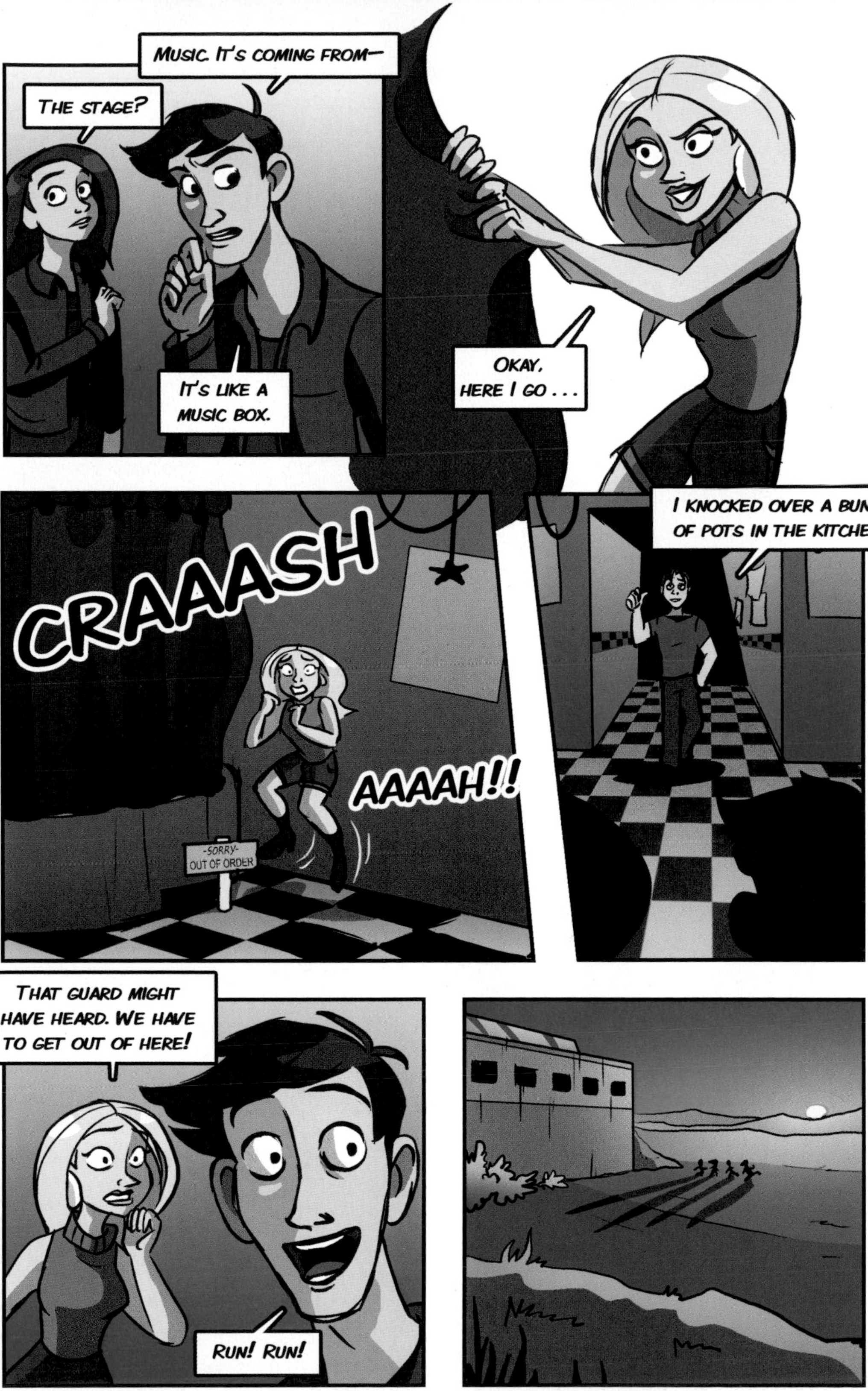
THE STAGE?
MUSIC. IT'S COMING FROM—
IT'S LIKE A MUSIC BOX.
OKAY, HERE I GO . . .
CRAAASH
AAAAH!!
-SORRY- OUT OF ORDER
I KNOCKED OVER A BUNCH OF POTS IN THE KITCHEN.
THAT GUARD MIGHT HAVE HEARD. WE HAVE TO GET OUT OF HERE!
RUN! RUN!

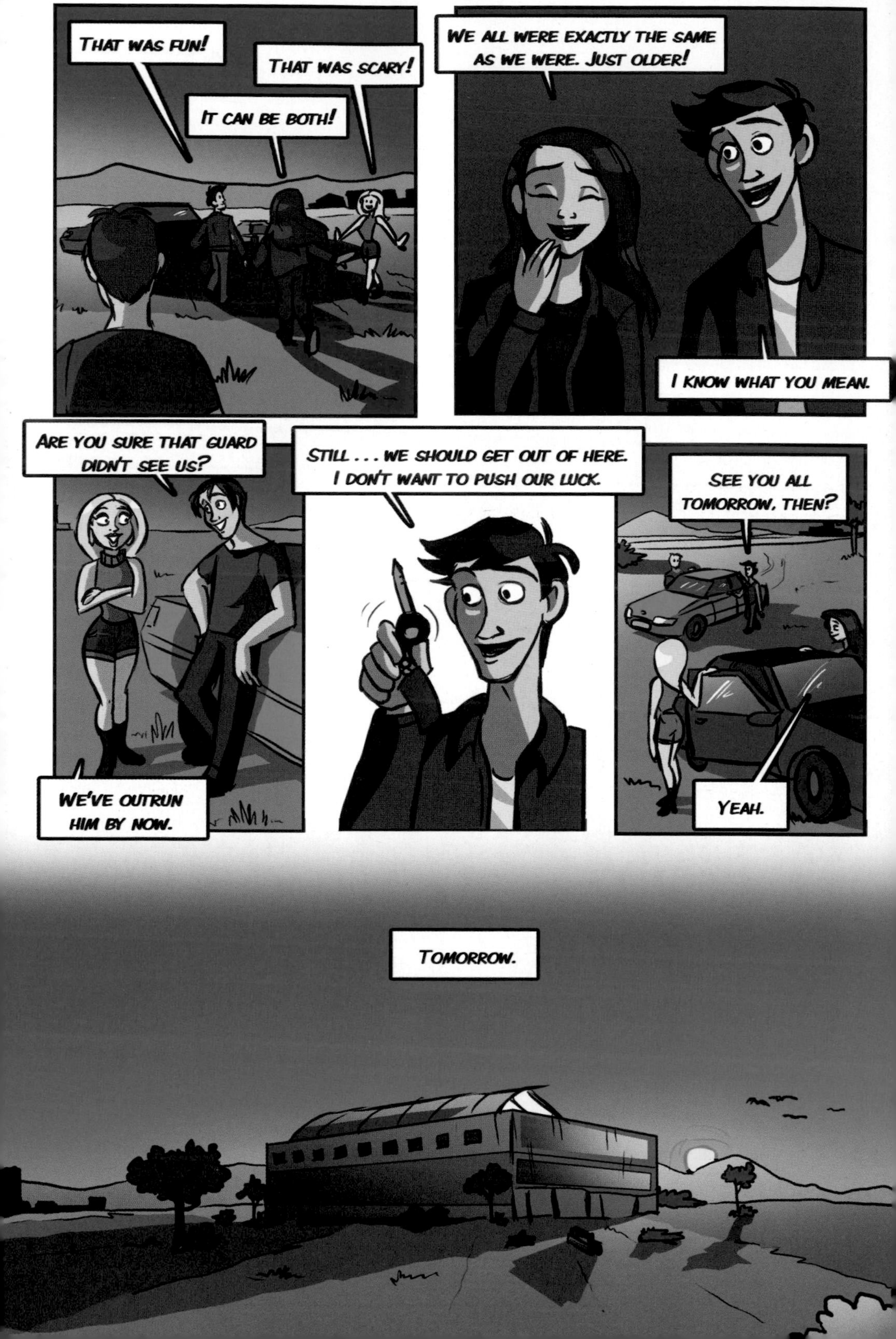
THAT WAS FUN!
THAT WAS SCARY!
IT CAN BE BOTH!
WE ALL WERE EXACTLY THE SAME AS WE WERE. JUST OLDER!
I KNOW WHAT YOU MEAN.
ARE YOU SURE THAT GUARD DIDN'T SEE US?
WE'VE OUTRUN HIM BY NOW.
STILL . . . WE SHOULD GET OUT OF HERE. I DON'T WANT TO PUSH OUR LUCK.
SEE YOU ALL TOMORROW, THEN?
YEAH.
TOMORROW.

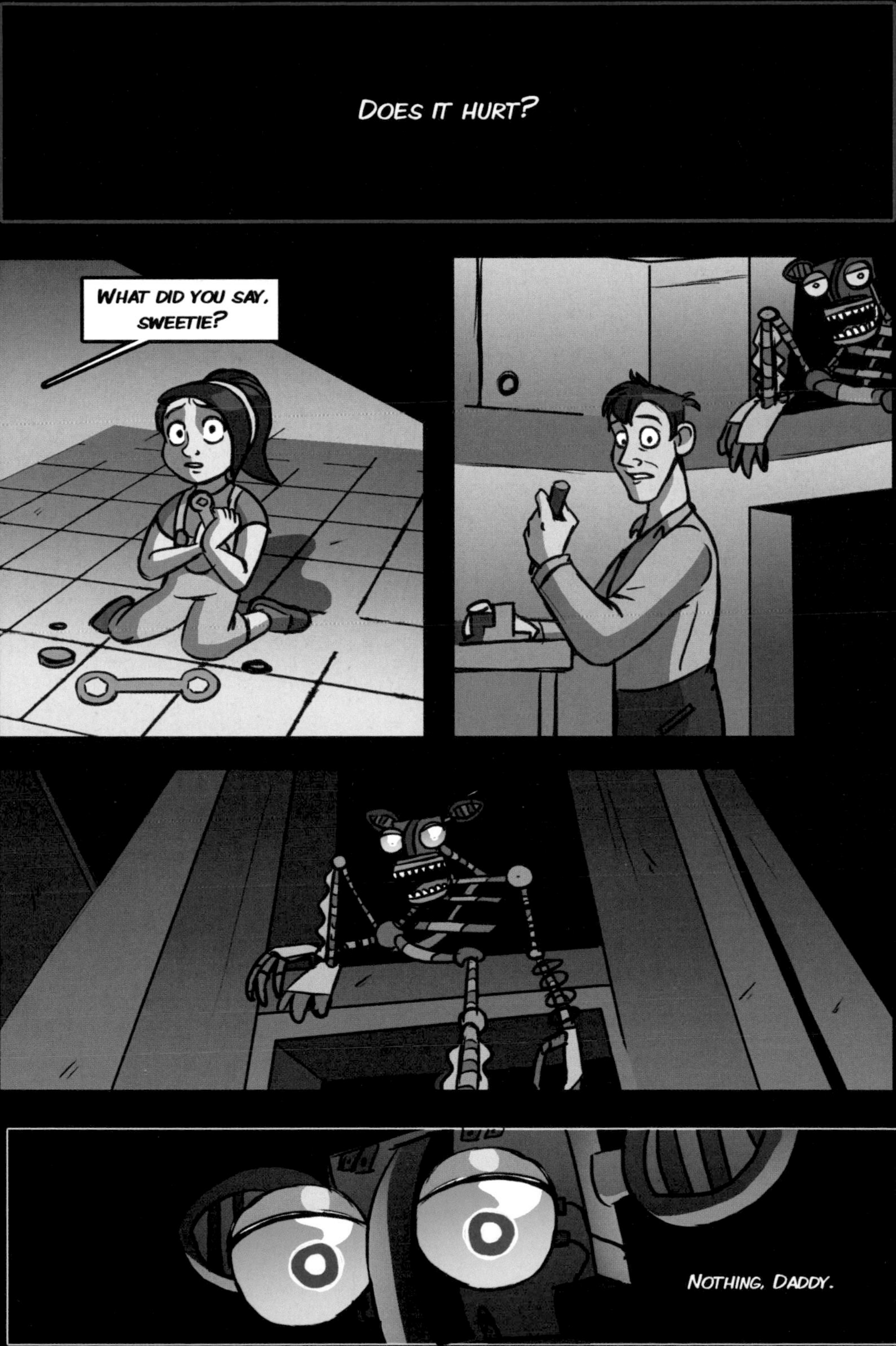
DOES IT HURT?
WHAT DID YOU SAY, SWEETIE?
NOTHING, DADDY.

CHAPTER 3

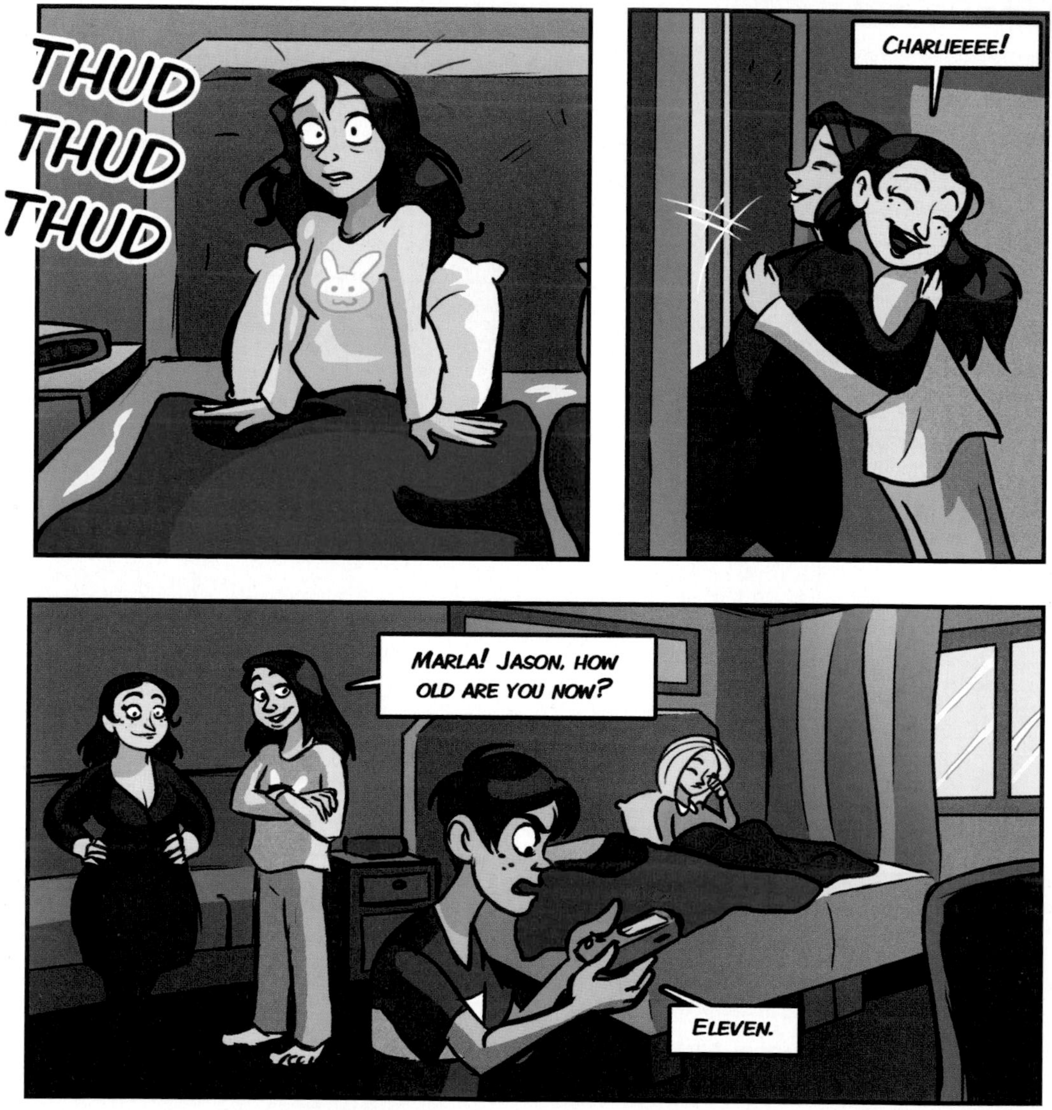
THUD
THUD
THUD
CHARLIEEEE!
MARLA! JASON, HOW OLD ARE YOU NOW?
ELEVEN.

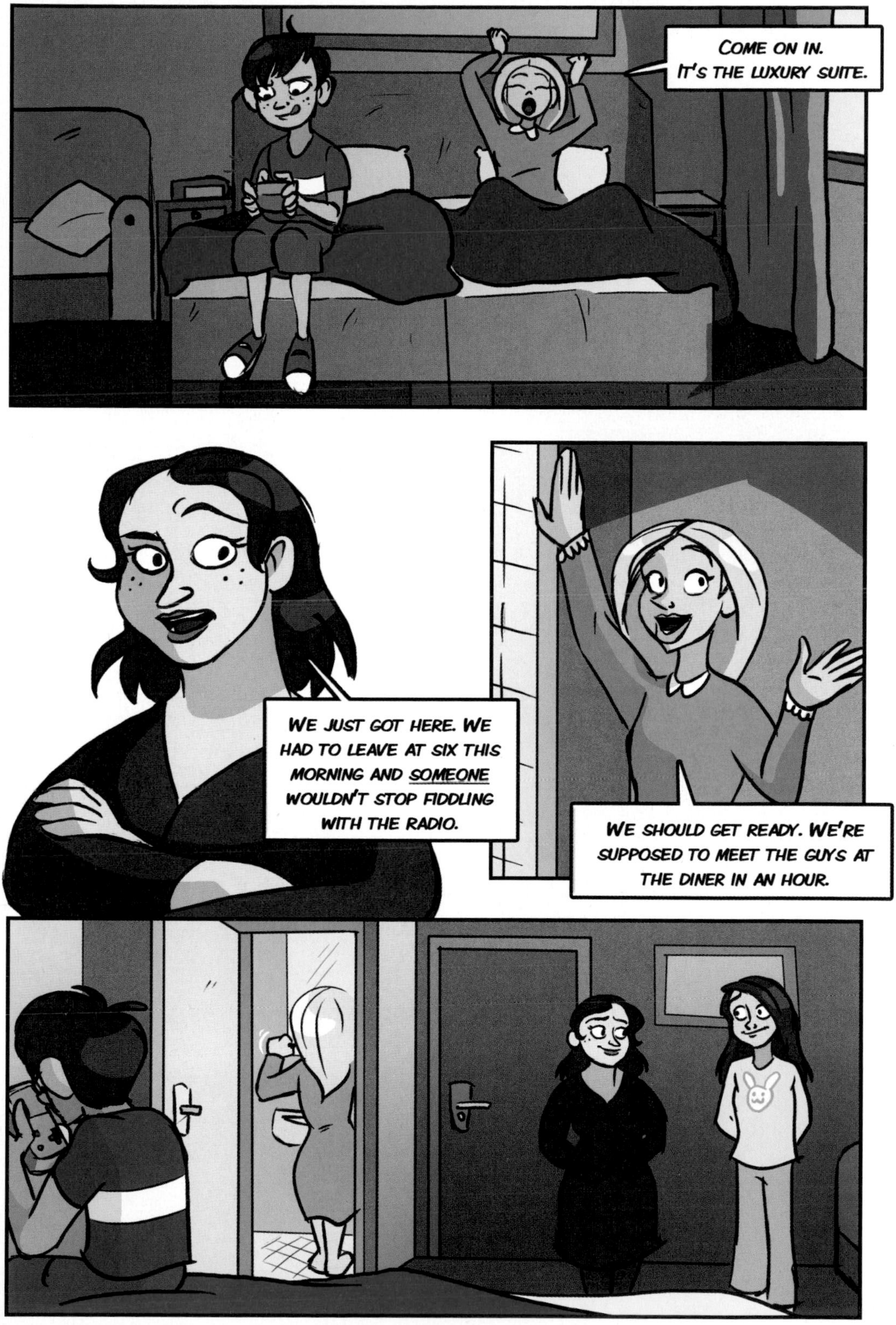
COME ON IN.
IT'S THE LUXURY SUITE.
WE JUST GOT HERE. WE HAD TO LEAVE AT SIX THIS MORNING AND SOMEONE WOULDN'T STOP FIDDLING WITH THE RADIO.
WE SHOULD GET READY. WE'RE SUPPOSED TO MEET THE GUYS AT THE DINER IN AN HOUR.

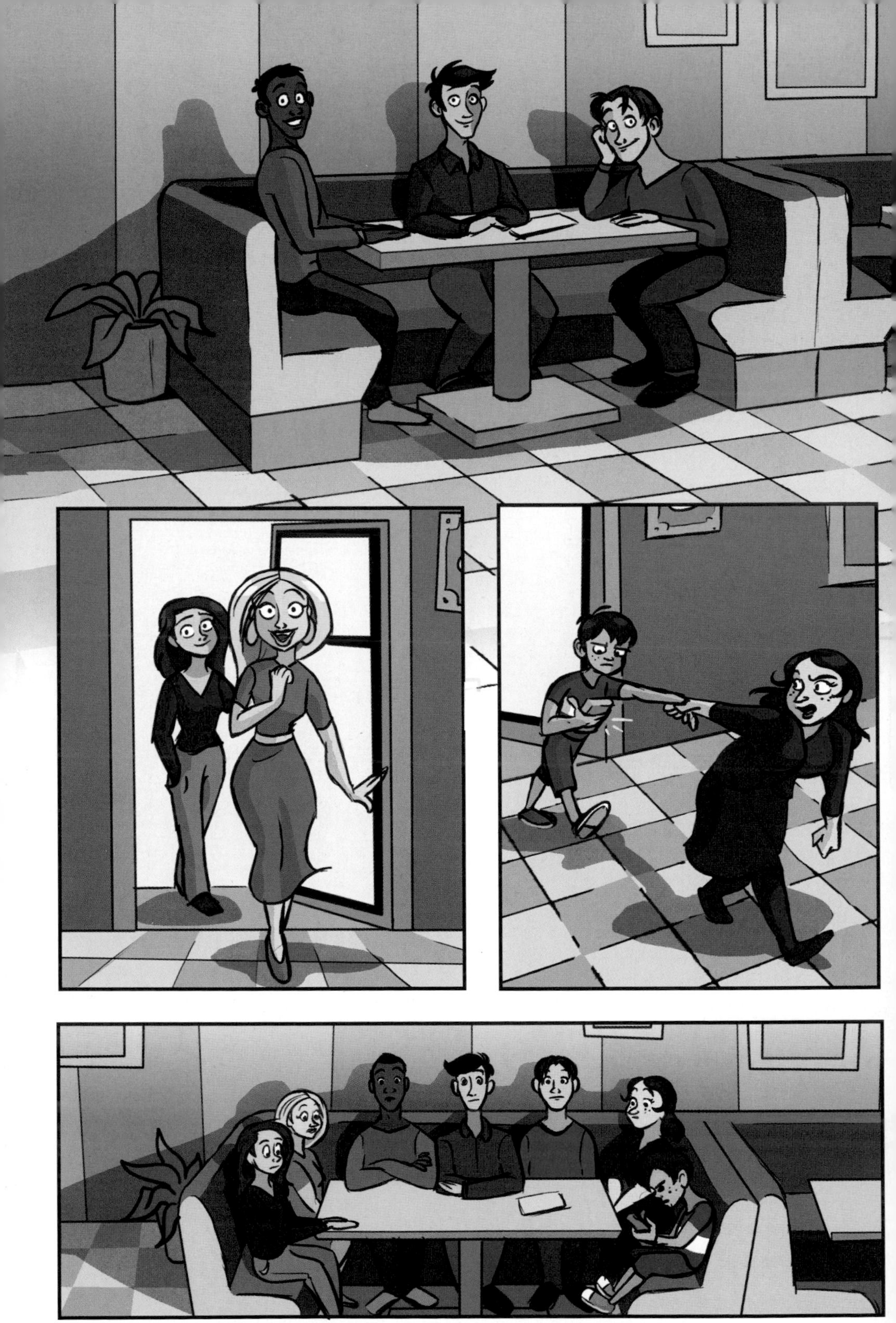

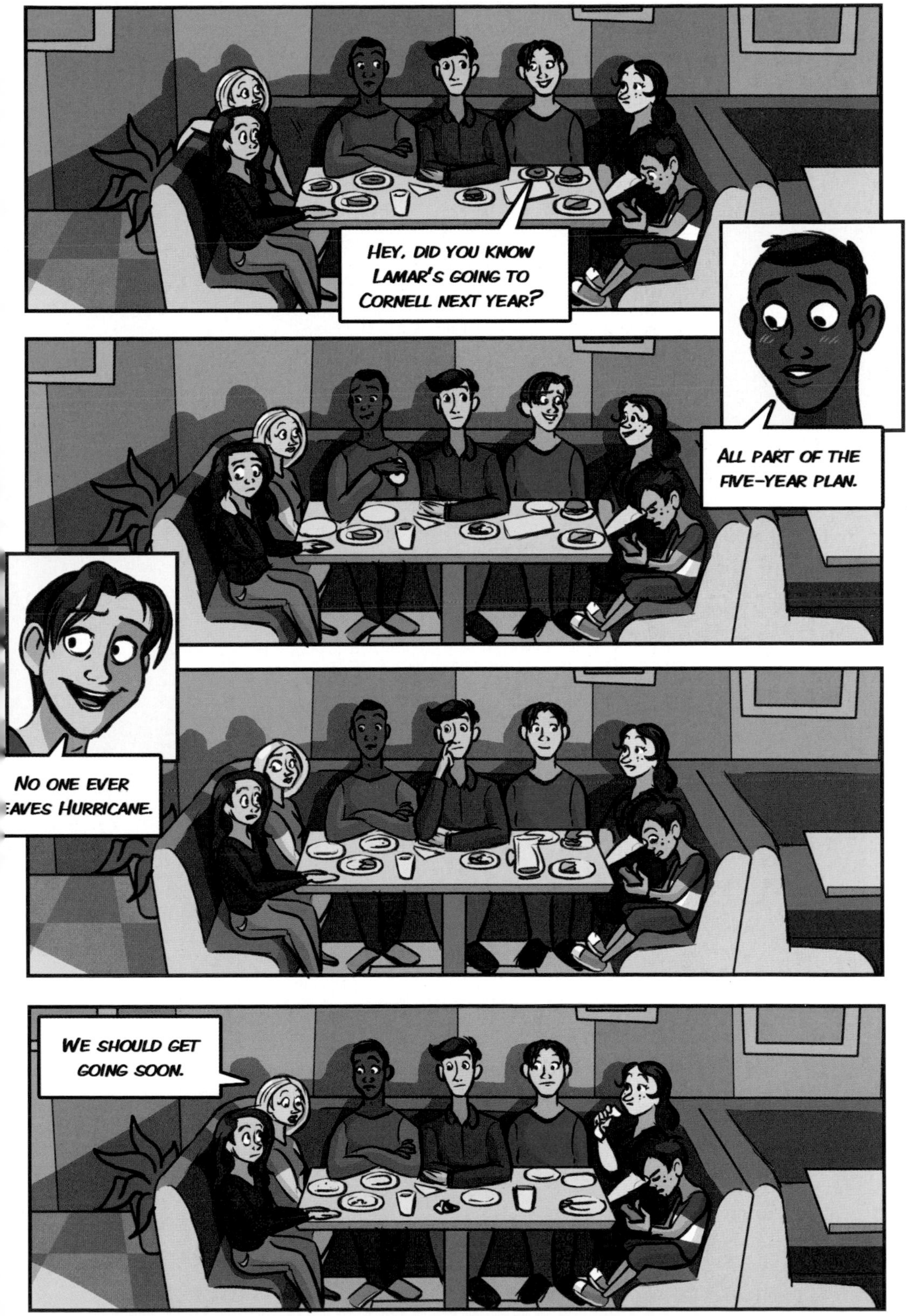
HEY, DID YOU KNOW LAMAR'S GOING TO CORNELL NEXT YEAR?
ALL PART OF THE FIVE-YEAR PLAN.
NO ONE EVER
EAVES HURRICANE.
WE SHOULD GET GOING SOON.

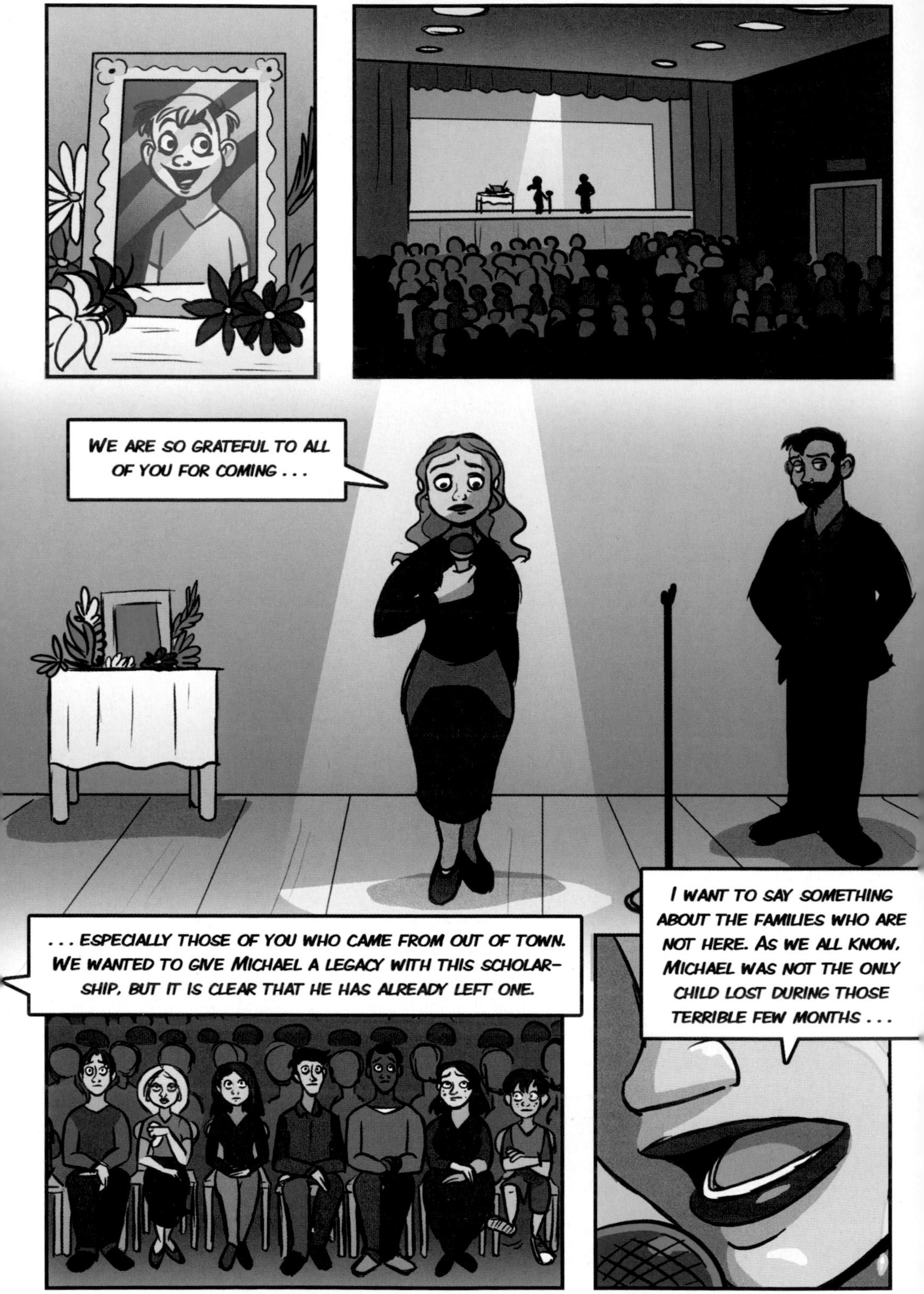
WE ARE SO GRATEFUL TO ALL OF YOU FOR COMING . . .
. . . ESPECIALLY THOSE OF YOU WHO CAME FROM OUT OF TOWN. WE WANTED TO GIVE MICHAEL A LEGACY WITH THIS SCHOLAR-SHIP, BUT IT IS CLEAR THAT HE HAS ALREADY LEFT ONE.
I WANT TO SAY SOMETHING ABOUT THE FAMILIES WHO ARE NOT HERE. AS WE ALL KNOW, MICHAEL WAS NOT THE ONLY CHILD LOST DURING THOSE TERRIBLE FEW MONTHS . . .

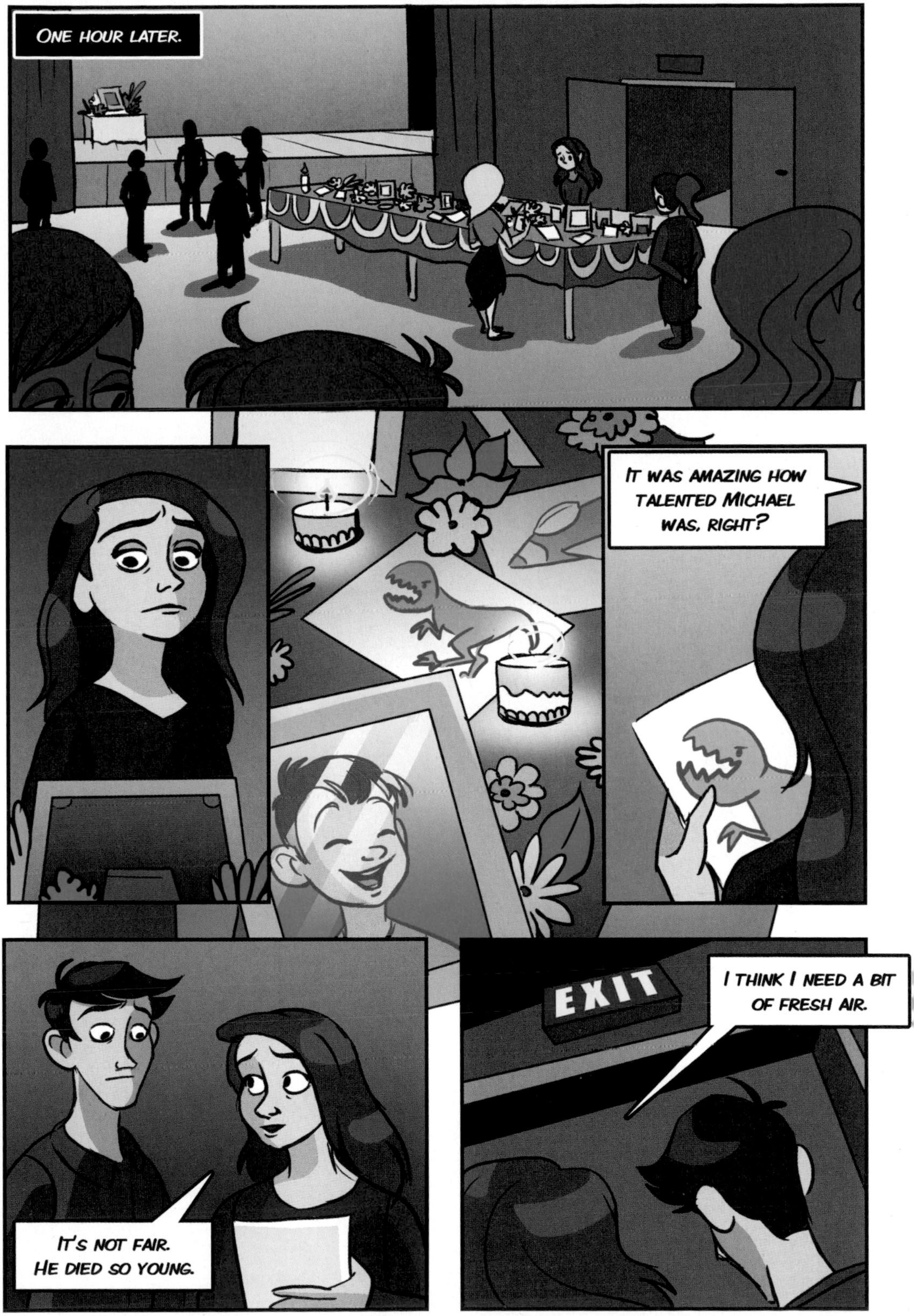
ONE HOUR LATER.
IT WAS AMAZING HOW TALENTED MICHAEL WAS, RIGHT?
IT'S NOT FAIR. HE DIED SO YOUNG.
EXIT
I THINK I NEED A BIT OF FRESH AIR.

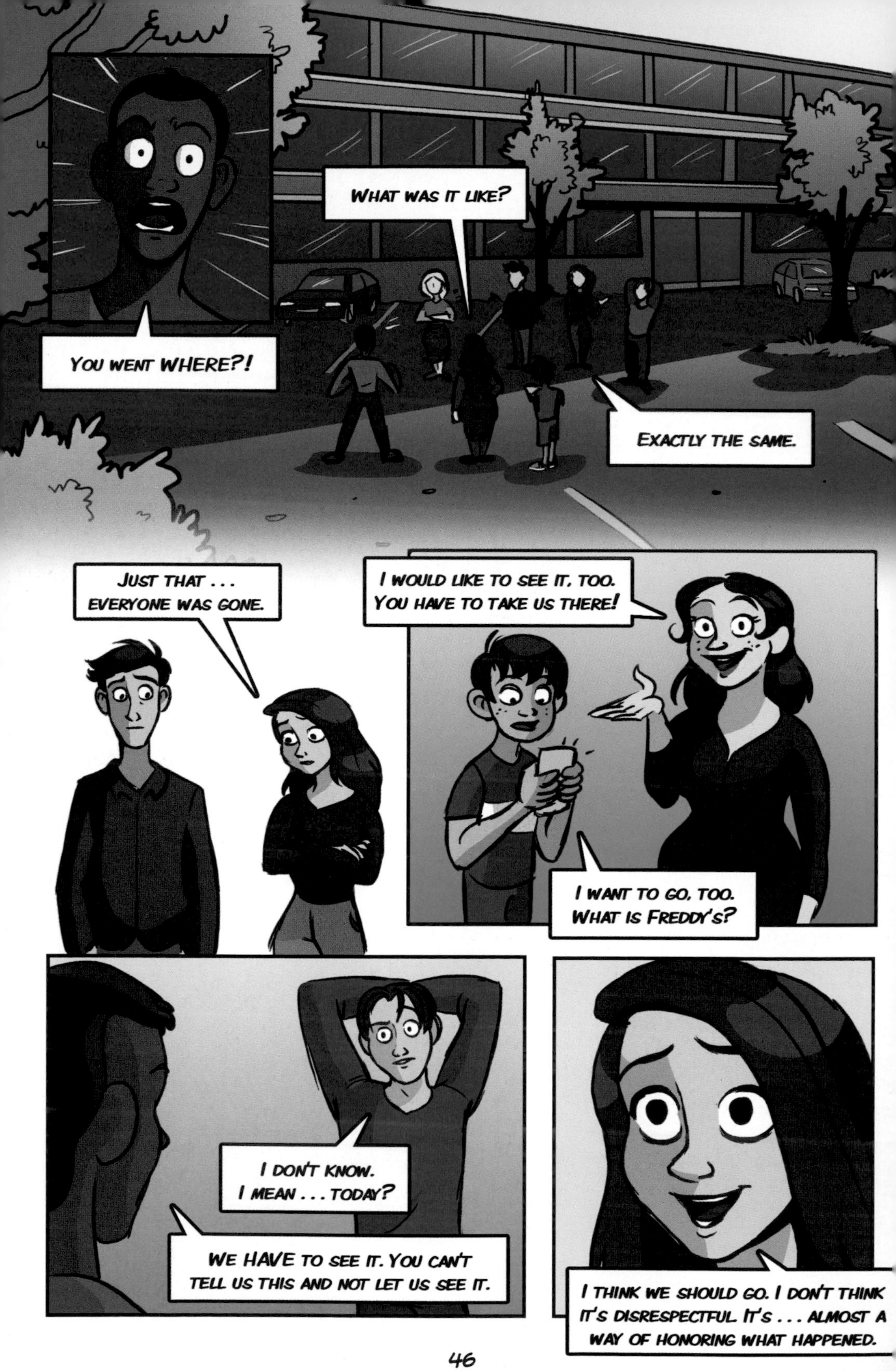

YOU WENT WHERE?!
WHAT WAS IT LIKE?
EXACTLY THE SAME.
JUST THAT . . . EVERYONE WAS GONE.
I WOULD LIKE TO SEE IT, TOO. YOU HAVE TO TAKE US THERE!
I WANT TO GO, TOO. WHAT IS FREDDY'S?
I DON'T KNOW. I MEAN . . . TODAY?
WE HAVE TO SEE IT. YOU CAN'T TELL US THIS AND NOT LET US SEE IT.
I THINK WE SHOULD GO. I DON'T THINK IT'S DISRESPECTFUL. IT'S . . . ALMOST A WAY OF HONORING WHAT HAPPENED.

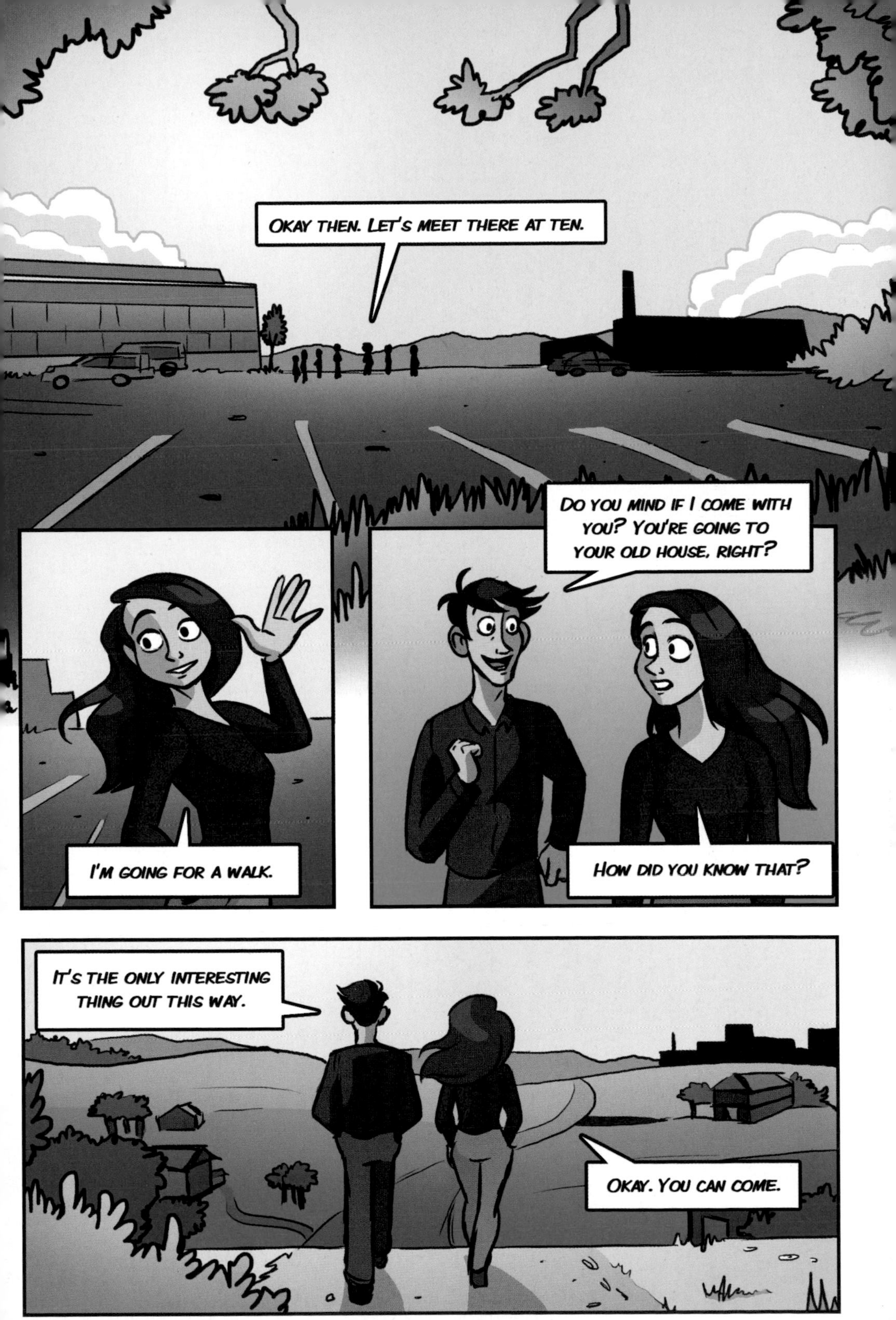
OKAY THEN. LET'S MEET THERE AT TEN.
I'M GOING FOR A WALK.
DO YOU MIND IF I COME WITH YOU? YOU'RE GOING TO YOUR OLD HOUSE, RIGHT?
HOW DID YOU KNOW THAT?
IT'S THE ONLY INTERESTING THING OUT THIS WAY.
OKAY. YOU CAN COME.

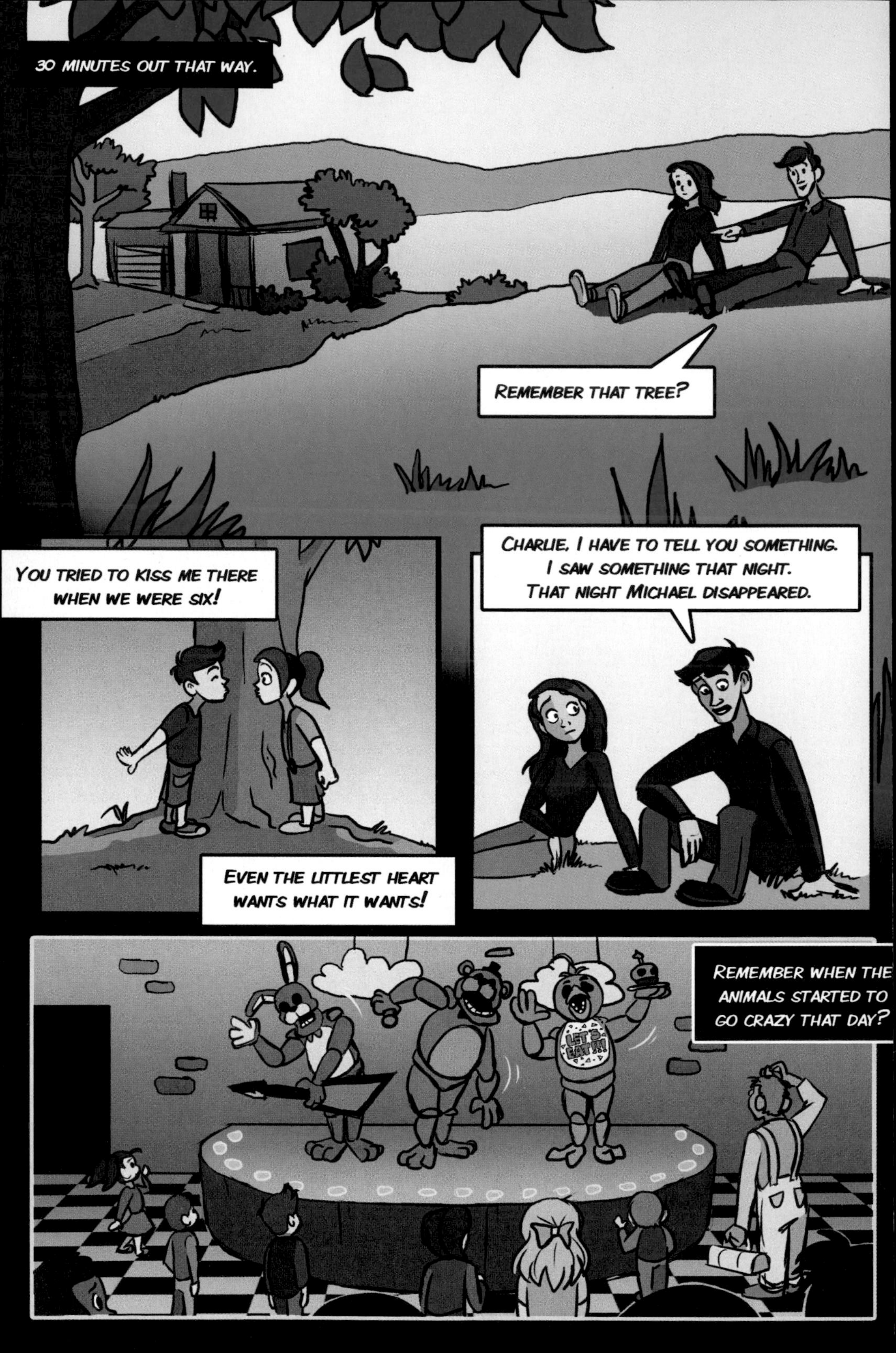

30 MINUTES OUT THAT WAY.
REMEMBER THAT TREE?
YOU TRIED TO KISS ME THERE WHEN WE WERE SIX!
EVEN THE LITTLEST HEART WANTS WHAT IT WANTS!
CHARLIE, I HAVE TO TELL YOU SOMETHING. I SAW SOMETHING THAT NIGHT. THAT NIGHT MICHAEL DISAPPEARED.
REMEMBER WHEN THE ANIMALS STARTED TO GO CRAZY THAT DAY?
LET'S EAT!!!

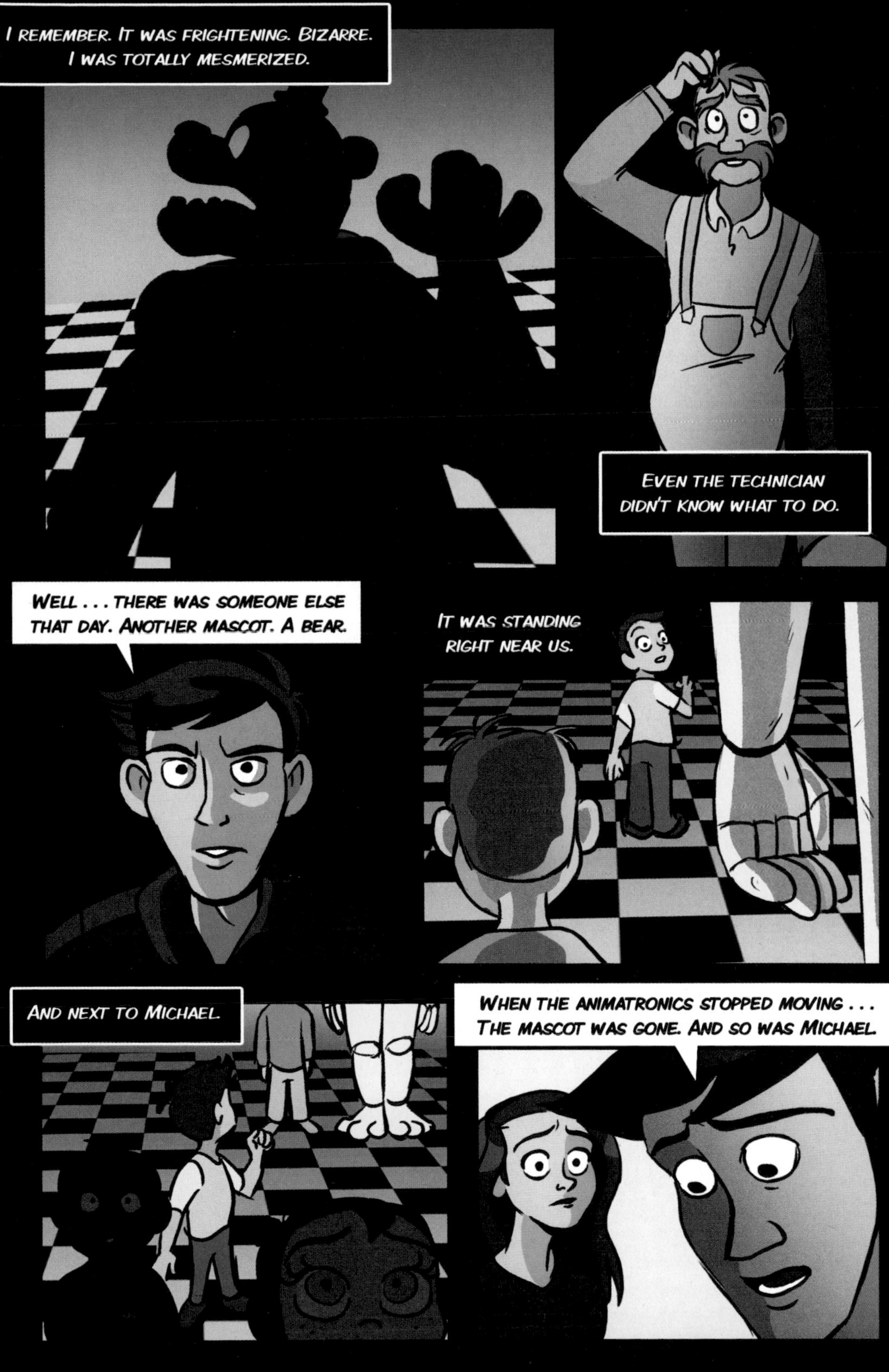
I REMEMBER. IT WAS FRIGHTENING. BIZARRE. I WAS TOTALLY MESMERIZED.
EVEN THE TECHNICIAN DIDN'T KNOW WHAT TO DO.
WELL . . . THERE WAS SOMEONE ELSE THAT DAY. ANOTHER MASCOT. A BEAR.
IT WAS STANDING RIGHT NEAR US.
AND NEXT TO MICHAEL.
WHEN THE ANIMATRONICS STOPPED MOVING . . . THE MASCOT WAS GONE. AND SO WAS MICHAEL.

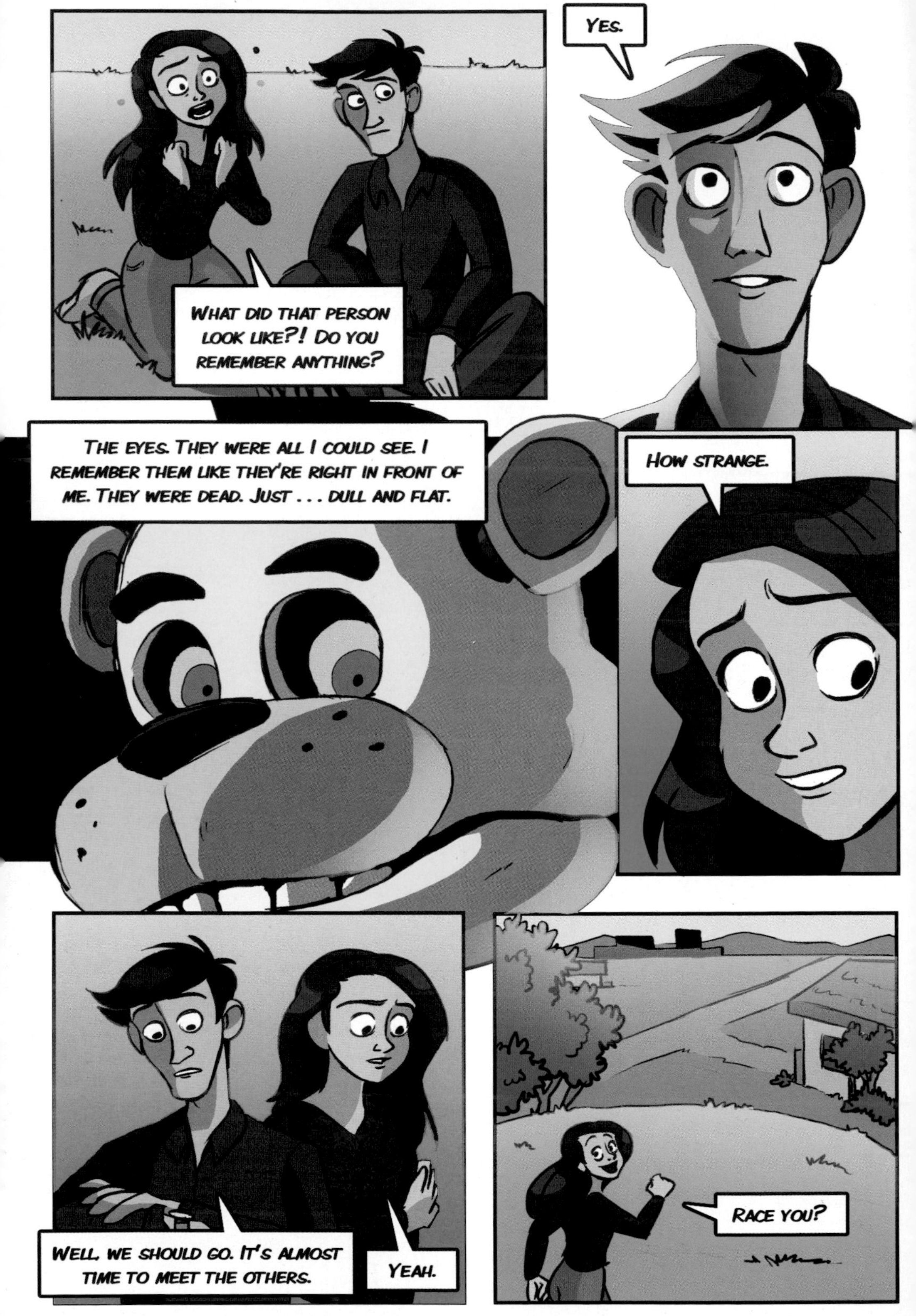
What did that person look like?! Do you remember anything?
Yes.
The eyes. They were all I could see. I remember them like they're right in front of me. They were dead. Just . . . dull and flat.
How strange.
Well, we should go. It's almost time to meet the others.
Yeah.
Race you?

CHAPTER 4

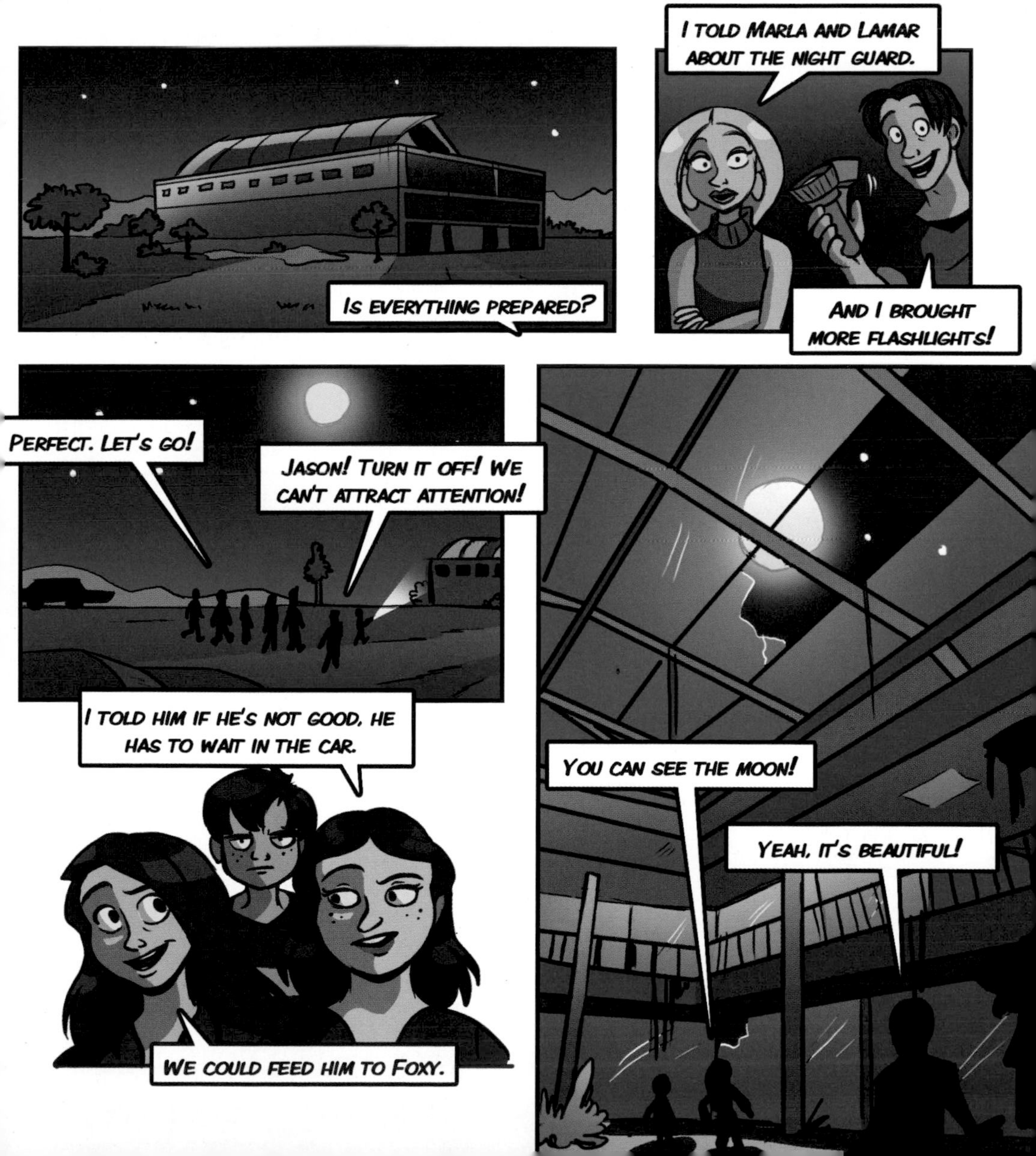

Is everything prepared?
I told Marla and Lamar about the night guard.
And I brought more flashlights!
Perfect. Let's go!
Jason! Turn it off! We can't attract attention!
I told him if he's not good, he has to wait in the car.
We could feed him to Foxy.
You can see the moon!
Yeah, it's beautiful!

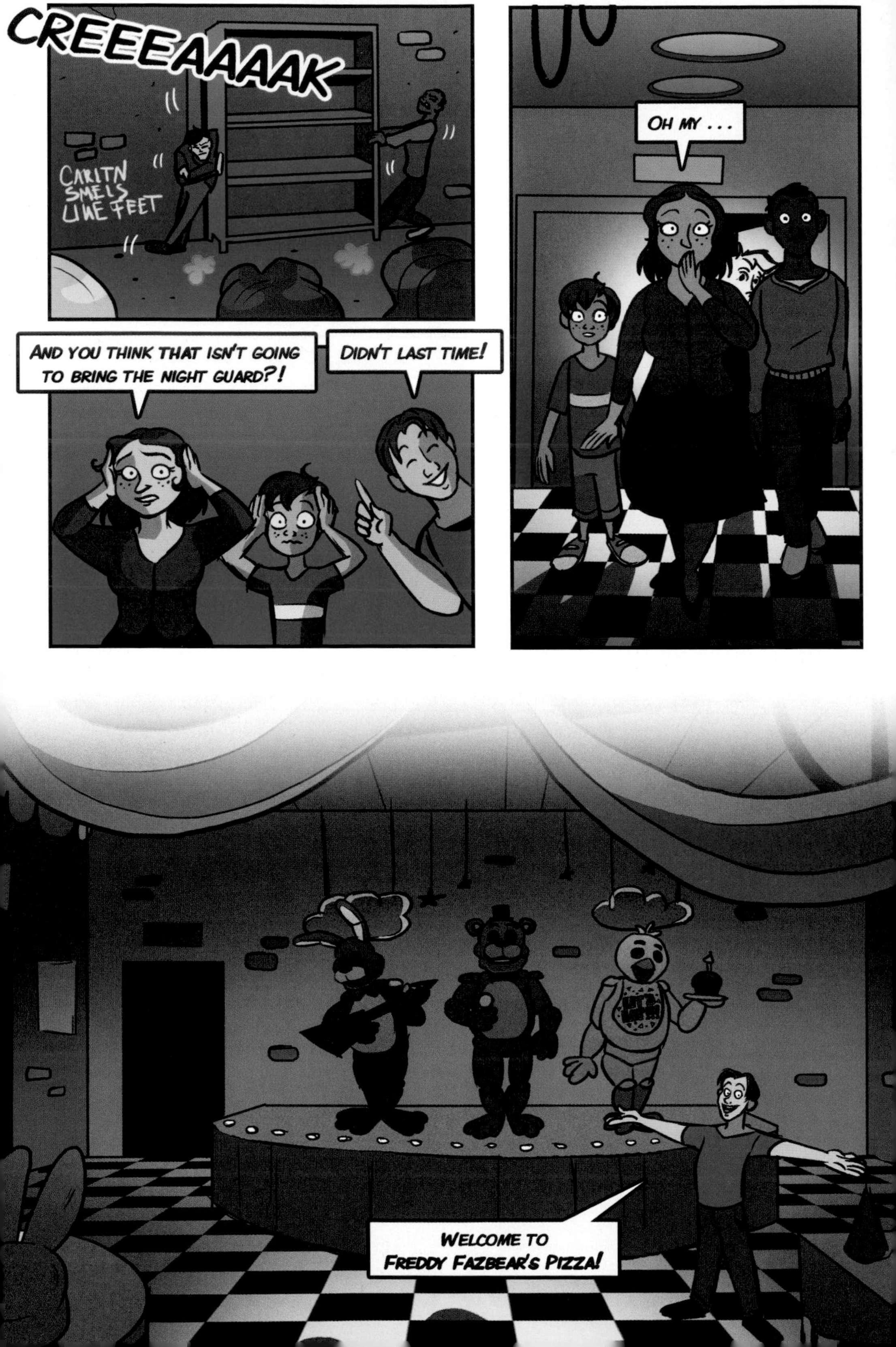
CREEEAAAAK
CARLTN SMELS LIKE FEET
AND YOU THINK THAT ISN'T GOING TO BRING THE NIGHT GUARD?!
DIDN'T LAST TIME!
OH MY . . .
WELCOME TO FREDDY FAZBEAR'S PIZZA!

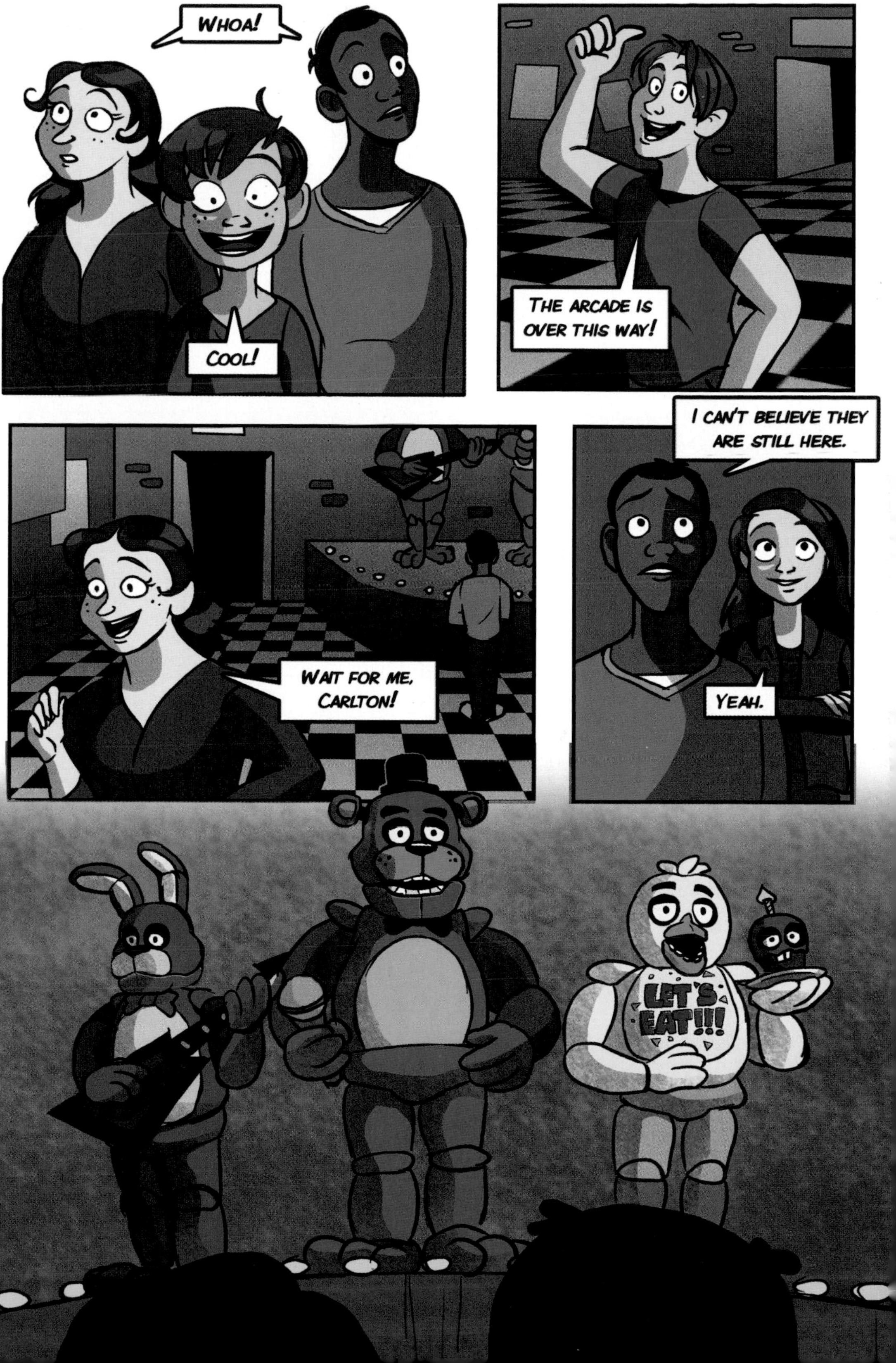
WHOA!
COOL!
THE ARCADE IS OVER THIS WAY!
WAIT FOR ME, CARLTON!
I CAN'T BELIEVE THEY ARE STILL HERE.
YEAH.
LET'S EAT!!!

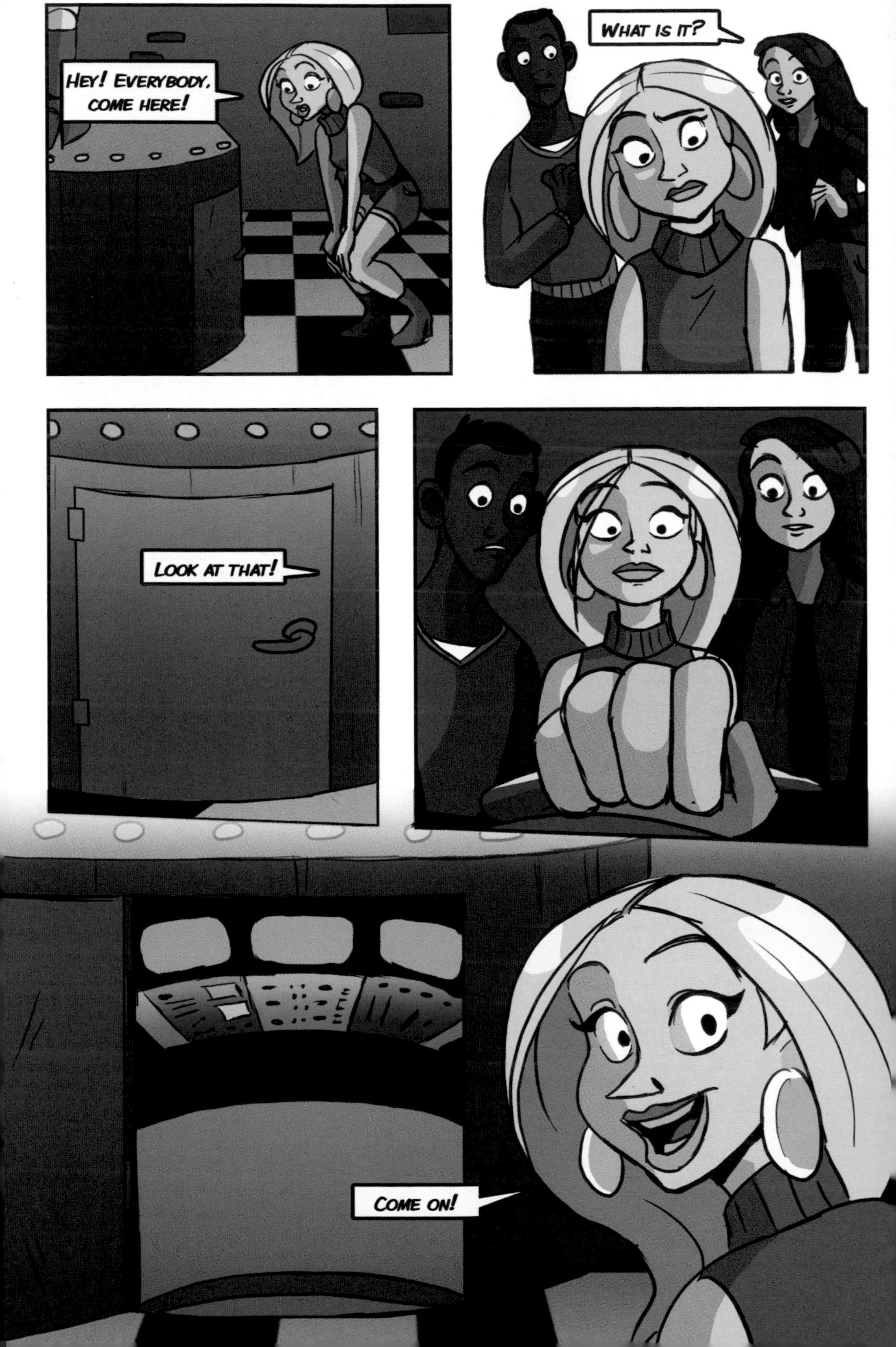
HEY! EVERYBODY, COME HERE!
WHAT IS IT?
LOOK AT THAT!
COME ON!

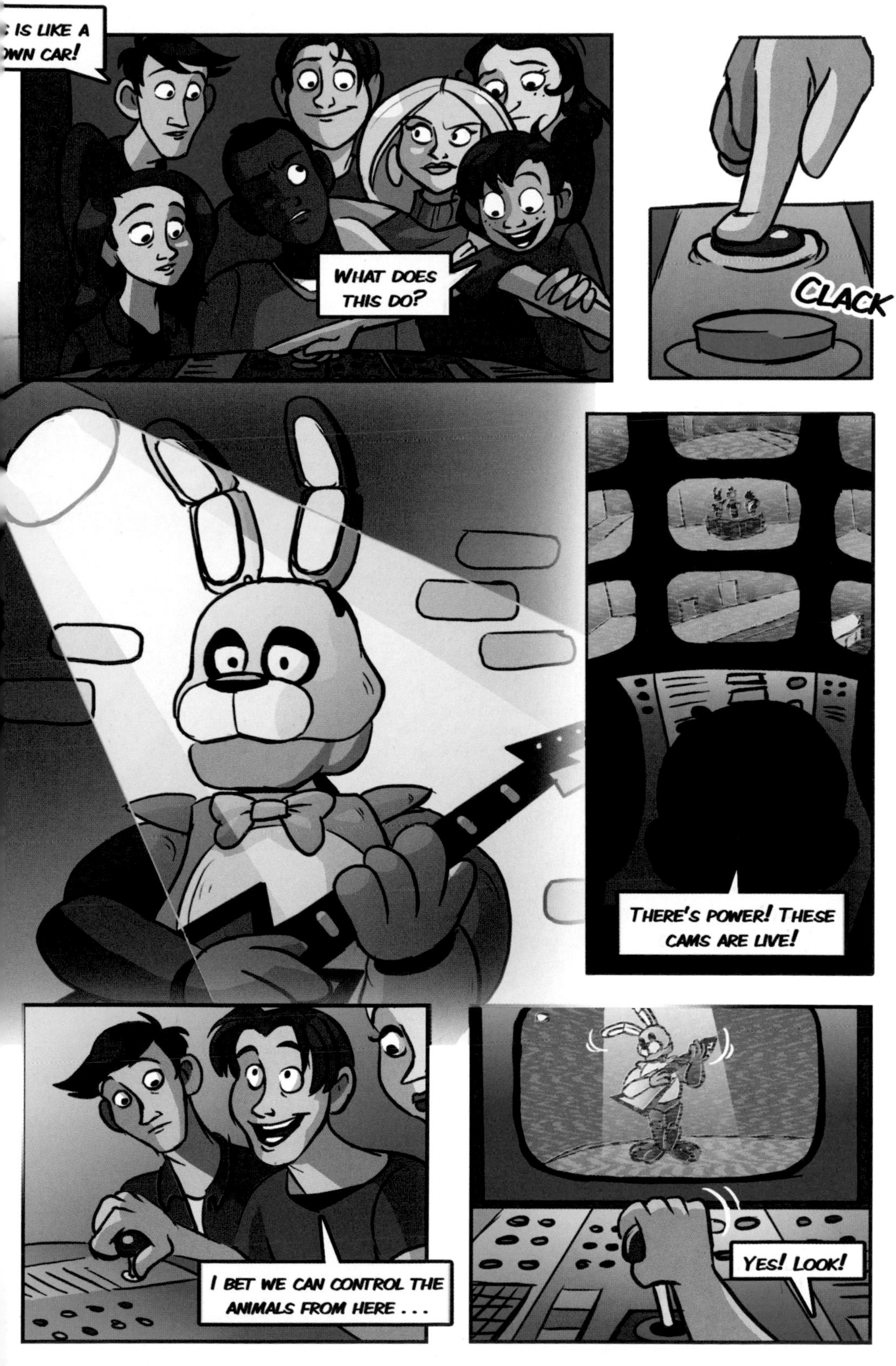

IS LIKE A
WN CAR!
WHAT DOES THIS DO?
CLACK
THERE'S POWER! THESE CAMS ARE LIVE!
I BET WE CAN CONTROL THE ANIMALS FROM HERE . . .
YES! LOOK!

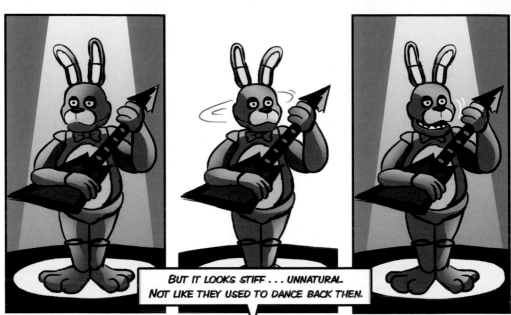

BUT IT LOOKS STIFF . . . UNNATURAL. NOT LIKE THEY USED TO DANCE BACK THEN.

I GUESS EACH BUTTON IS FOR A SINGLE MOVEMENT.

IT'S TOO STUFFY IN HERE!

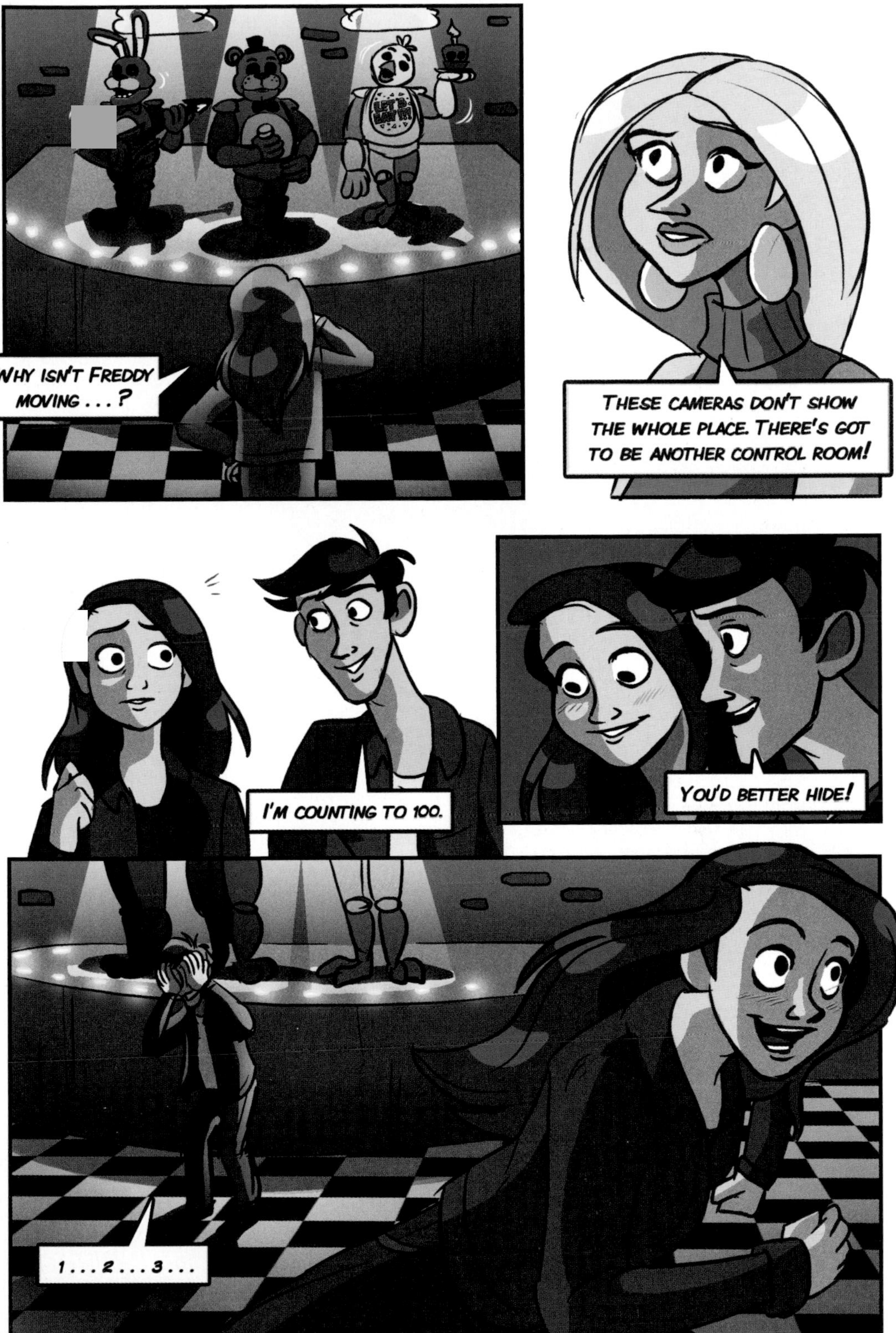
WHY ISN'T FREDDY MOVING . . . ?
THESE CAMERAS DON'T SHOW THE WHOLE PLACE. THERE'S GOT TO BE ANOTHER CONTROL ROOM!
I'M COUNTING TO 100.
YOU'D BETTER HIDE!
1 . . . 2 . . . 3 . . .

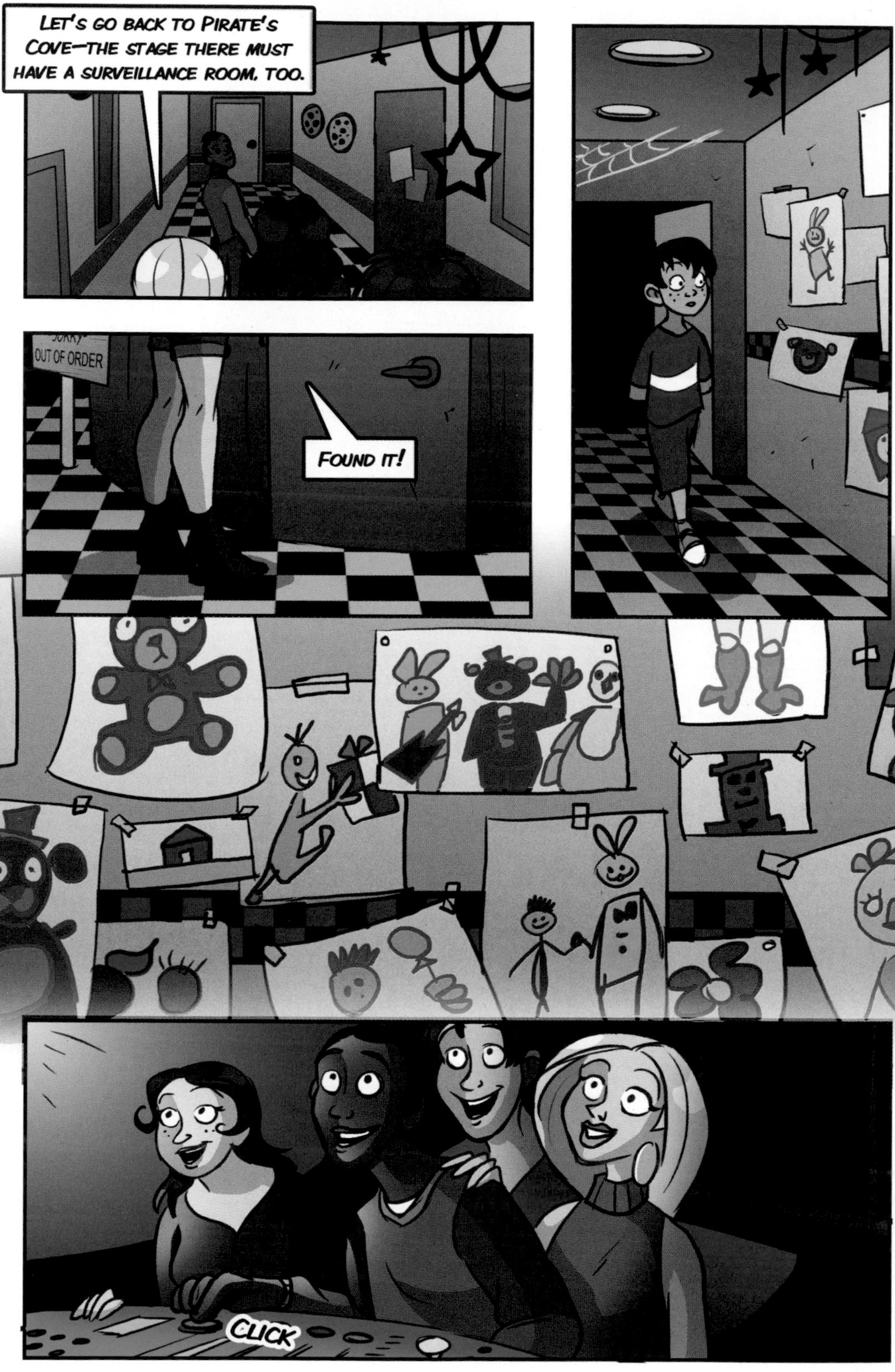
LET'S GO BACK TO PIRATE'S COVE—THE STAGE THERE MUST HAVE A SURVEILLANCE ROOM, TOO.
OUT OF ORDER
FOUND IT!
CLICK

100! I'M COMING!

I'LL FIND YOU, CHARLIE!

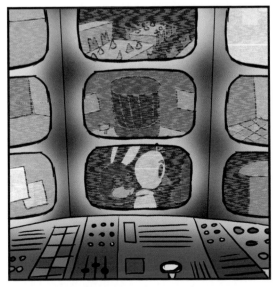

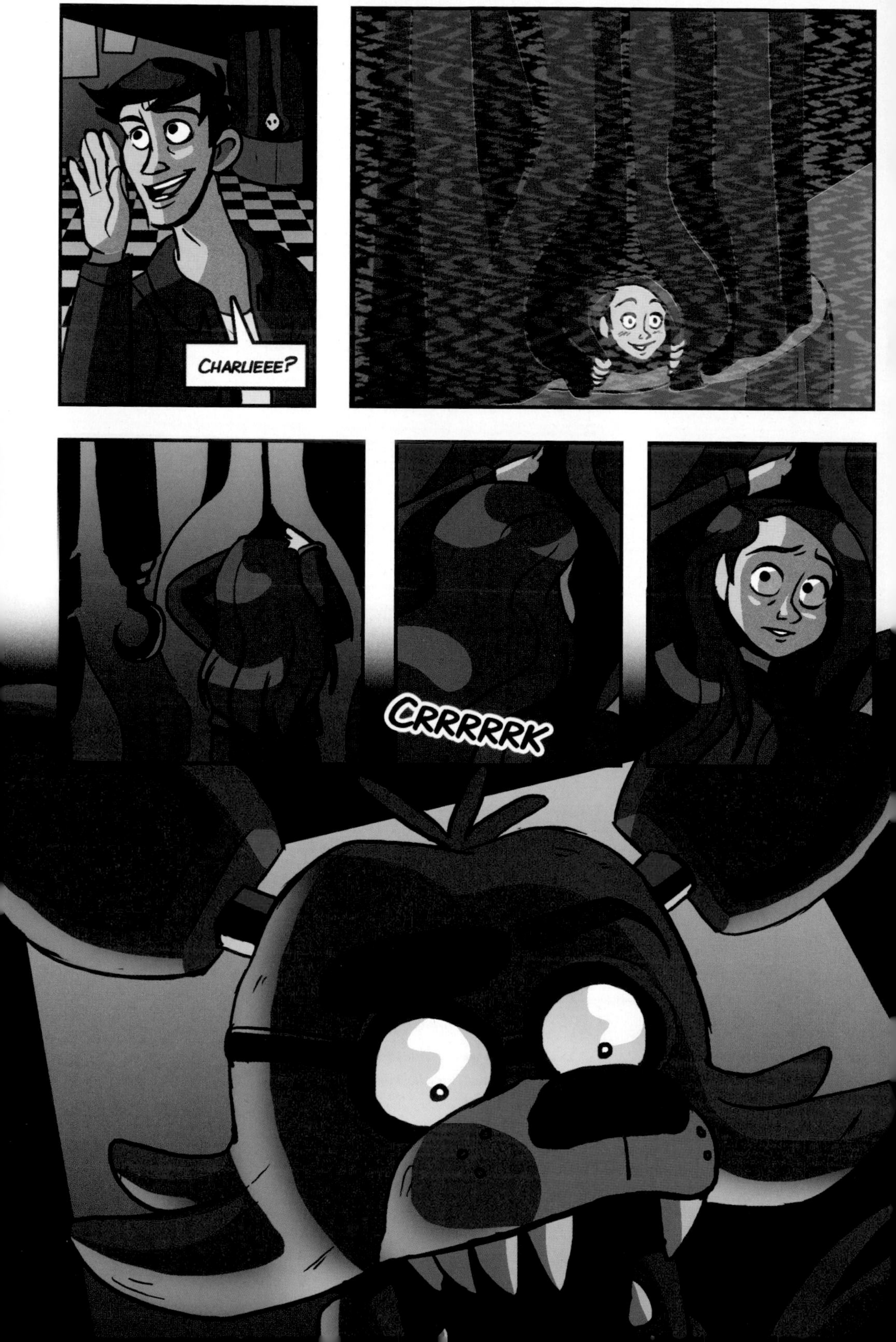
CHARLIEEE?
CRRRRRK

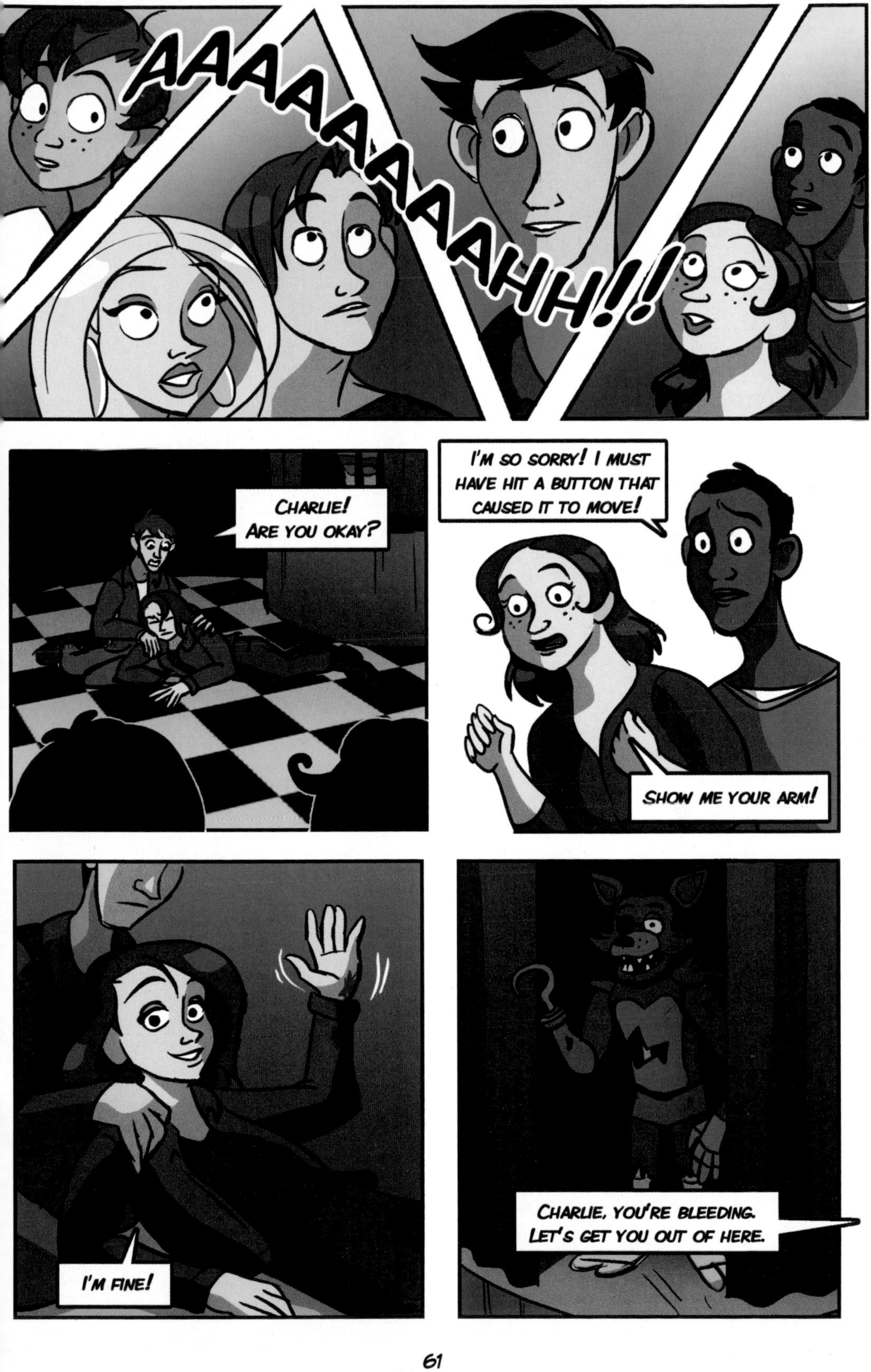
AAAAAAAAAAHH!!!
CHARLIE! ARE YOU OKAY?
I'M SO SORRY! I MUST HAVE HIT A BUTTON THAT CAUSED IT TO MOVE!
SHOW ME YOUR ARM!
I'M FINE!
CHARLIE, YOU'RE BLEEDING. LET'S GET YOU OUT OF HERE.

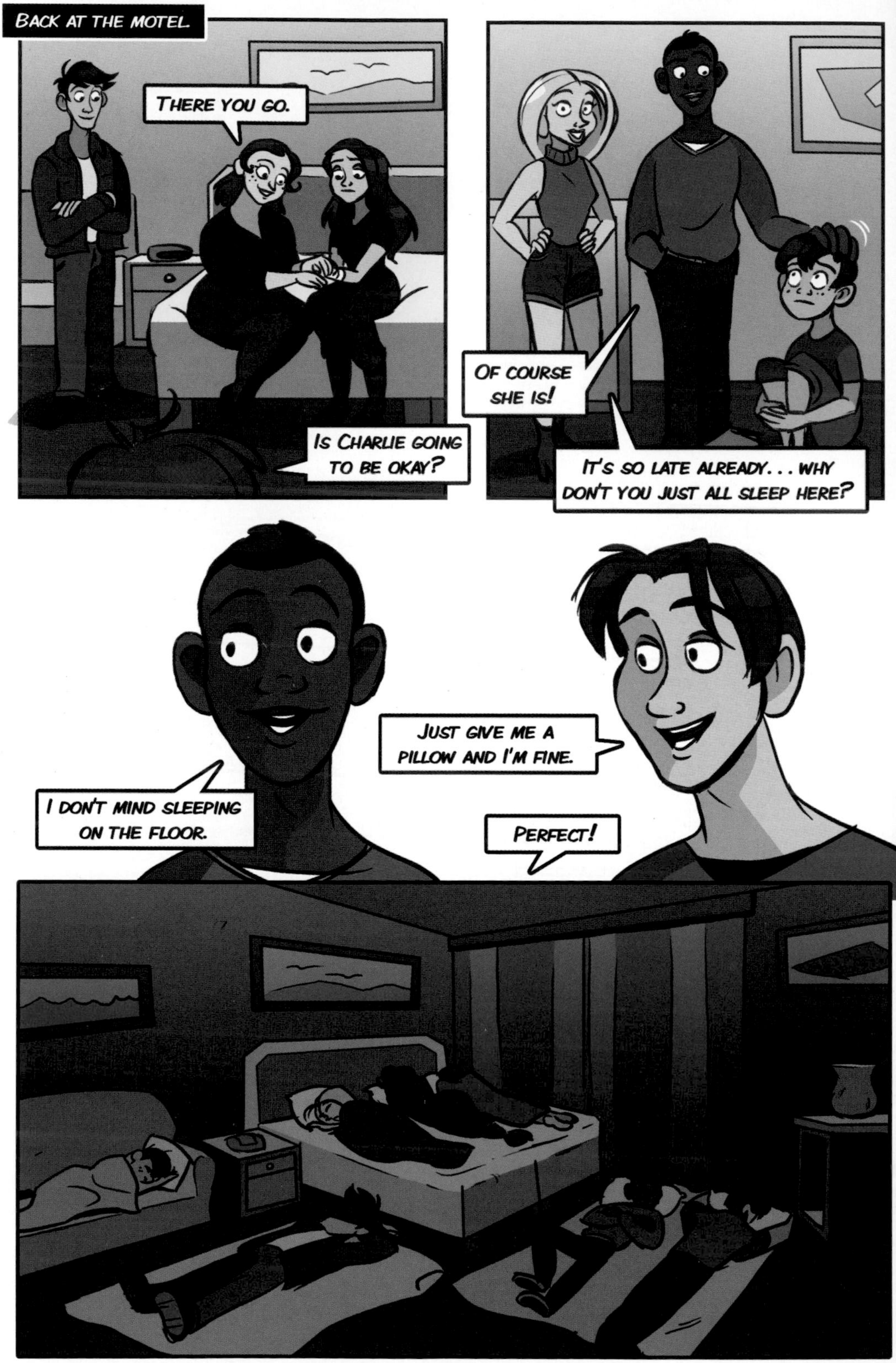
BACK AT THE MOTEL
THERE YOU GO.
IS CHARLIE GOING TO BE OKAY?
OF COURSE SHE IS!
IT'S SO LATE ALREADY. . . WHY DON'T YOU JUST ALL SLEEP HERE?
I DON'T MIND SLEEPING ON THE FLOOR.
JUST GIVE ME A PILLOW AND I'M FINE.
PERFECT!

CHAPTER 5

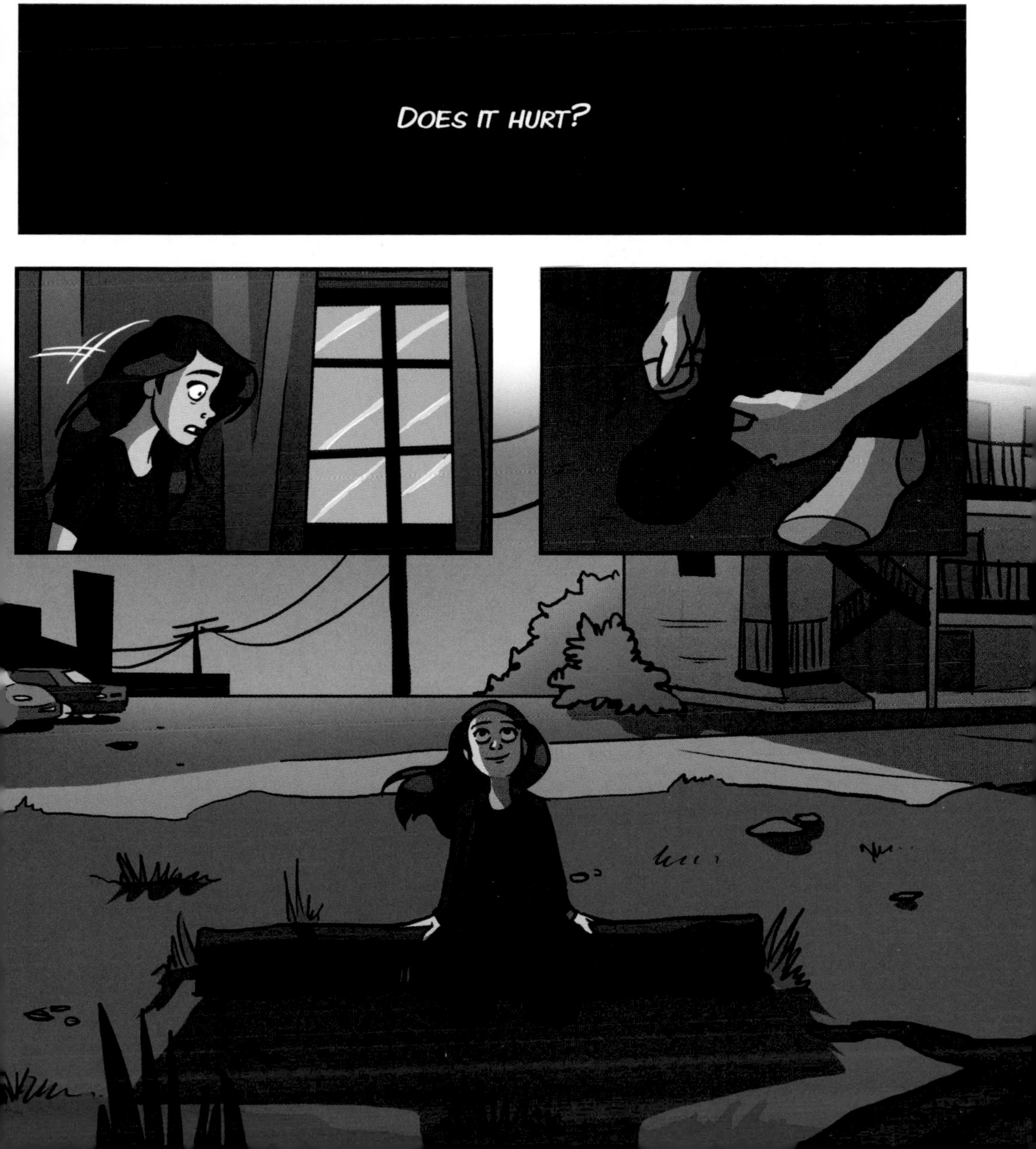
Does it hurt?

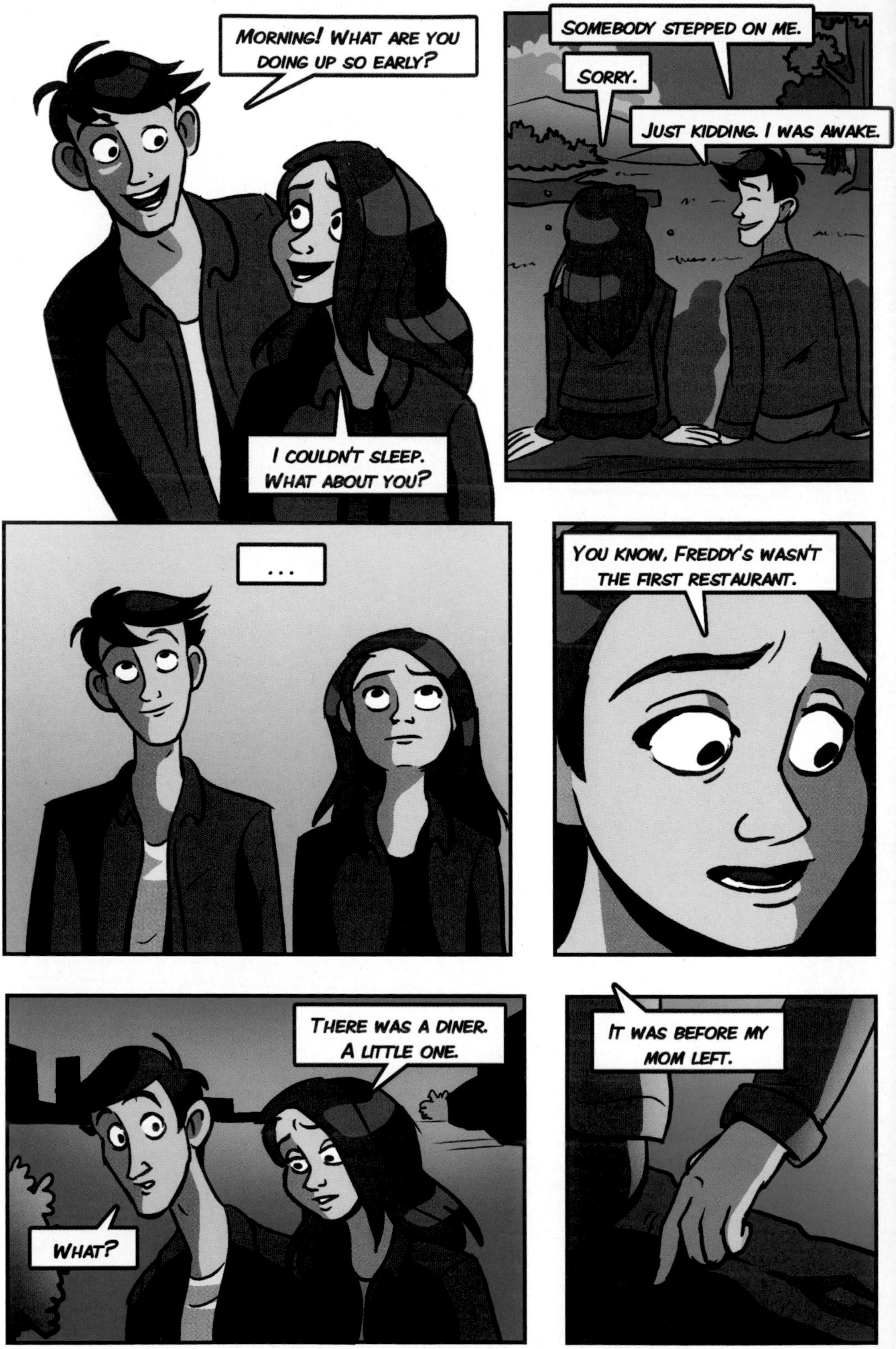
MORNING! WHAT ARE YOU DOING UP SO EARLY?
I COULDN'T SLEEP. WHAT ABOUT YOU?
SOMEBODY STEPPED ON ME.
SORRY.
JUST KIDDING. I WAS AWAKE.
. . .
YOU KNOW, FREDDY'S WASN'T THE FIRST RESTAURANT.
THERE WAS A DINER. A LITTLE ONE.
WHAT?
IT WAS BEFORE MY MOM LEFT.

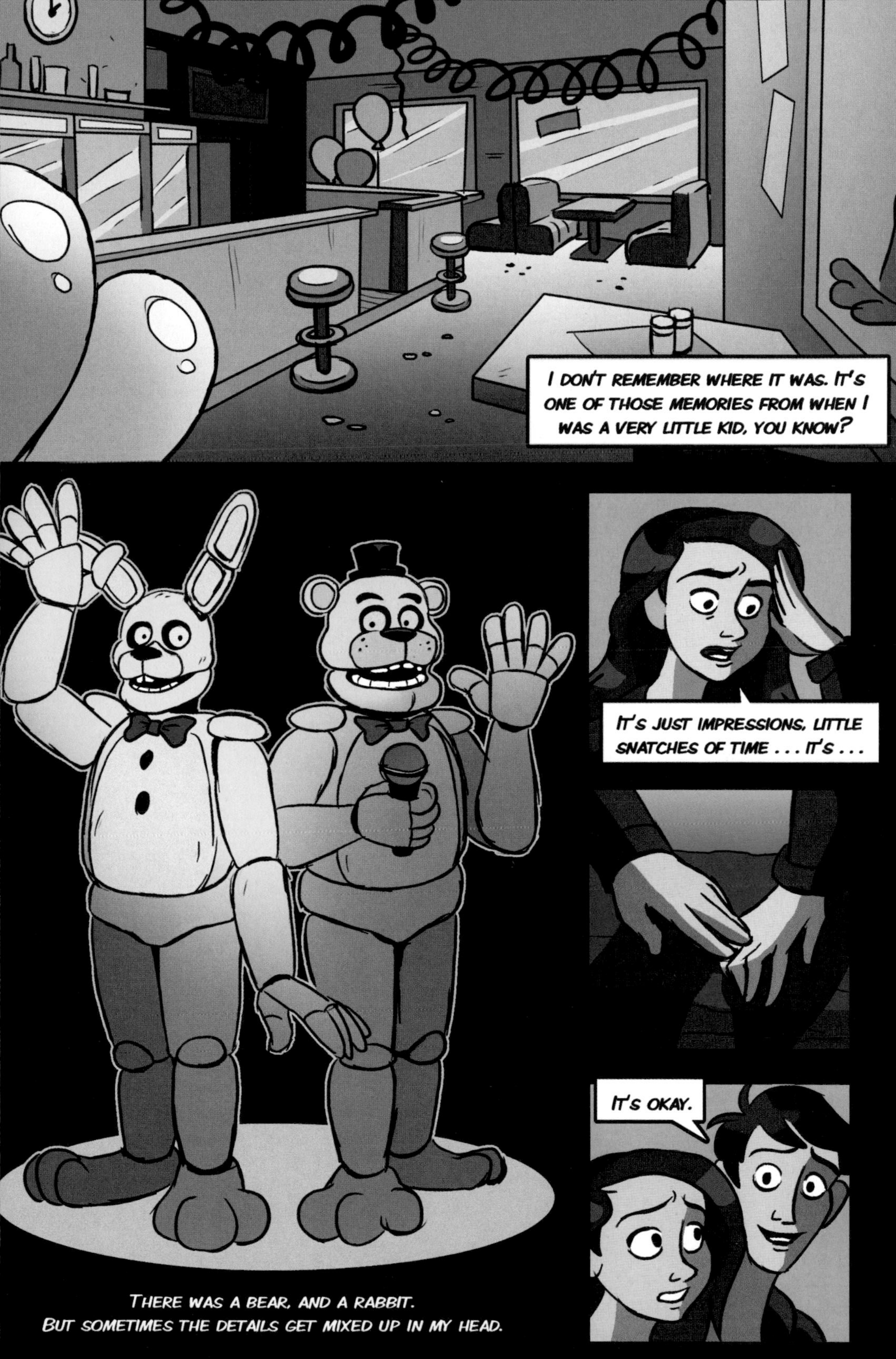
I DON'T REMEMBER WHERE IT WAS. IT'S ONE OF THOSE MEMORIES FROM WHEN I WAS A VERY LITTLE KID, YOU KNOW?
THERE WAS A BEAR, AND A RABBIT.
BUT SOMETIMES THE DETAILS GET MIXED UP IN MY HEAD.
IT'S JUST IMPRESSIONS, LITTLE SNATCHES OF TIME . . . IT'S . . .
IT'S OKAY.

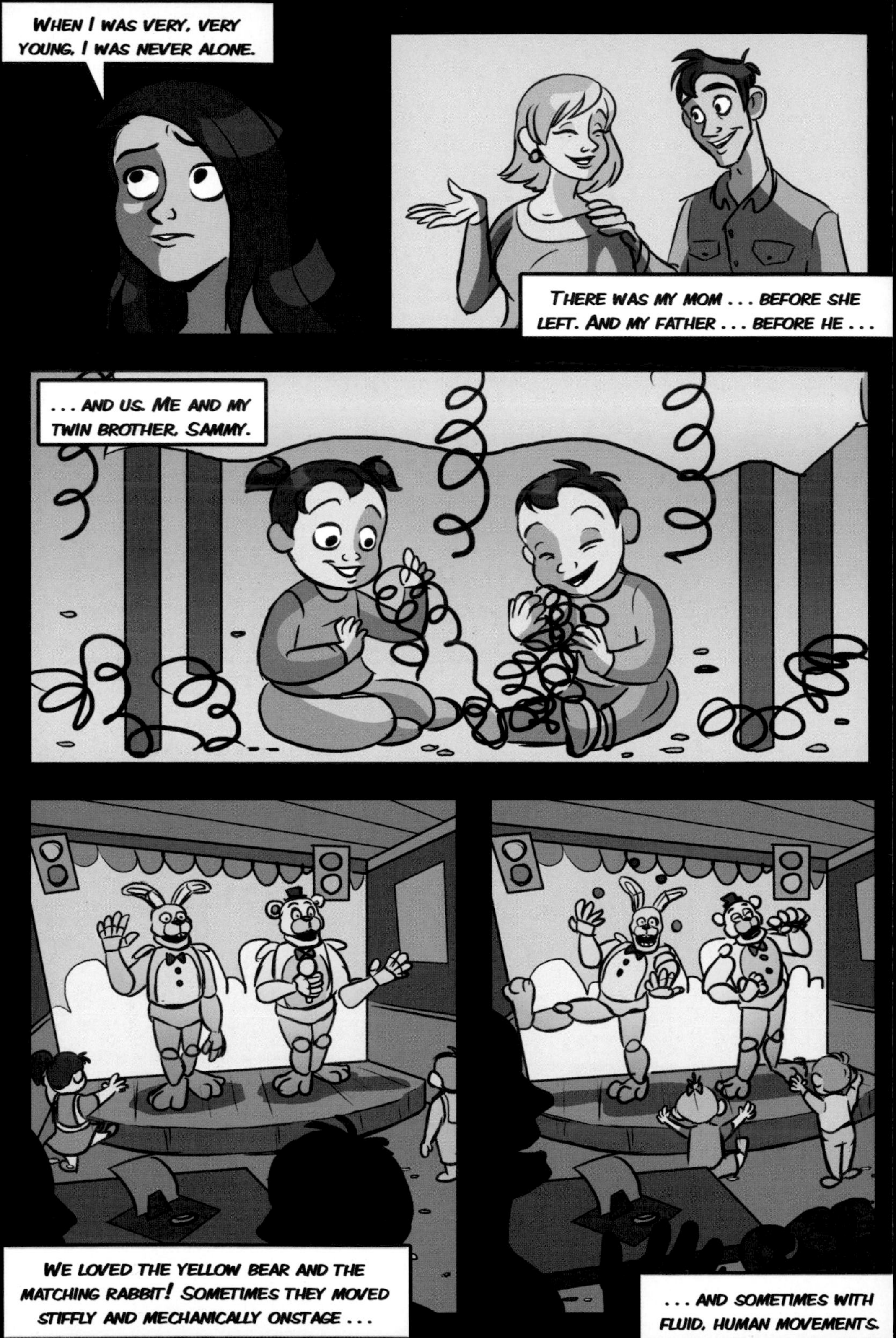

WHEN I WAS VERY, VERY YOUNG, I WAS NEVER ALONE.
THERE WAS MY MOM . . . BEFORE SHE LEFT. AND MY FATHER . . . BEFORE HE . . .
. . . AND US. ME AND MY TWIN BROTHER, SAMMY.
WE LOVED THE YELLOW BEAR AND THE MATCHING RABBIT! SOMETIMES THEY MOVED STIFFLY AND MECHANICALLY ONSTAGE . . .
. . . AND SOMETIMES WITH FLUID, HUMAN MOVEMENTS.

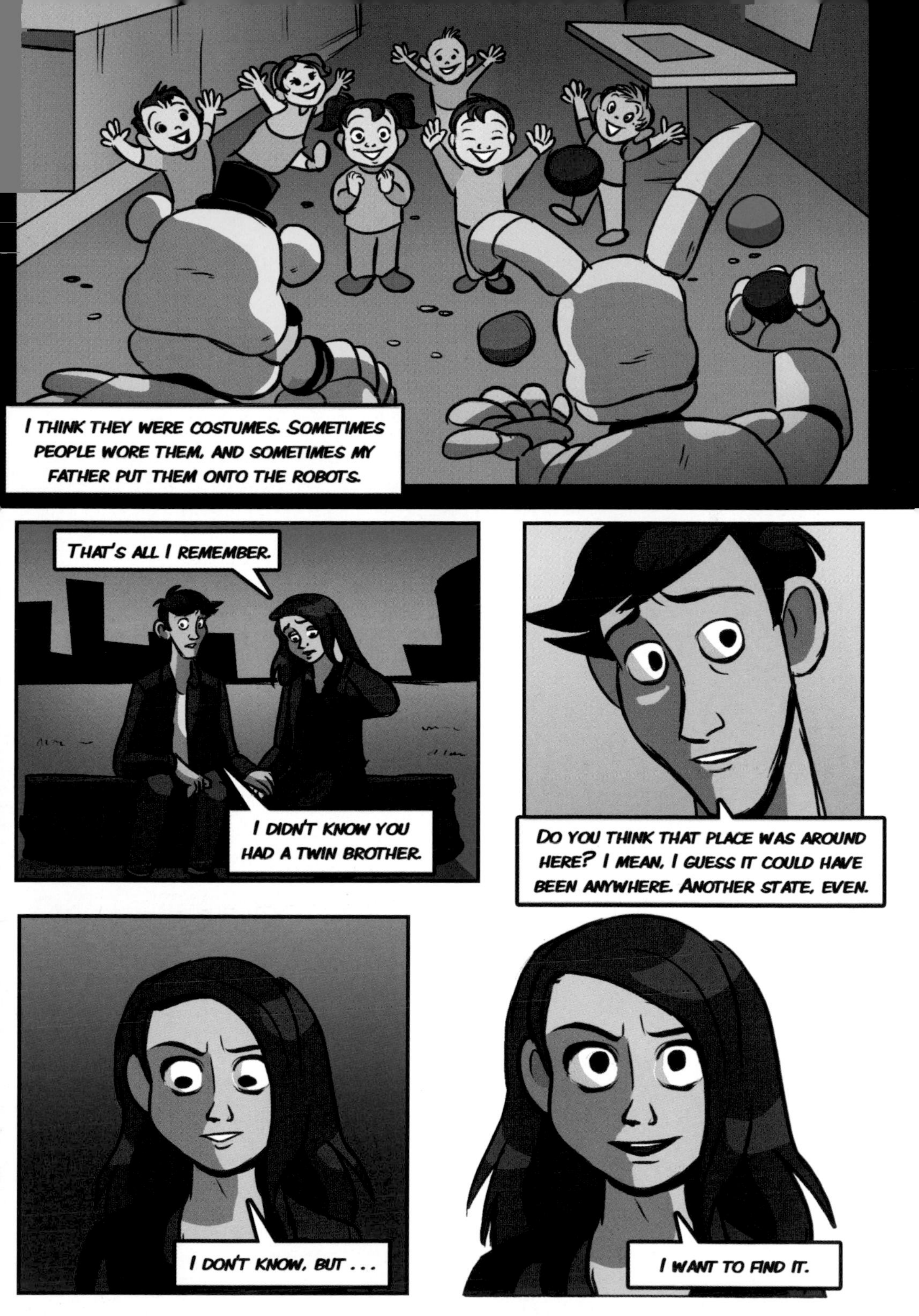
I THINK THEY WERE COSTUMES. SOMETIMES PEOPLE WORE THEM, AND SOMETIMES MY FATHER PUT THEM ONTO THE ROBOTS.
THAT'S ALL I REMEMBER.
I DIDN'T KNOW YOU HAD A TWIN BROTHER.
DO YOU THINK THAT PLACE WAS AROUND HERE? I MEAN, I GUESS IT COULD HAVE BEEN ANYWHERE. ANOTHER STATE, EVEN.
I DON'T KNOW, BUT . . .
I WANT TO FIND IT.

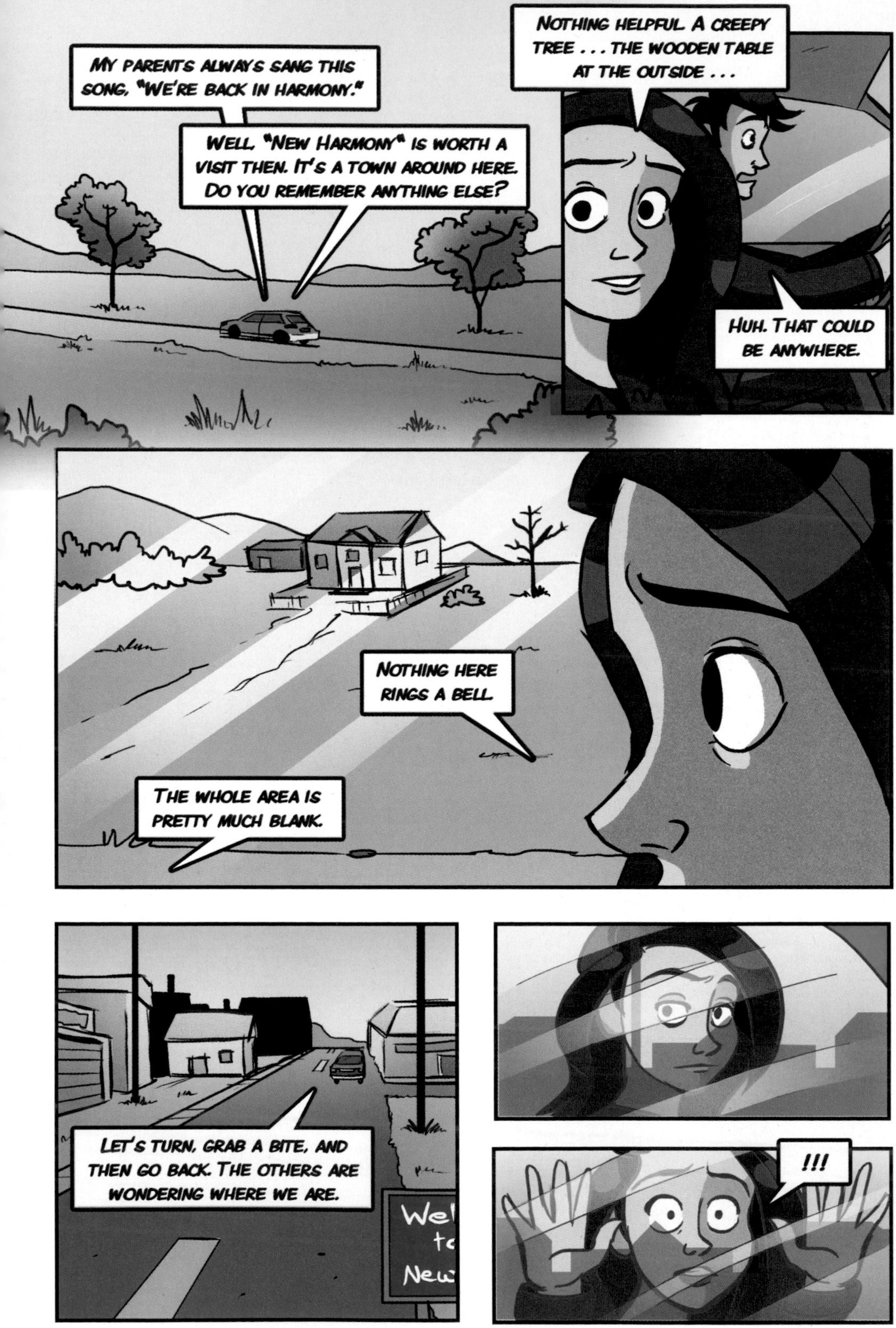
MY PARENTS ALWAYS SANG THIS SONG, "WE'RE BACK IN HARMONY."
WELL, "NEW HARMONY" IS WORTH A VISIT THEN. IT'S A TOWN AROUND HERE. DO YOU REMEMBER ANYTHING ELSE?
NOTHING HELPFUL. A CREEPY TREE . . . THE WOODEN TABLE AT THE OUTSIDE . . .
HUH. THAT COULD BE ANYWHERE.
NOTHING HERE RINGS A BELL.
THE WHOLE AREA IS PRETTY MUCH BLANK.
LET'S TURN, GRAB A BITE, AND THEN GO BACK. THE OTHERS ARE WONDERING WHERE WE ARE.
!!!

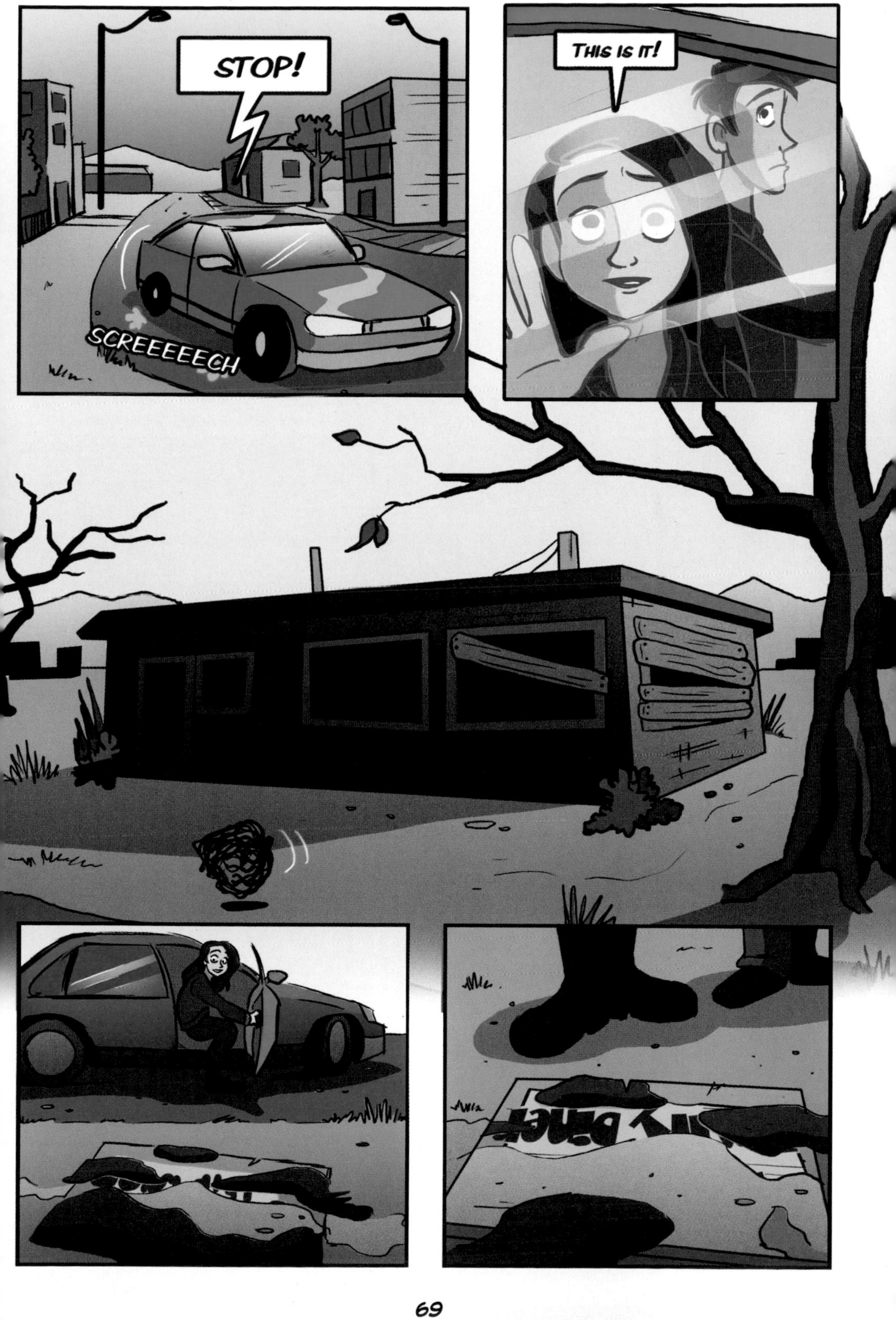
STOP!
SCREEEEEECH
THIS IS IT!

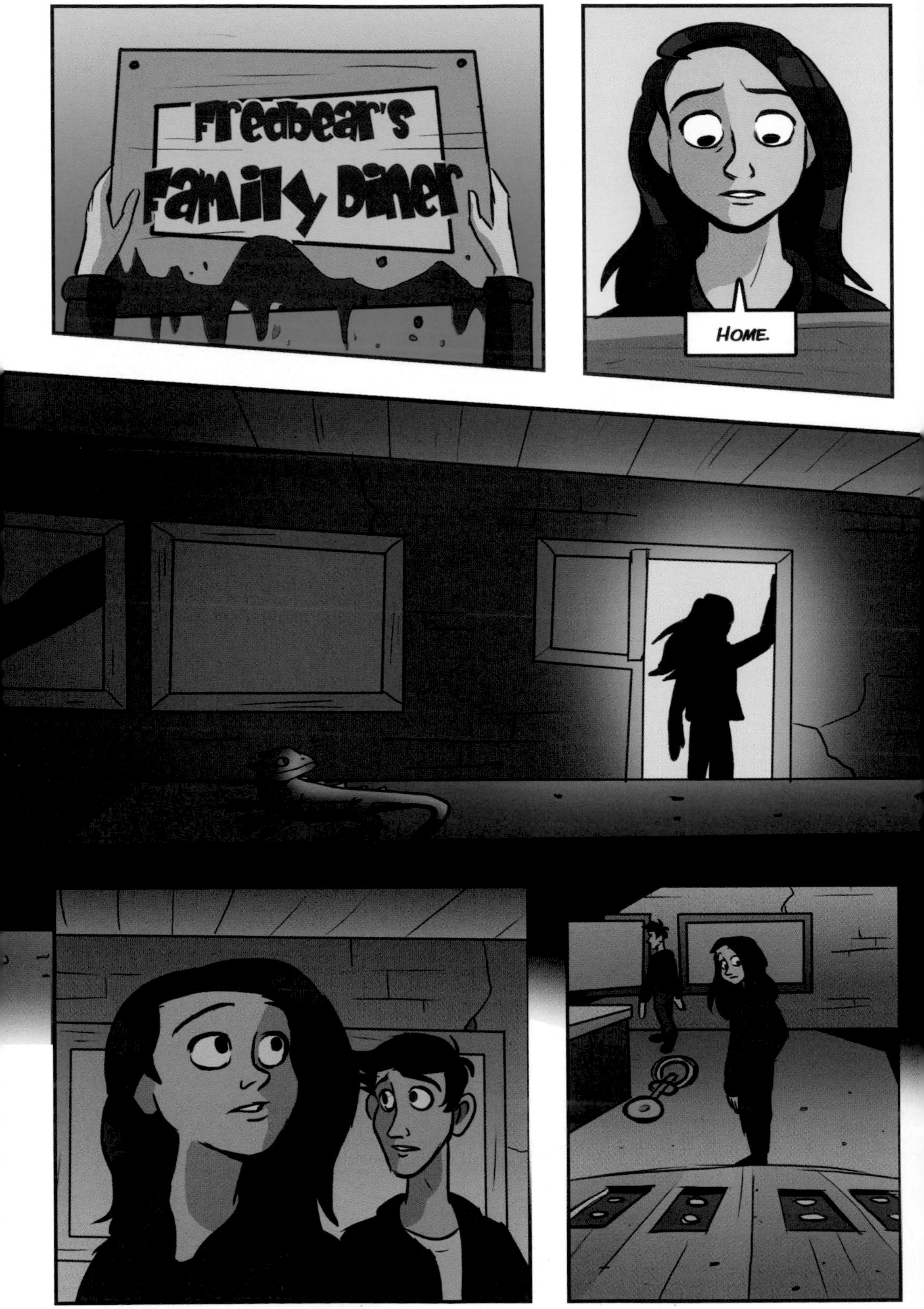
Fredbear's
Family Diner
HOME.

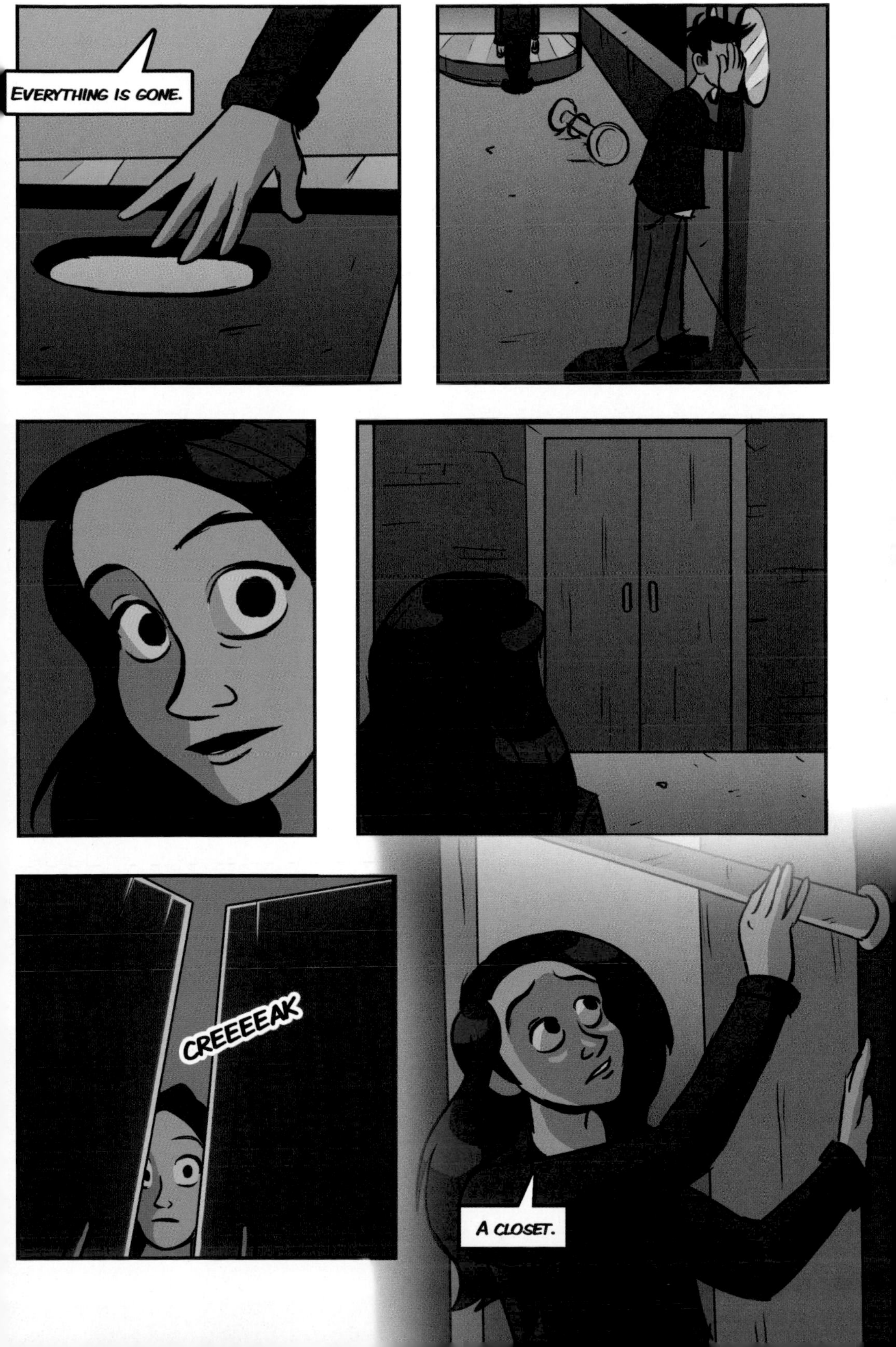
EVERYTHING IS GONE.
CREEEEAK
A CLOSET.

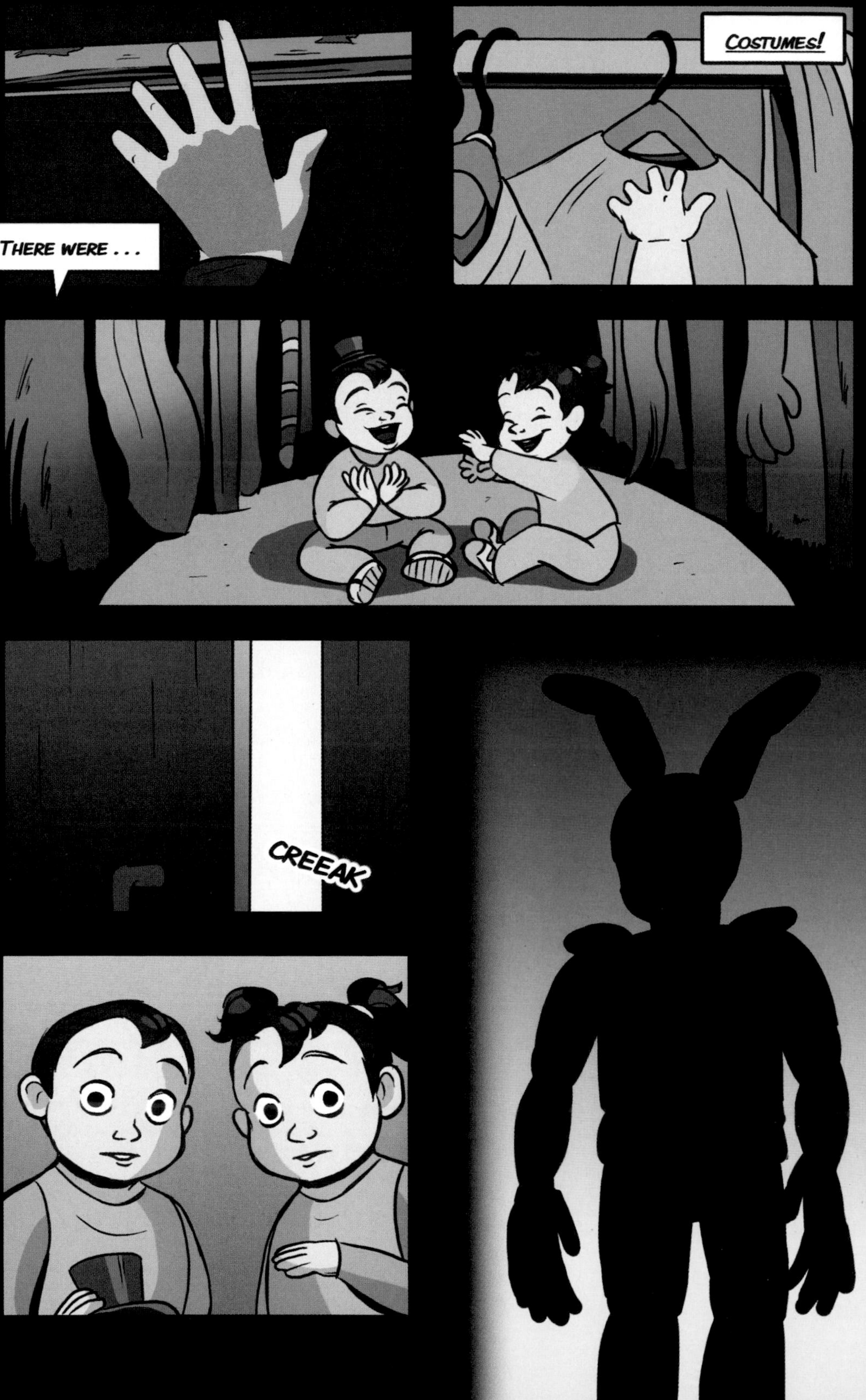

THERE WERE . . .
COSTUMES!
CREEAK

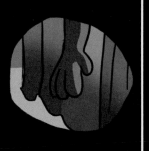

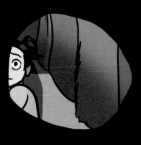

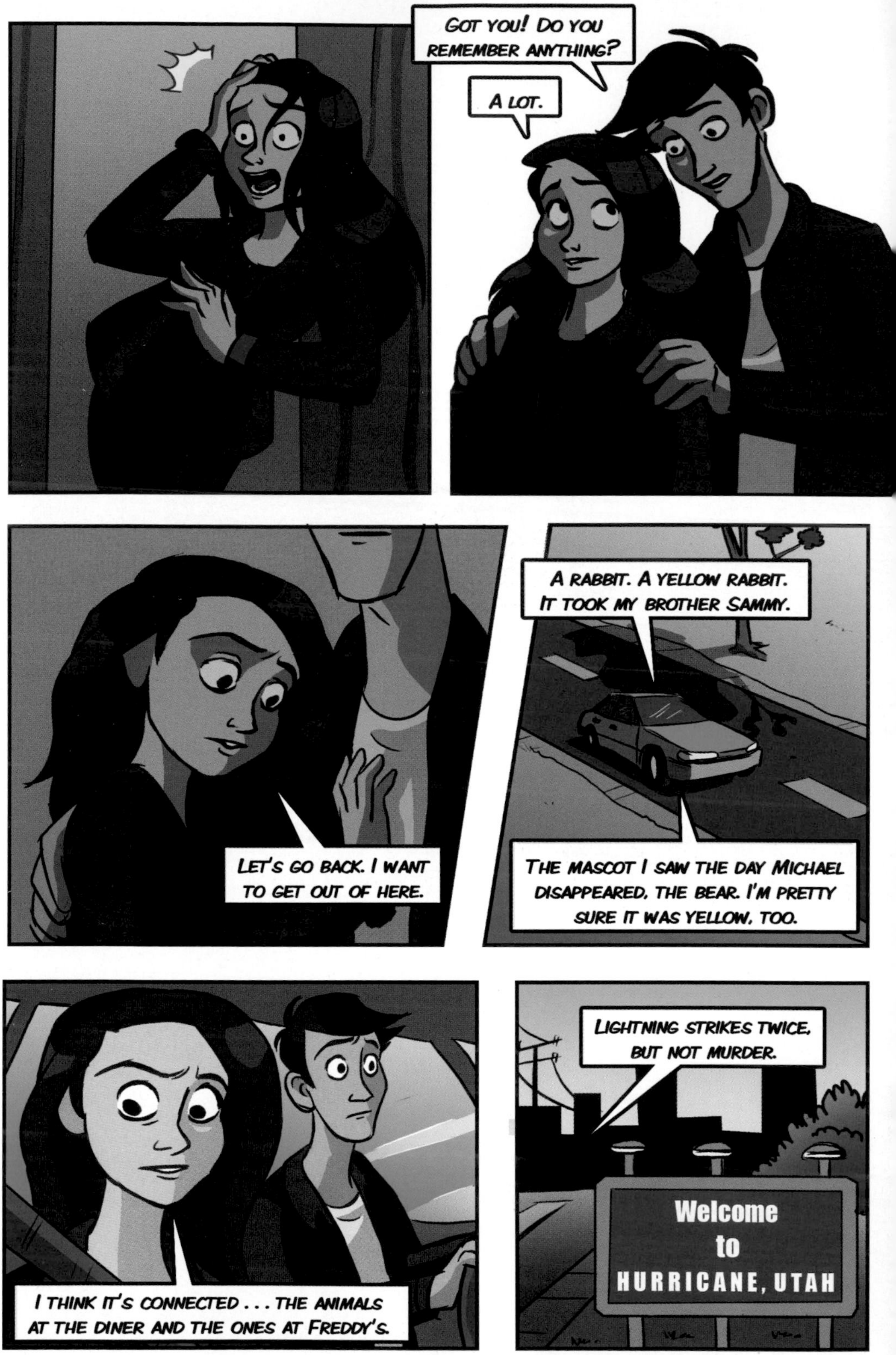
GOT YOU! DO YOU REMEMBER ANYTHING?
A LOT.
LET'S GO BACK. I WANT TO GET OUT OF HERE.
A RABBIT. A YELLOW RABBIT. IT TOOK MY BROTHER SAMMY.
THE MASCOT I SAW THE DAY MICHAEL DISAPPEARED, THE BEAR. I'M PRETTY SURE IT WAS YELLOW, TOO.
I THINK IT'S CONNECTED . . . THE ANIMALS AT THE DINER AND THE ONES AT FREDDY'S.
LIGHTNING STRIKES TWICE, BUT NOT MURDER.
Welcome to HURRICANE, UTAH

CHAPTER 6

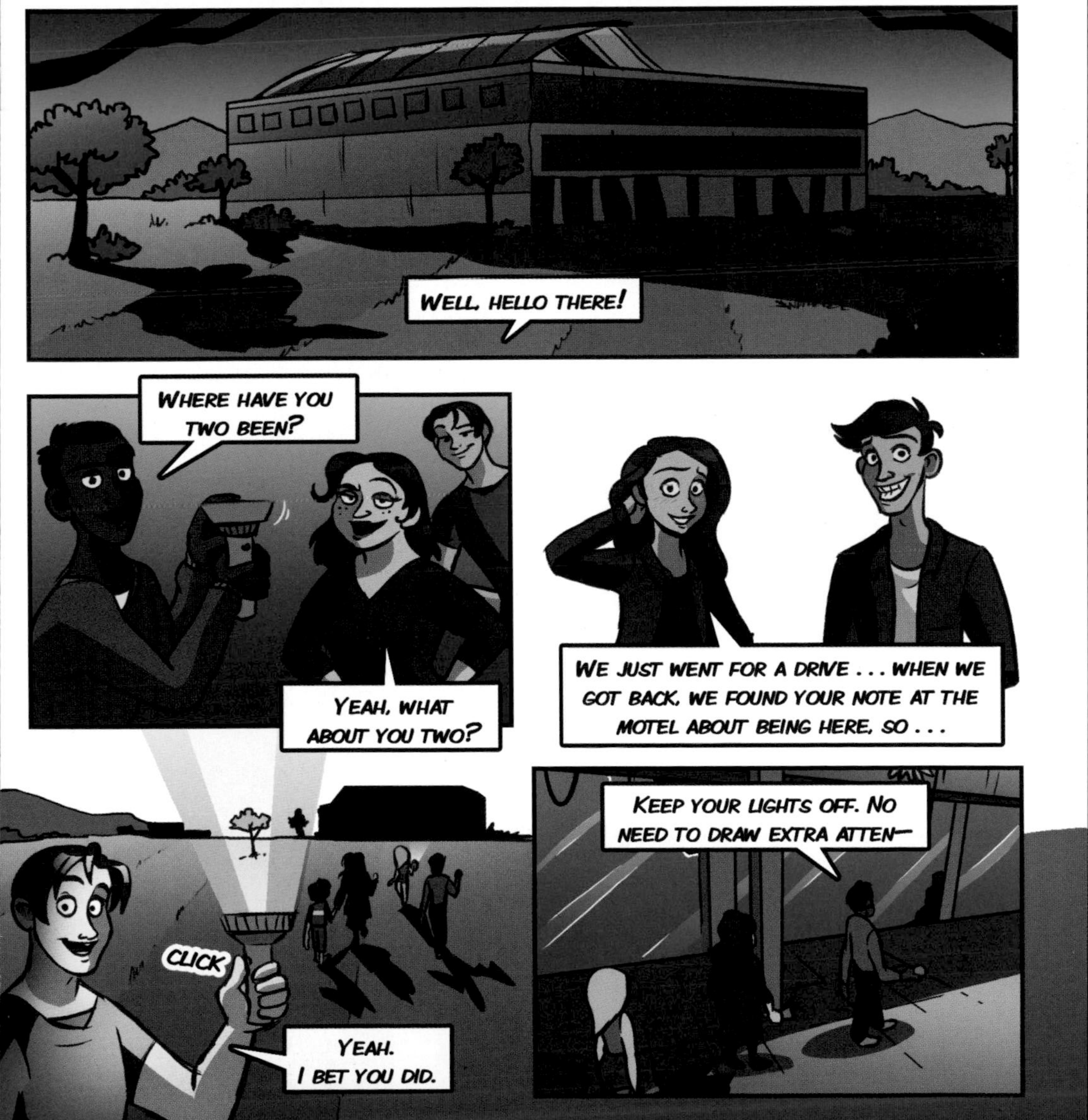
WELL, HELLO THERE!
WHERE HAVE YOU TWO BEEN?
YEAH, WHAT ABOUT YOU TWO?
WE JUST WENT FOR A DRIVE . . . WHEN WE GOT BACK, WE FOUND YOUR NOTE AT THE MOTEL ABOUT BEING HERE, SO . . .
CLICK
YEAH. I BET YOU DID.
KEEP YOUR LIGHTS OFF. NO NEED TO DRAW EXTRA ATTEN—

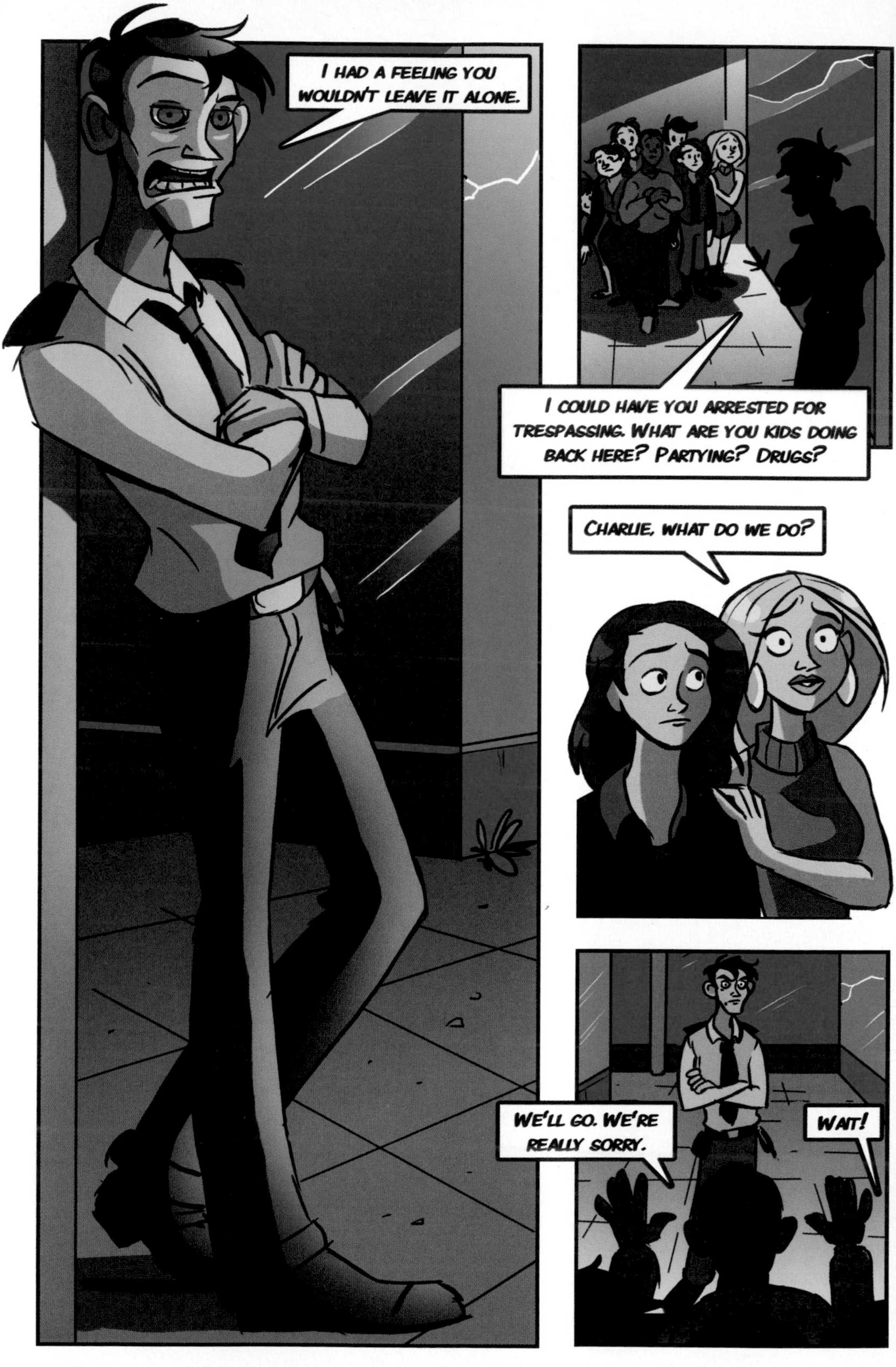
I HAD A FEELING YOU WOULDN'T LEAVE IT ALONE.
I COULD HAVE YOU ARRESTED FOR TRESPASSING. WHAT ARE YOU KIDS DOING BACK HERE? PARTYING? DRUGS?
CHARLIE, WHAT DO WE DO?
WE'LL GO. WE'RE REALLY SORRY.
WAIT!

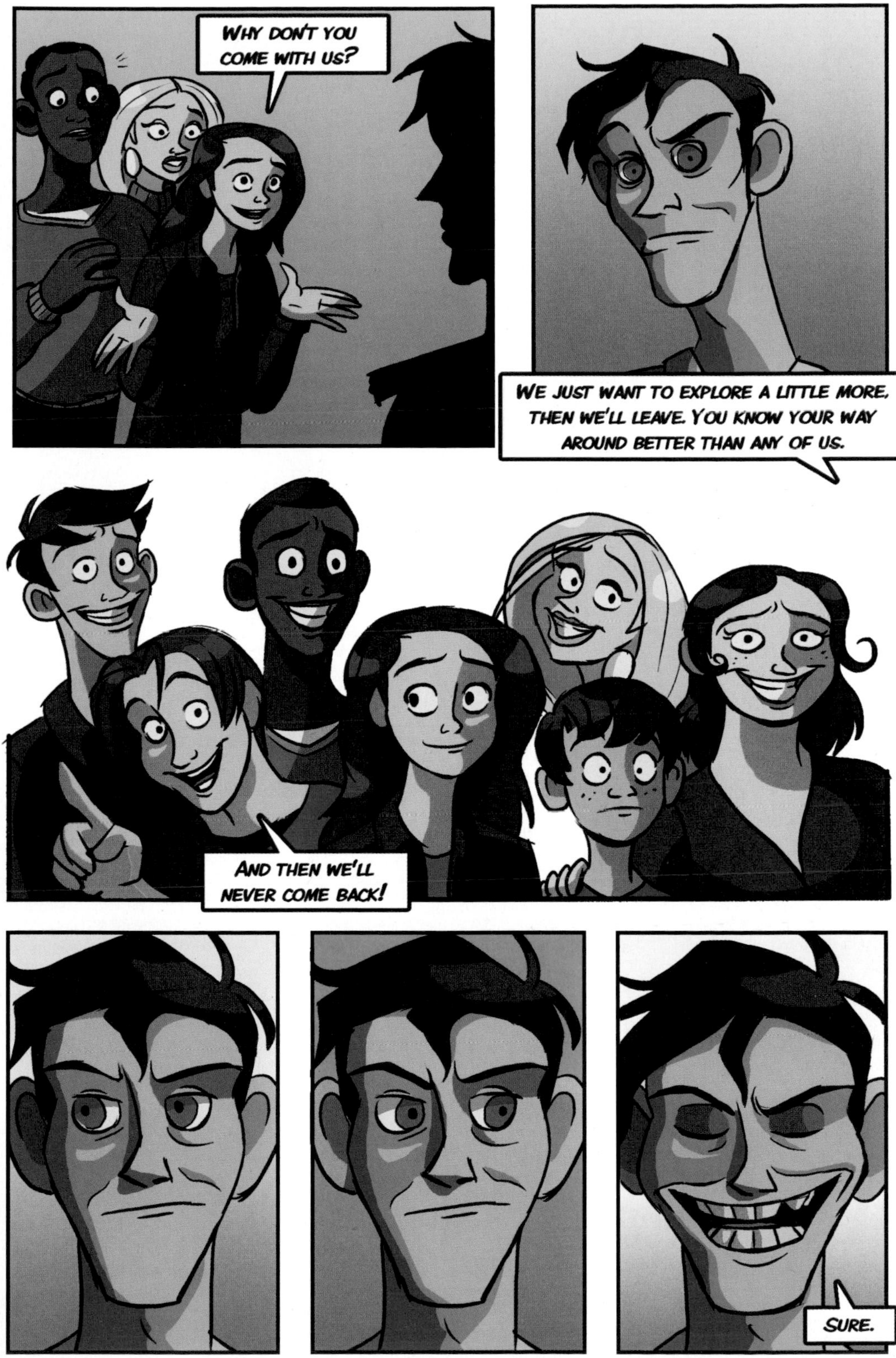
WHY DON'T YOU COME WITH US?
WE JUST WANT TO EXPLORE A LITTLE MORE, THEN WE'LL LEAVE. YOU KNOW YOUR WAY AROUND BETTER THAN ANY OF US.
AND THEN WE'LL NEVER COME BACK!
SURE.

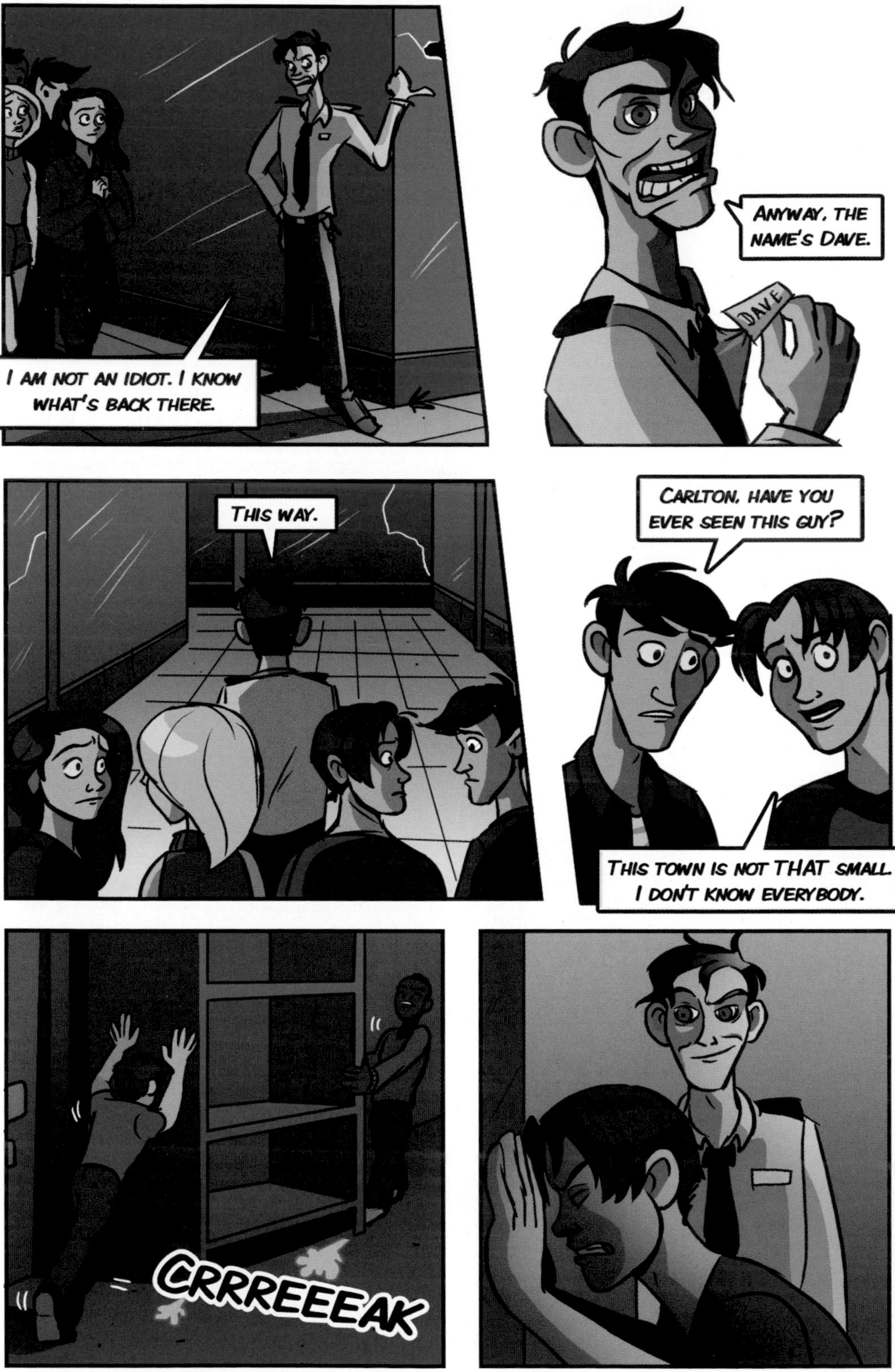
I AM NOT AN IDIOT. I KNOW WHAT'S BACK THERE.
ANYWAY, THE NAME'S DAVE.
DAVE
THIS WAY.
CARLTON, HAVE YOU EVER SEEN THIS GUY?
THIS TOWN IS NOT THAT SMALL. I DON'T KNOW EVERYBODY.
CRRREEEAK

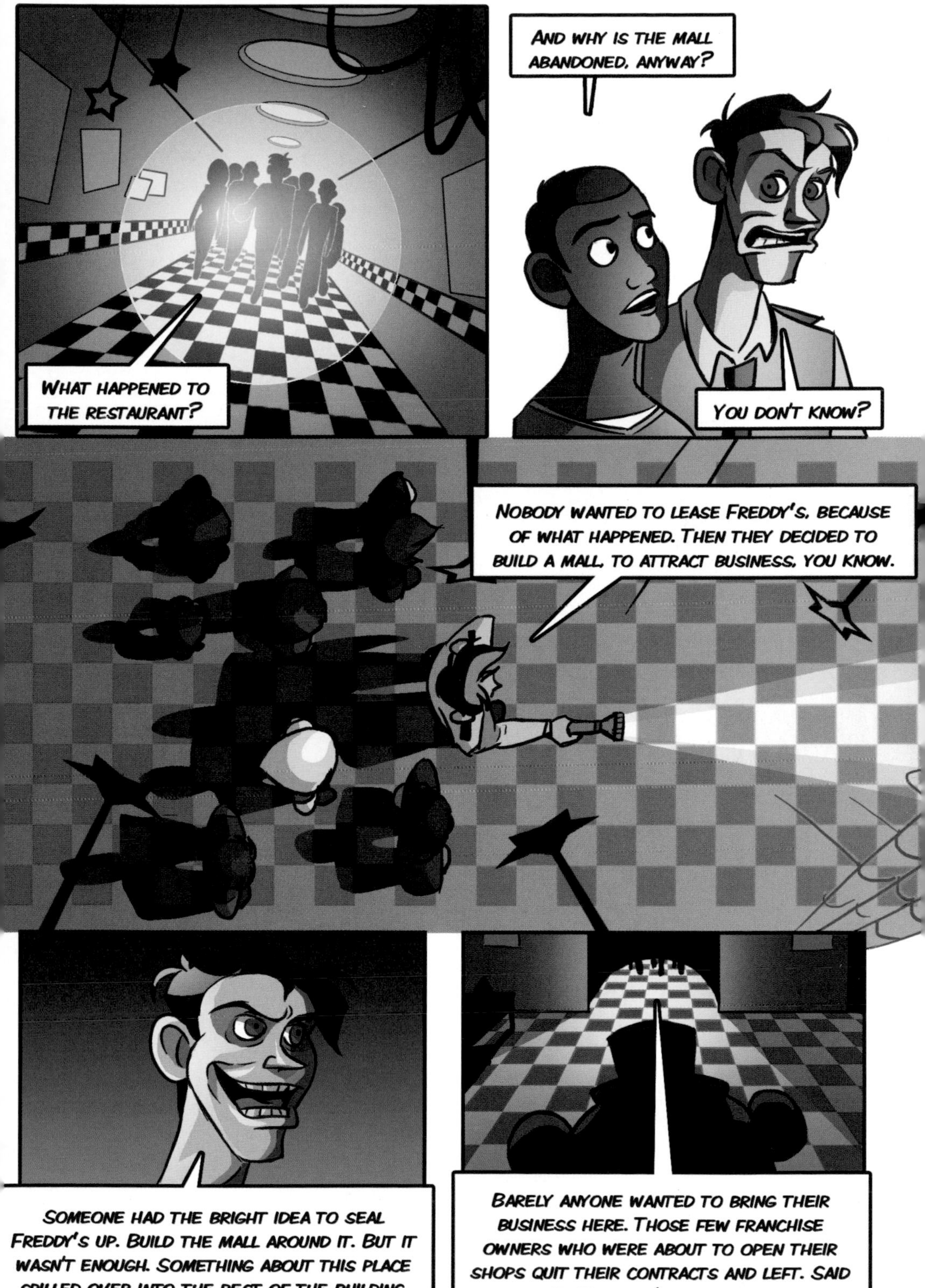
WHAT HAPPENED TO THE RESTAURANT?
AND WHY IS THE MALL ABANDONED, ANYWAY?
YOU DON'T KNOW?
NOBODY WANTED TO LEASE FREDDY'S, BECAUSE OF WHAT HAPPENED. THEN THEY DECIDED TO BUILD A MALL, TO ATTRACT BUSINESS, YOU KNOW.
SOMEONE HAD THE BRIGHT IDEA TO SEAL FREDDY'S UP. BUILD THE MALL AROUND IT. BUT IT WASN'T ENOUGH. SOMETHING ABOUT THIS PLACE SPILLED OVER INTO THE REST OF THE BUILDING.
BARELY ANYONE WANTED TO BRING THEIR BUSINESS HERE. THOSE FEW FRANCHISE OWNERS WHO WERE ABOUT TO OPEN THEIR SHOPS QUIT THEIR CONTRACTS AND LEFT. SAID IT JUST DIDN'T FEEL RIGHT.

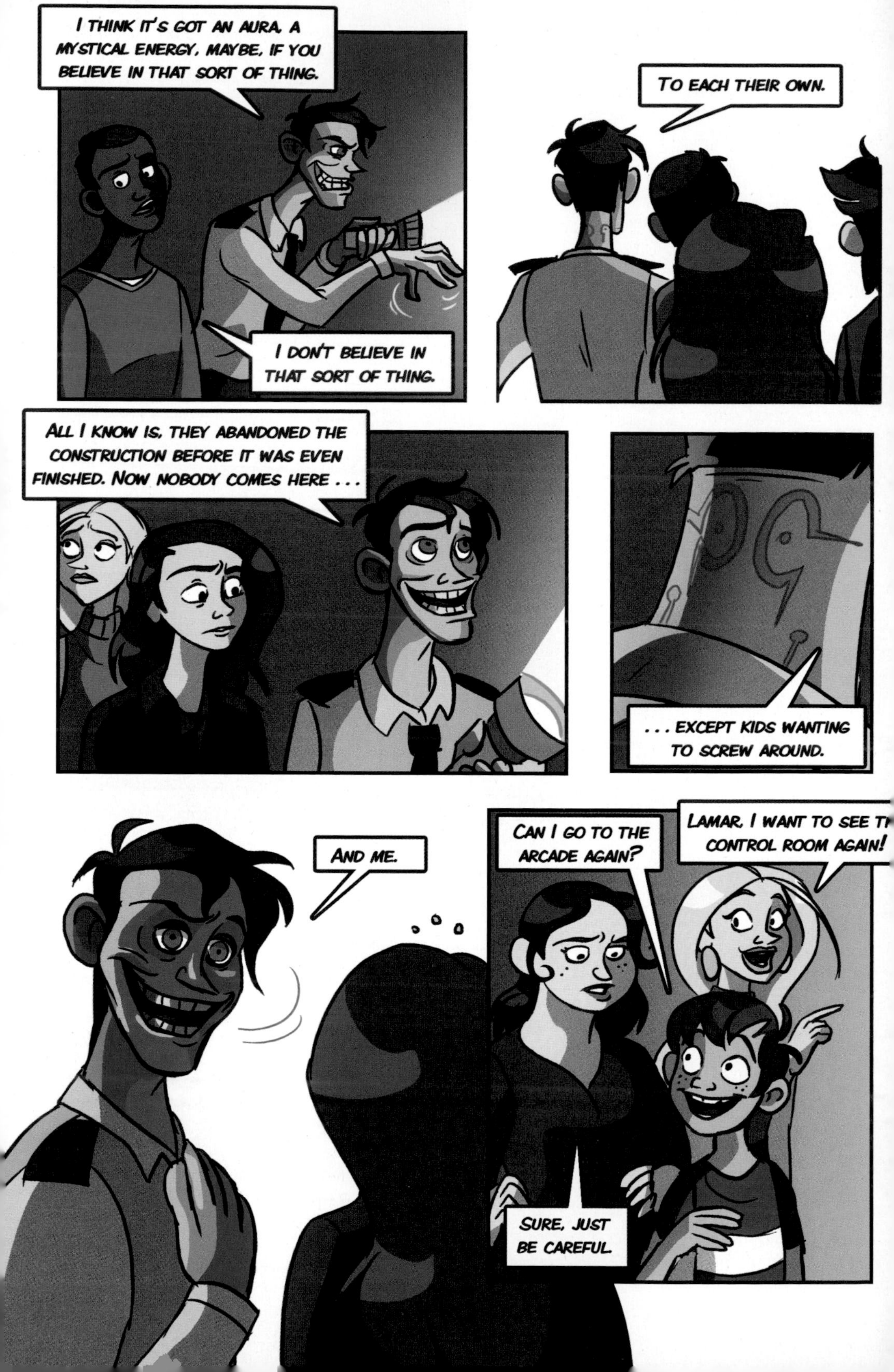
I THINK IT'S GOT AN AURA, A MYSTICAL ENERGY, MAYBE, IF YOU BELIEVE IN THAT SORT OF THING.
I DON'T BELIEVE IN THAT SORT OF THING.
TO EACH THEIR OWN.
ALL I KNOW IS, THEY ABANDONED THE CONSTRUCTION BEFORE IT WAS EVEN FINISHED. NOW NOBODY COMES HERE . . .
. . . EXCEPT KIDS WANTING TO SCREW AROUND.
AND ME.
CAN I GO TO THE ARCADE AGAIN?
CONTROL ROOM AGAIN!
SURE, JUST BE CAREFUL.

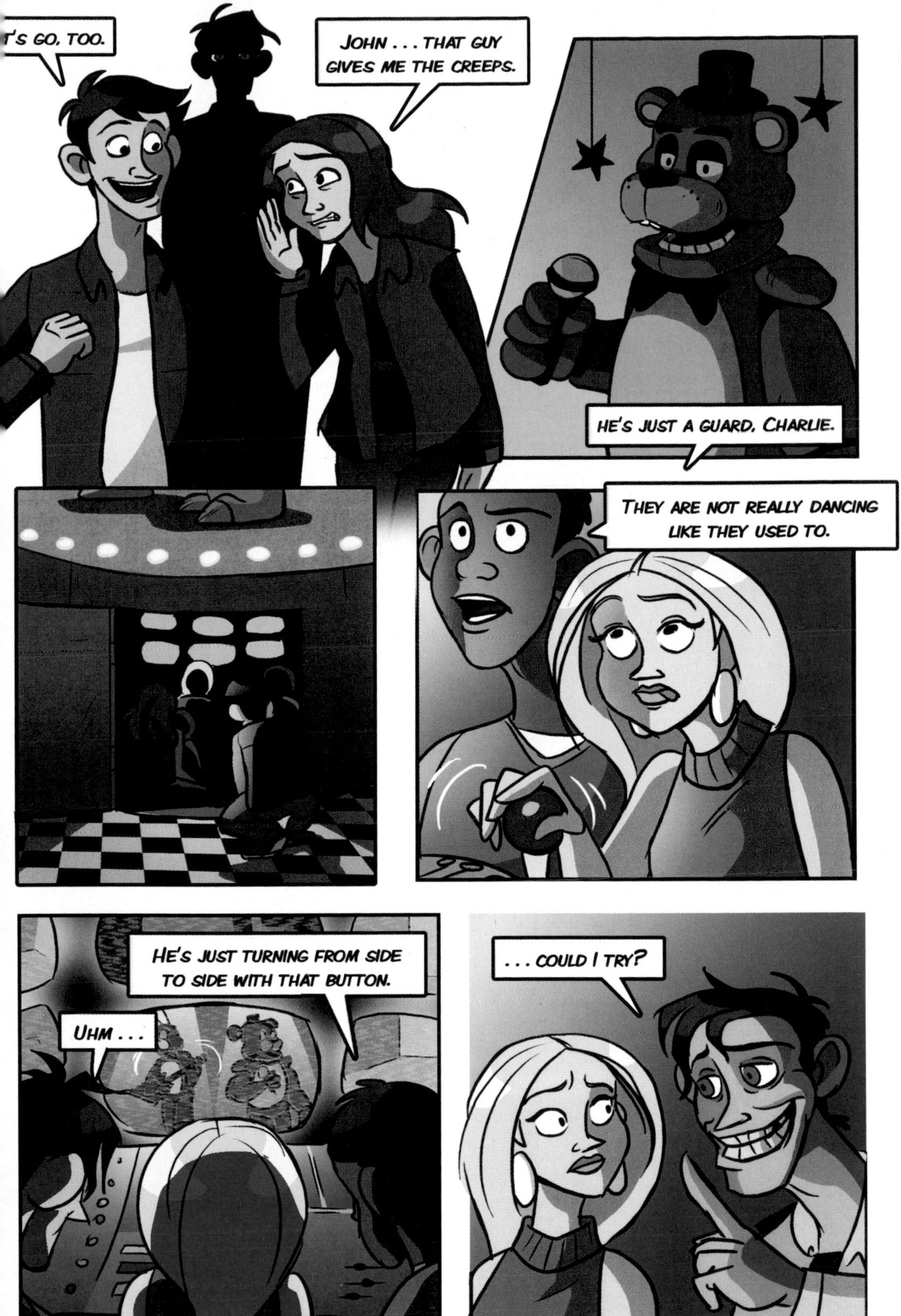

T'S GO, TOO.
JOHN . . . THAT GUY GIVES ME THE CREEPS.
HE'S JUST A GUARD, CHARLIE.
THEY ARE NOT REALLY DANCING LIKE THEY USED TO.
HE'S JUST TURNING FROM SIDE TO SIDE WITH THAT BUTTON.
UHM . . .
. . . COULD I TRY?

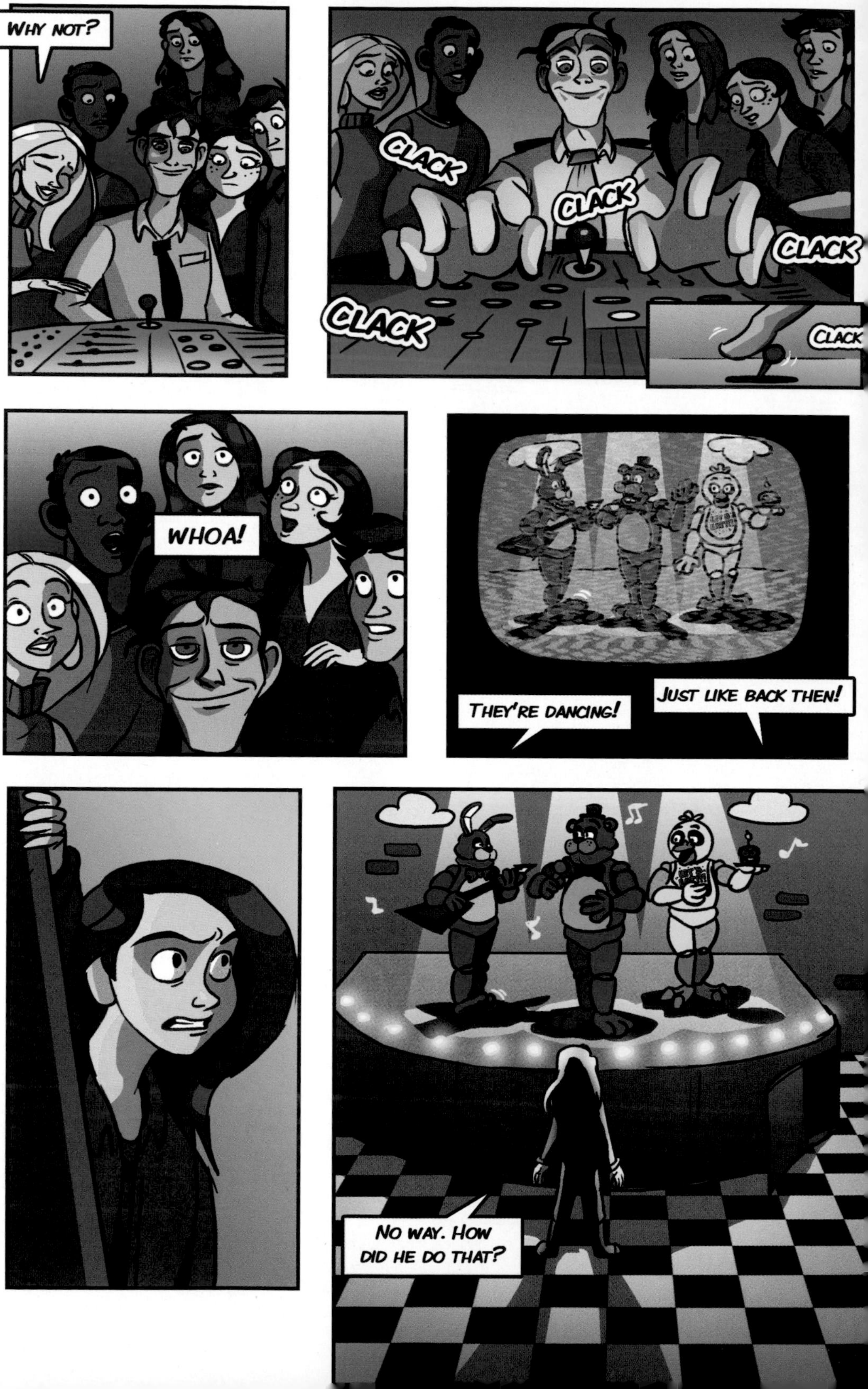
WHY NOT?
CLACK
CLACK
CLACK
CLACK
CLACK
WHOA!
THEY'RE DANCING!
JUST LIKE BACK THEN!
NO WAY. HOW DID HE DO THAT?

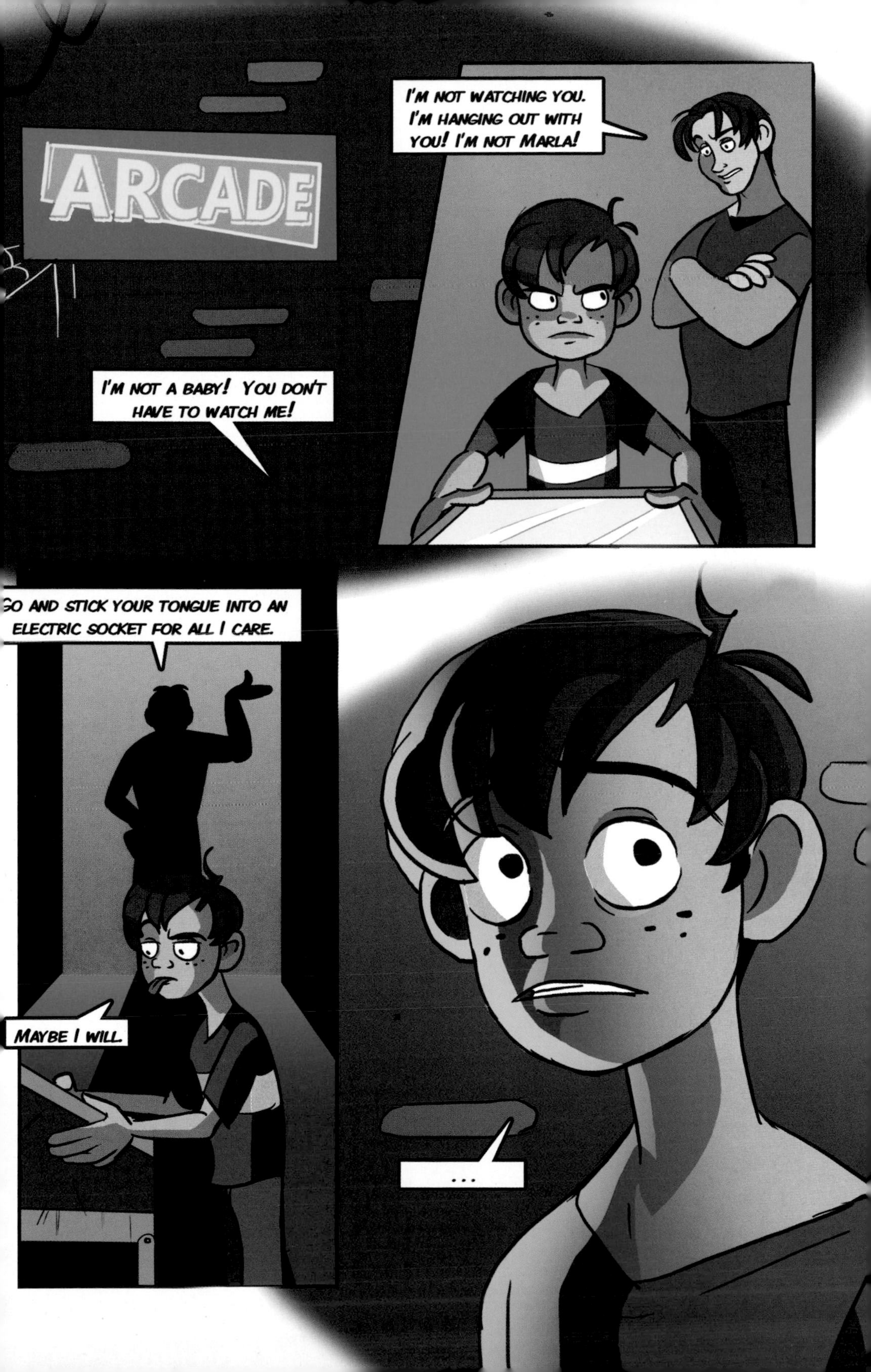
ARCADE
I'M NOT A BABY! YOU DON'T HAVE TO WATCH ME!
I'M NOT WATCHING YOU. I'M HANGING OUT WITH YOU! I'M NOT MARLA!
GO AND STICK YOUR TONGUE INTO AN ELECTRIC SOCKET FOR ALL I CARE.
MAYBE I WILL.
...

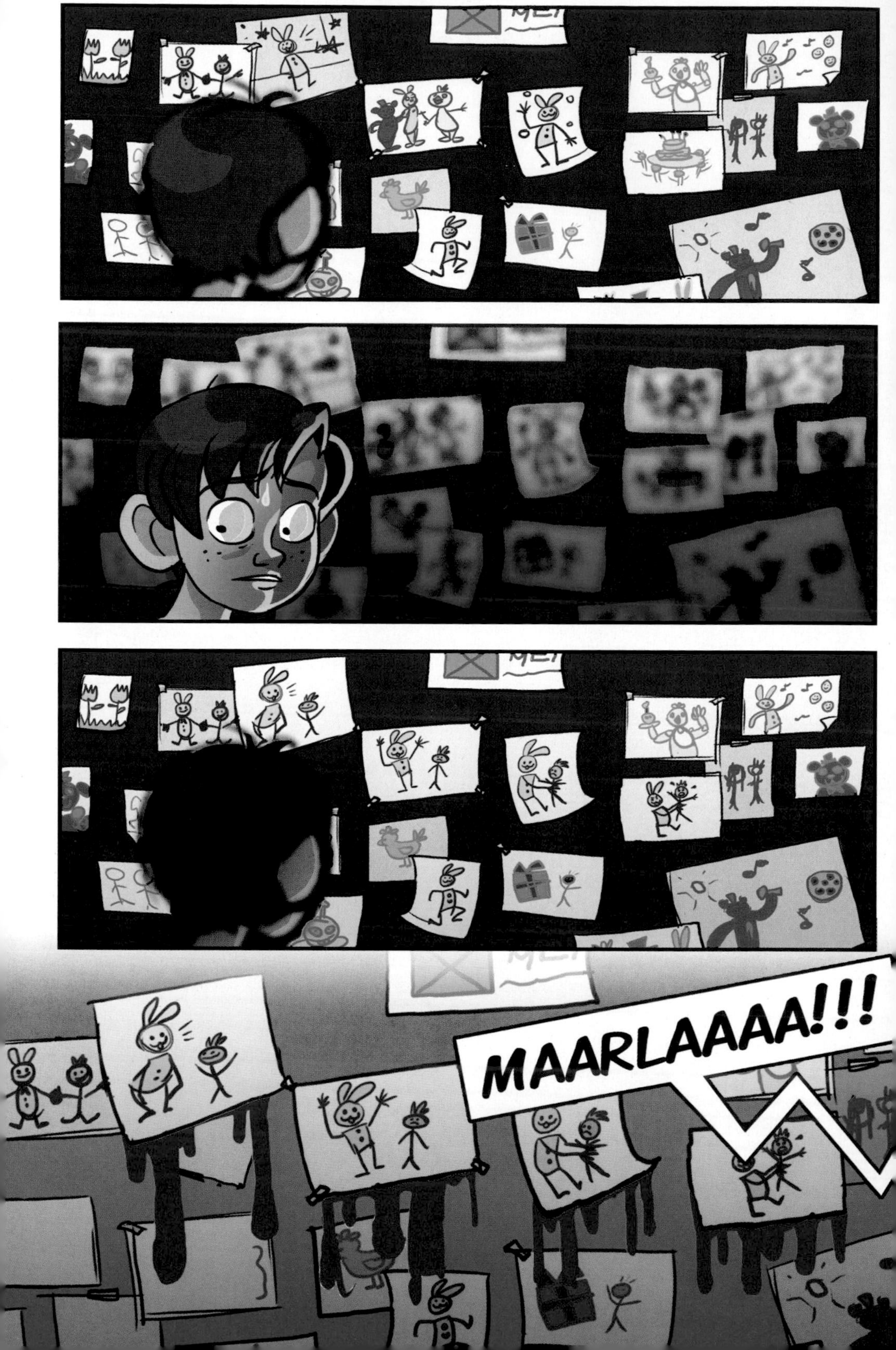
MAARLAAAA!!!

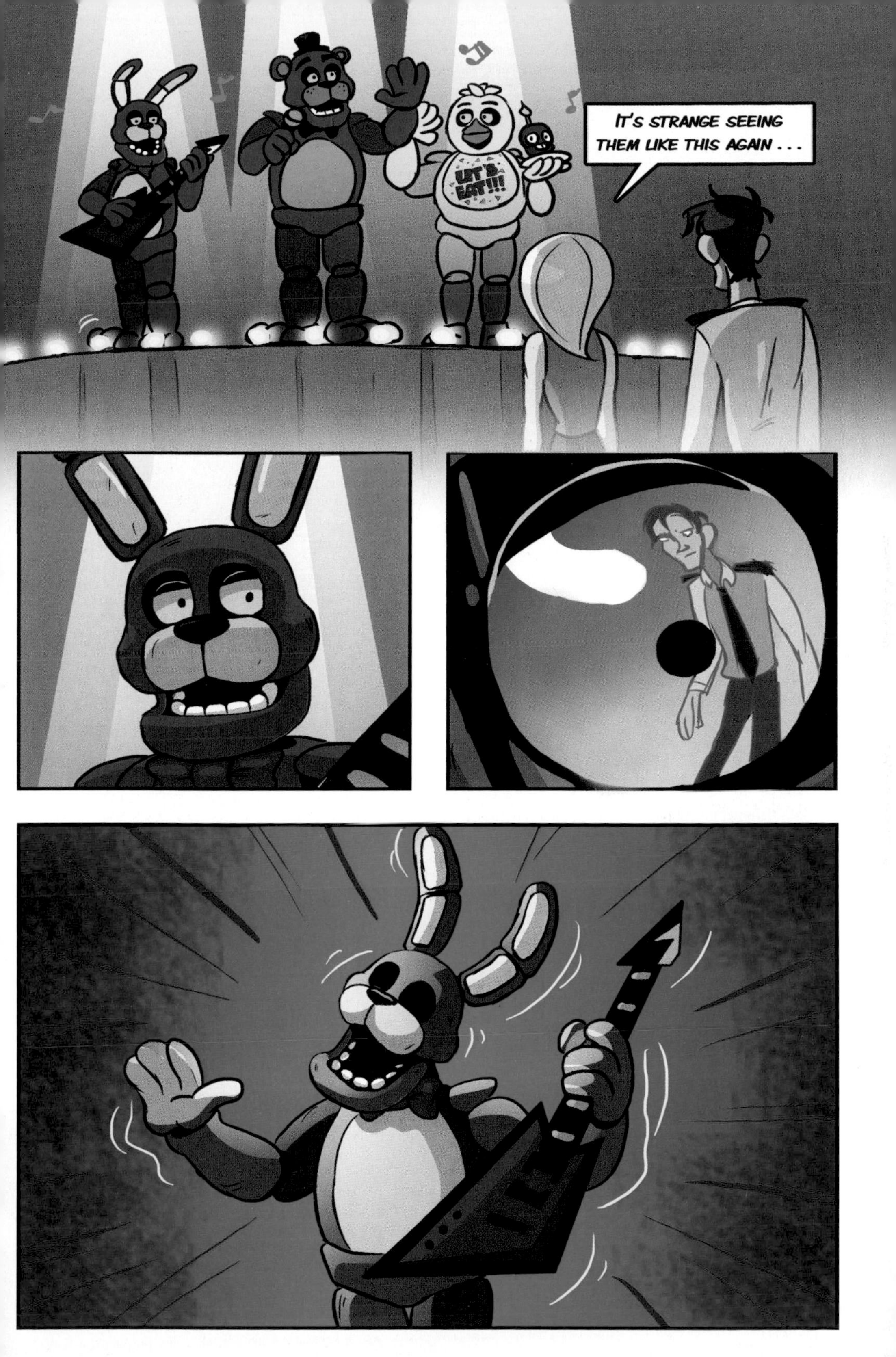
IT'S STRANGE SEEING THEM LIKE THIS AGAIN . . .
LET'S EAT!!!

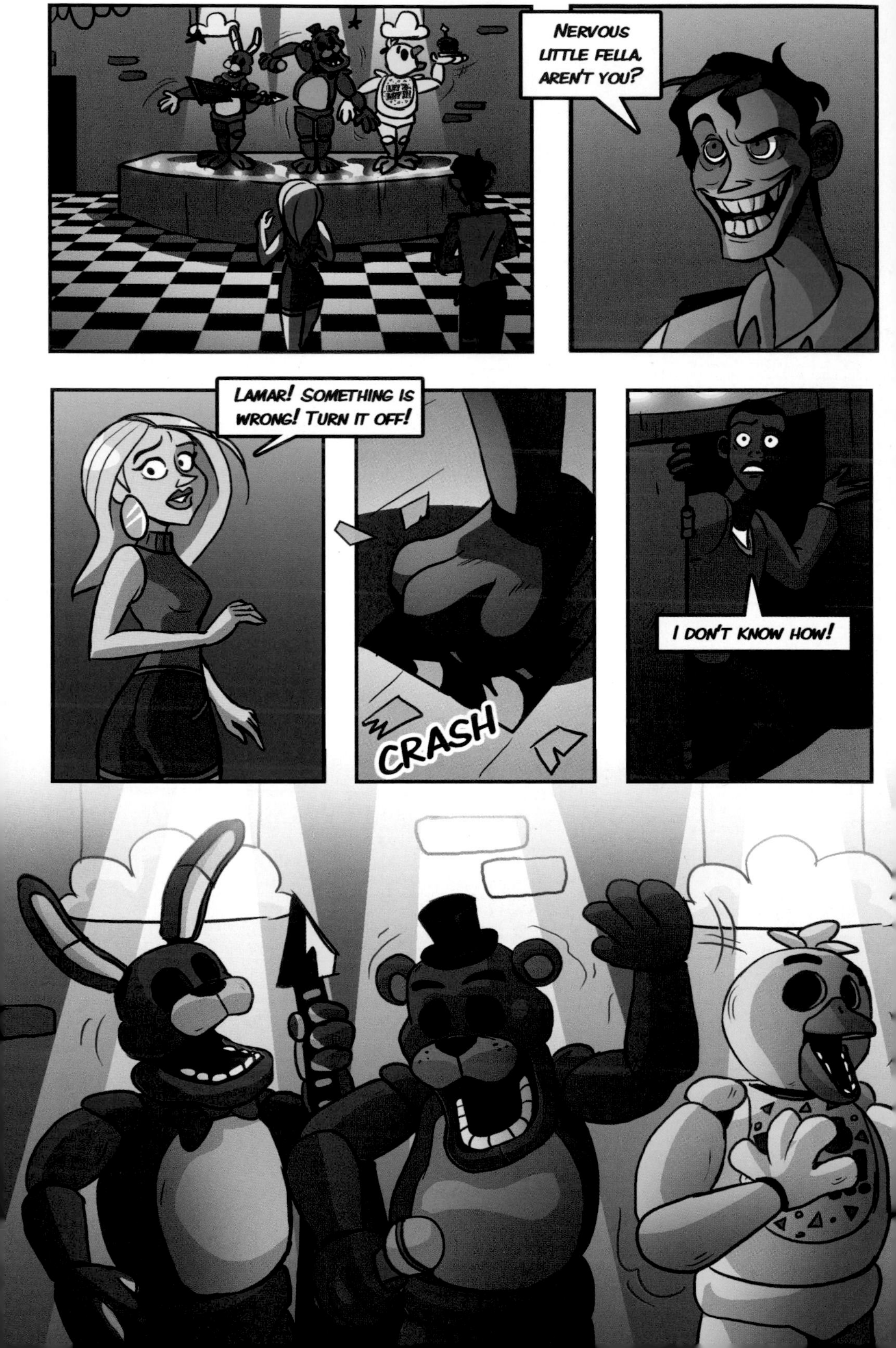
NERVOUS LITTLE FELLA, AREN'T YOU?
LAMAR! SOMETHING IS WRONG! TURN IT OFF!
CRASH
I DON'T KNOW HOW!

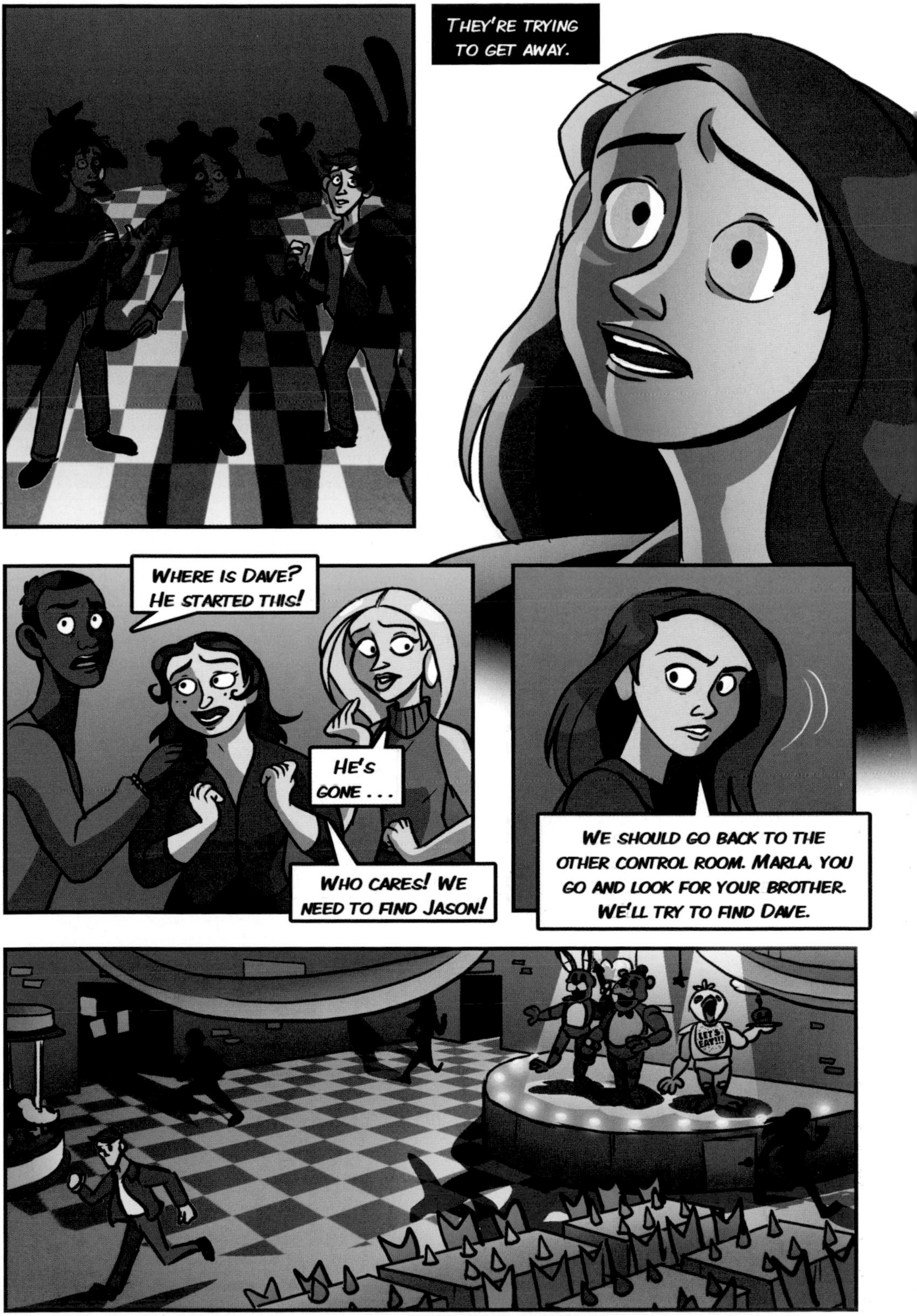
THEY'RE TRYING TO GET AWAY.
WHERE IS DAVE? HE STARTED THIS!
HE'S GONE . . .
WHO CARES! WE NEED TO FIND JASON!
WE SHOULD GO BACK TO THE OTHER CONTROL ROOM. MARLA, YOU GO AND LOOK FOR YOUR BROTHER. WE'LL TRY TO FIND DAVE.
LET'S EAT!!!

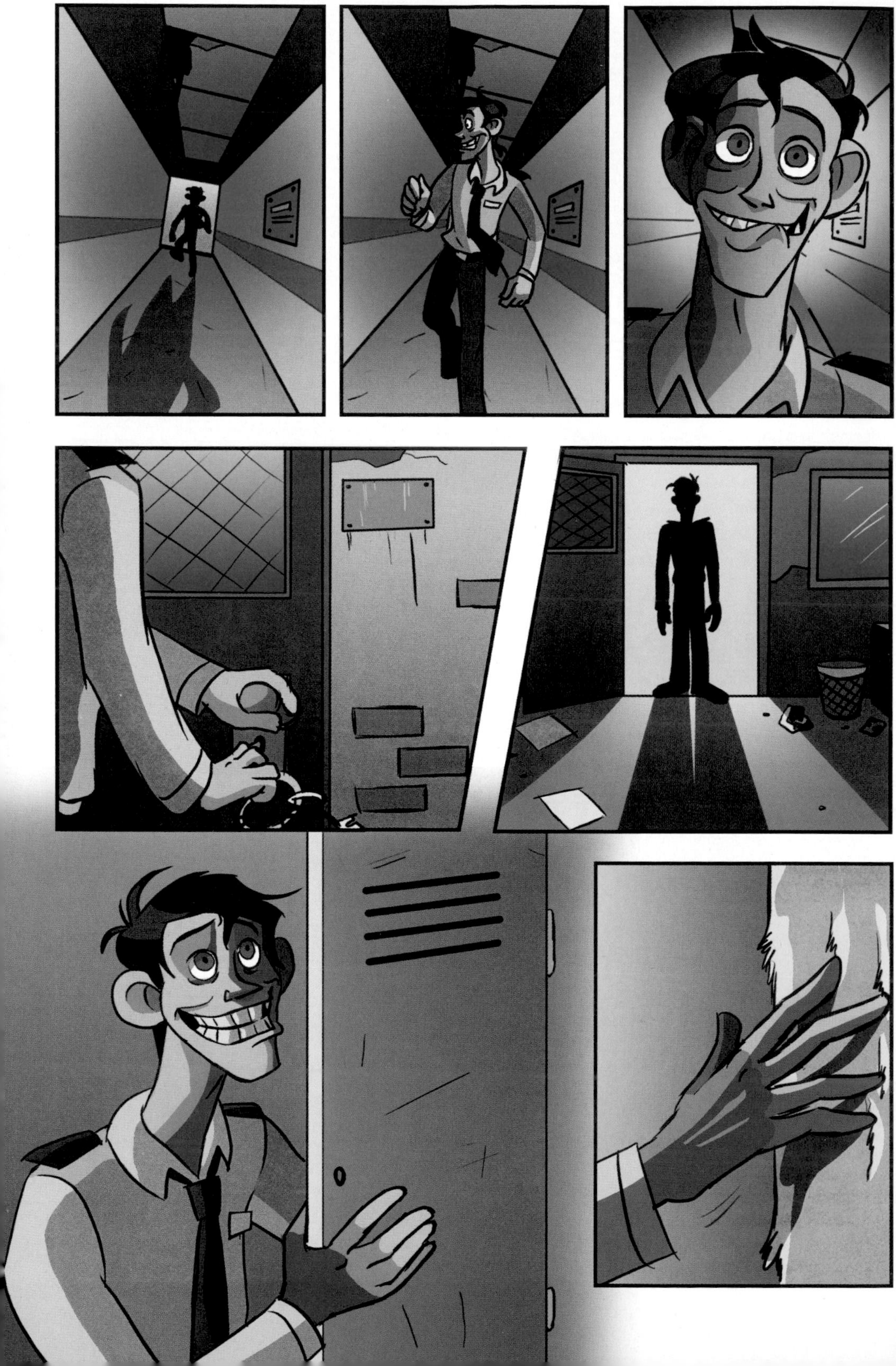

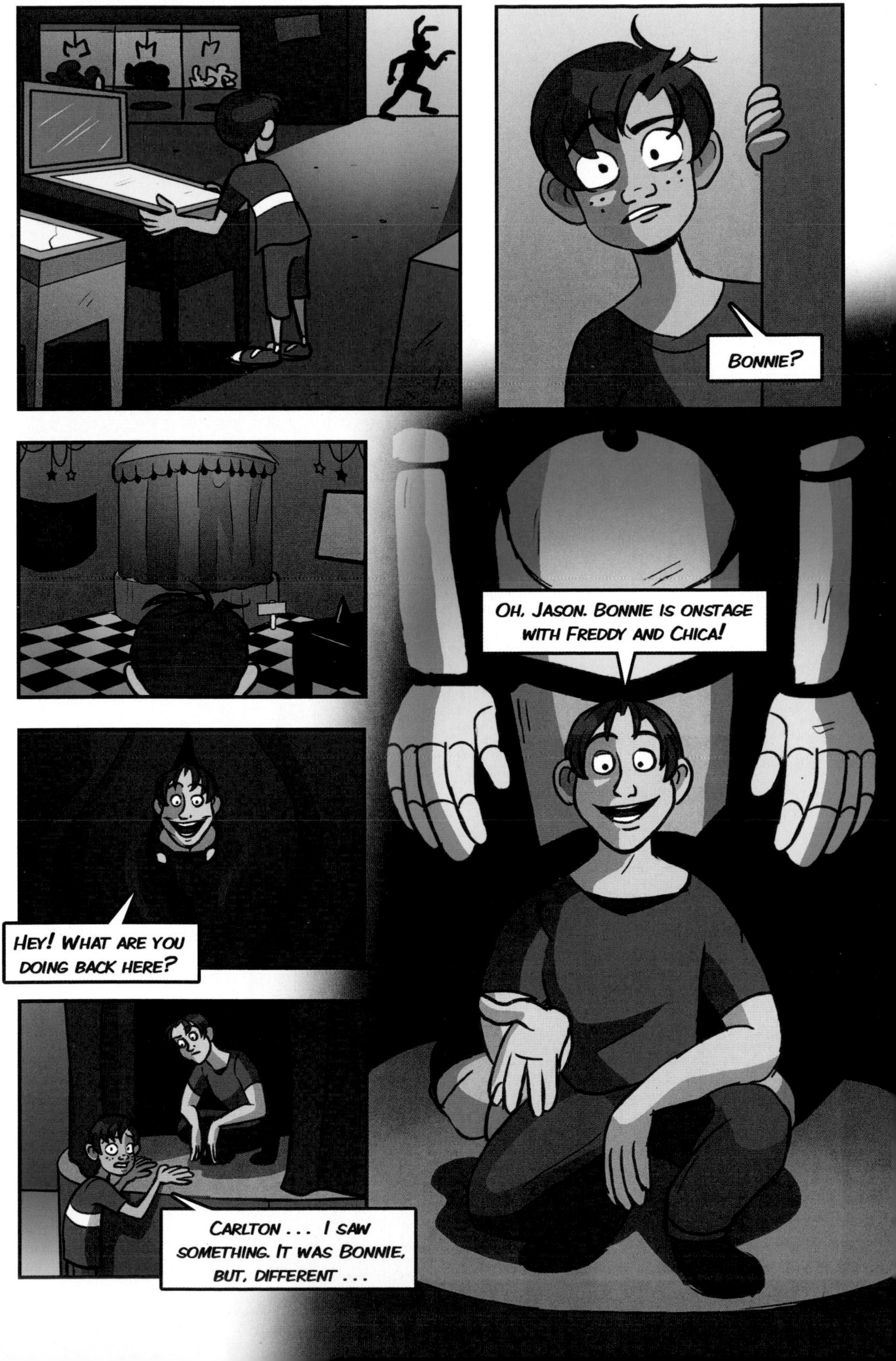
BONNIE?
HEY! WHAT ARE YOU DOING BACK HERE?
CARLTON . . . I SAW SOMETHING. IT WAS BONNIE, BUT, DIFFERENT . . .
OH, JASON. BONNIE IS ONSTAGE WITH FREDDY AND CHICA!

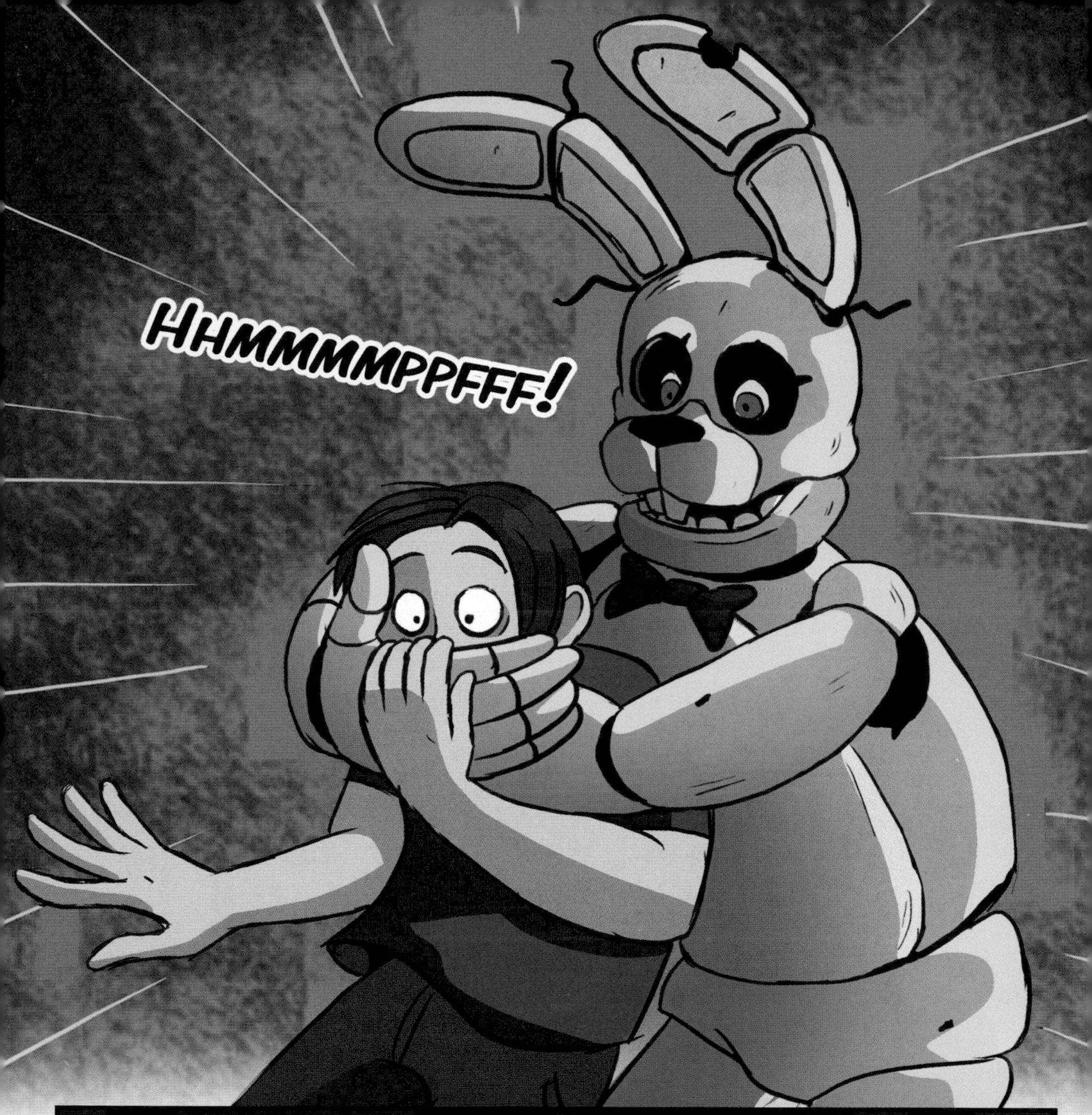
HHMMMMMPPFFF!

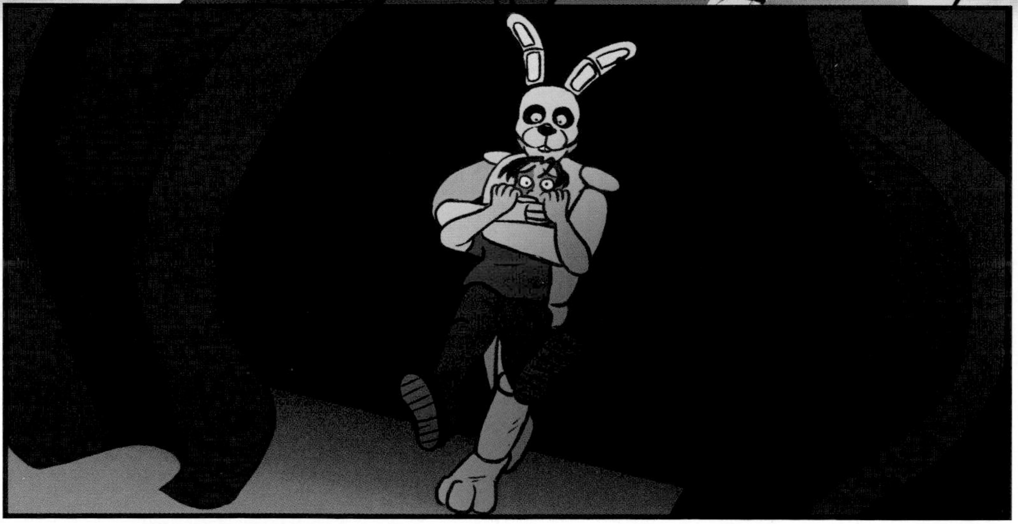

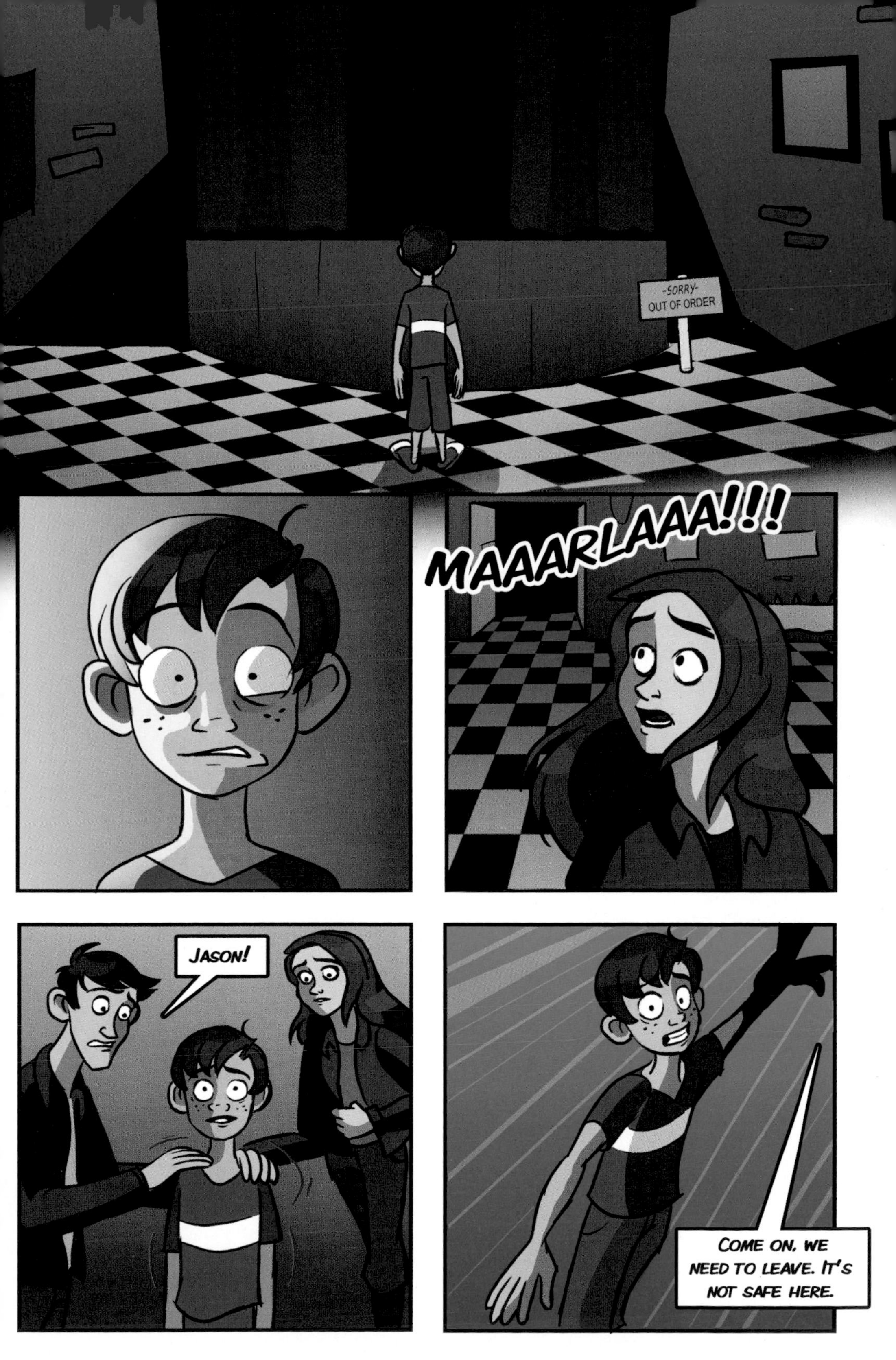
-SORRY-
OUT OF ORDER
MAAARLAAA!!!
JASON!
COME ON, WE NEED TO LEAVE. IT'S NOT SAFE HERE.

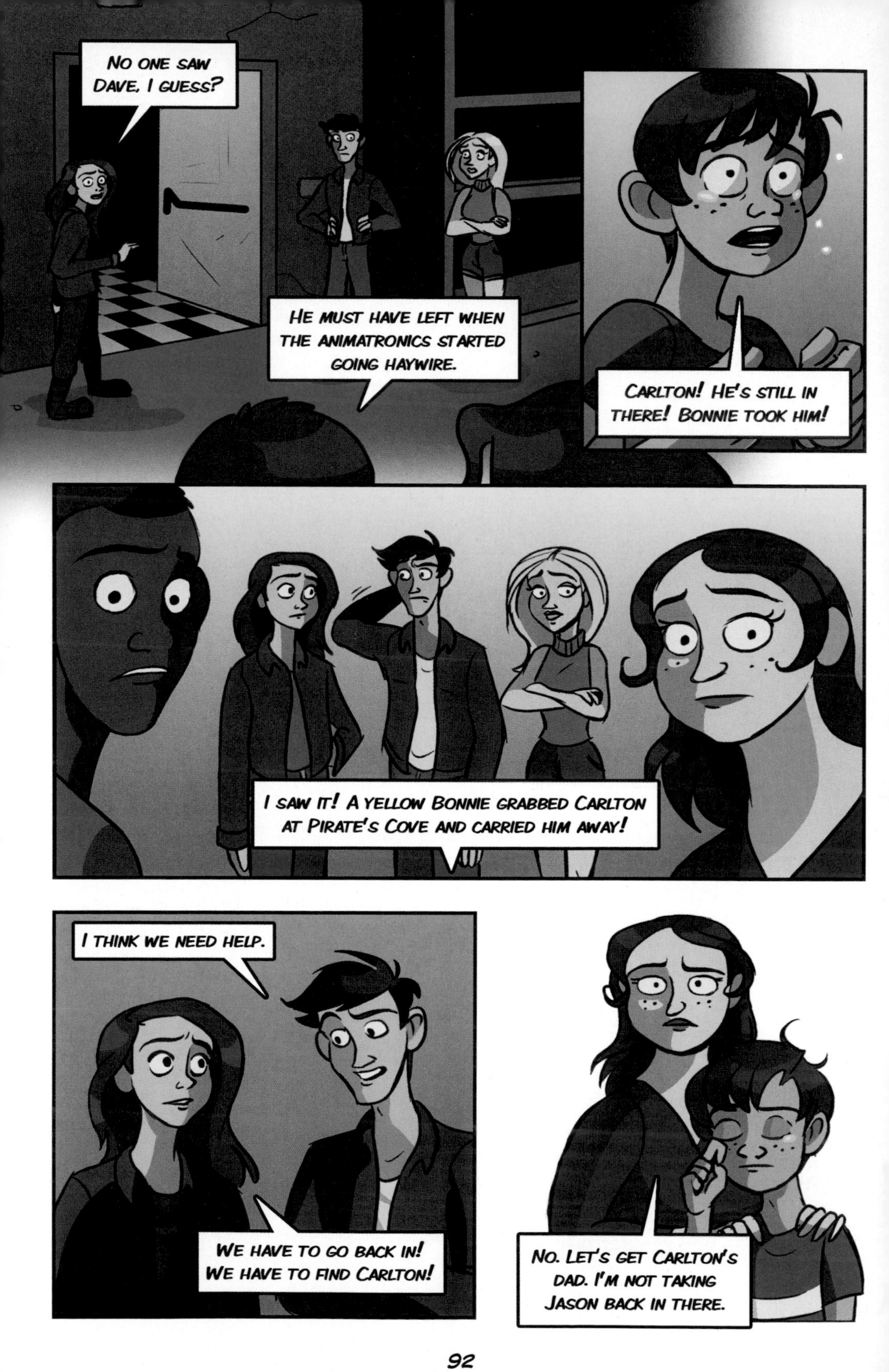
NO ONE SAW DAVE, I GUESS?
HE MUST HAVE LEFT WHEN THE ANIMATRONICS STARTED GOING HAYWIRE.
CARLTON! HE'S STILL IN THERE! BONNIE TOOK HIM!
I SAW IT! A YELLOW BONNIE GRABBED CARLTON AT PIRATE'S COVE AND CARRIED HIM AWAY!
I THINK WE NEED HELP.
WE HAVE TO GO BACK IN! WE HAVE TO FIND CARLTON!
NO. LET'S GET CARLTON'S DAD. I'M NOT TAKING JASON BACK IN THERE.

CHAPTER 7

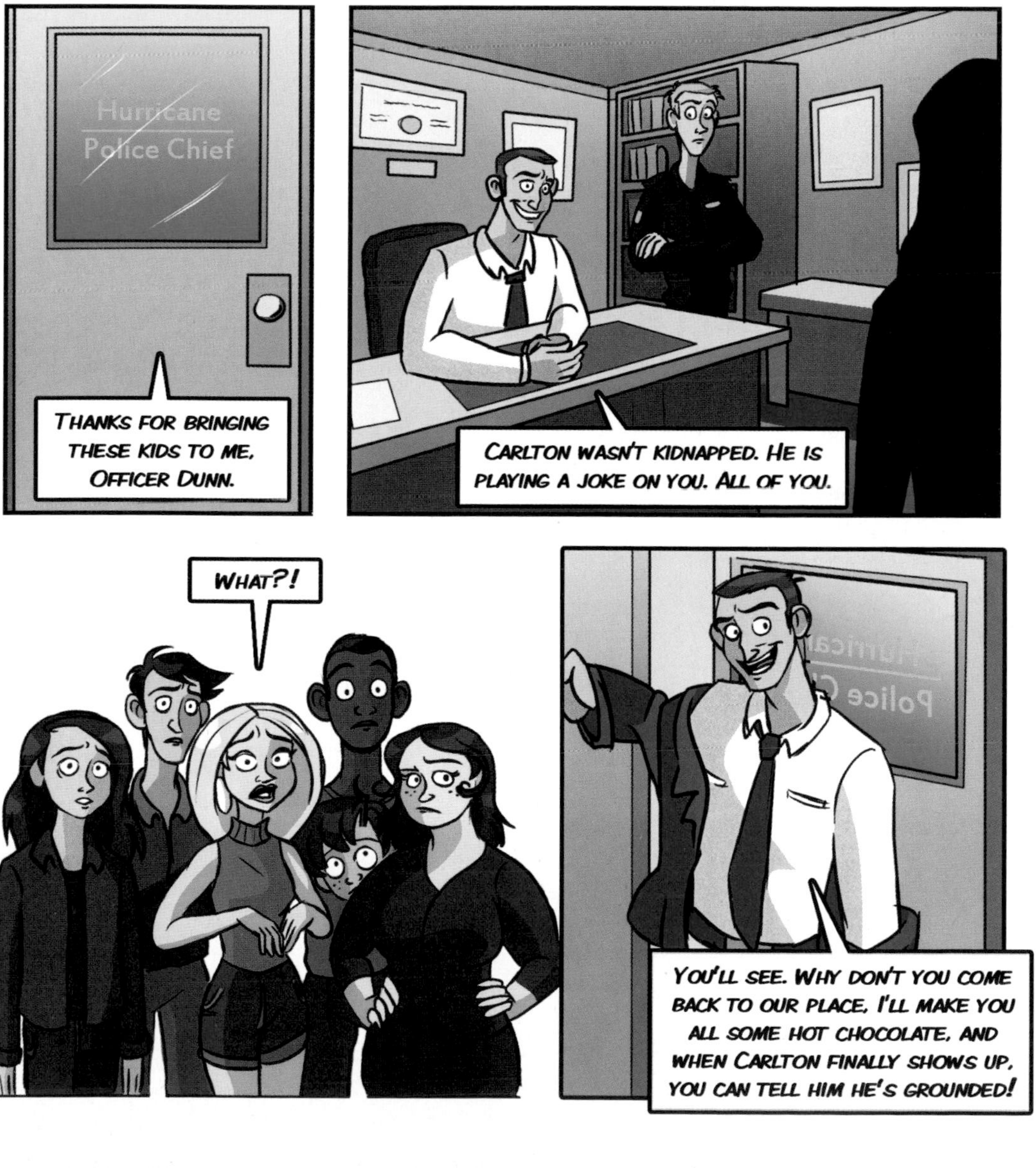
Hurricane
Police Chief
THANKS FOR BRINGING THESE KIDS TO ME, OFFICER DUNN.
CARLTON WASN'T KIDNAPPED. HE IS PLAYING A JOKE ON YOU. ALL OF YOU.
WHAT?!
YOU'LL SEE. WHY DON'T YOU COME BACK TO OUR PLACE, I'LL MAKE YOU ALL SOME HOT CHOCOLATE, AND WHEN CARLTON FINALLY SHOWS UP, YOU CAN TELL HIM HE'S GROUNDED!

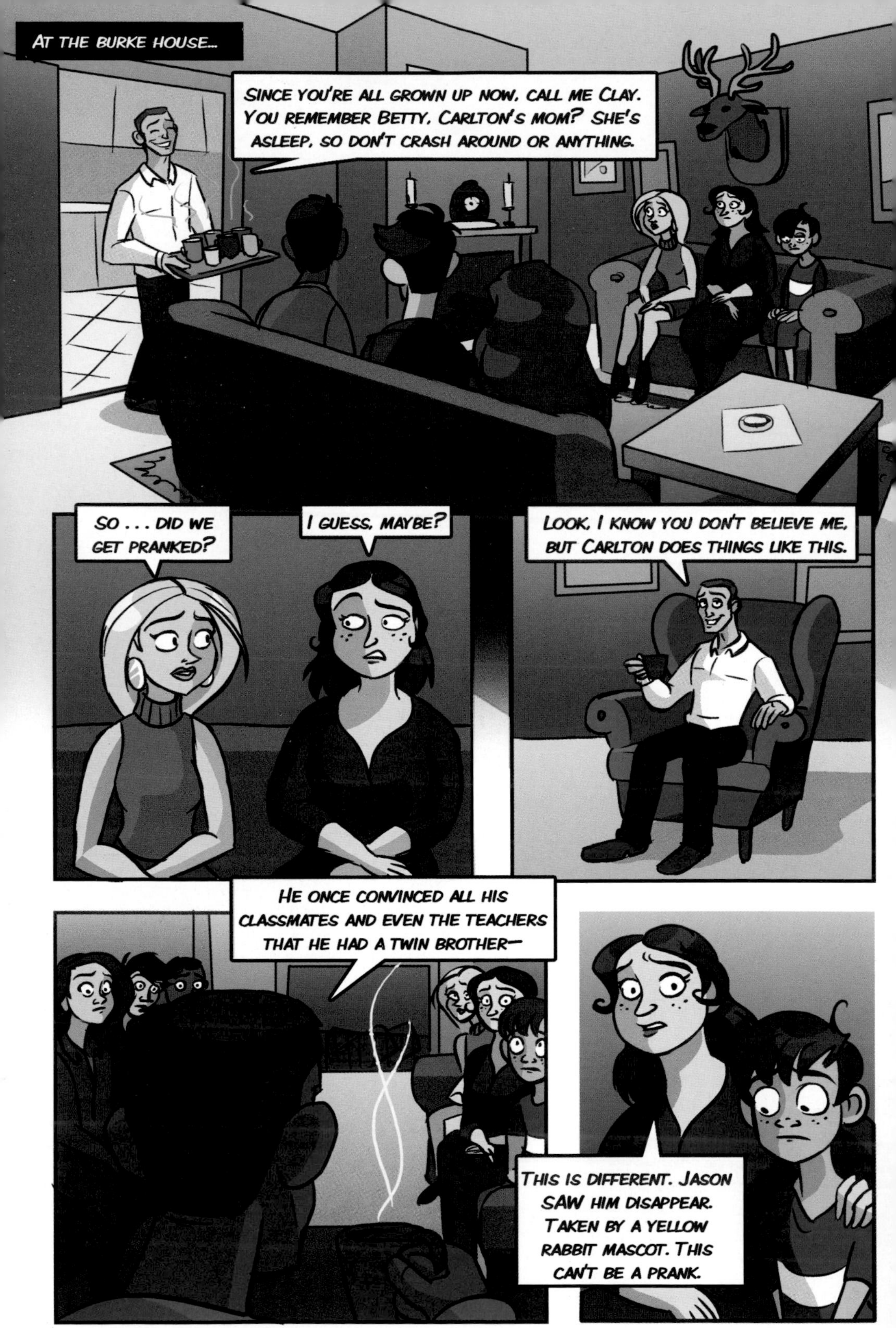

AT THE BURKE HOUSE...
SINCE YOU'RE ALL GROWN UP NOW, CALL ME CLAY. YOU REMEMBER BETTY, CARLTON'S MOM? SHE'S ASLEEP, SO DON'T CRASH AROUND OR ANYTHING.
SO . . . DID WE GET PRANKED?
I GUESS, MAYBE?
LOOK, I KNOW YOU DON'T BELIEVE ME, BUT CARLTON DOES THINGS LIKE THIS.
HE ONCE CONVINCED ALL HIS CLASSMATES AND EVEN THE TEACHERS THAT HE HAD A TWIN BROTHER—
THIS IS DIFFERENT. JASON SAW HIM DISAPPEAR. TAKEN BY A YELLOW RABBIT MASCOT. THIS CAN'T BE A PRANK.

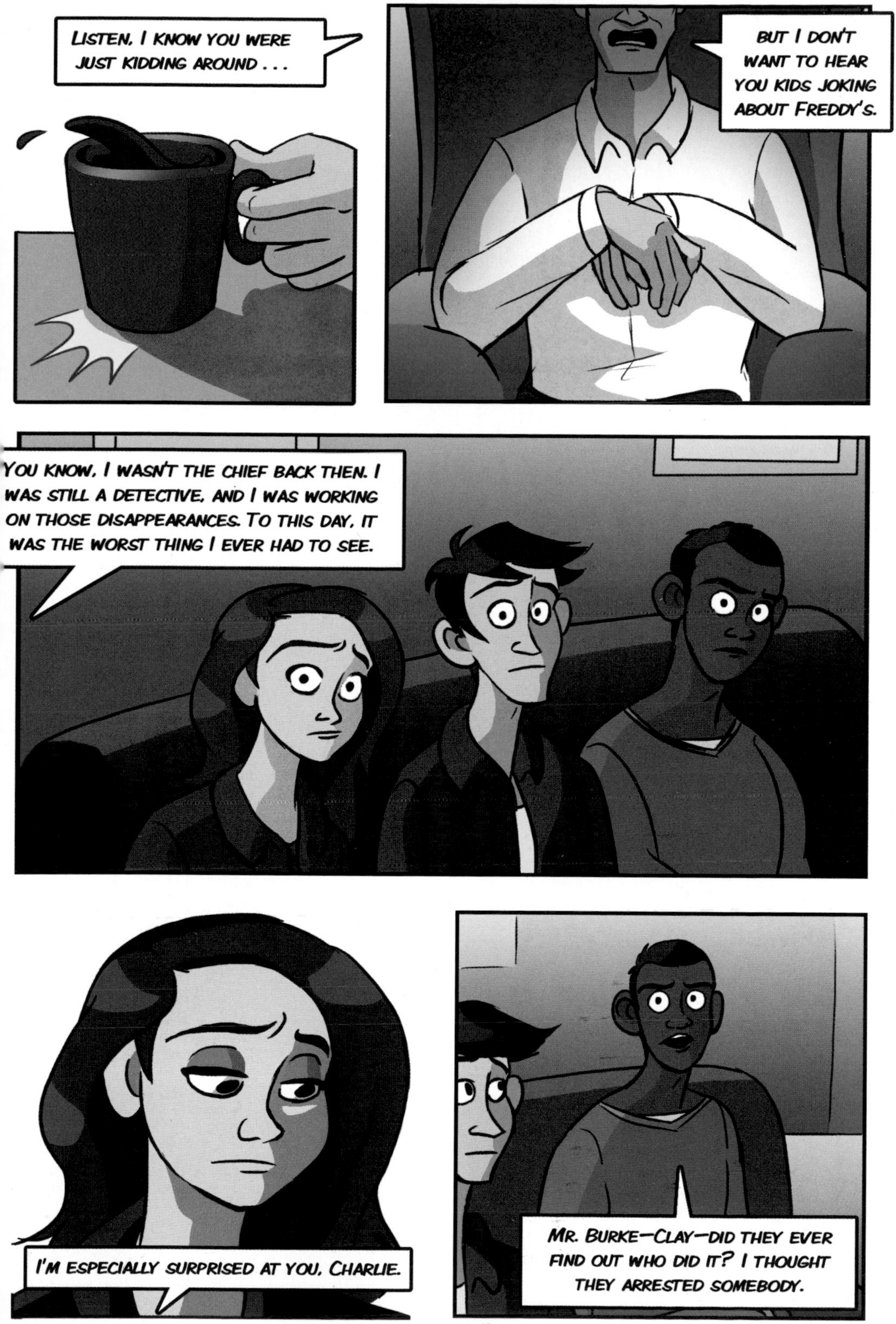
LISTEN, I KNOW YOU WERE JUST KIDDING AROUND . . .
BUT I DON'T WANT TO HEAR YOU KIDS JOKING ABOUT FREDDY'S.
YOU KNOW, I WASN'T THE CHIEF BACK THEN. I WAS STILL A DETECTIVE, AND I WAS WORKING ON THOSE DISAPPEARANCES. TO THIS DAY, IT WAS THE WORST THING I EVER HAD TO SEE.
I'M ESPECIALLY SURPRISED AT YOU, CHARLIE.
MR. BURKE—CLAY—DID THEY EVER FIND OUT WHO DID IT? I THOUGHT THEY ARRESTED SOMEBODY.

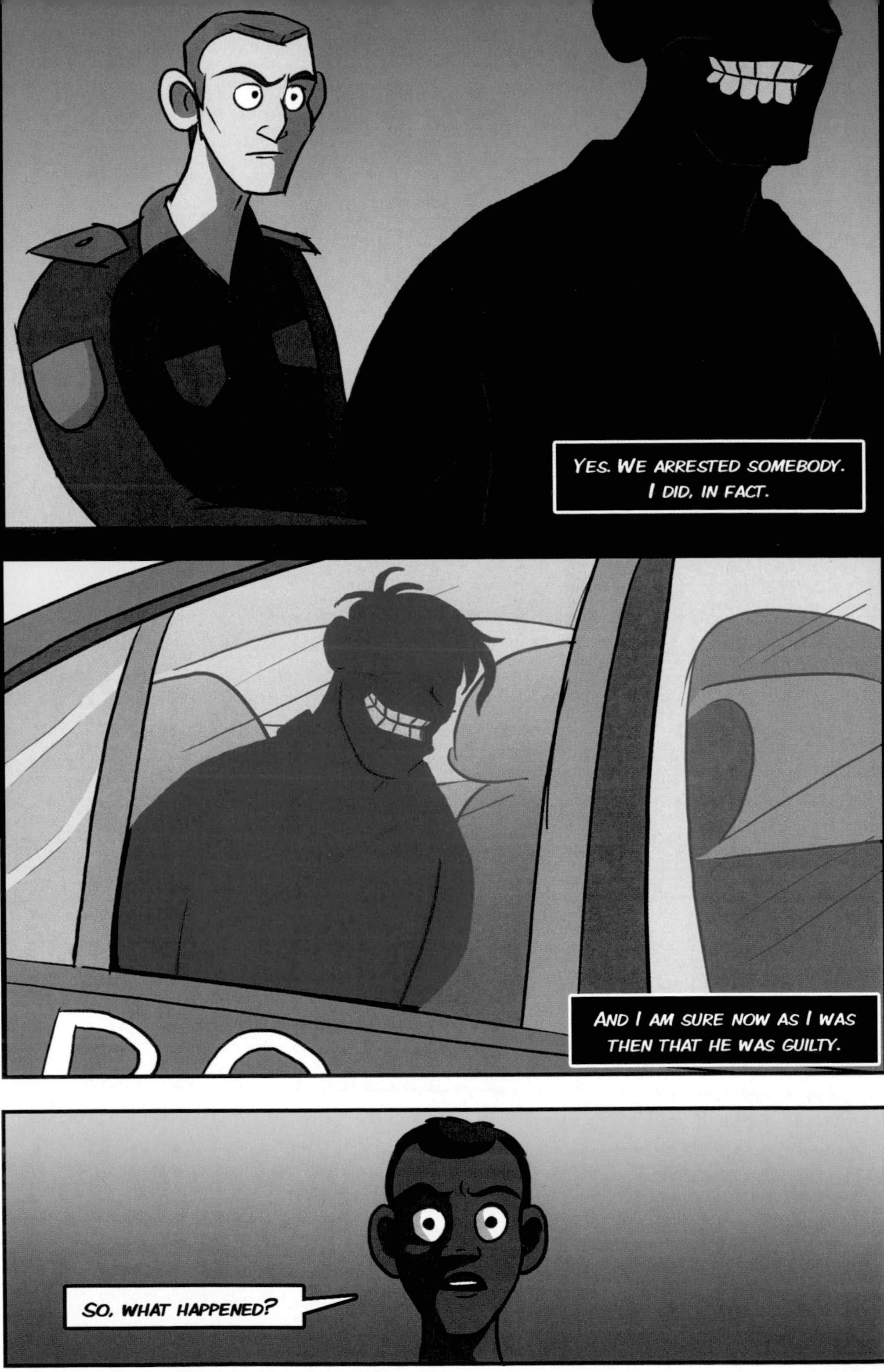
YES. WE ARRESTED SOMEBODY. I DID, IN FACT.
AND I AM SURE NOW AS I WAS THEN THAT HE WAS GUILTY.
SO, WHAT HAPPENED?

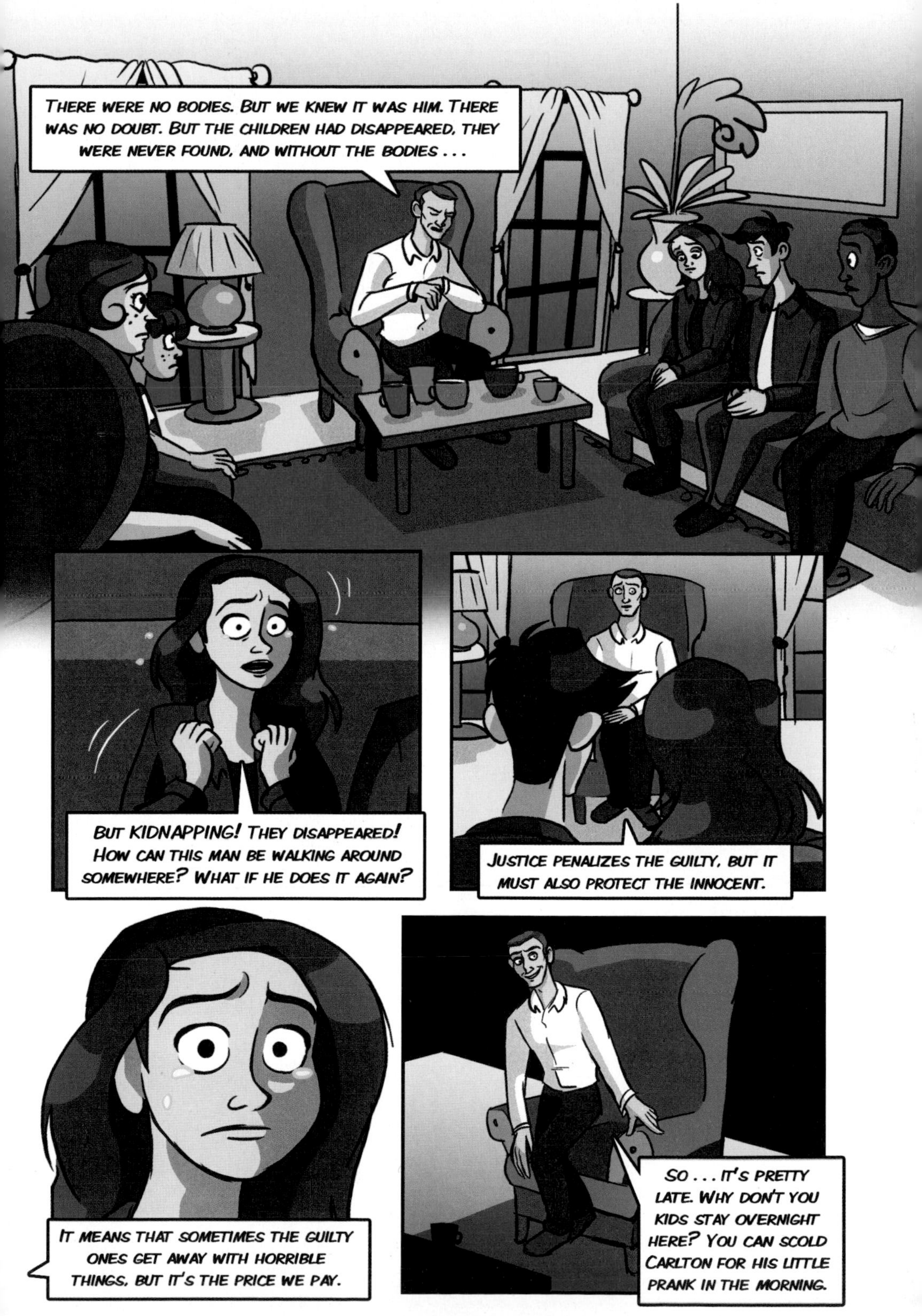
THERE WERE NO BODIES. BUT WE KNEW IT WAS HIM. THERE WAS NO DOUBT. BUT THE CHILDREN HAD DISAPPEARED, THEY WERE NEVER FOUND, AND WITHOUT THE BODIES . . .
BUT KIDNAPPING! THEY DISAPPEARED! HOW CAN THIS MAN BE WALKING AROUND SOMEWHERE? WHAT IF HE DOES IT AGAIN?
JUSTICE PENALIZES THE GUILTY, BUT IT MUST ALSO PROTECT THE INNOCENT.
IT MEANS THAT SOMETIMES THE GUILTY ONES GET AWAY WITH HORRIBLE THINGS, BUT IT'S THE PRICE WE PAY.
SO . . . IT'S PRETTY LATE. WHY DON'T YOU KIDS STAY OVERNIGHT HERE? YOU CAN SCOLD CARLTON FOR HIS LITTLE PRANK IN THE MORNING.

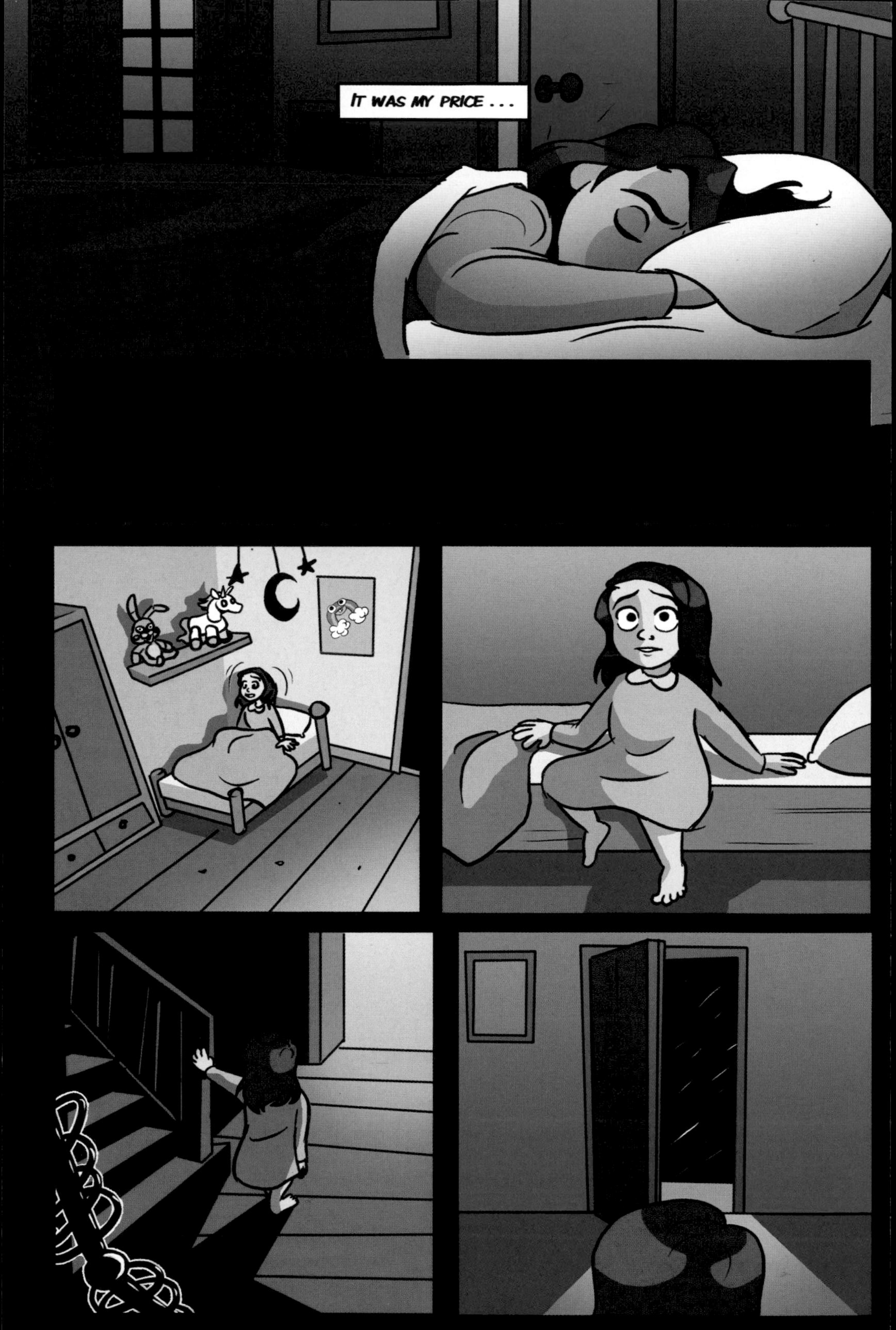
IT WAS MY PRICE . . .

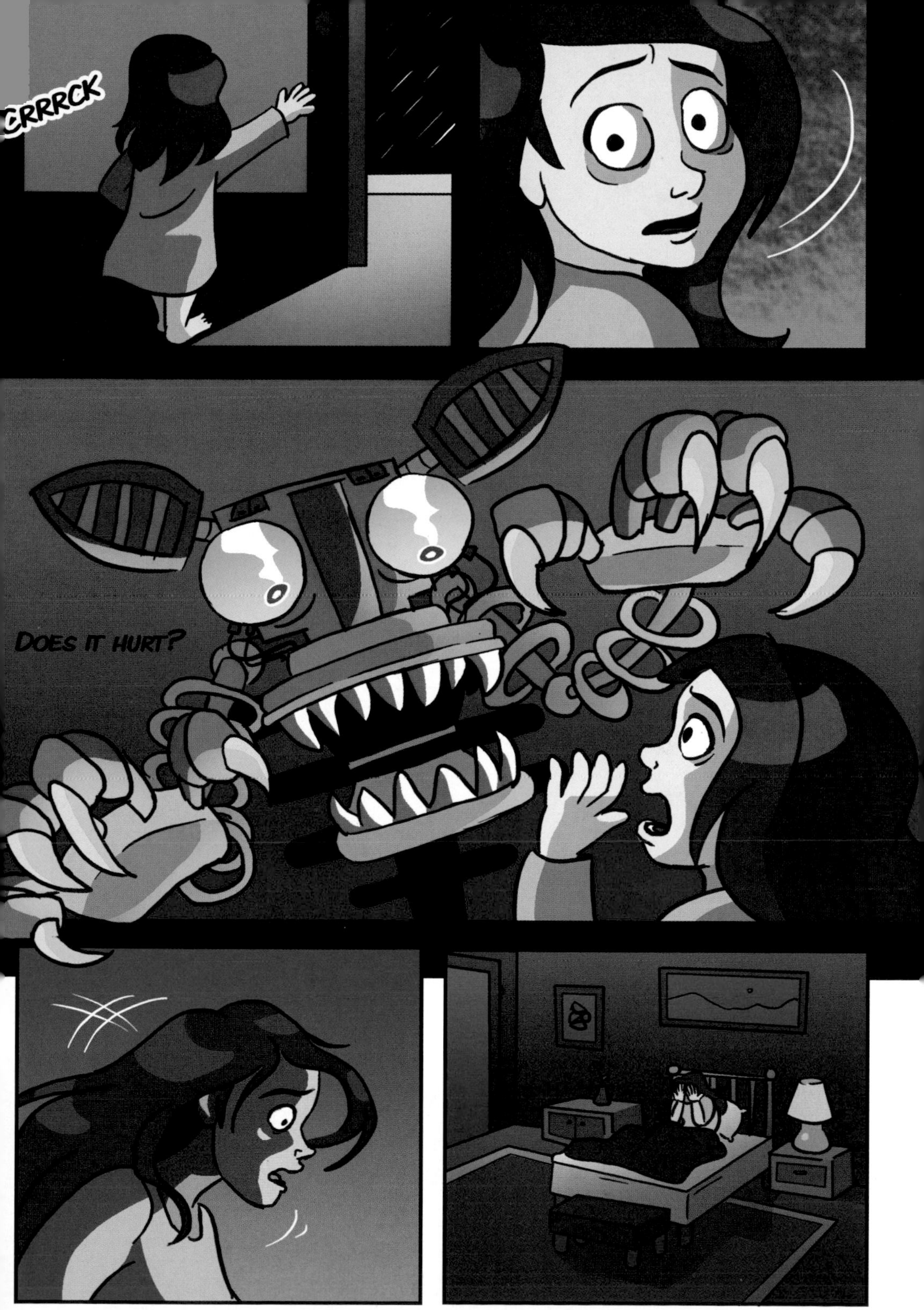
CRRRCK
DOES IT HURT?

CHAPTER 8

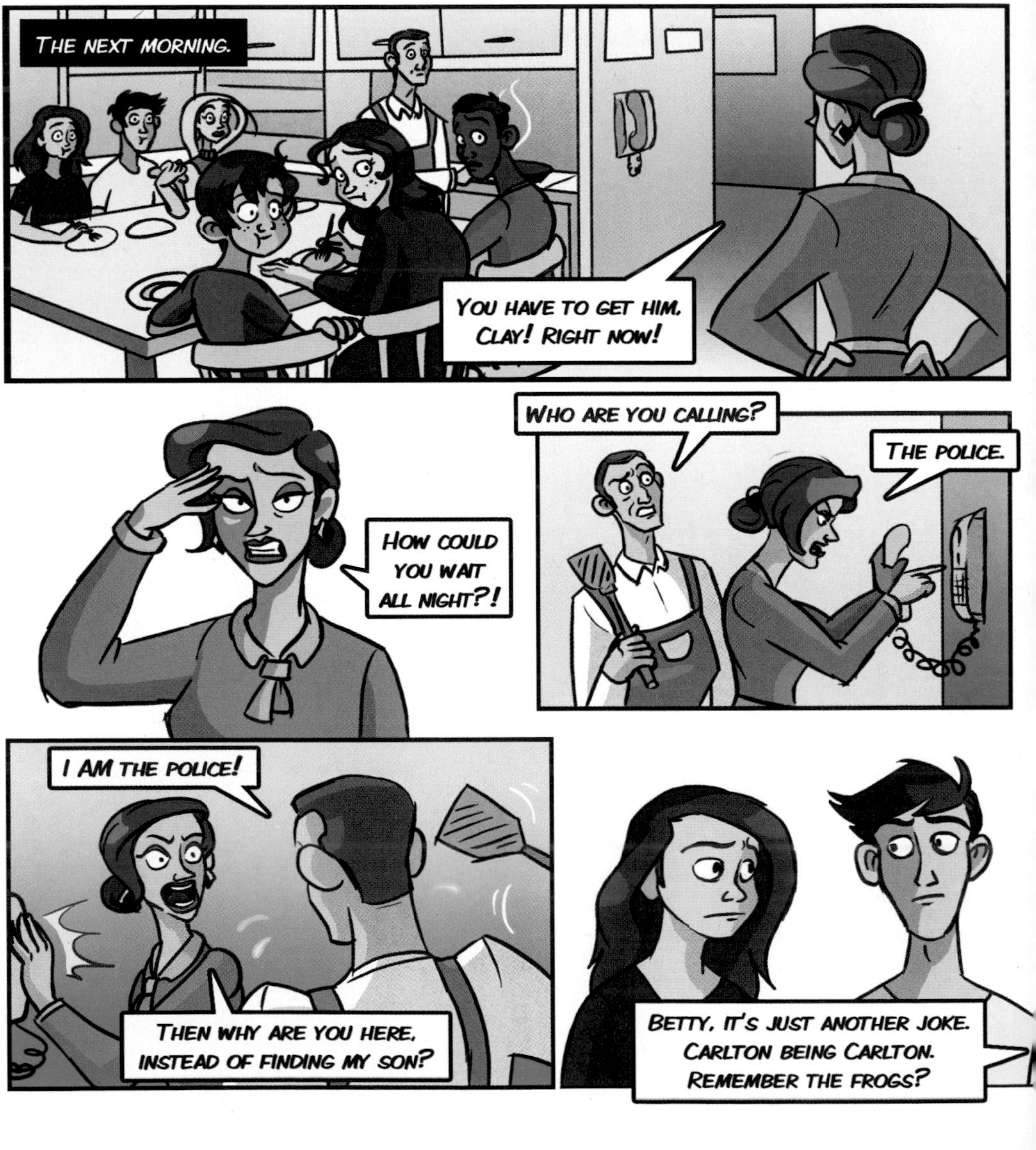
THE NEXT MORNING.
YOU HAVE TO GET HIM, CLAY! RIGHT NOW!
HOW COULD YOU WAIT ALL NIGHT?!
WHO ARE YOU CALLING?
THE POLICE.
I AM THE POLICE!
THEN WHY ARE YOU HERE, INSTEAD OF FINDING MY SON?
BETTY, IT'S JUST ANOTHER JOKE. CARLTON BEING CARLTON. REMEMBER THE FROGS?

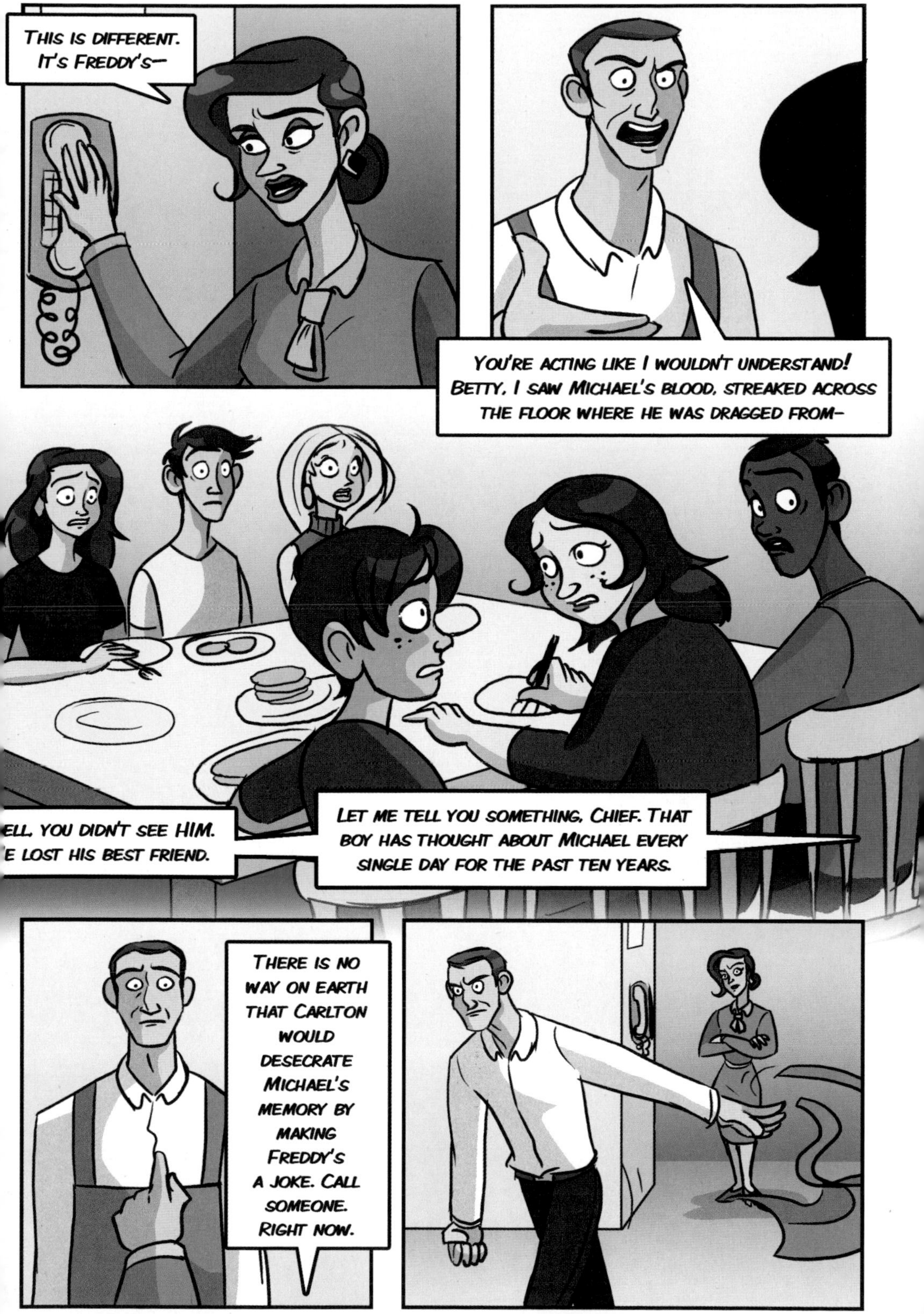
THIS IS DIFFERENT. IT'S FREDDY'S—
YOU'RE ACTING LIKE I WOULDN'T UNDERSTAND! BETTY, I SAW MICHAEL'S BLOOD, STREAKED ACROSS THE FLOOR WHERE HE WAS DRAGGED FROM—
ELL, YOU DIDN'T SEE HIM. E LOST HIS BEST FRIEND.
LET ME TELL YOU SOMETHING, CHIEF. THAT BOY HAS THOUGHT ABOUT MICHAEL EVERY SINGLE DAY FOR THE PAST TEN YEARS.
THERE IS NO WAY ON EARTH THAT CARLTON WOULD DESECRATE MICHAEL'S MEMORY BY MAKING FREDDY'S A JOKE. CALL SOMEONE. RIGHT NOW.

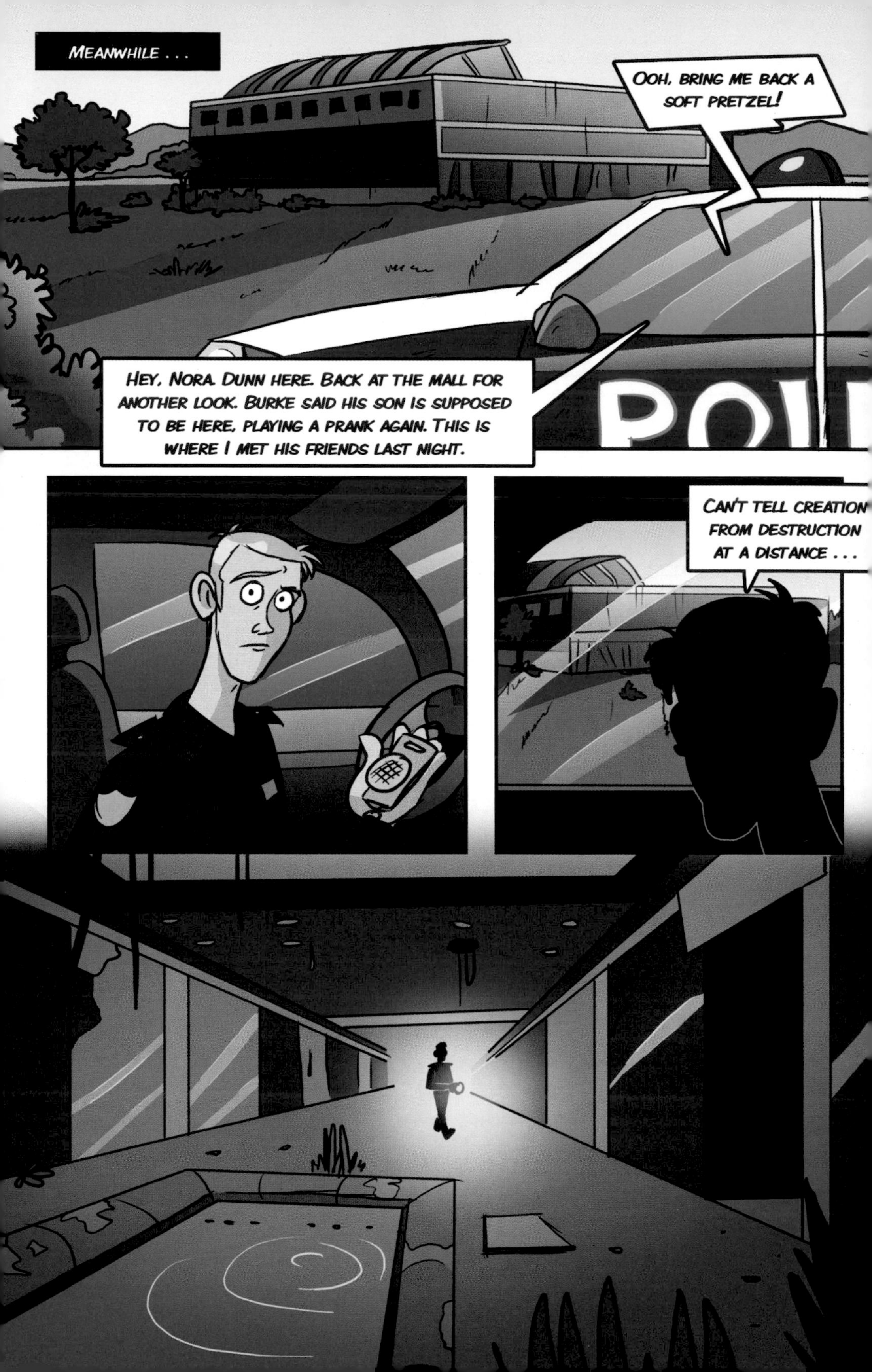
MEANWHILE . . .
OOH, BRING ME BACK A SOFT PRETZEL!
HEY, NORA. DUNN HERE. BACK AT THE MALL FOR ANOTHER LOOK. BURKE SAID HIS SON IS SUPPOSED TO BE HERE, PLAYING A PRANK AGAIN. THIS IS WHERE I MET HIS FRIENDS LAST NIGHT.
CAN'T TELL CREATION FROM DESTRUCTION AT A DISTANCE . . .

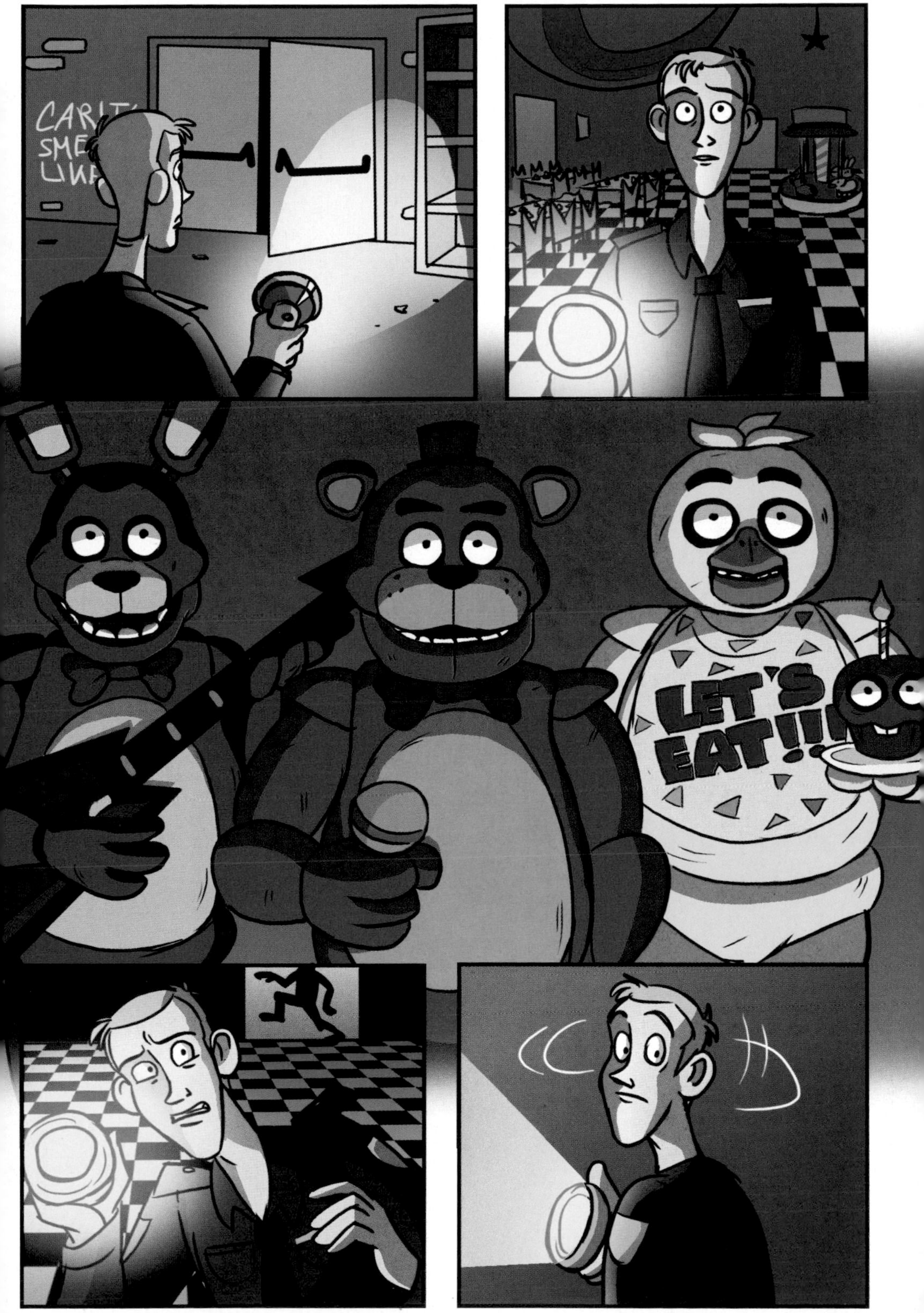
LET'S EAT!!!

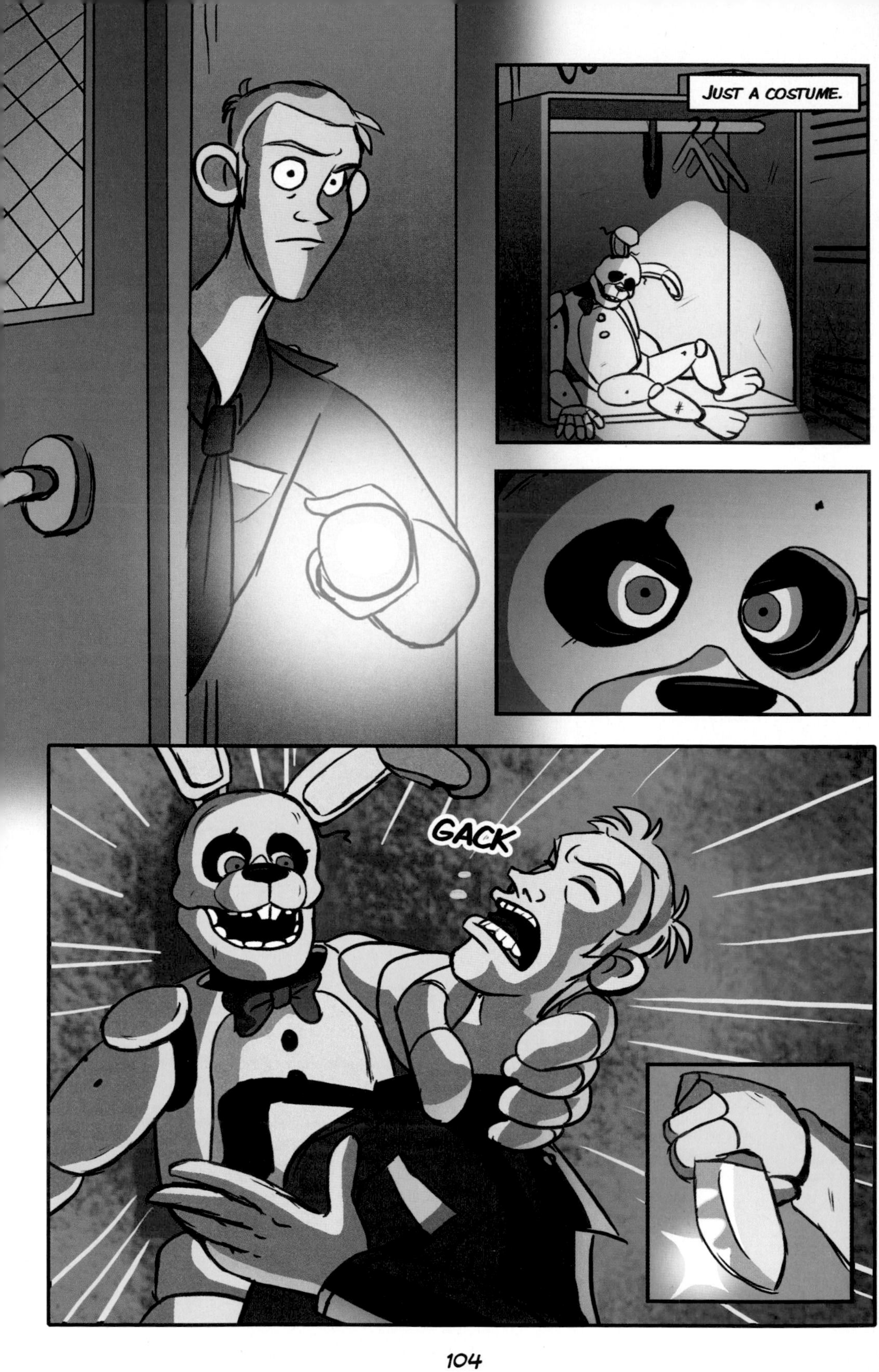
JUST A COSTUME.
GACK

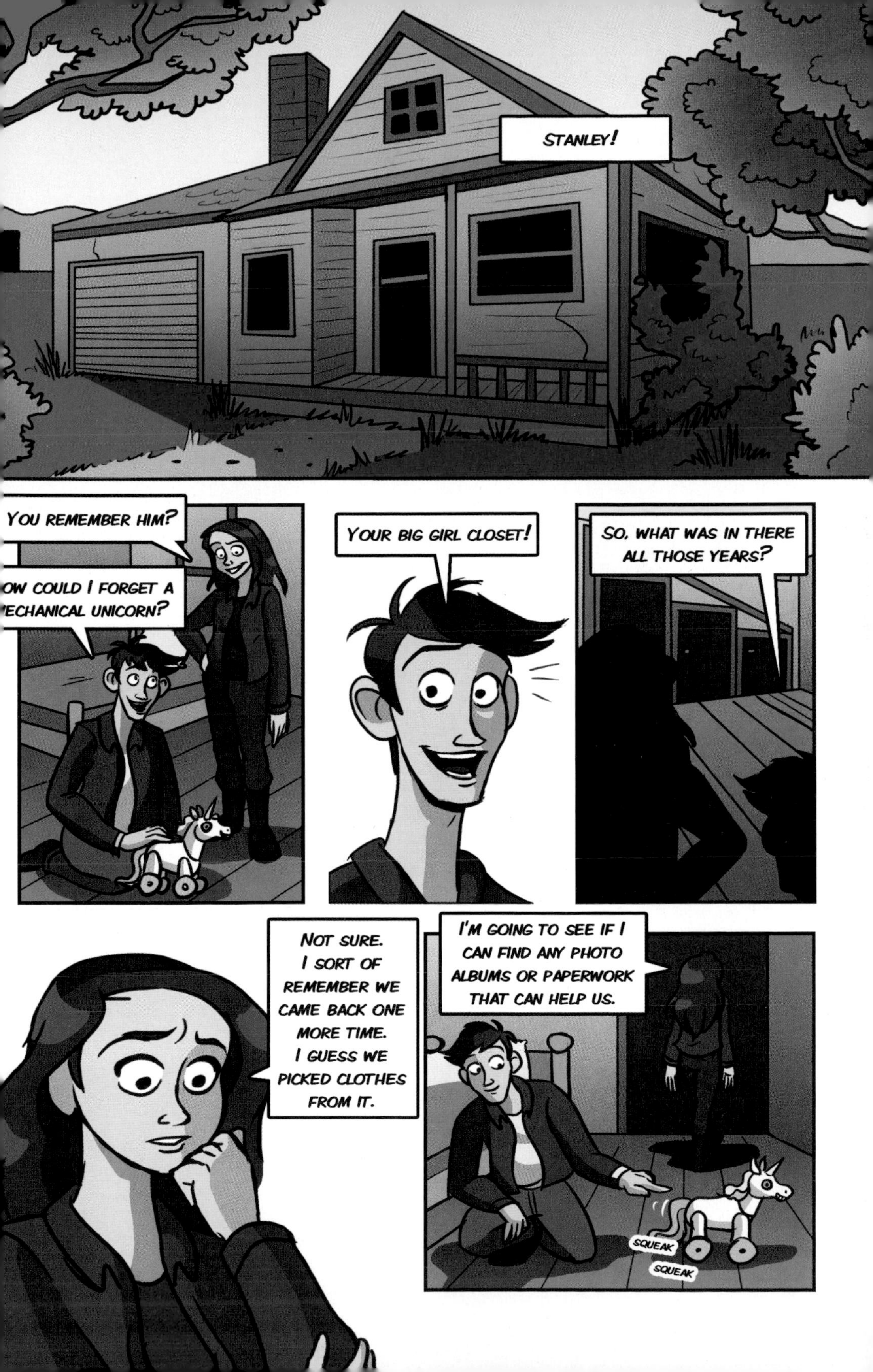
STANLEY!
YOU REMEMBER HIM?
OW COULD I FORGET A 'ECHANICAL UNICORN?
YOUR BIG GIRL CLOSET!
SO, WHAT WAS IN THERE ALL THOSE YEARS?
NOT SURE. I SORT OF REMEMBER WE CAME BACK ONE MORE TIME. I GUESS WE PICKED CLOTHES FROM IT.
I'M GOING TO SEE IF I CAN FIND ANY PHOTO ALBUMS OR PAPERWORK THAT CAN HELP US.
SQUEAK
SQUEAK

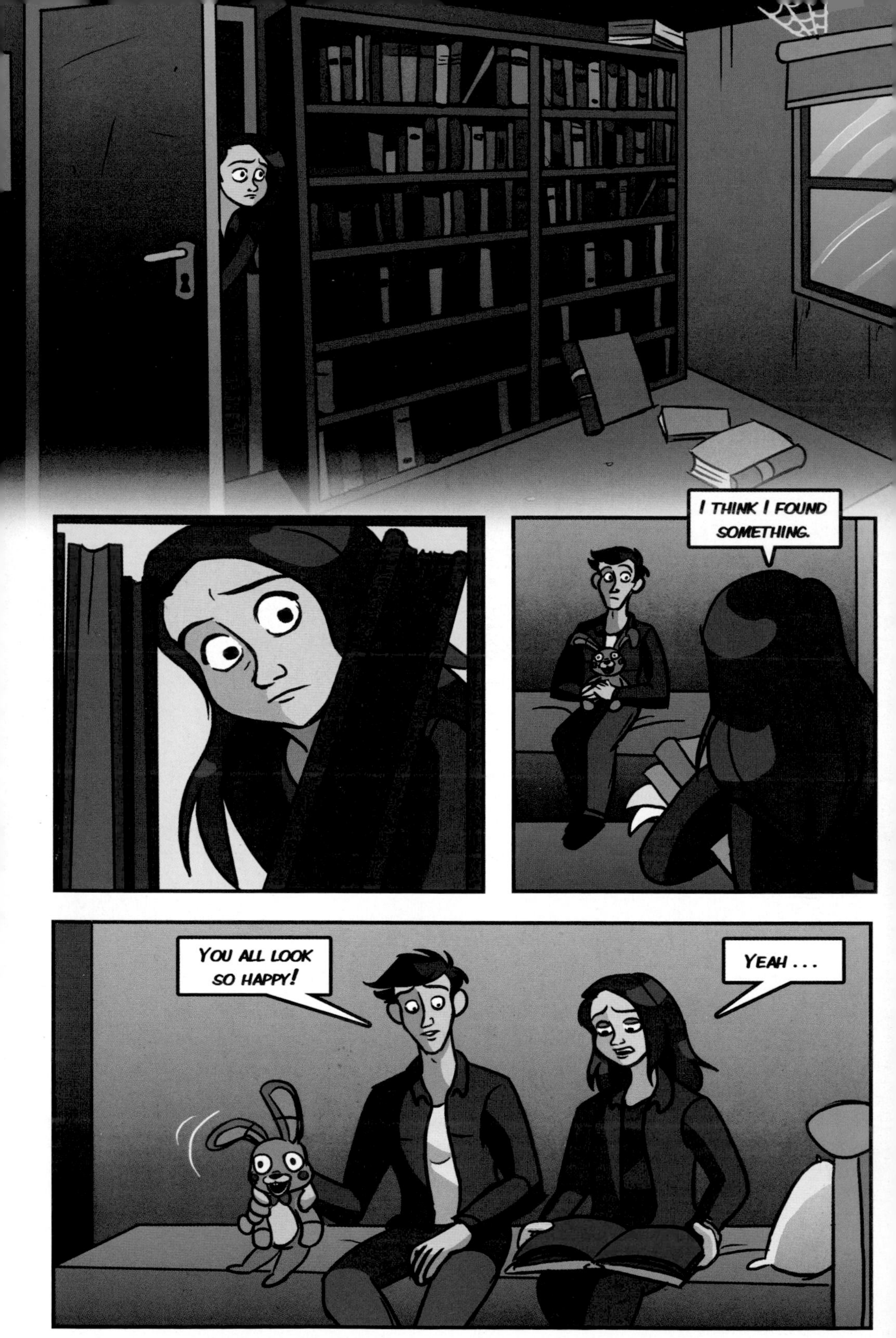
I THINK I FOUND SOMETHING.
YOU ALL LOOK SO HAPPY!
YEAH . . .

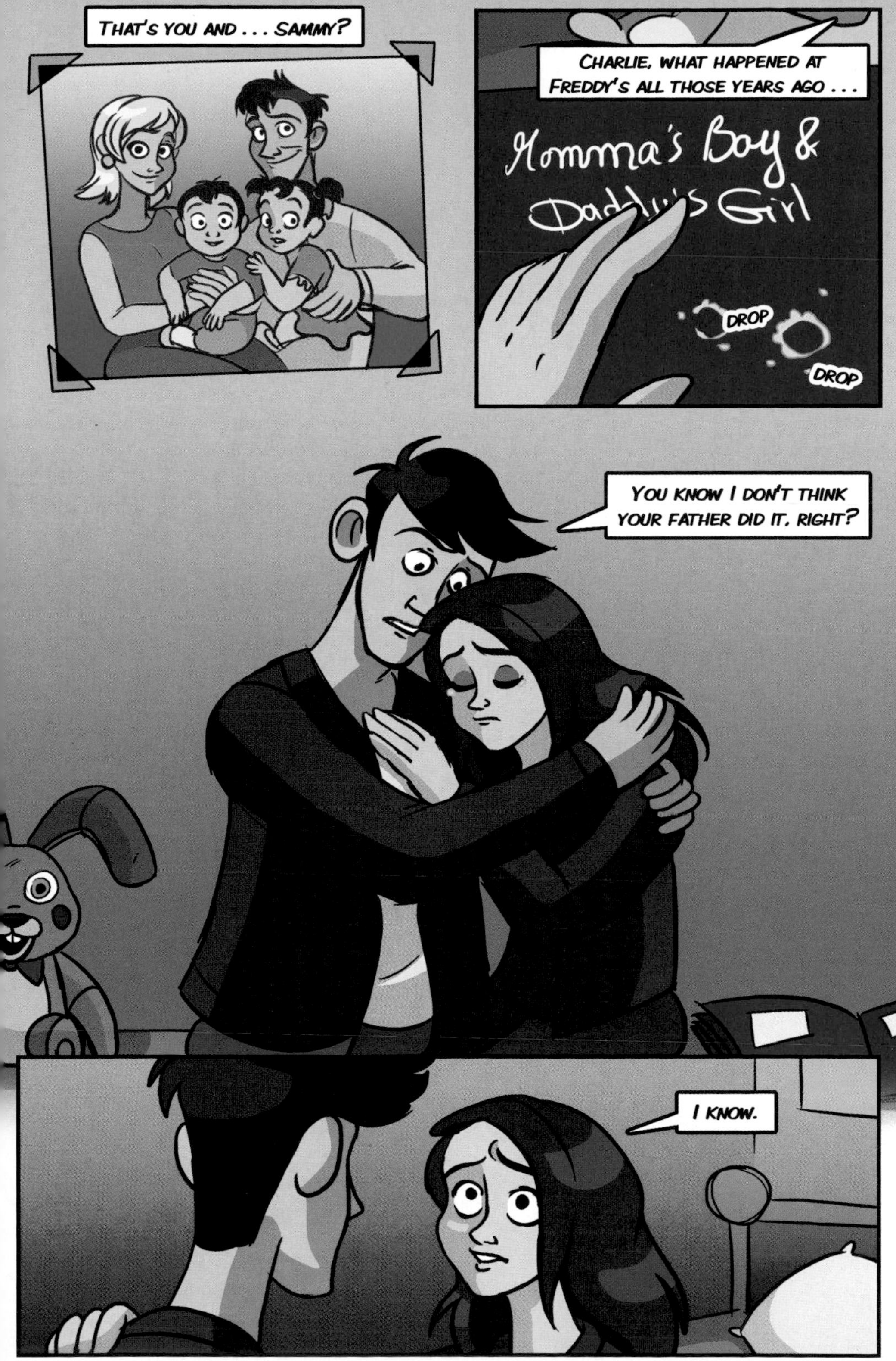
THAT'S YOU AND . . . SAMMY?
CHARLIE, WHAT HAPPENED AT FREDDY'S ALL THOSE YEARS AGO . . .
Momma's Boy &
Daddy's Girl
DROP
DROP
YOU KNOW I DON'T THINK YOUR FATHER DID IT, RIGHT?
I KNOW.

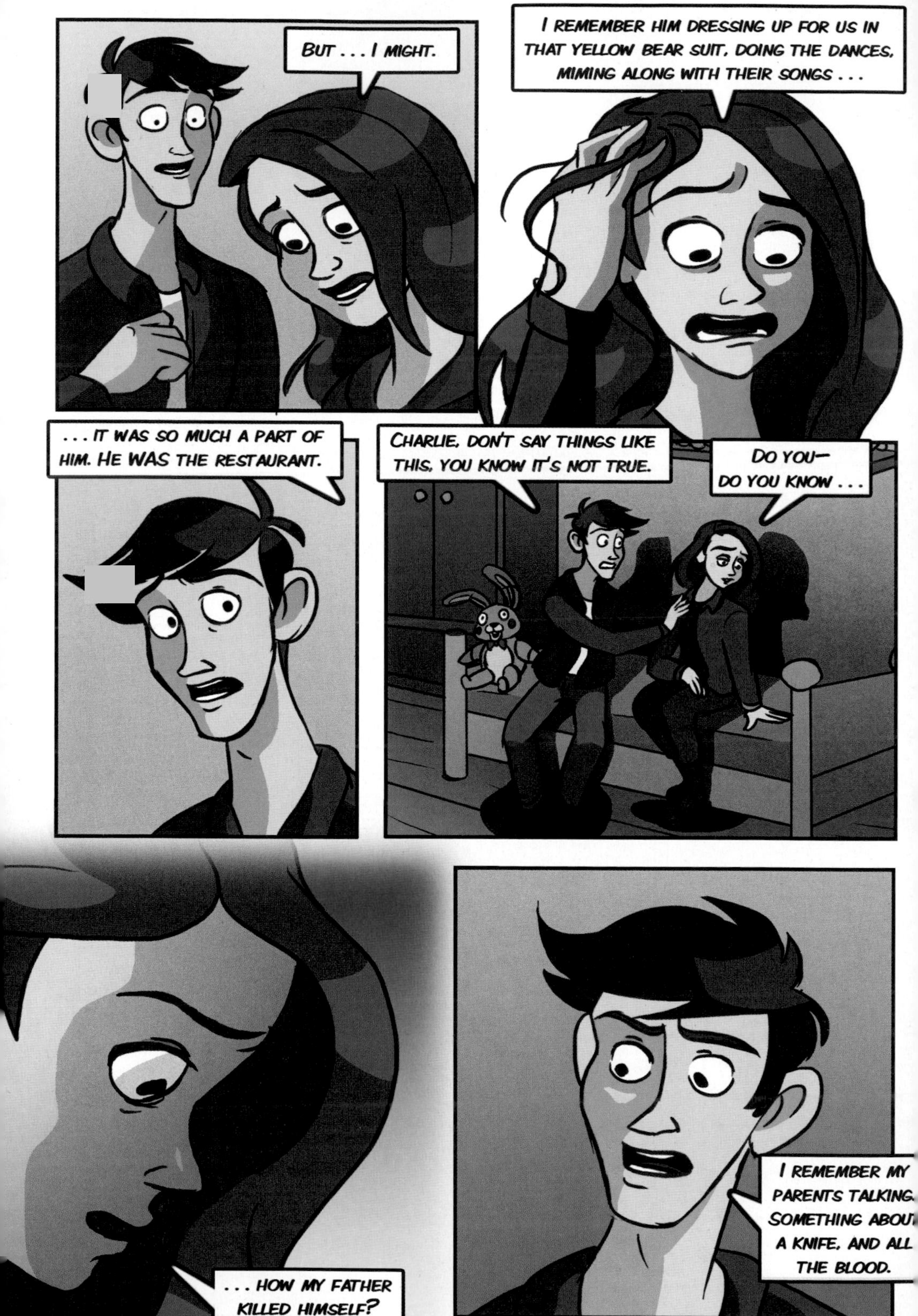

BUT . . . I MIGHT.
I REMEMBER HIM DRESSING UP FOR US IN THAT YELLOW BEAR SUIT, DOING THE DANCES, MIMING ALONG WITH THEIR SONGS . . .
. . . IT WAS SO MUCH A PART OF HIM. HE WAS THE RESTAURANT.
CHARLIE, DON'T SAY THINGS LIKE THIS, YOU KNOW IT'S NOT TRUE.
DO YOU— DO YOU KNOW . . .
. . . HOW MY FATHER KILLED HIMSELF?
I REMEMBER MY PARENTS TALKING. SOMETHING ABOU A KNIFE, AND ALL THE BLOOD.

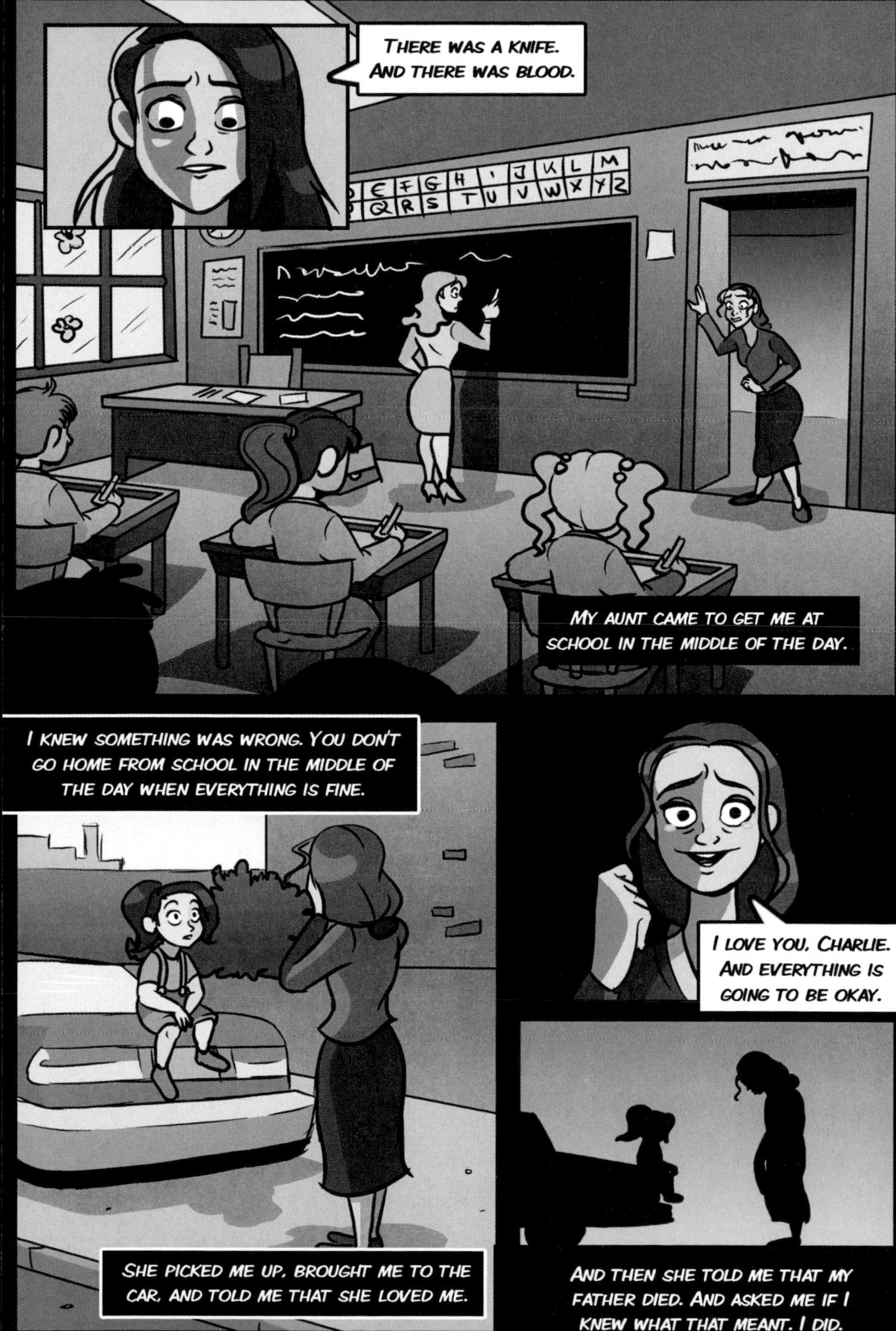
THERE WAS A KNIFE. AND THERE WAS BLOOD.
MY AUNT CAME TO GET ME AT SCHOOL IN THE MIDDLE OF THE DAY.
I KNEW SOMETHING WAS WRONG. YOU DON'T GO HOME FROM SCHOOL IN THE MIDDLE OF THE DAY WHEN EVERYTHING IS FINE.
I LOVE YOU, CHARLIE. AND EVERYTHING IS GOING TO BE OKAY.
SHE PICKED ME UP, BROUGHT ME TO THE CAR, AND TOLD ME THAT SHE LOVED ME.
AND THEN SHE TOLD ME THAT MY FATHER DIED. AND ASKED ME IF I KNEW WHAT THAT MEANT. I DID.

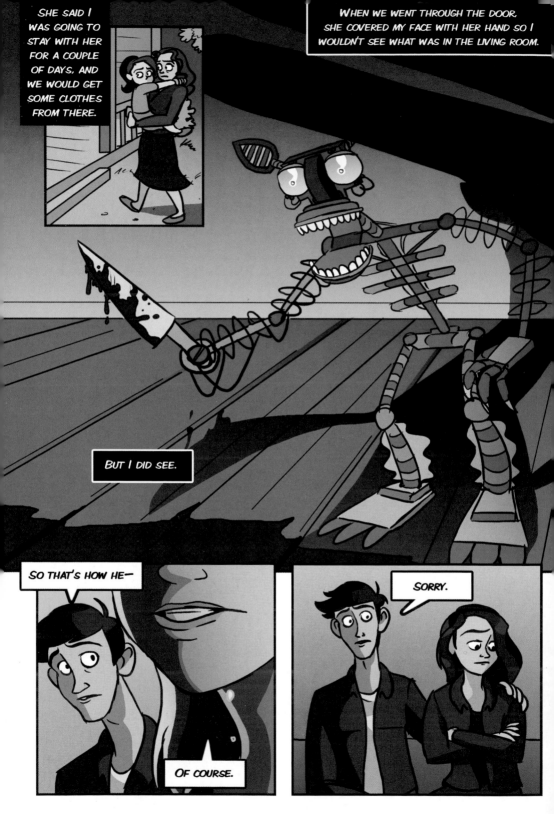

SHE SAID I WAS GOING TO STAY WITH HER FOR A COUPLE OF DAYS, AND WE WOULD GET SOME CLOTHES FROM THERE.

WHEN WE WENT THROUGH THE DOOR, SHE COVERED MY FACE WITH HER HAND SO I WOULDN'T SEE WHAT WAS IN THE LIVING ROOM.

BUT I DID SEE.

SO THAT'S HOW HE—

OF COURSE.

SORRY.

110

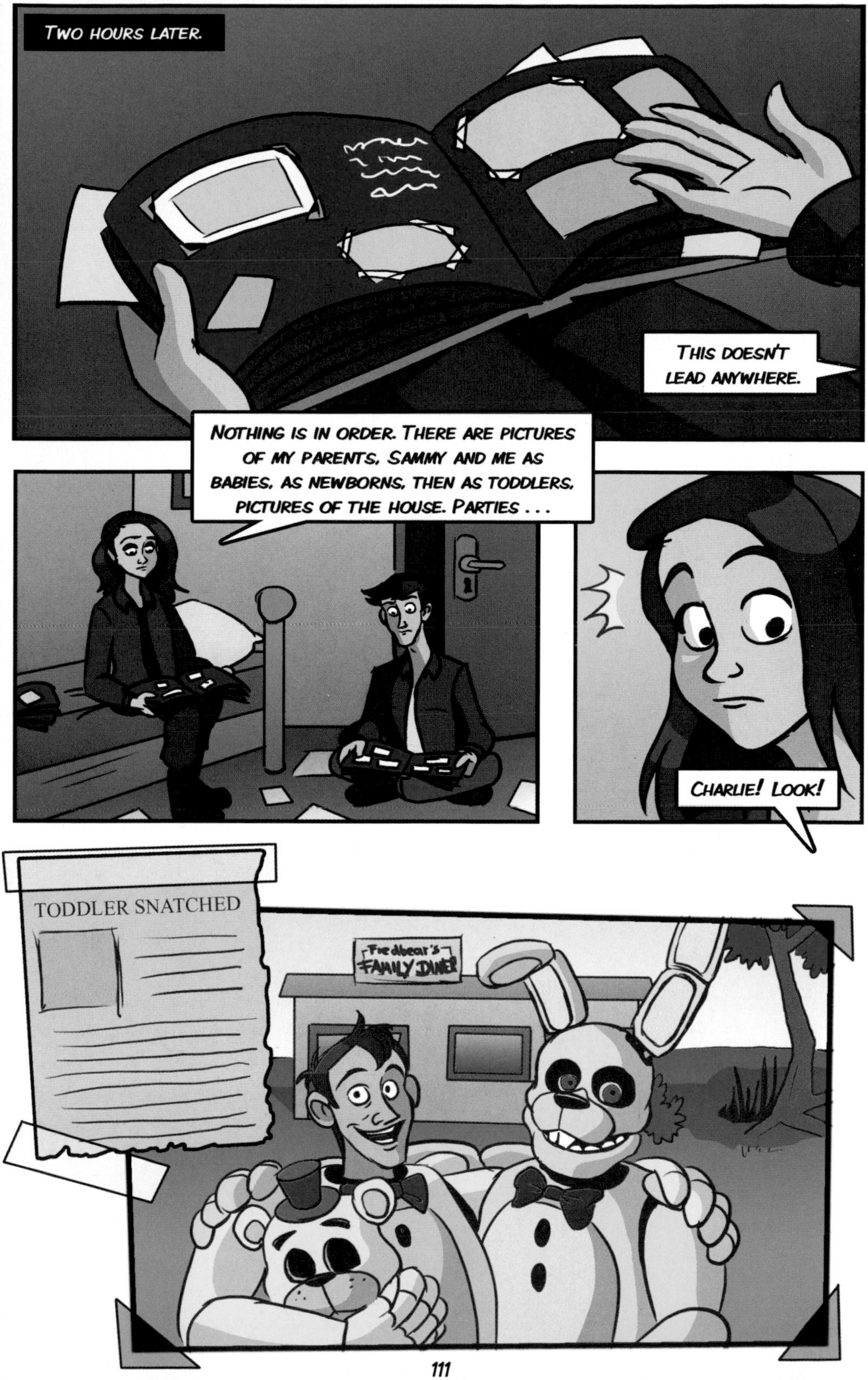
TWO HOURS LATER.
THIS DOESN'T LEAD ANYWHERE.
NOTHING IS IN ORDER. THERE ARE PICTURES OF MY PARENTS, SAMMY AND ME AS BABIES, AS NEWBORNS, THEN AS TODDLERS, PICTURES OF THE HOUSE. PARTIES . . .
CHARLIE! LOOK!
TODDLER SNATCHED
Fredbear's FAMILY DINER

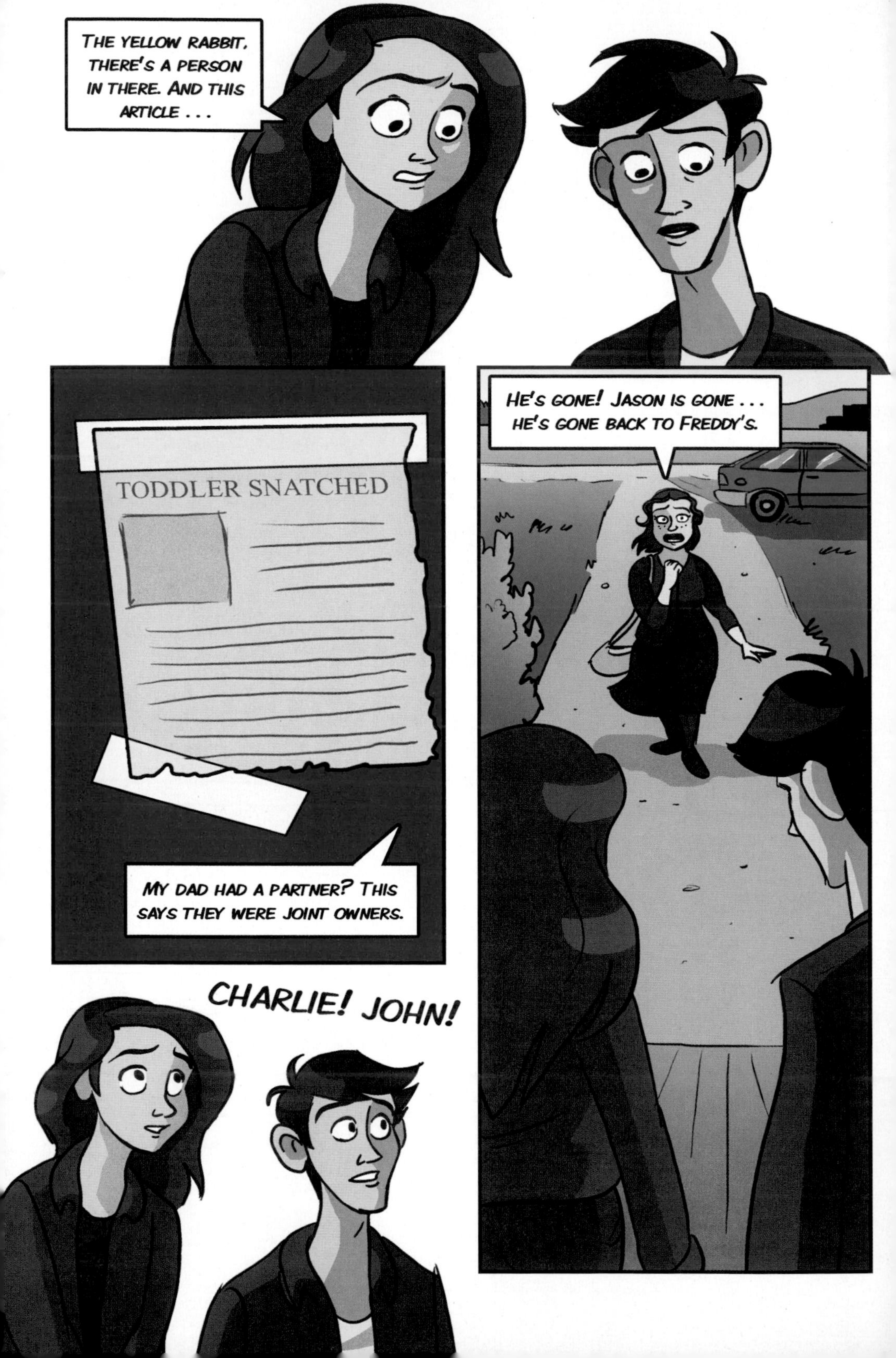
THE YELLOW RABBIT, THERE'S A PERSON IN THERE. AND THIS ARTICLE . . .
TODDLER SNATCHED
MY DAD HAD A PARTNER? THIS SAYS THEY WERE JOINT OWNERS.
HE'S GONE! JASON IS GONE . . . HE'S GONE BACK TO FREDDY'S.
CHARLIE! JOHN!

CHAPTER 9

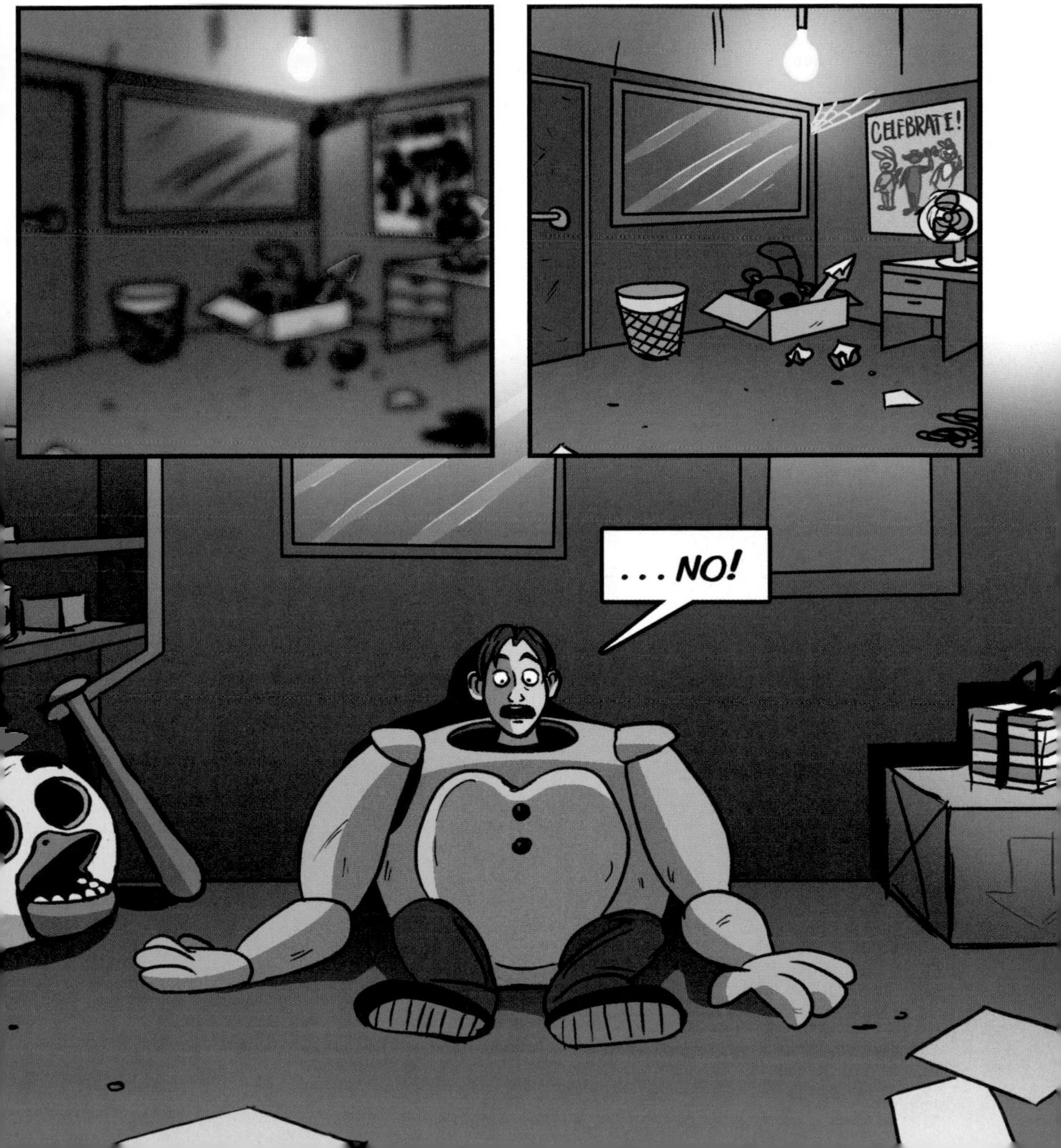
CELEBRATE!
. . . NO!

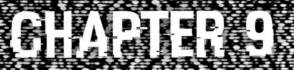

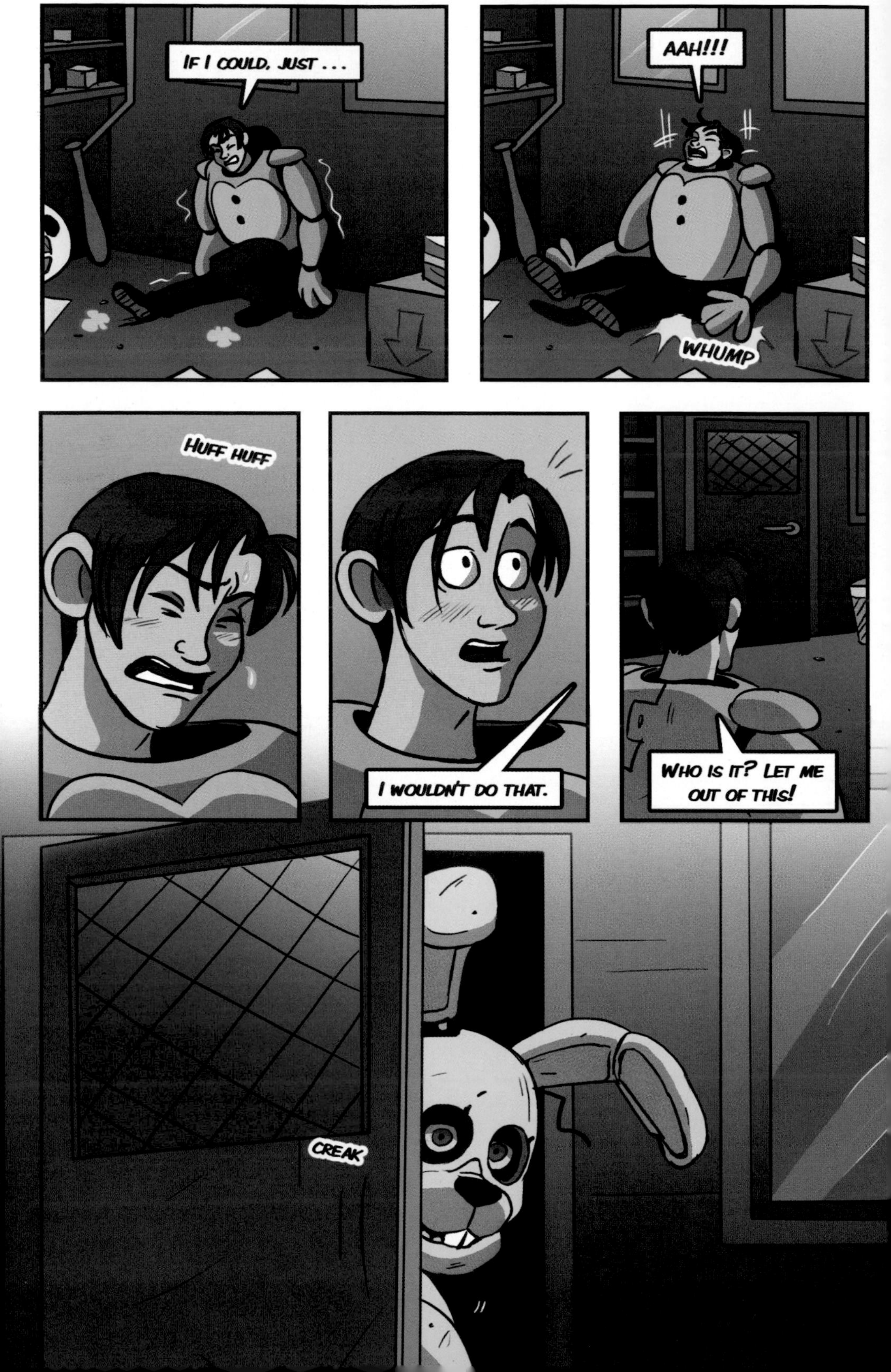
IF I COULD, JUST . . .
AAH!!!
WHUMP
HUFF HUFF
I WOULDN'T DO THAT.
WHO IS IT? LET ME OUT OF THIS!
CREAK

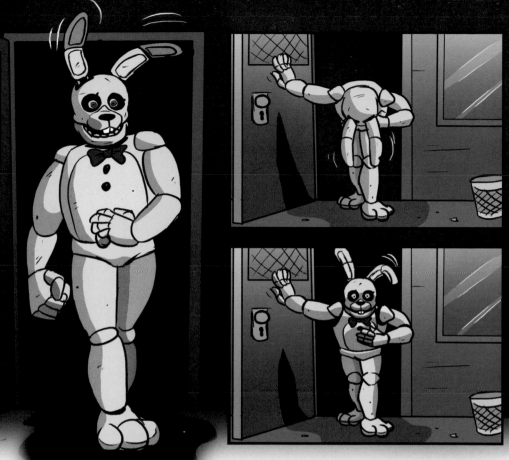

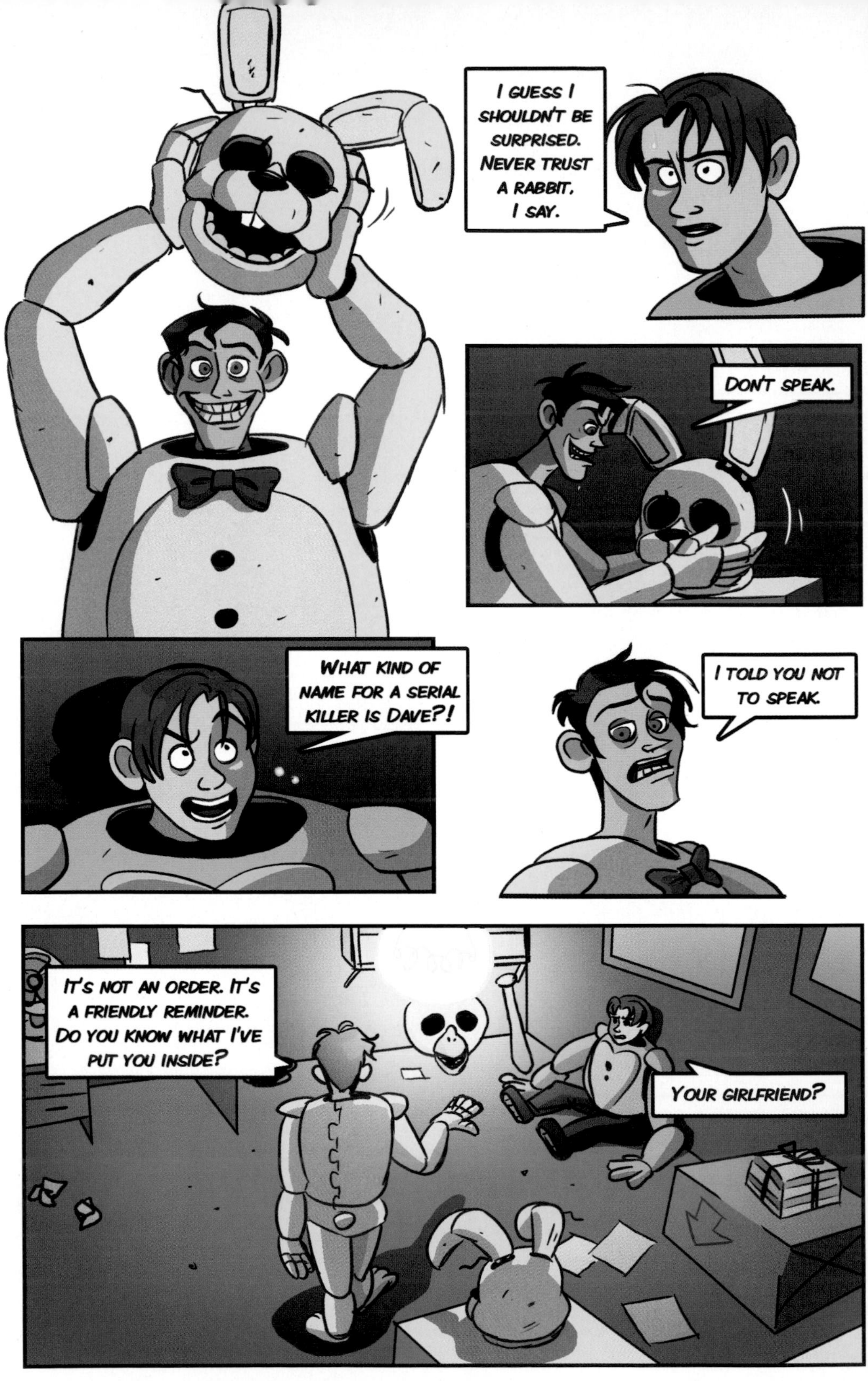

I GUESS I SHOULDN'T BE SURPRISED. NEVER TRUST A RABBIT, I SAY.
DON'T SPEAK.
WHAT KIND OF NAME FOR A SERIAL KILLER IS DAVE?!
I TOLD YOU NOT TO SPEAK.
IT'S NOT AN ORDER. IT'S A FRIENDLY REMINDER. DO YOU KNOW WHAT I'VE PUT YOU INSIDE?
YOUR GIRLFRIEND?

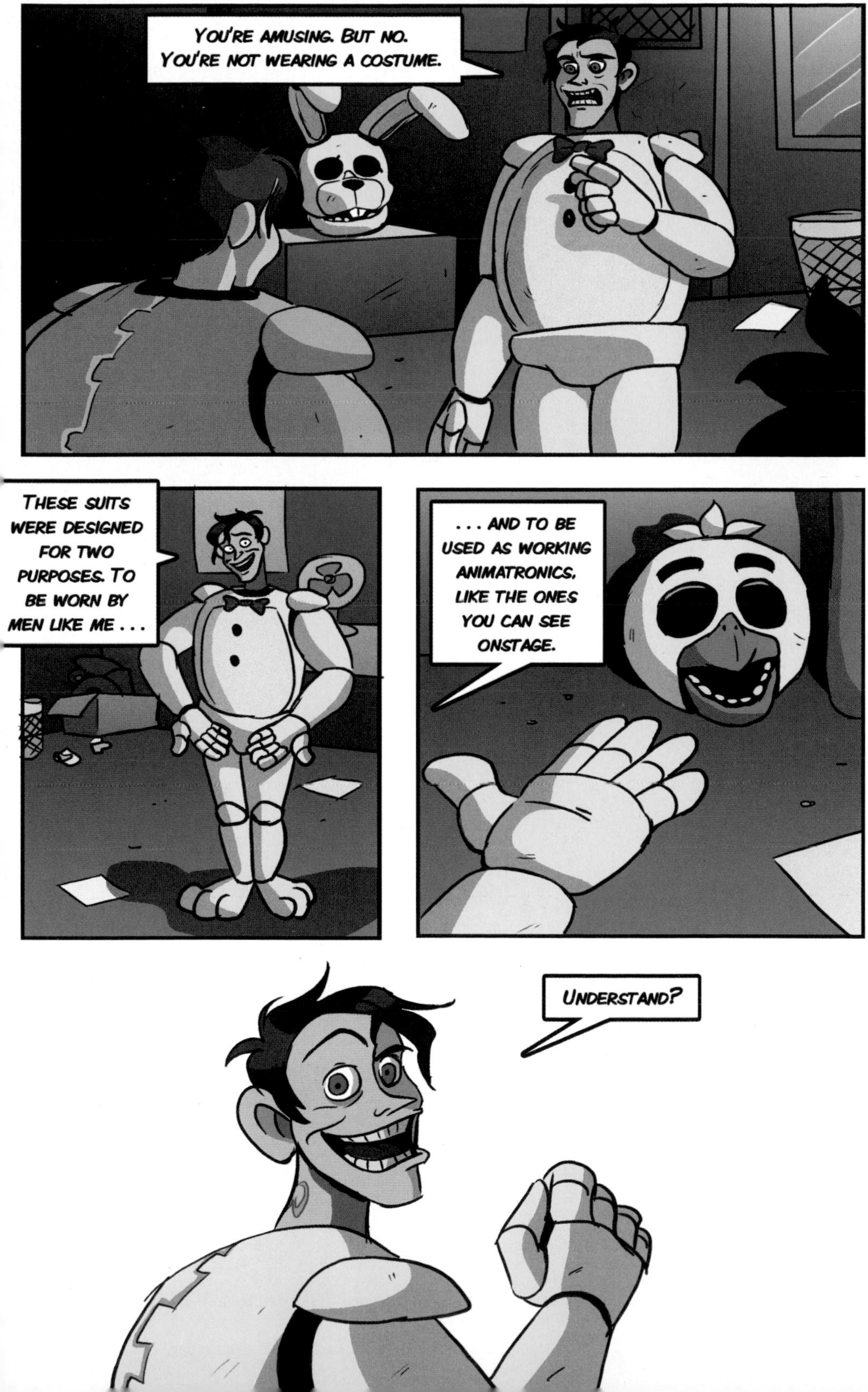
YOU'RE AMUSING. BUT NO. YOU'RE NOT WEARING A COSTUME.
THESE SUITS WERE DESIGNED FOR TWO PURPOSES. TO BE WORN BY MEN LIKE ME . . .
. . . AND TO BE USED AS WORKING ANIMATRONICS, LIKE THE ONES YOU CAN SEE ONSTAGE.
UNDERSTAND?

. . .

YOU SEE, ALL OF THE ANIMATRONIC PARTS IN THIS SUIT ARE STILL IN IT; THEY ARE SIMPLY HELD BACK BY SPRING LOCKS.

LIKE THIS.

THESE ARE SPRING LOCKS. WATCH.

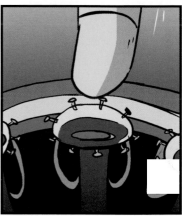

SNAP

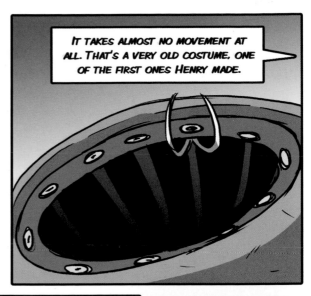

IT TAKES ALMOST NO MOVEMENT AT ALL. THAT'S A VERY OLD COSTUME, ONE OF THE FIRST ONES HENRY MADE.

YOU CAN TRIP THOSE SPRING LOCKS VERY, VERY EASILY.

HENRY . . . WHO'S HENRY?

HENRY. YOUR FRIEND CHARLIE'S FATHER. DID YOU NOT KNOW THAT HE MADE THE PLACE?

WELL, THAT'S ONE OF HIS FIRST SUITS. AND IF YOU TRIGGER THOSE SPRING LOCKS, TWO THINGS WILL HAPPEN:

FIRST THE LOCKS THEMSELVES WILL SNAP RIGHT INTO YOU, MAKING DEEP CUTS ALL OVER YOUR BODY. AND A SPLIT SECOND LATER . . .

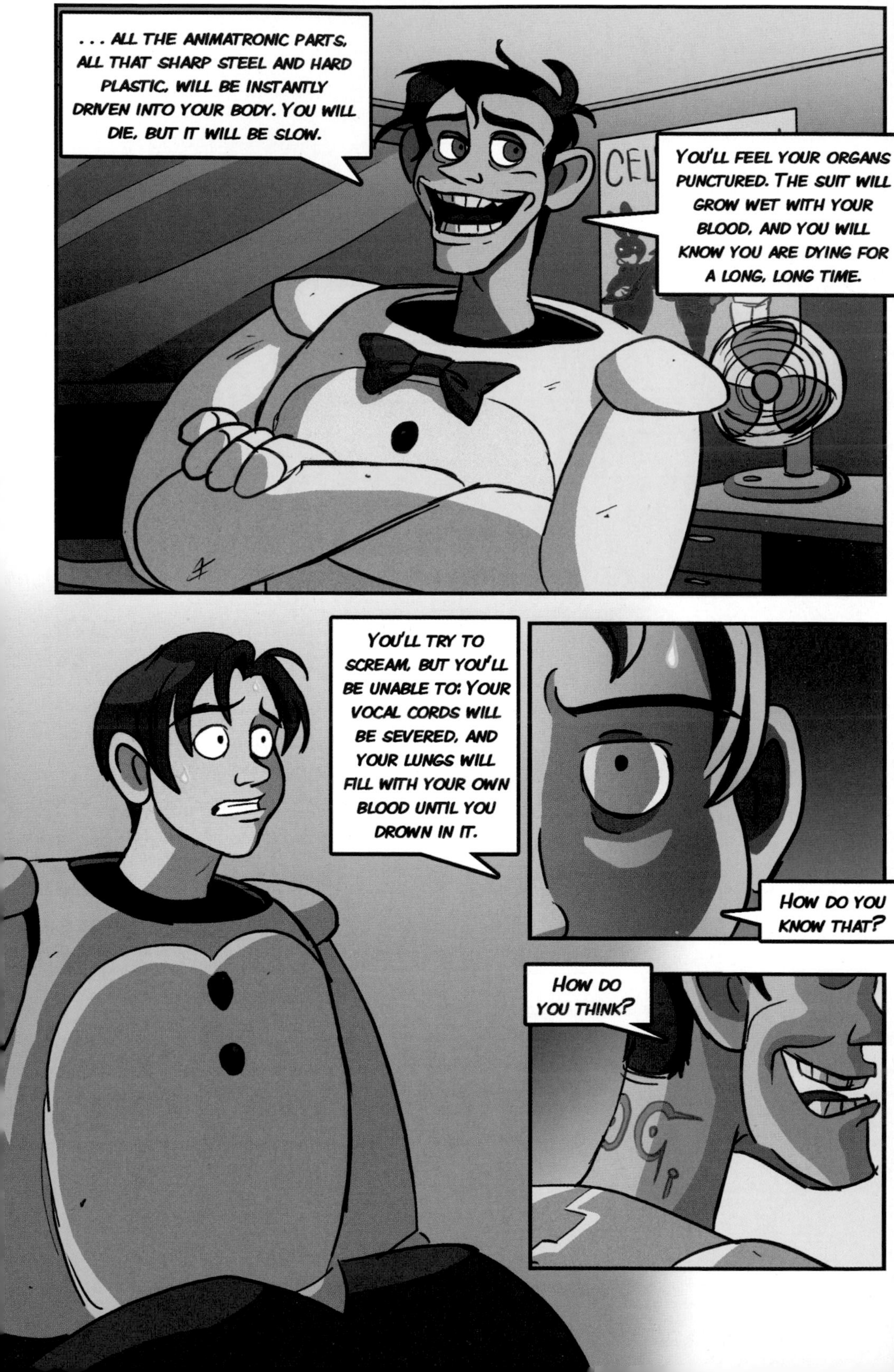
. . . ALL THE ANIMATRONIC PARTS, ALL THAT SHARP STEEL AND HARD PLASTIC, WILL BE INSTANTLY DRIVEN INTO YOUR BODY. YOU WILL DIE, BUT IT WILL BE SLOW.
YOU'LL FEEL YOUR ORGANS PUNCTURED. THE SUIT WILL GROW WET WITH YOUR BLOOD, AND YOU WILL KNOW YOU ARE DYING FOR A LONG, LONG TIME.
YOU'LL TRY TO SCREAM, BUT YOU'LL BE UNABLE TO: YOUR VOCAL CORDS WILL BE SEVERED, AND YOUR LUNGS WILL FILL WITH YOUR OWN BLOOD UNTIL YOU DROWN IN IT.
HOW DO YOU KNOW THAT?
HOW DO YOU THINK?

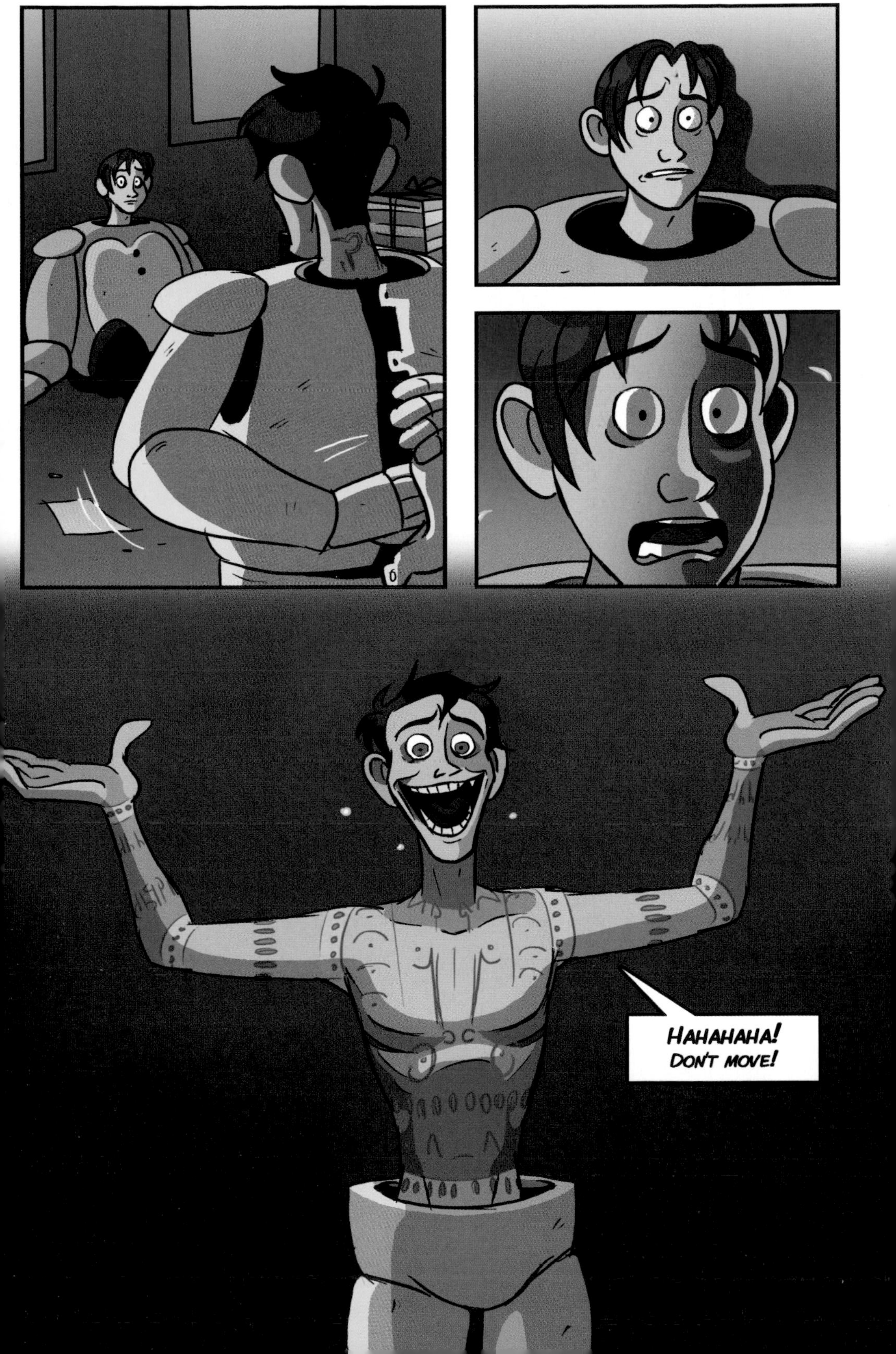
HAHAHAHA! DON'T MOVE!

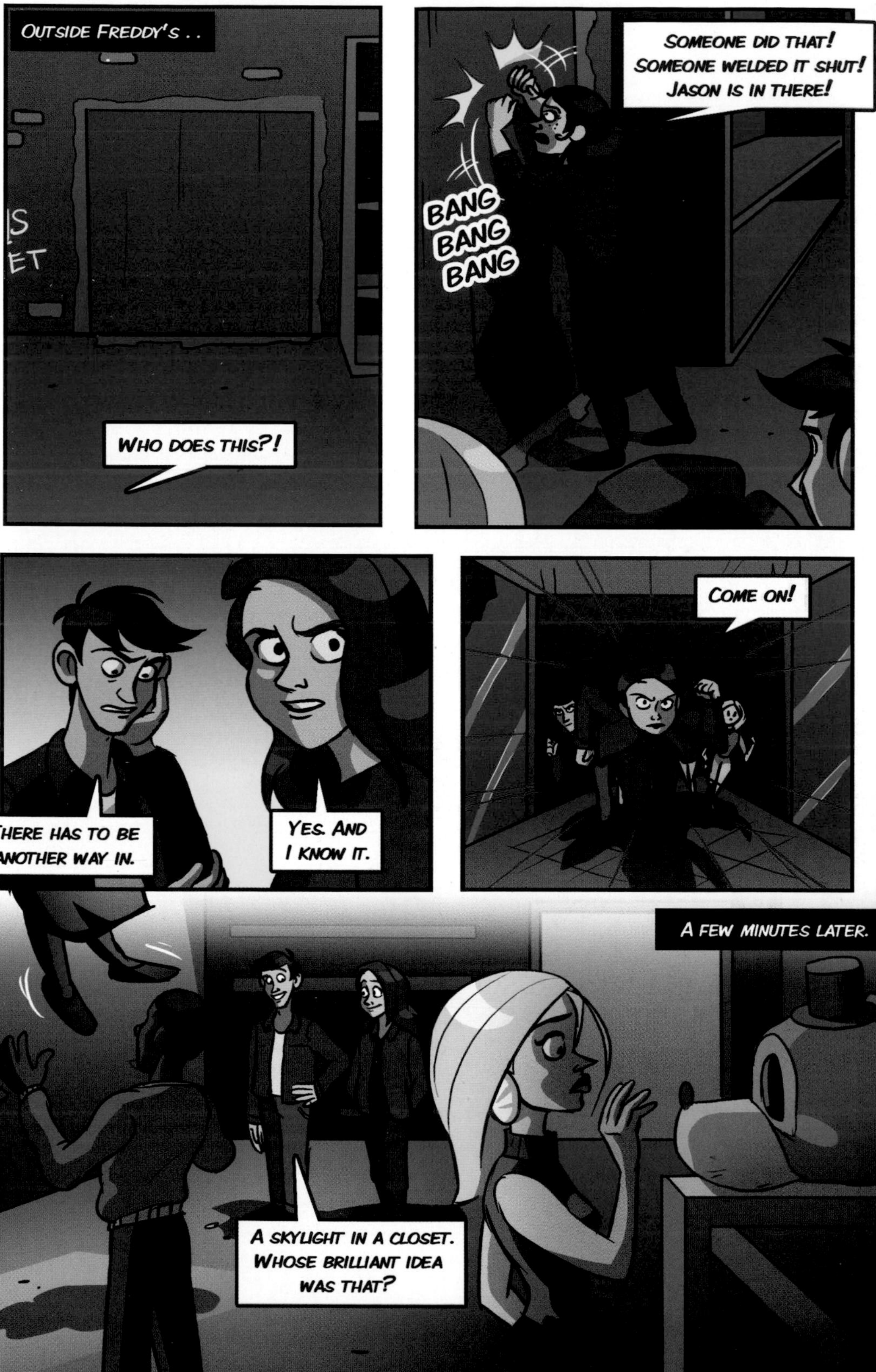

OUTSIDE FREDDY'S . .
WHO DOES THIS?!
SOMEONE DID THAT! SOMEONE WELDED IT SHUT! JASON IS IN THERE!
BANG BANG BANG
THERE HAS TO BE ANOTHER WAY IN.
YES. AND I KNOW IT.
COME ON!
A FEW MINUTES LATER.
A SKYLIGHT IN A CLOSET. WHOSE BRILLIANT IDEA WAS THAT?

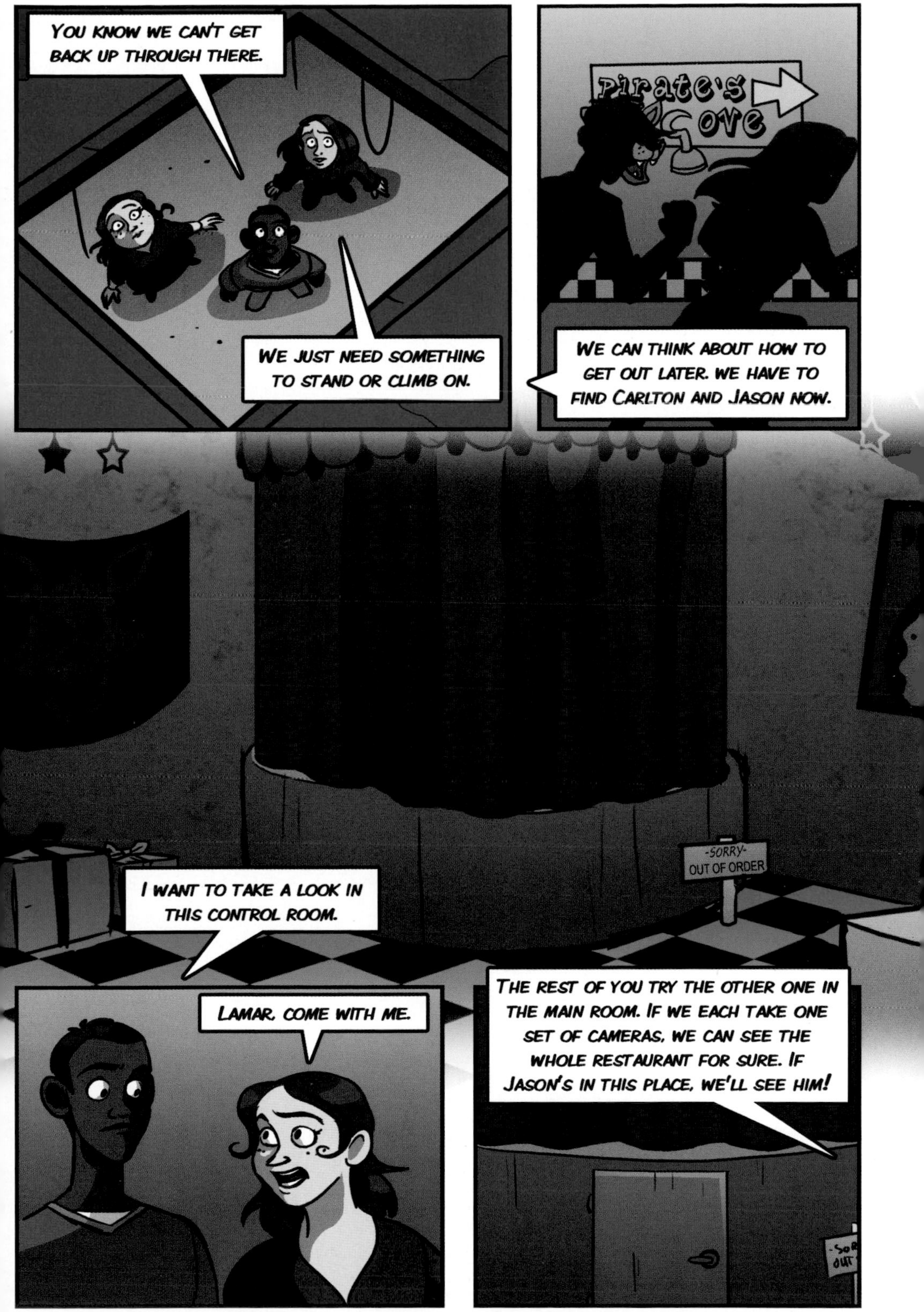
YOU KNOW WE CAN'T GET BACK UP THROUGH THERE.
WE JUST NEED SOMETHING TO STAND OR CLIMB ON.
Pirate's Cove
WE CAN THINK ABOUT HOW TO GET OUT LATER. WE HAVE TO FIND CARLTON AND JASON NOW.
-SORRY- OUT OF ORDER
I WANT TO TAKE A LOOK IN THIS CONTROL ROOM.
LAMAR, COME WITH ME.
THE REST OF YOU TRY THE OTHER ONE IN THE MAIN ROOM. IF WE EACH TAKE ONE SET OF CAMERAS, WE CAN SEE THE WHOLE RESTAURANT FOR SURE. IF JASON'S IN THIS PLACE, WE'LL SEE HIM!

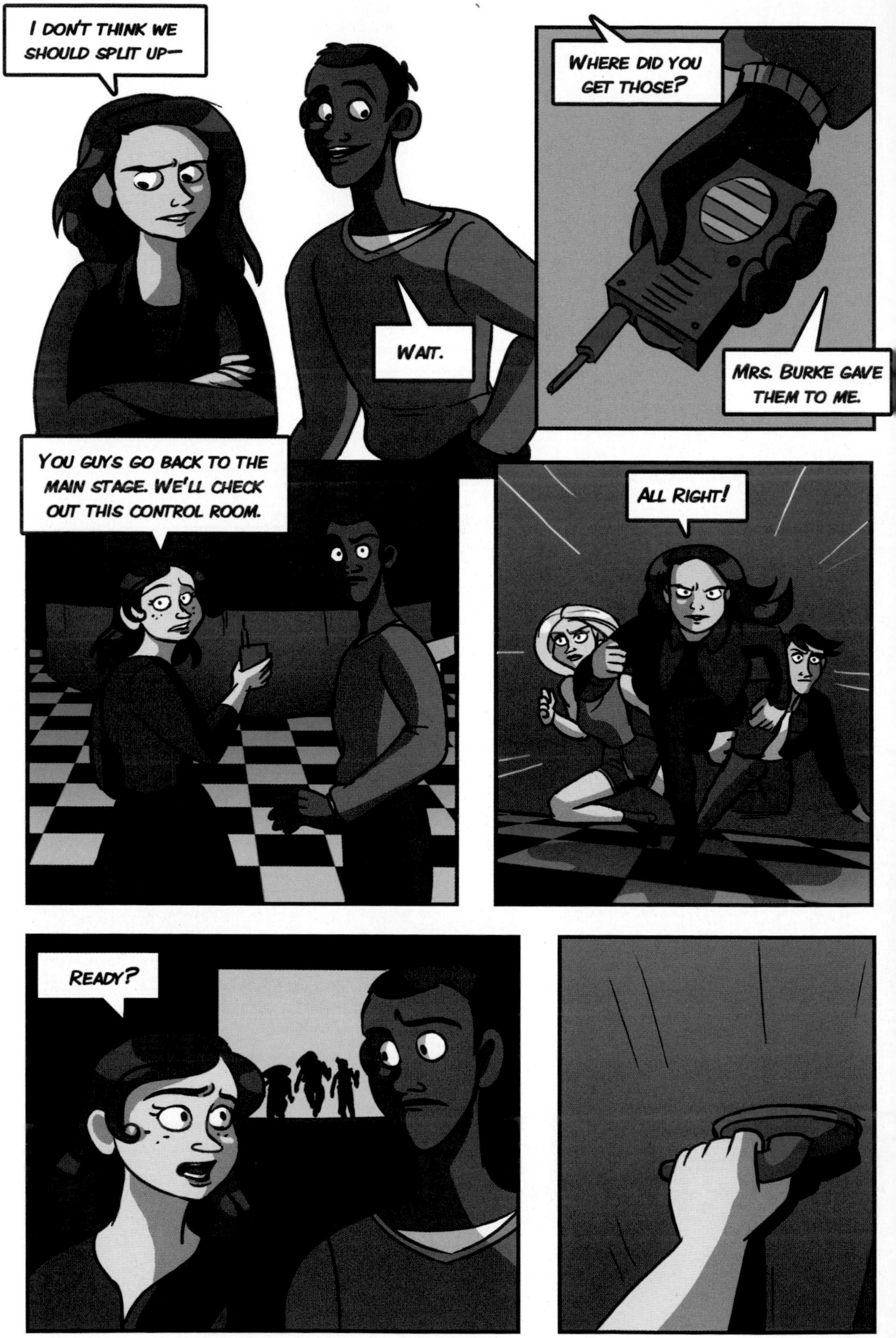
I DON'T THINK WE SHOULD SPLIT UP—
WAIT.
WHERE DID YOU GET THOSE?
MRS. BURKE GAVE THEM TO ME.
YOU GUYS GO BACK TO THE MAIN STAGE. WE'LL CHECK OUT THIS CONTROL ROOM.
ALL RIGHT!
READY?

MAARLAAA!!!

CHARLIE? WE FOUND JASON ALREADY.

JASON!

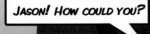

JASON! HOW COULD YOU?

THE VENT!

YEAH, REALLY—HOW?

YOU COULD HAVE BEEN KILLED!

OKAY, OKAY! GLAD TO KNOW I'M IMPORTANT AND EVERYBODY MISSED ME!

YOU ARE IMPORTANT!

OKAY. LET'S SEE WHAT WE CAN SEE . . .

CLICK

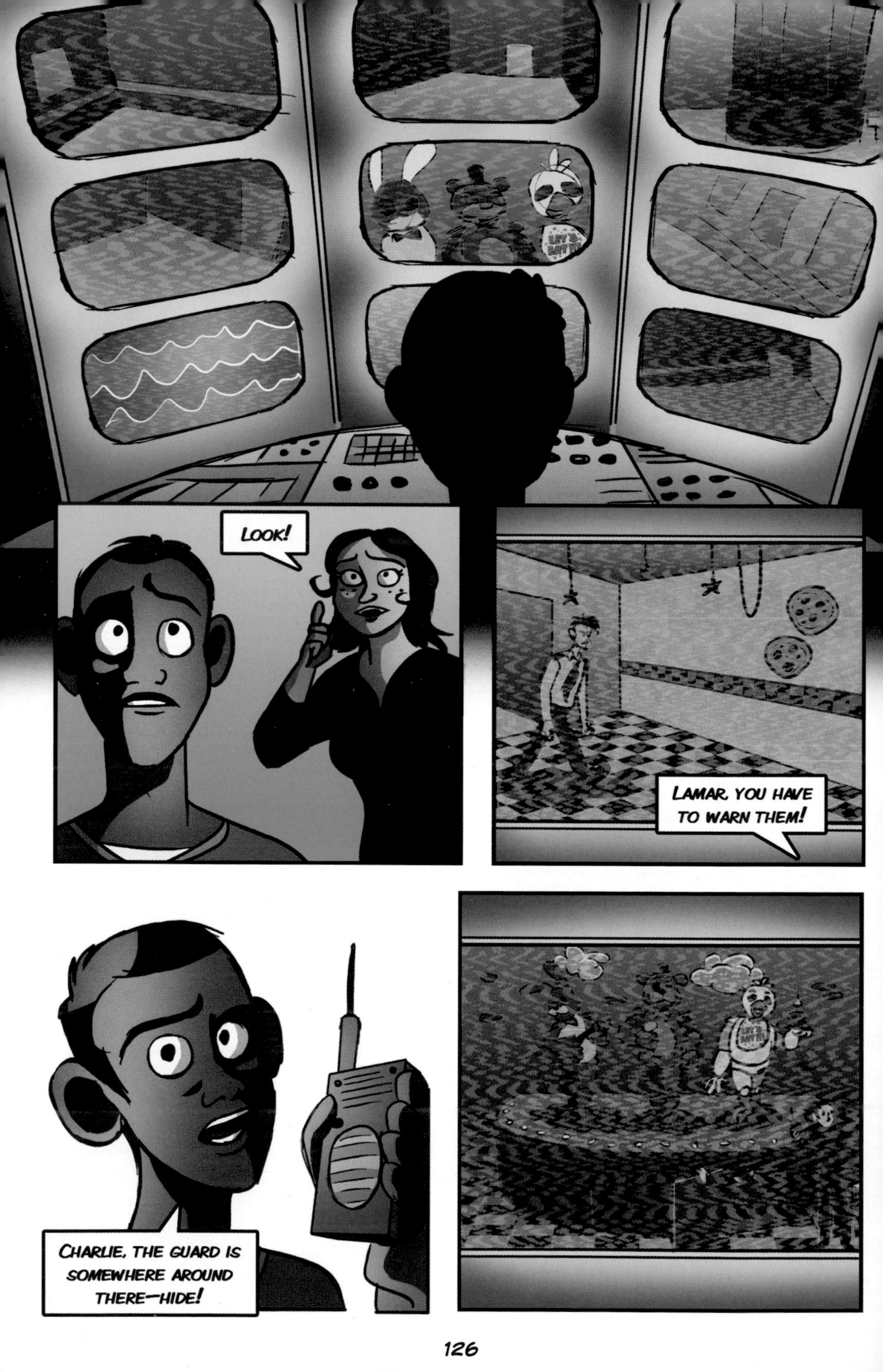
LOOK!
LAMAR, YOU HAVE TO WARN THEM!
CHARLIE, THE GUARD IS SOMEWHERE AROUND THERE—HIDE!

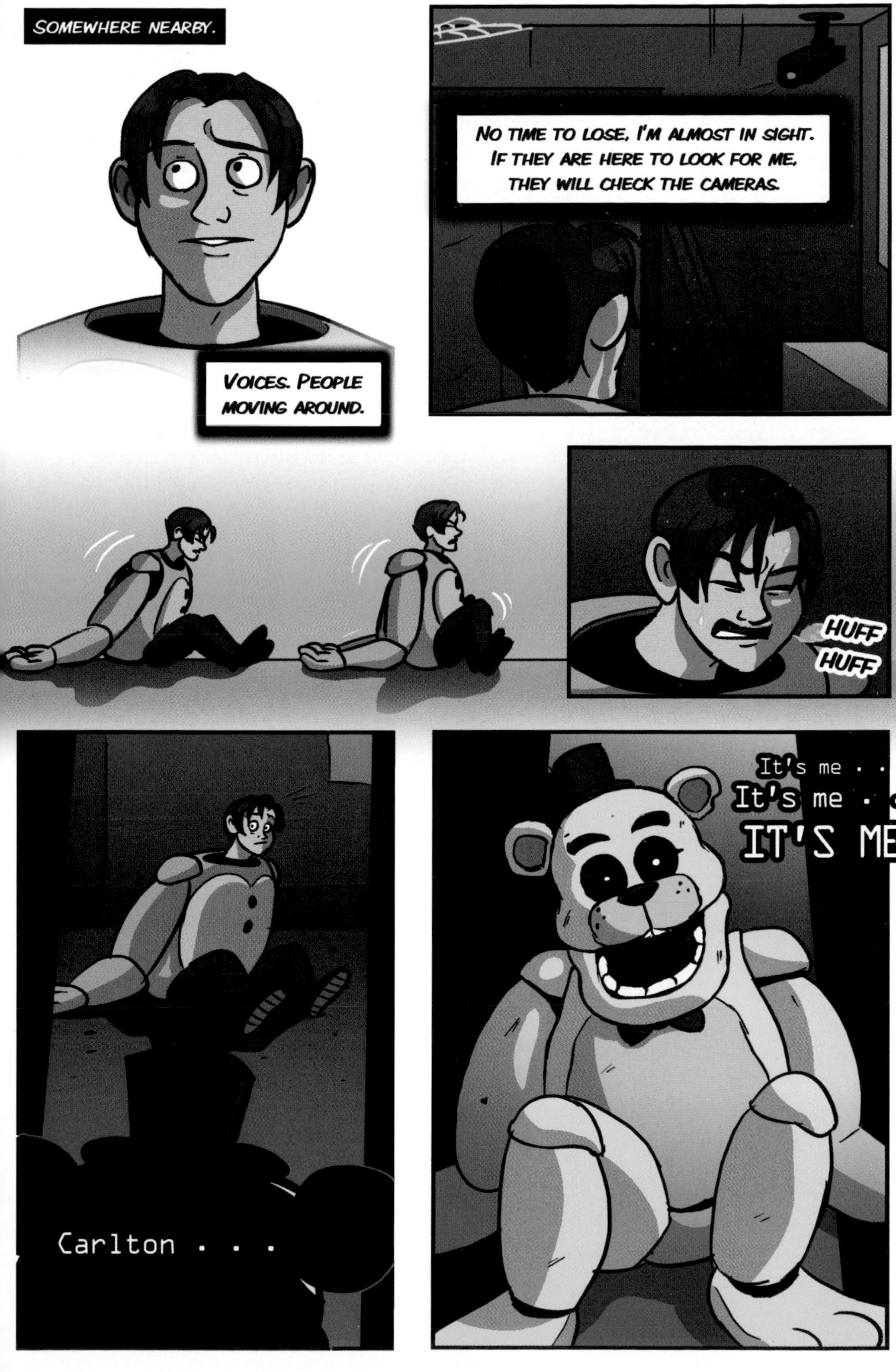
SOMEWHERE NEARBY.
VOICES. PEOPLE MOVING AROUND.
NO TIME TO LOSE, I'M ALMOST IN SIGHT. IF THEY ARE HERE TO LOOK FOR ME, THEY WILL CHECK THE CAMERAS.
HUFF HUFF
Carlton . . .
It's me . . .
It's me . . .
IT'S ME.

CHAPTER 10

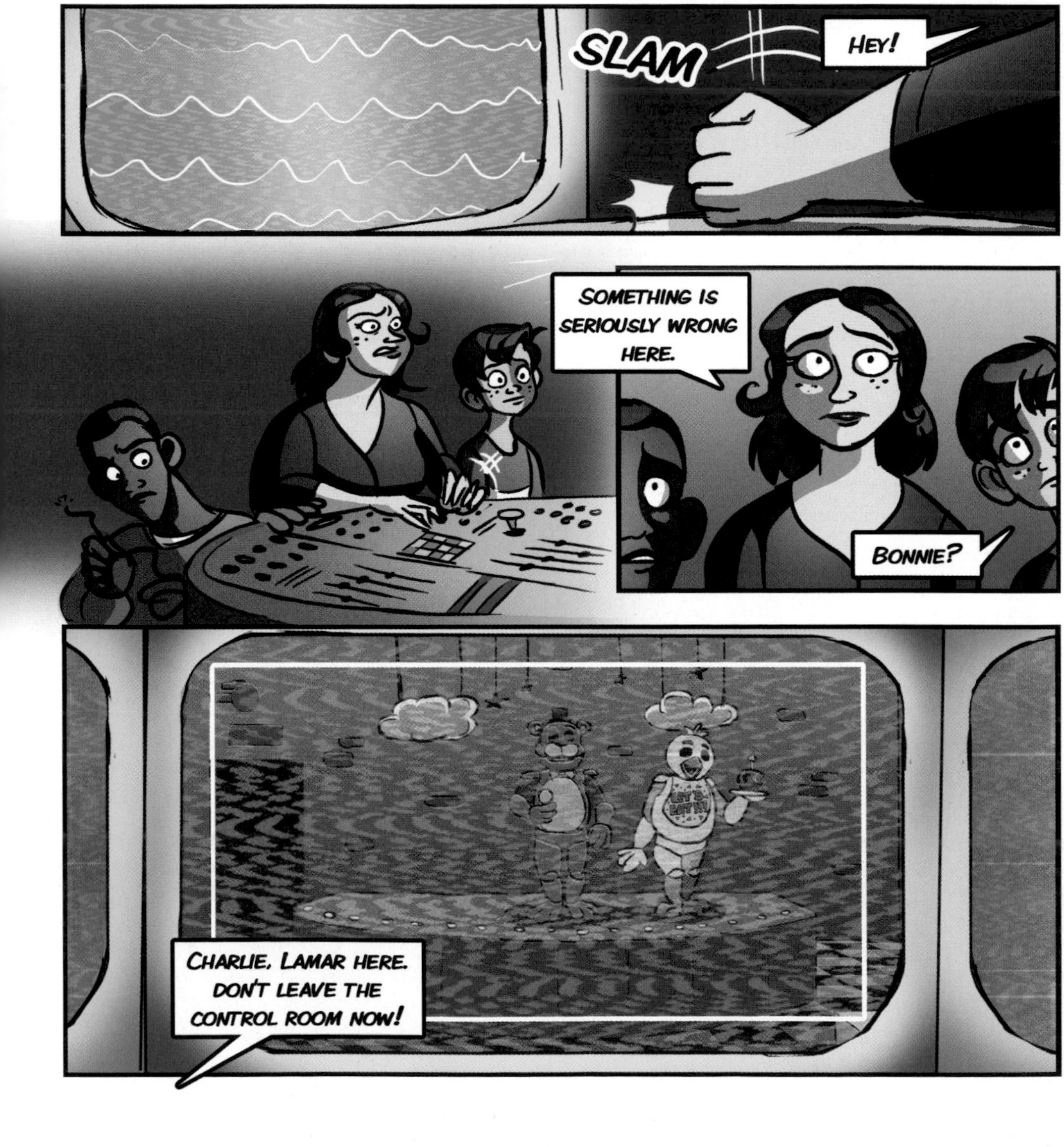
SLAM
HEY!
SOMETHING IS SERIOUSLY WRONG HERE.
BONNIE?
CHARLIE, LAMAR HERE. DON'T LEAVE THE CONTROL ROOM NOW!

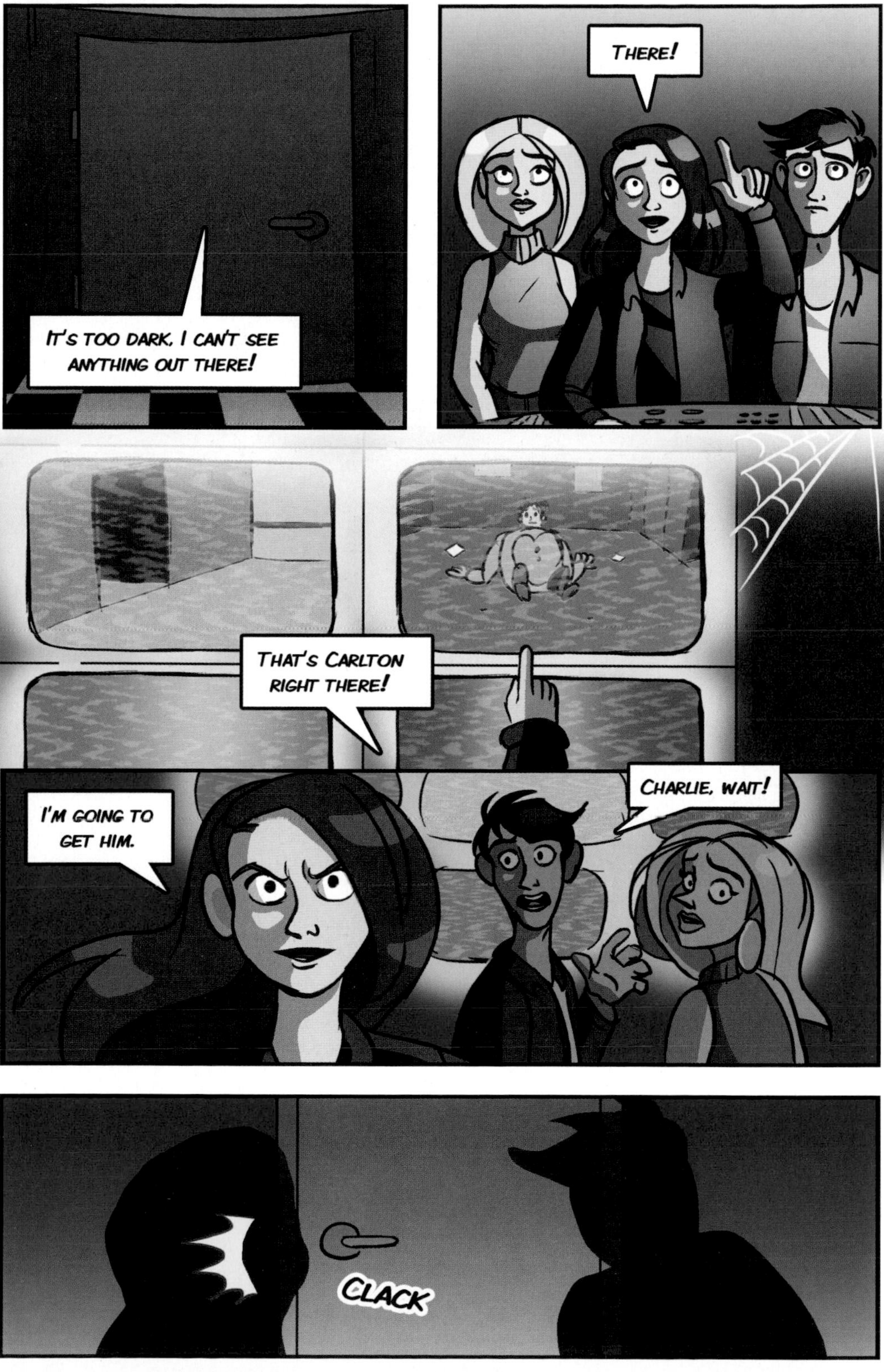
IT'S TOO DARK. I CAN'T SEE ANYTHING OUT THERE!
THERE!
THAT'S CARLTON RIGHT THERE!
I'M GOING TO GET HIM.
CHARLIE, WAIT!
CLACK

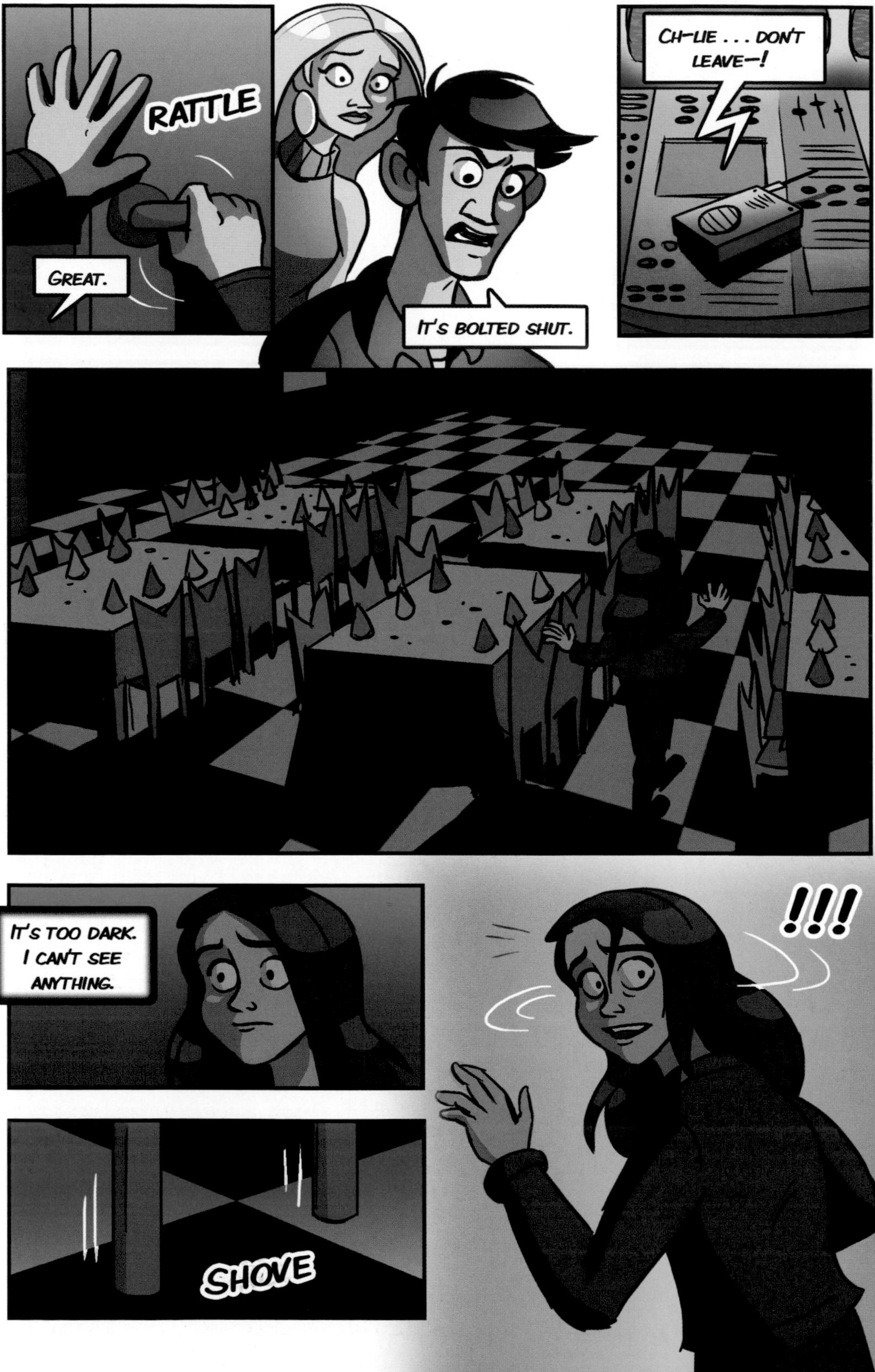
RATTLE
GREAT.
IT'S BOLTED SHUT.
CH-LIE . . . DON'T LEAVE—!
IT'S TOO DARK. I CAN'T SEE ANYTHING.
!!!
SHOVE

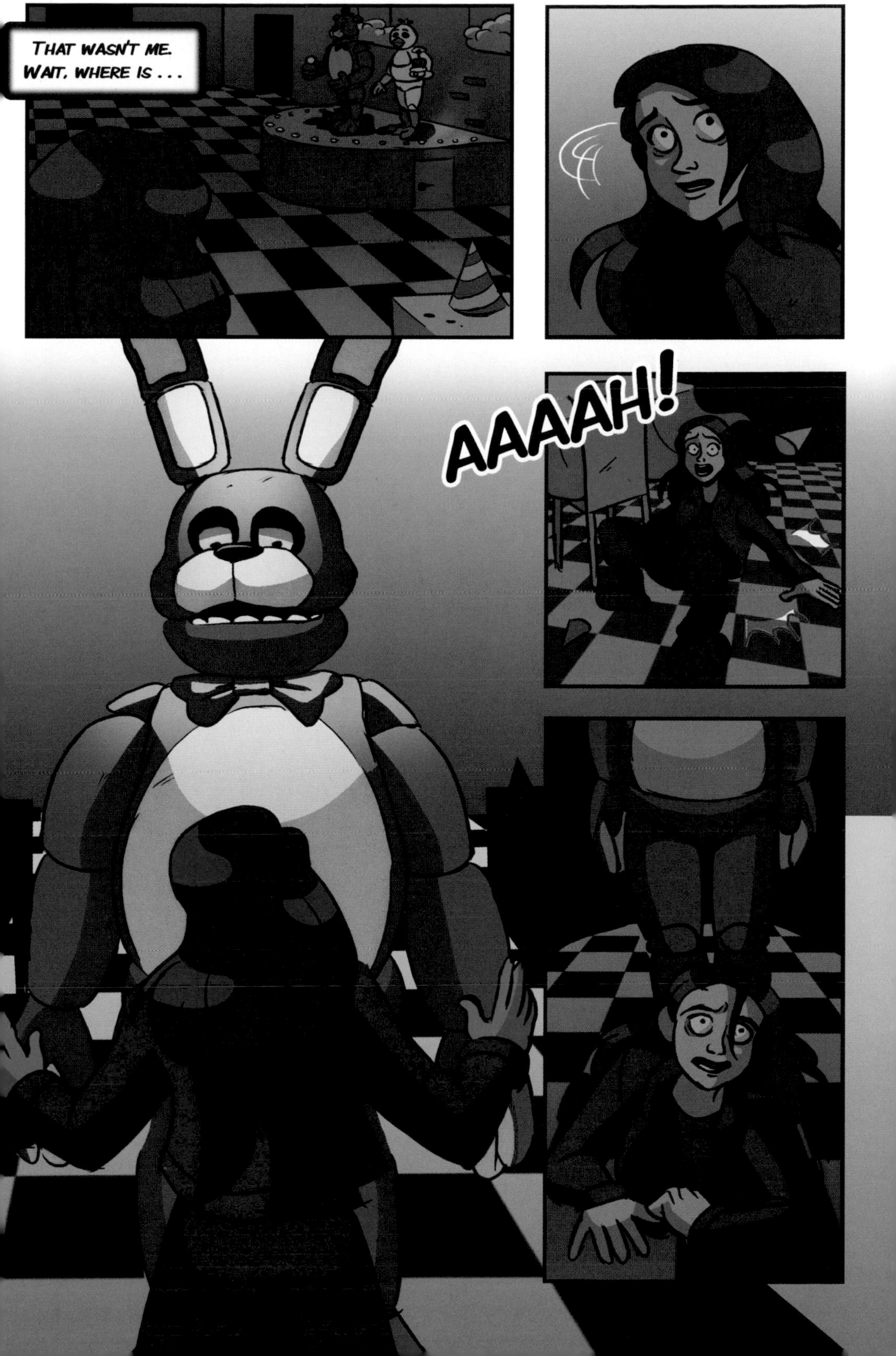
THAT WASN'T ME.
WAIT, WHERE IS . . .
AAAAH!

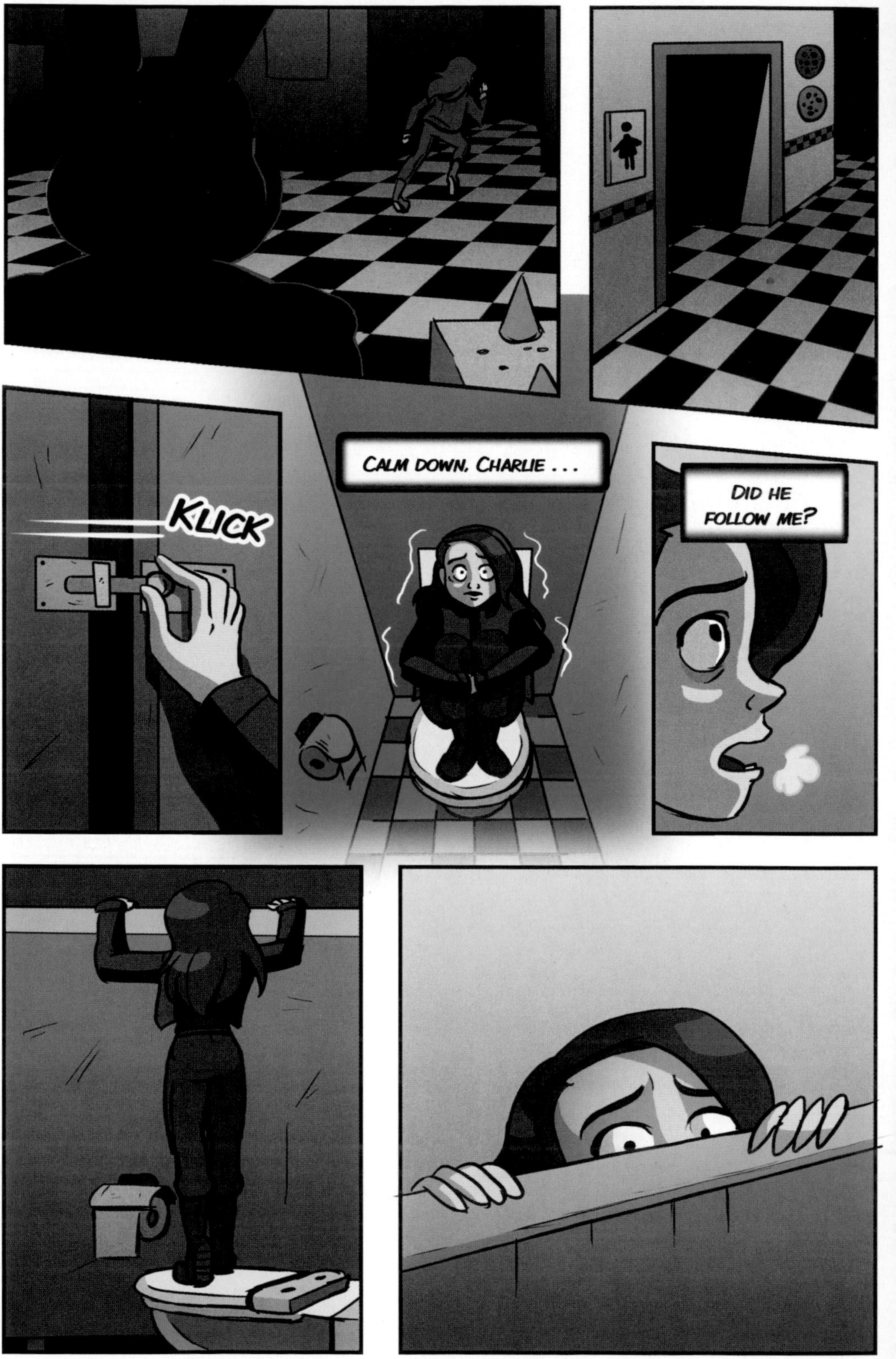
KLICK
CALM DOWN, CHARLIE . . .
DID HE FOLLOW ME?

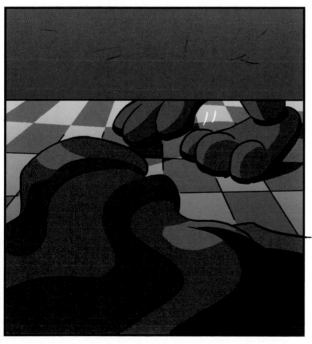

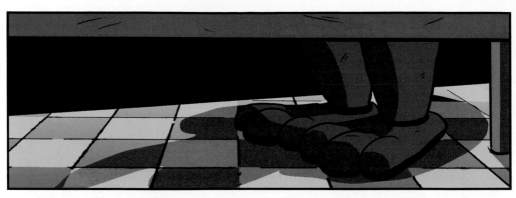

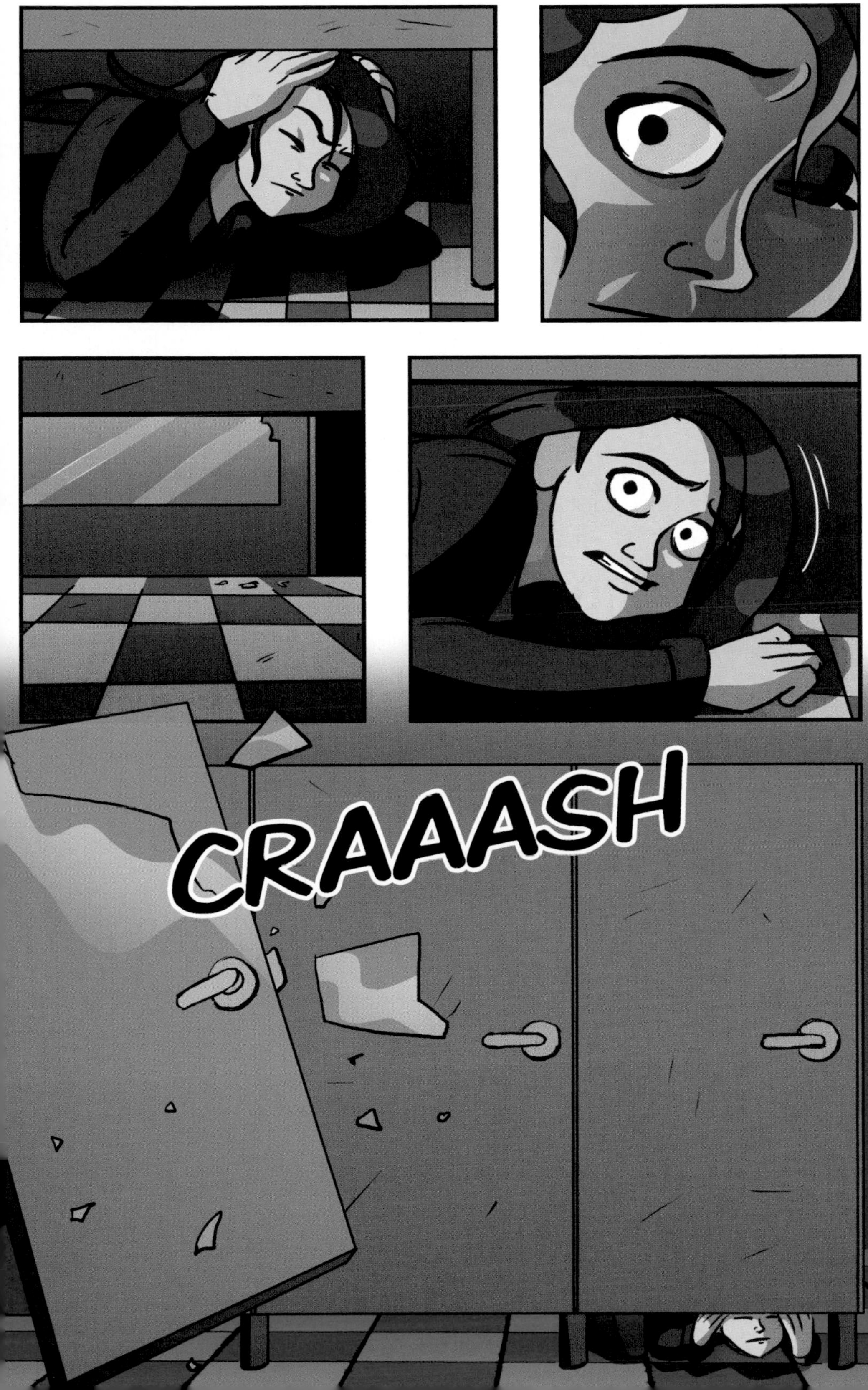
CRAAASH

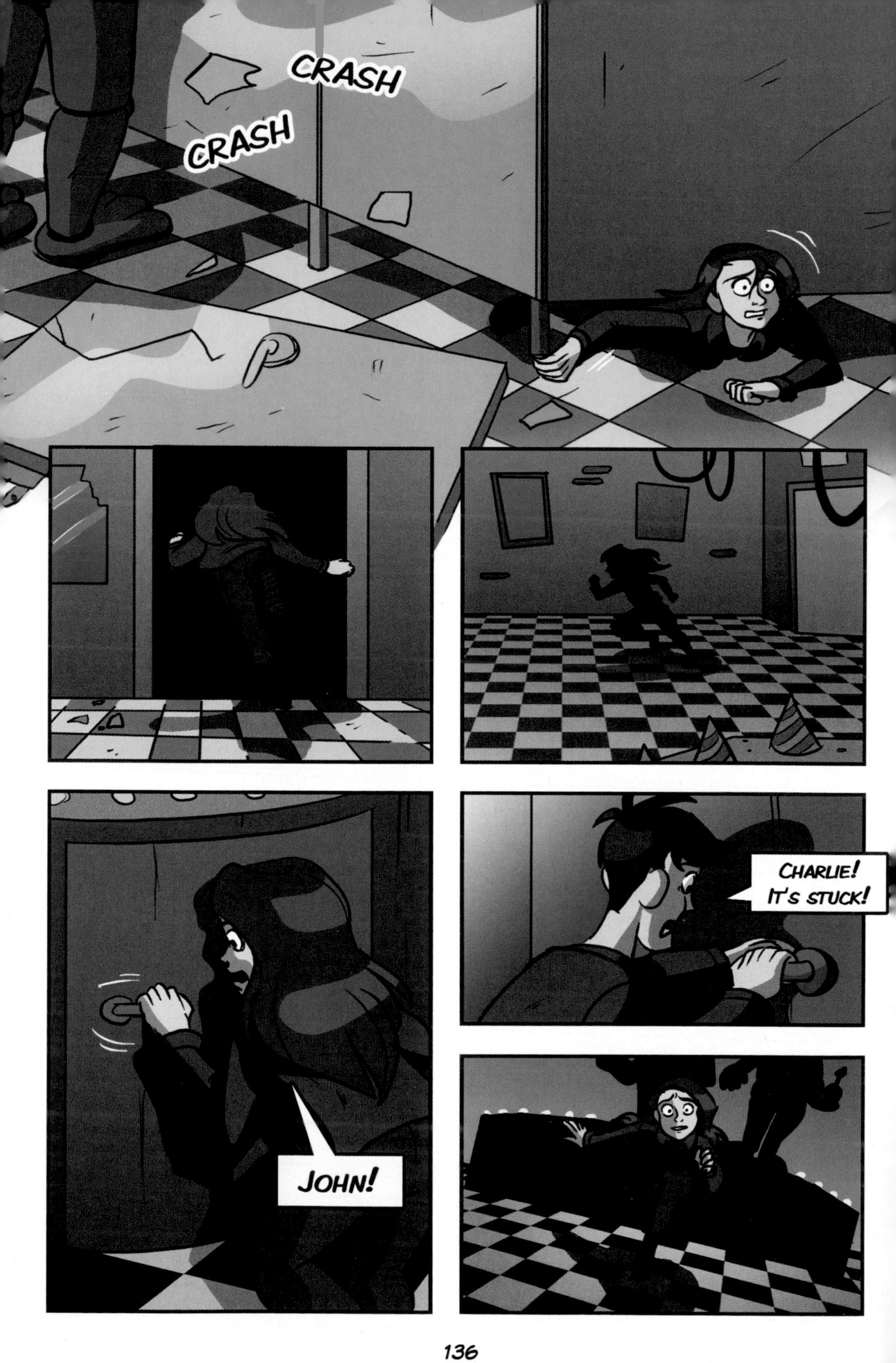
CRASH
CRASH
JOHN!
CHARLIE! IT'S STUCK!

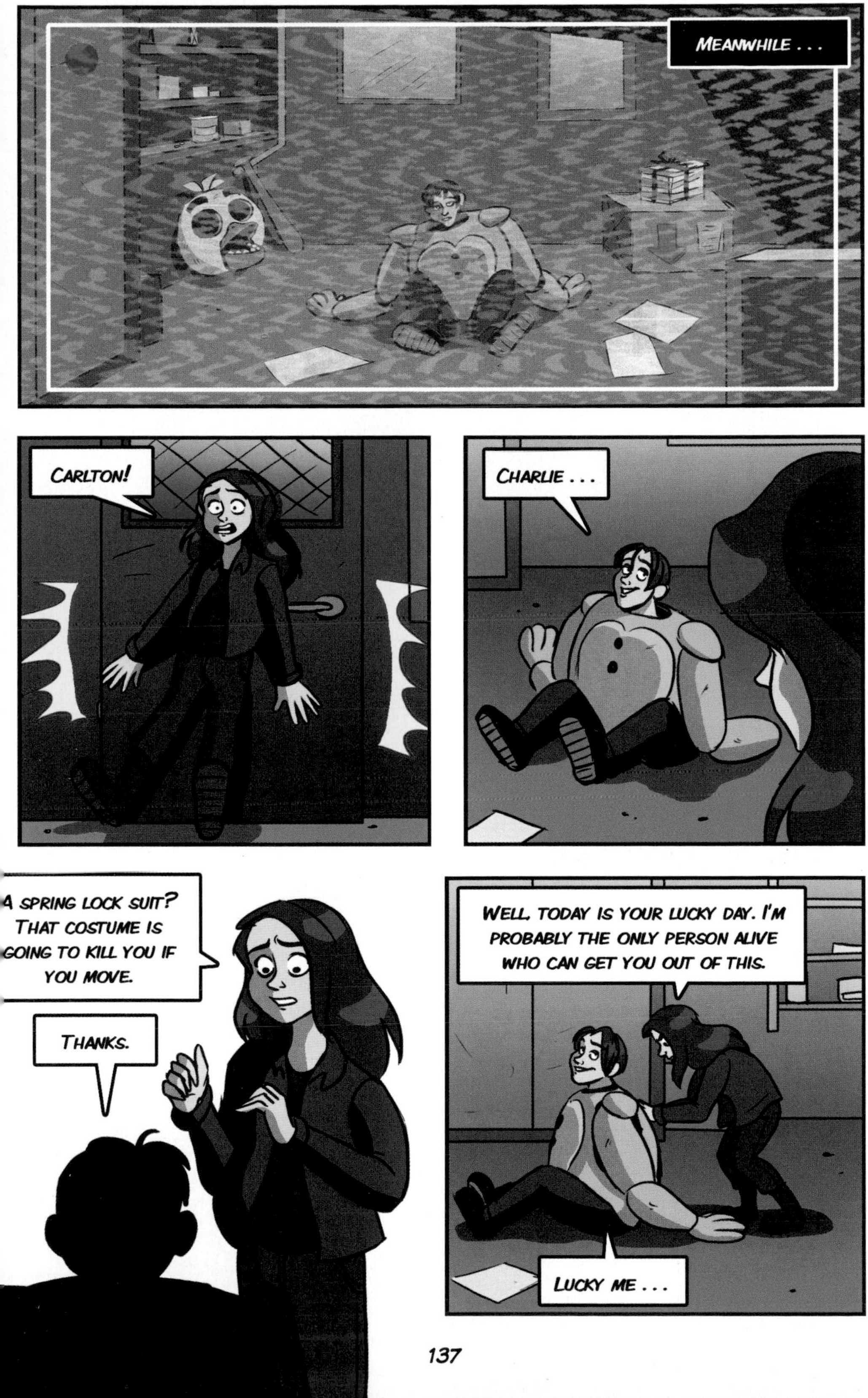
MEANWHILE . . .
CARLTON!
CHARLIE . . .
A SPRING LOCK SUIT? THAT COSTUME IS GOING TO KILL YOU IF YOU MOVE.
THANKS.
WELL, TODAY IS YOUR LUCKY DAY. I'M PROBABLY THE ONLY PERSON ALIVE WHO CAN GET YOU OUT OF THIS.
LUCKY ME . . .

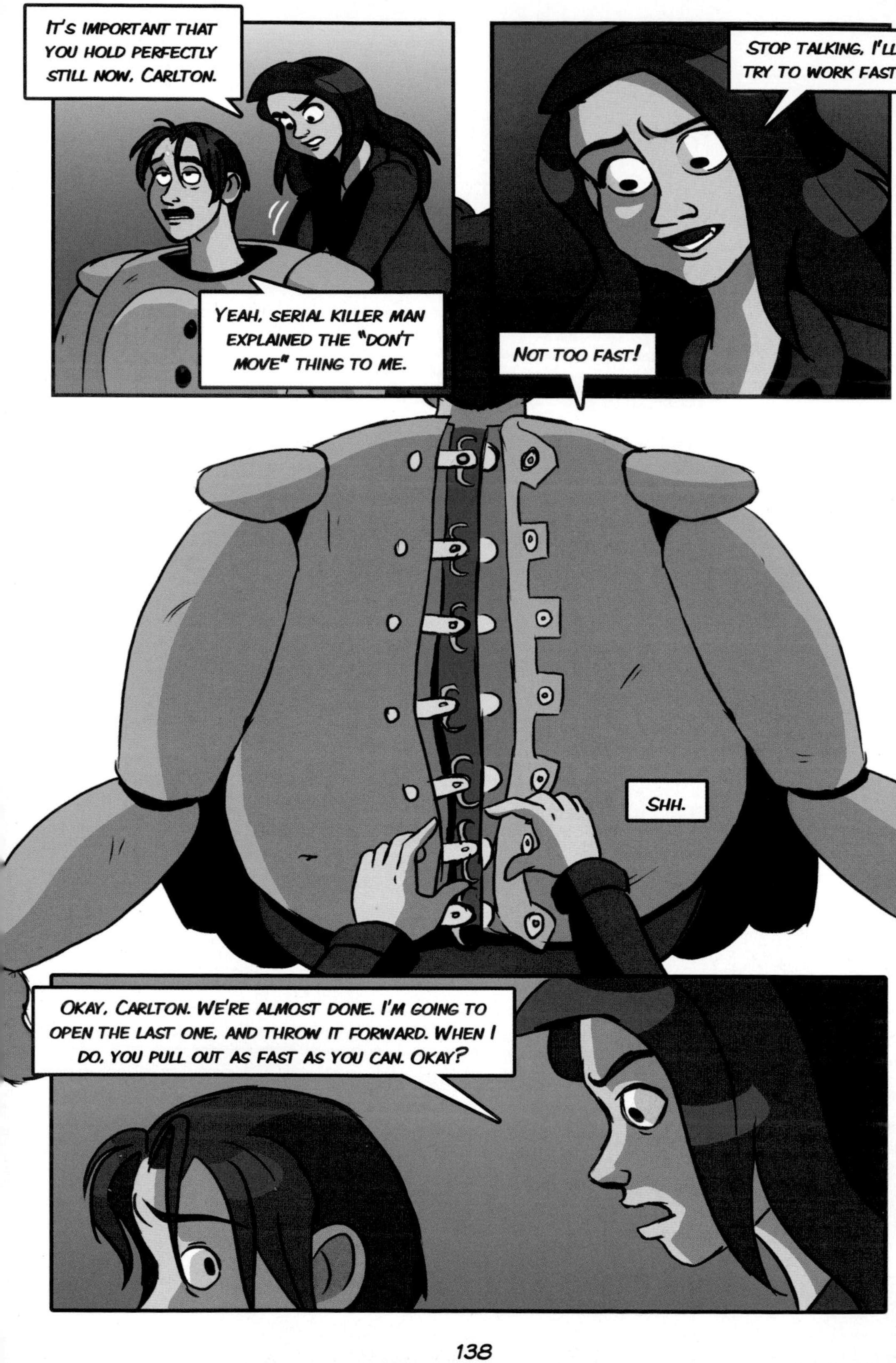
IT'S IMPORTANT THAT YOU HOLD PERFECTLY STILL NOW, CARLTON.
YEAH, SERIAL KILLER MAN EXPLAINED THE "DON'T MOVE" THING TO ME.
STOP TALKING. I'LL TRY TO WORK FAST.
NOT TOO FAST!
SHH.
OKAY, CARLTON. WE'RE ALMOST DONE. I'M GOING TO OPEN THE LAST ONE, AND THROW IT FORWARD. WHEN I DO, YOU PULL OUT AS FAST AS YOU CAN. OKAY?

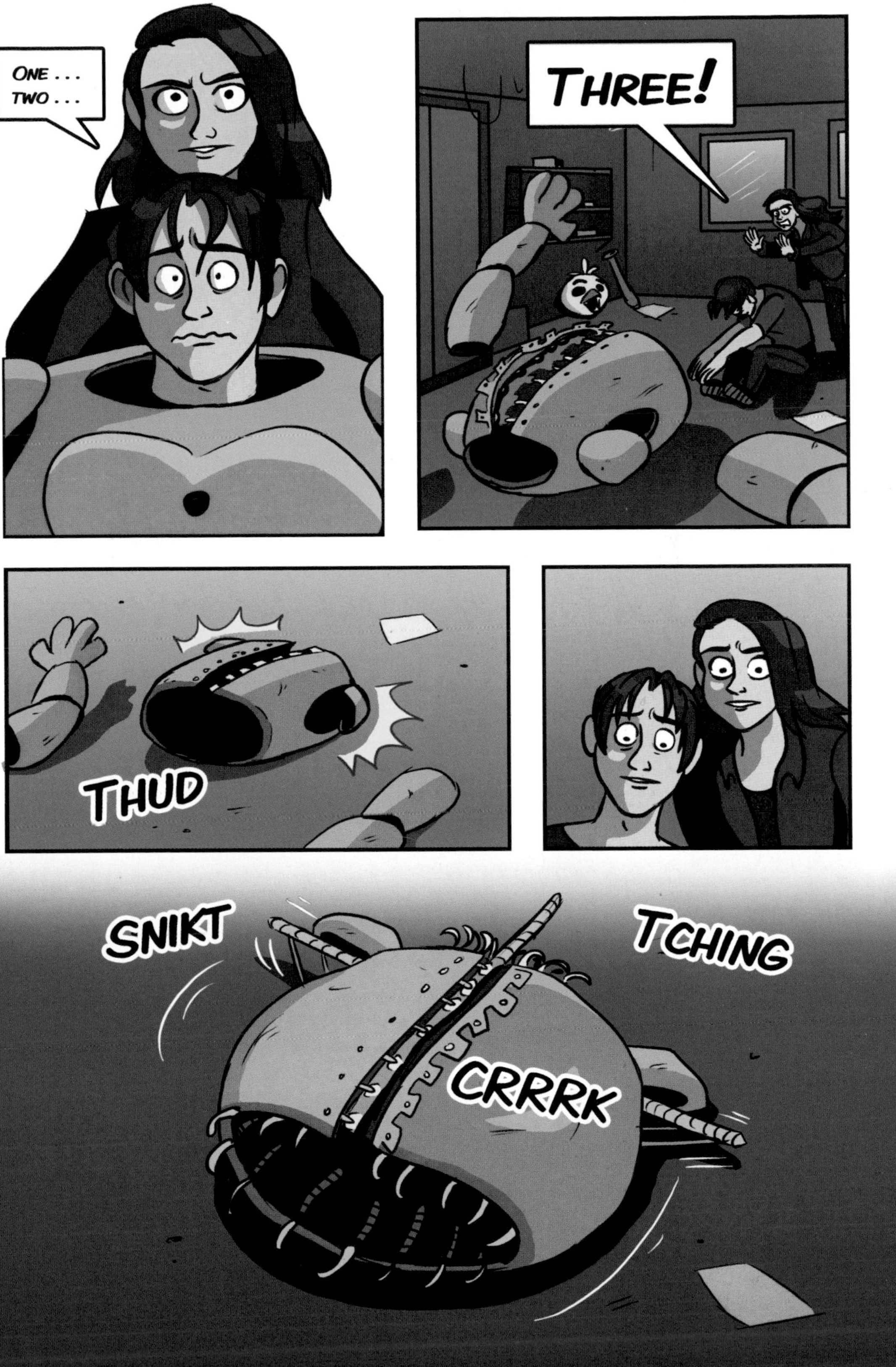
ONE . . .
TWO . . .
THREE!
THUD
SNIKT
TCHING
CRRRK

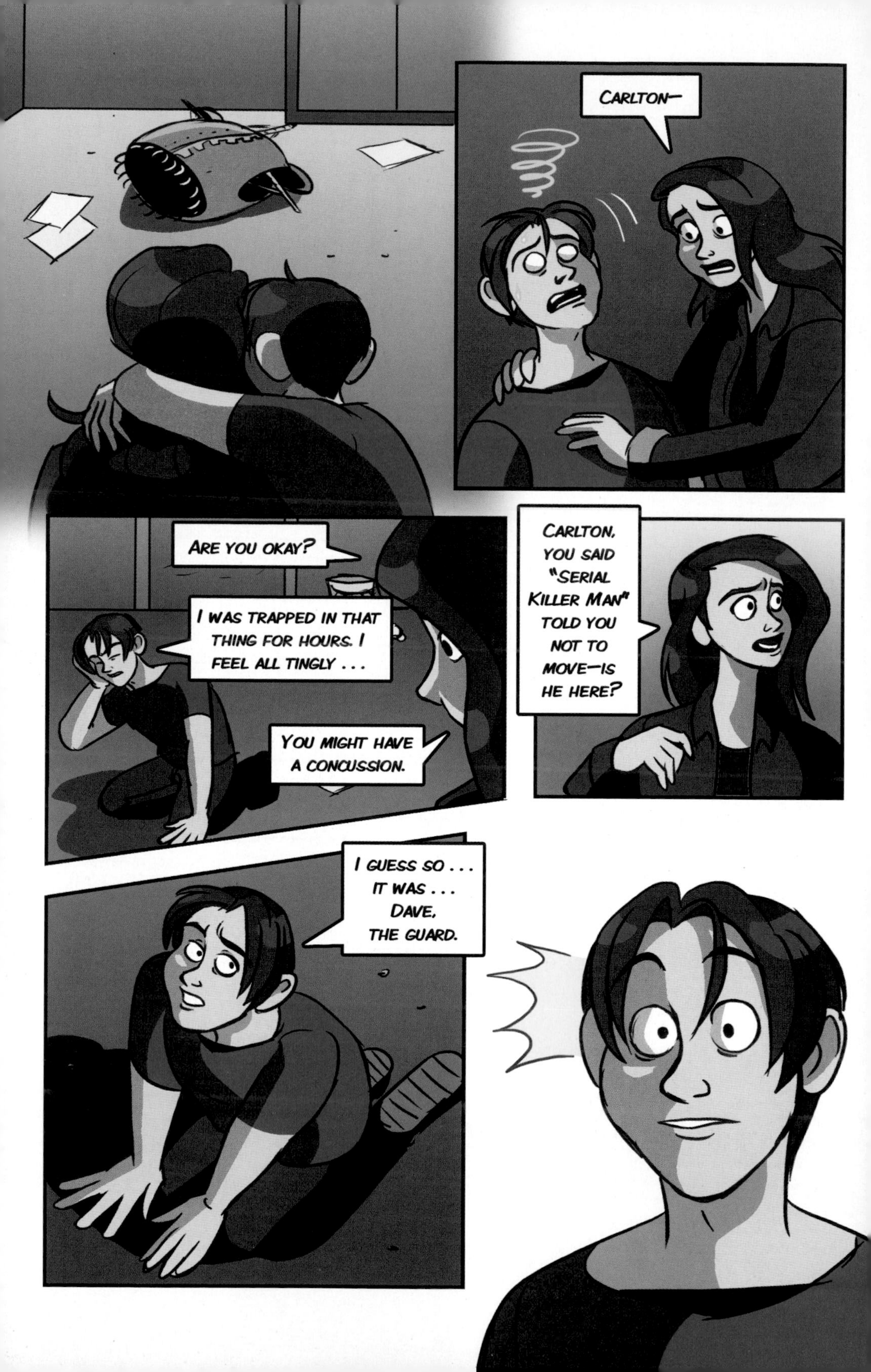
CARLTON—
ARE YOU OKAY?
I WAS TRAPPED IN THAT THING FOR HOURS. I FEEL ALL TINGLY . . .
YOU MIGHT HAVE A CONCUSSION.
CARLTON, YOU SAID "SERIAL KILLER MAN" TOLD YOU NOT TO MOVE—IS HE HERE?
I GUESS SO . . . IT WAS . . . DAVE, THE GUARD.

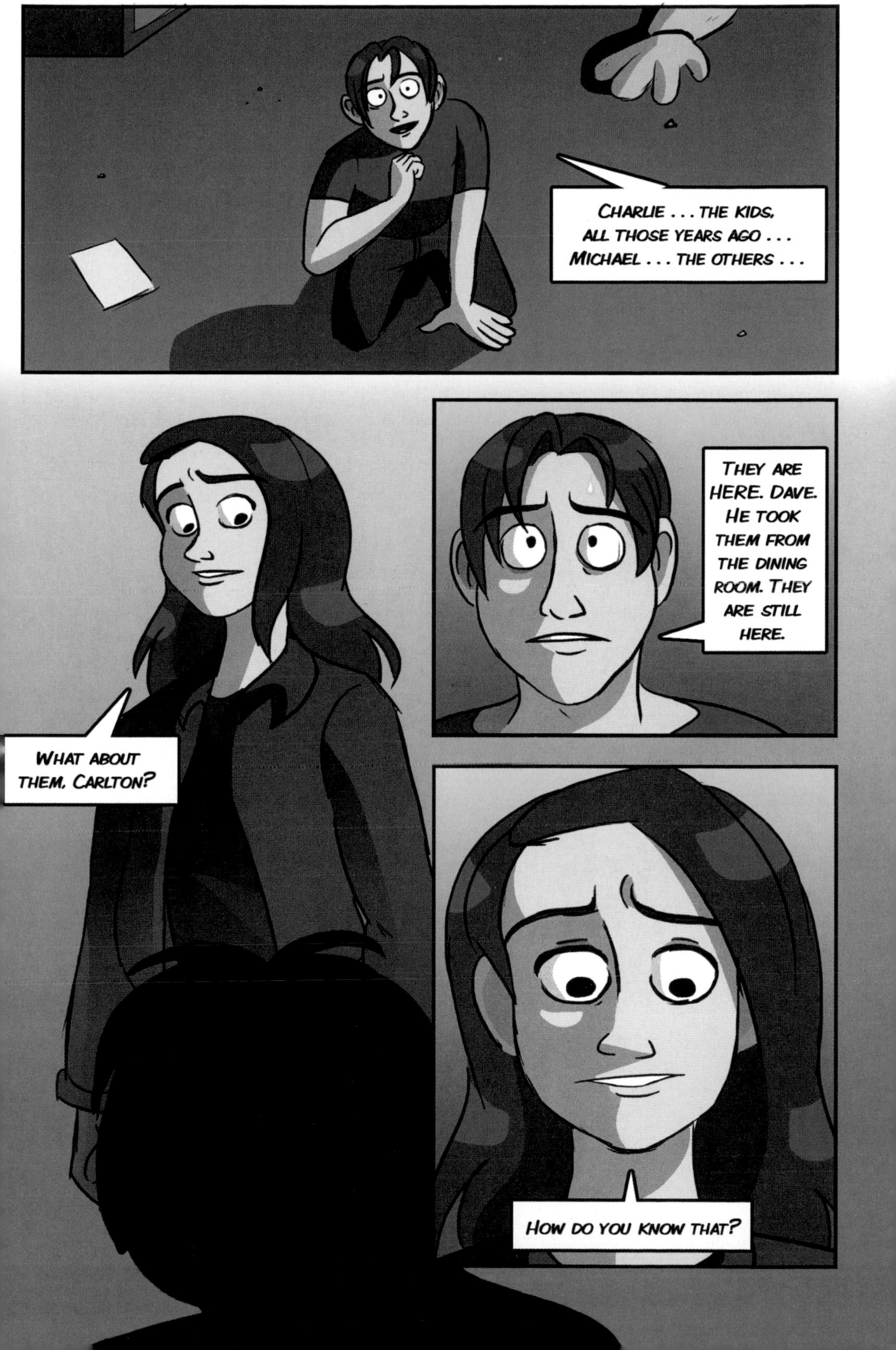
CHARLIE . . . THE KIDS, ALL THOSE YEARS AGO . . . MICHAEL . . . THE OTHERS . . .
WHAT ABOUT THEM, CARLTON?
THEY ARE HERE. DAVE. HE TOOK THEM FROM THE DINING ROOM. THEY ARE STILL HERE.
HOW DO YOU KNOW THAT?

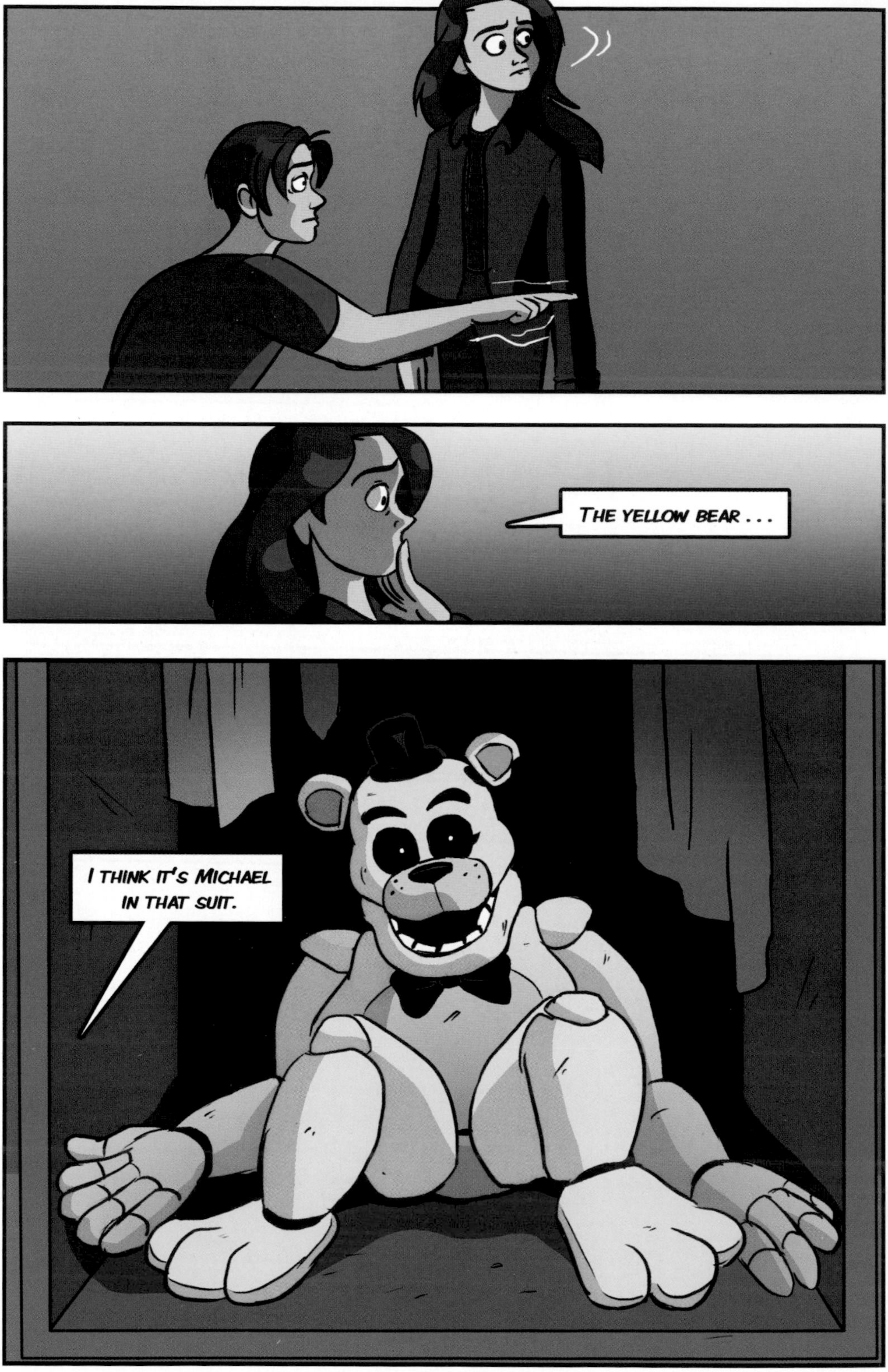
THE YELLOW BEAR . . .
I THINK IT'S MICHAEL IN THAT SUIT.

CHAPTER 11

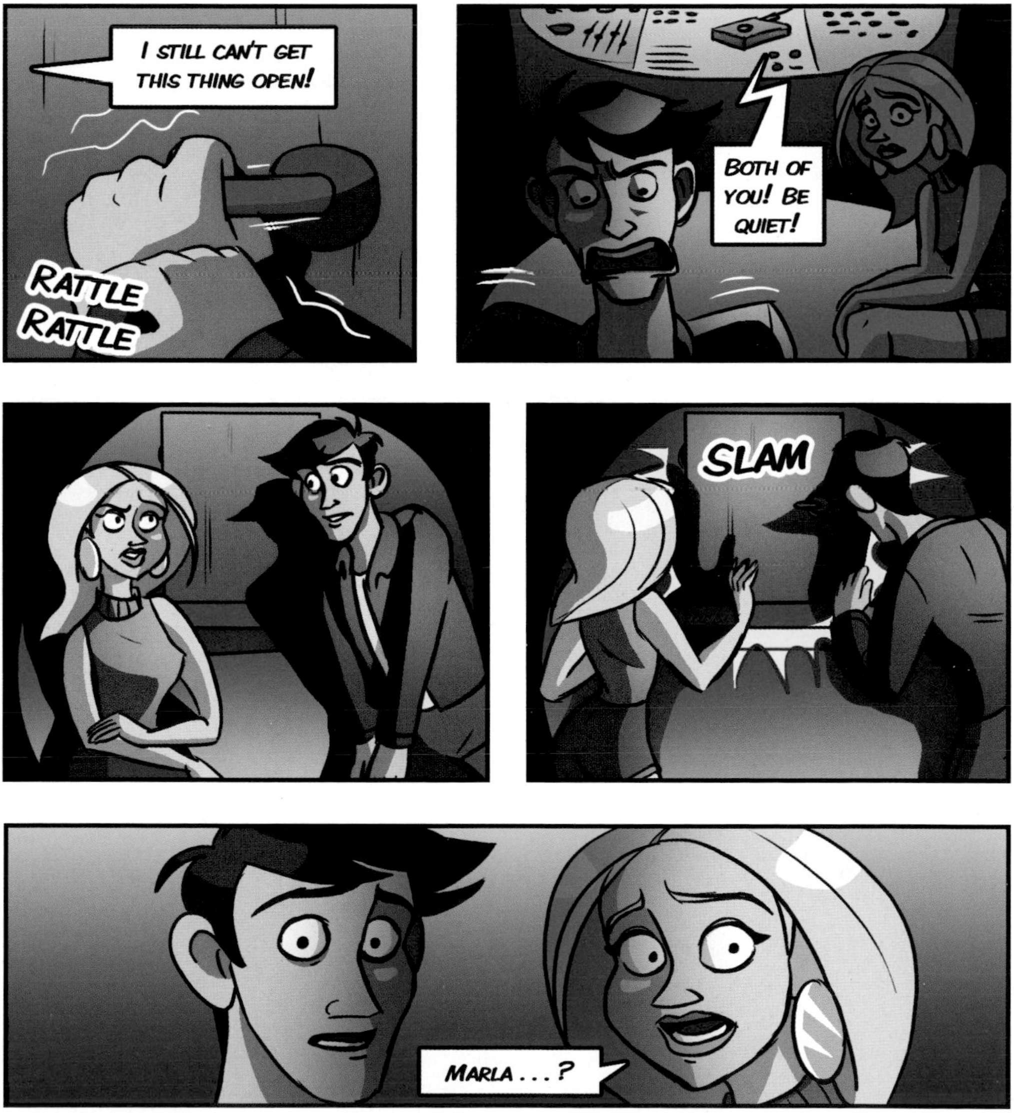
I STILL CAN'T GET THIS THING OPEN!
RATTLE RATTLE
BOTH OF YOU! BE QUIET!
SLAM
MARLA . . . ?

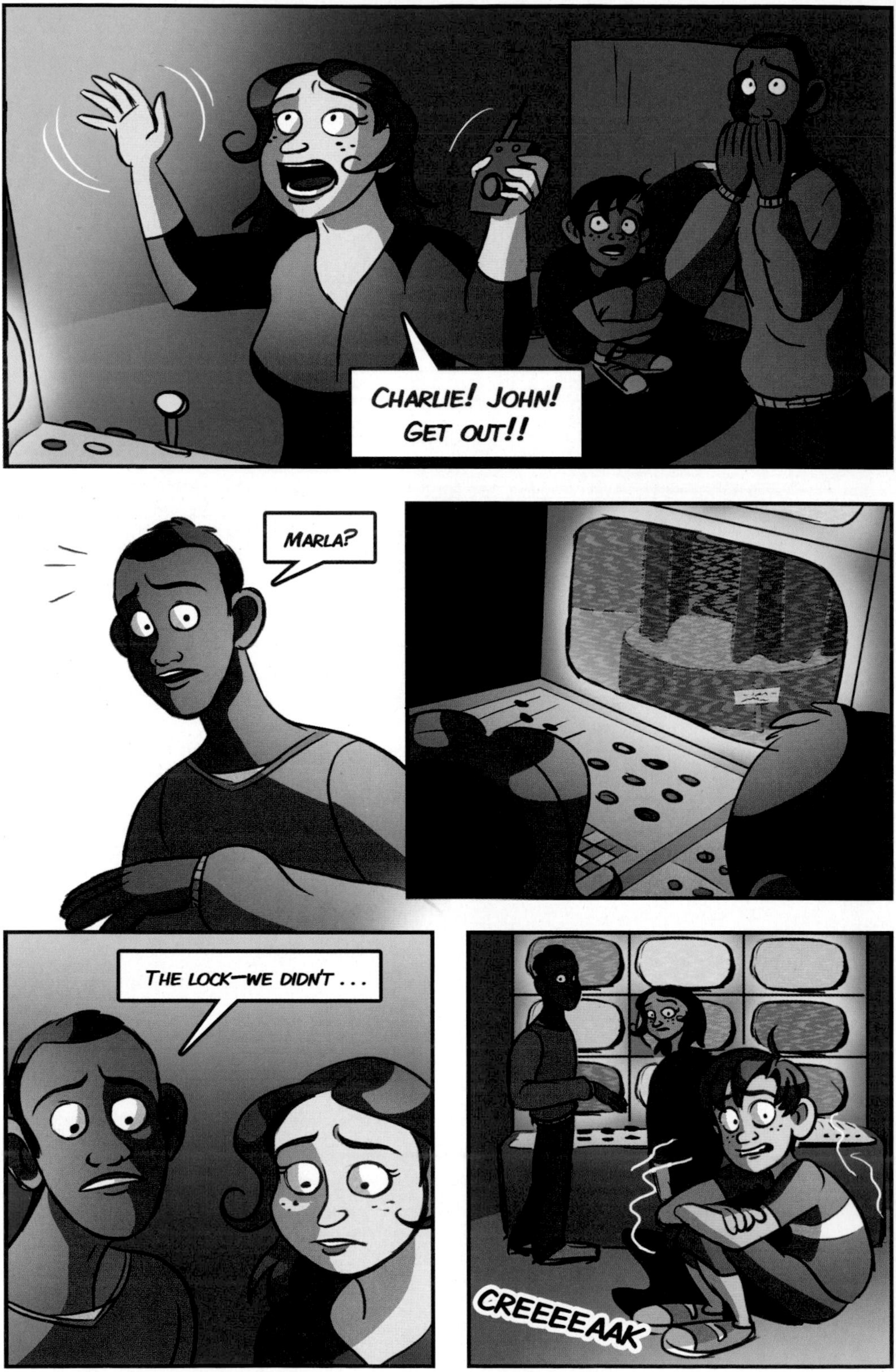
CHARLIE! JOHN!
GET OUT!!
MARLA?
THE LOCK—WE DIDN'T . . .
CREEEEAAK

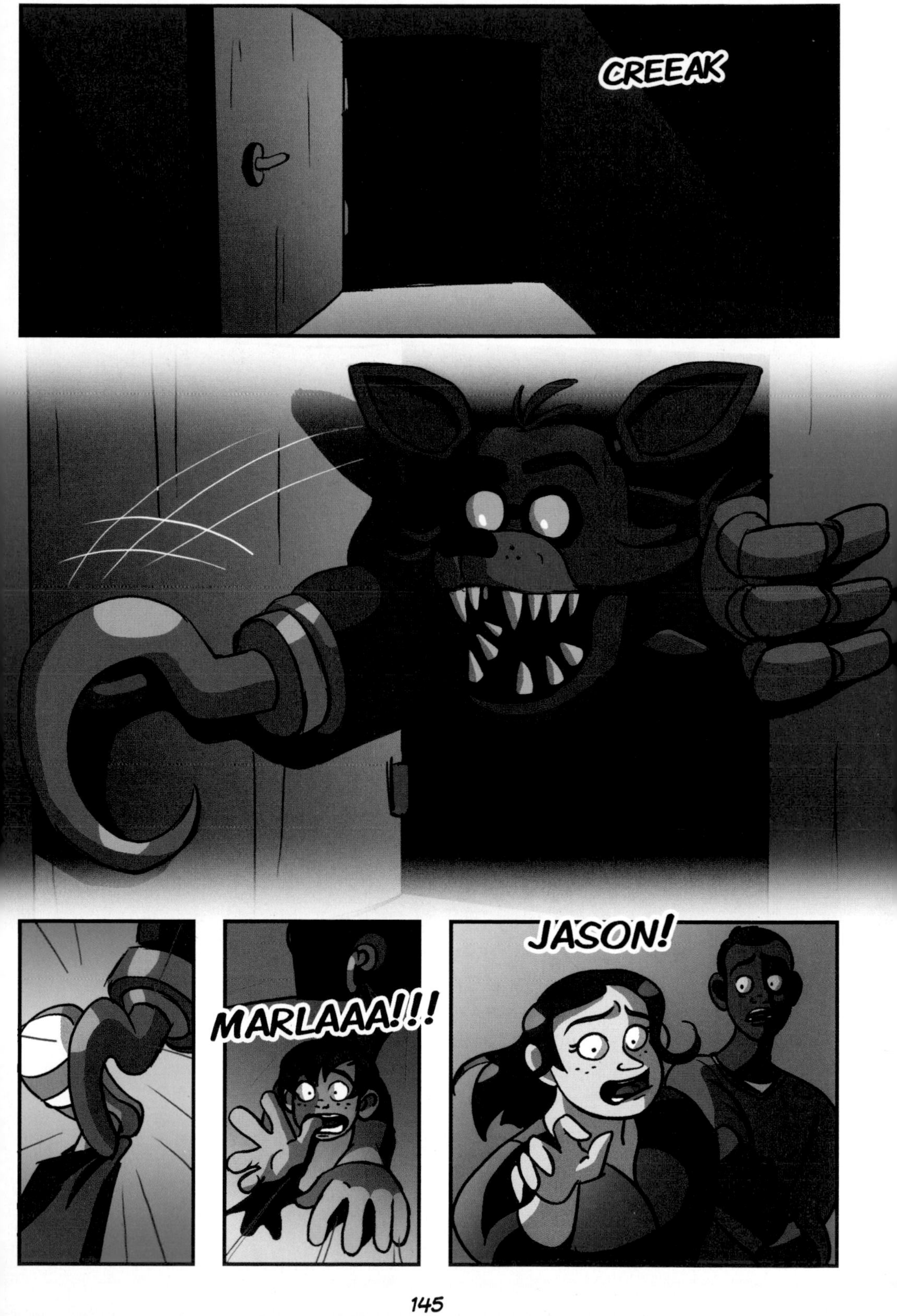
CREEAK
MARLAAA!!!
JASON!

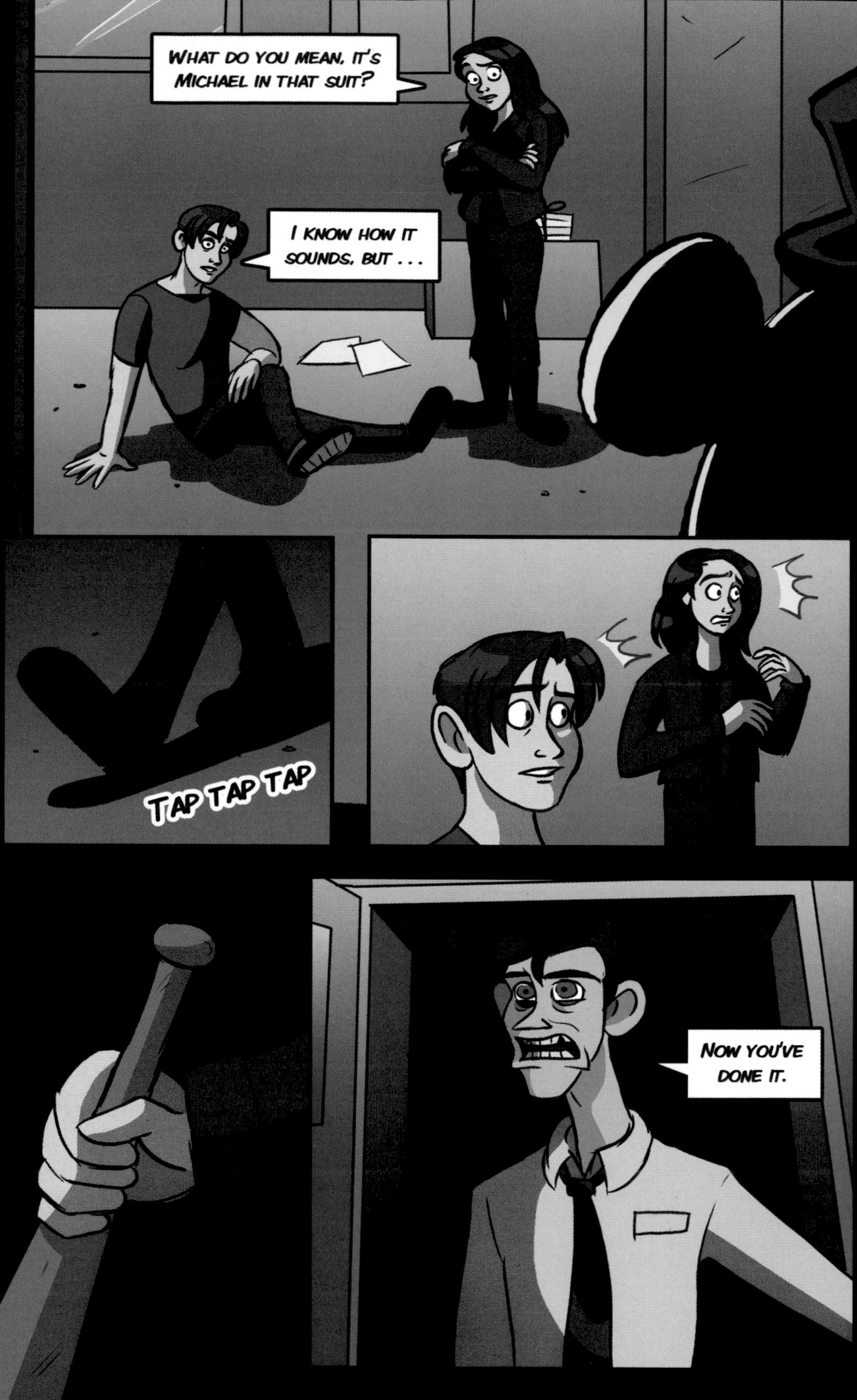
WHAT DO YOU MEAN, IT'S MICHAEL IN THAT SUIT?
I KNOW HOW IT SOUNDS, BUT . . .
TAP TAP TAP
NOW YOU'VE DONE IT.

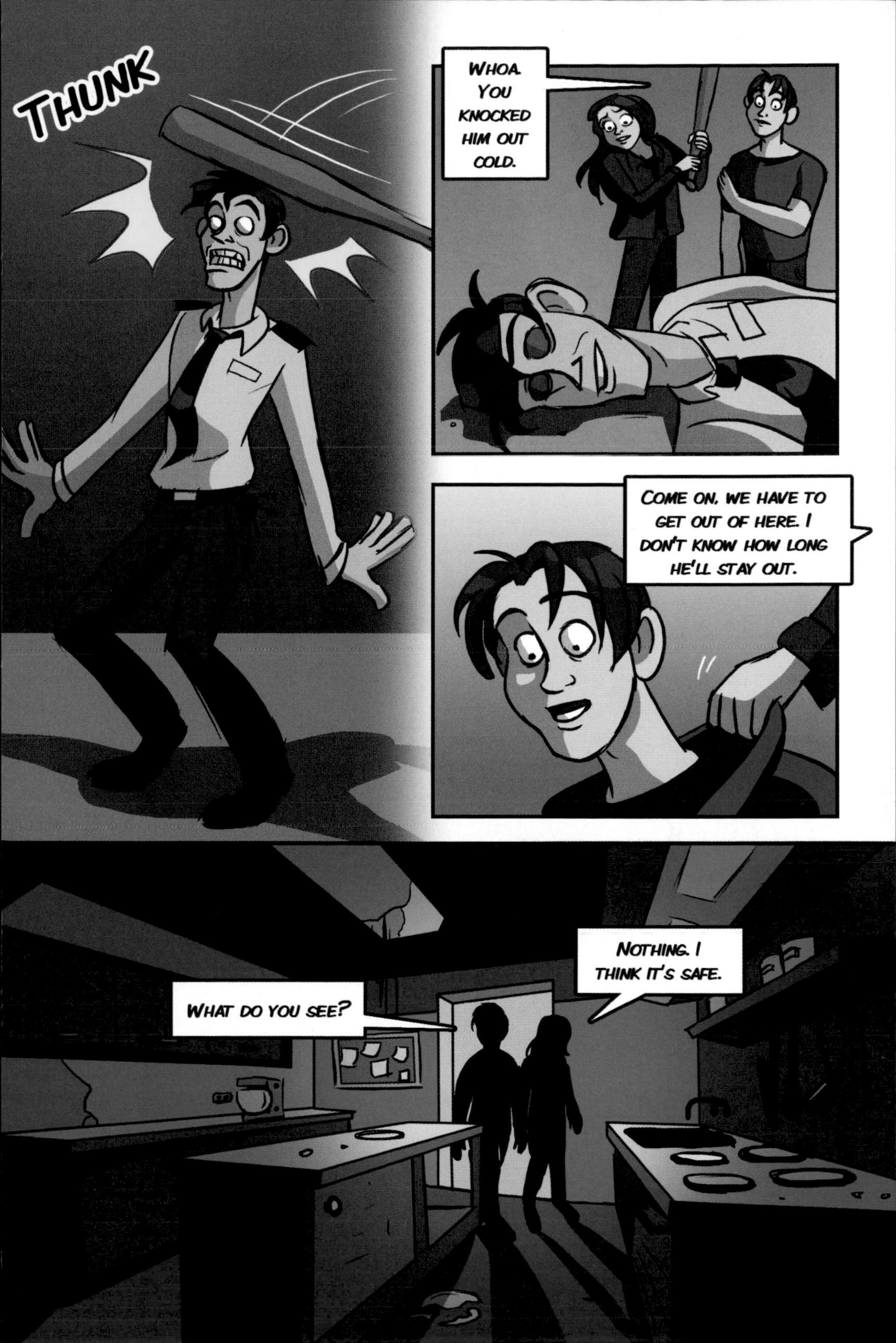
THUNK
WHOA. YOU KNOCKED HIM OUT COLD.
COME ON, WE HAVE TO GET OUT OF HERE. I DON'T KNOW HOW LONG HE'LL STAY OUT.
WHAT DO YOU SEE?
NOTHING. I THINK IT'S SAFE.

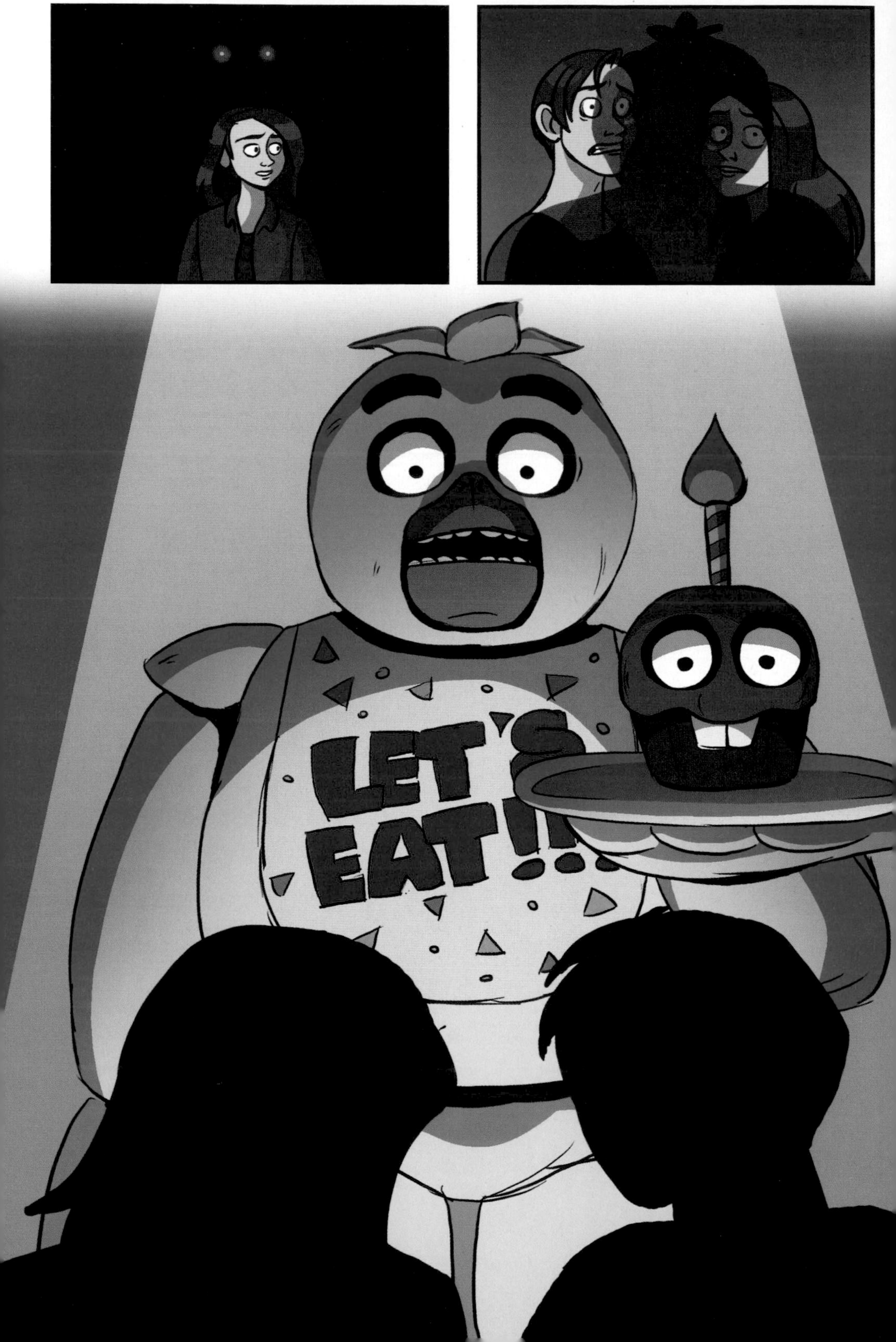
LET'S EAT!!!

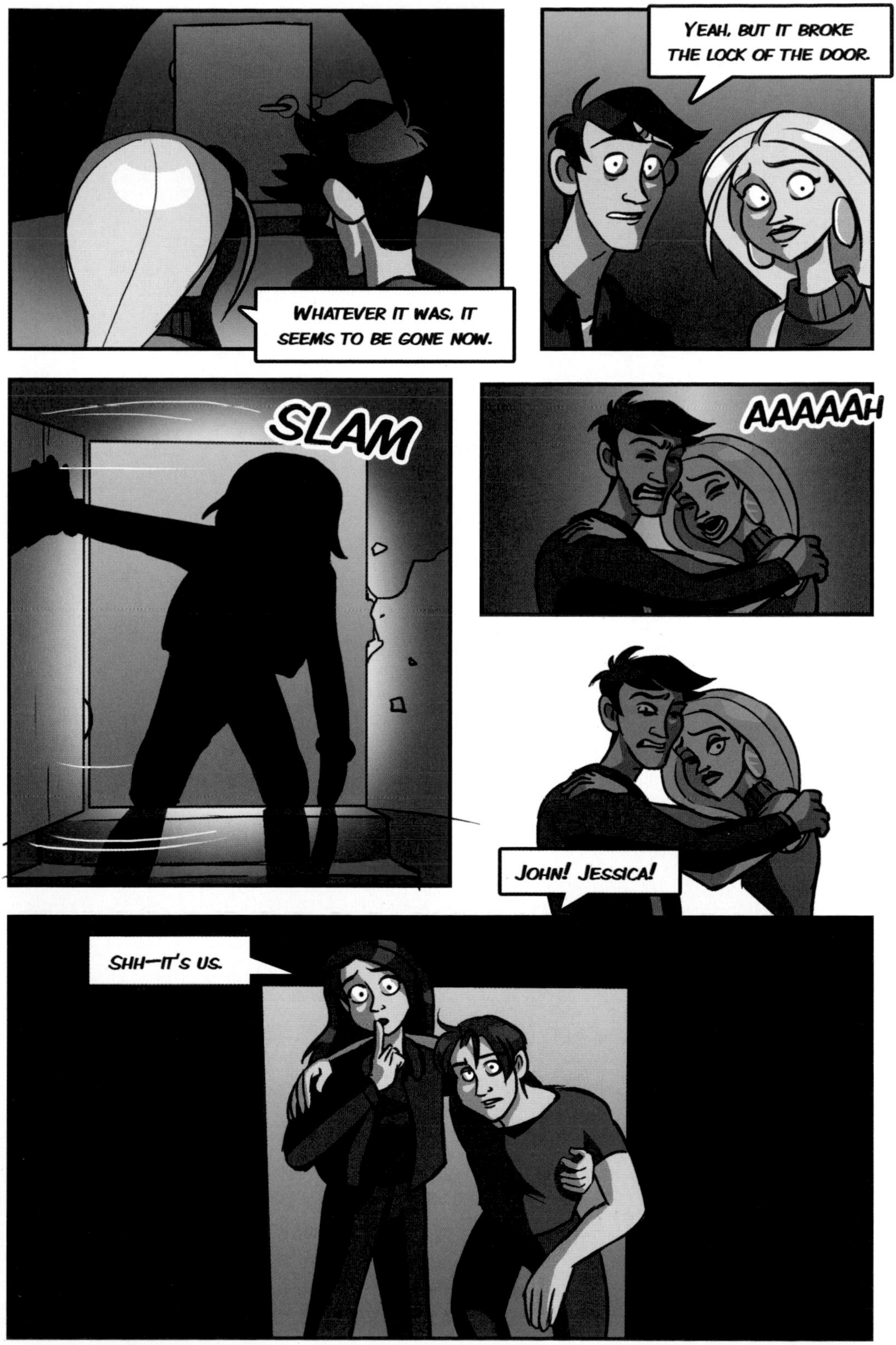
WHATEVER IT WAS, IT SEEMS TO BE GONE NOW.
YEAH, BUT IT BROKE THE LOCK OF THE DOOR.
SLAM
AAAAAH
JOHN! JESSICA!
SHH—IT'S US.

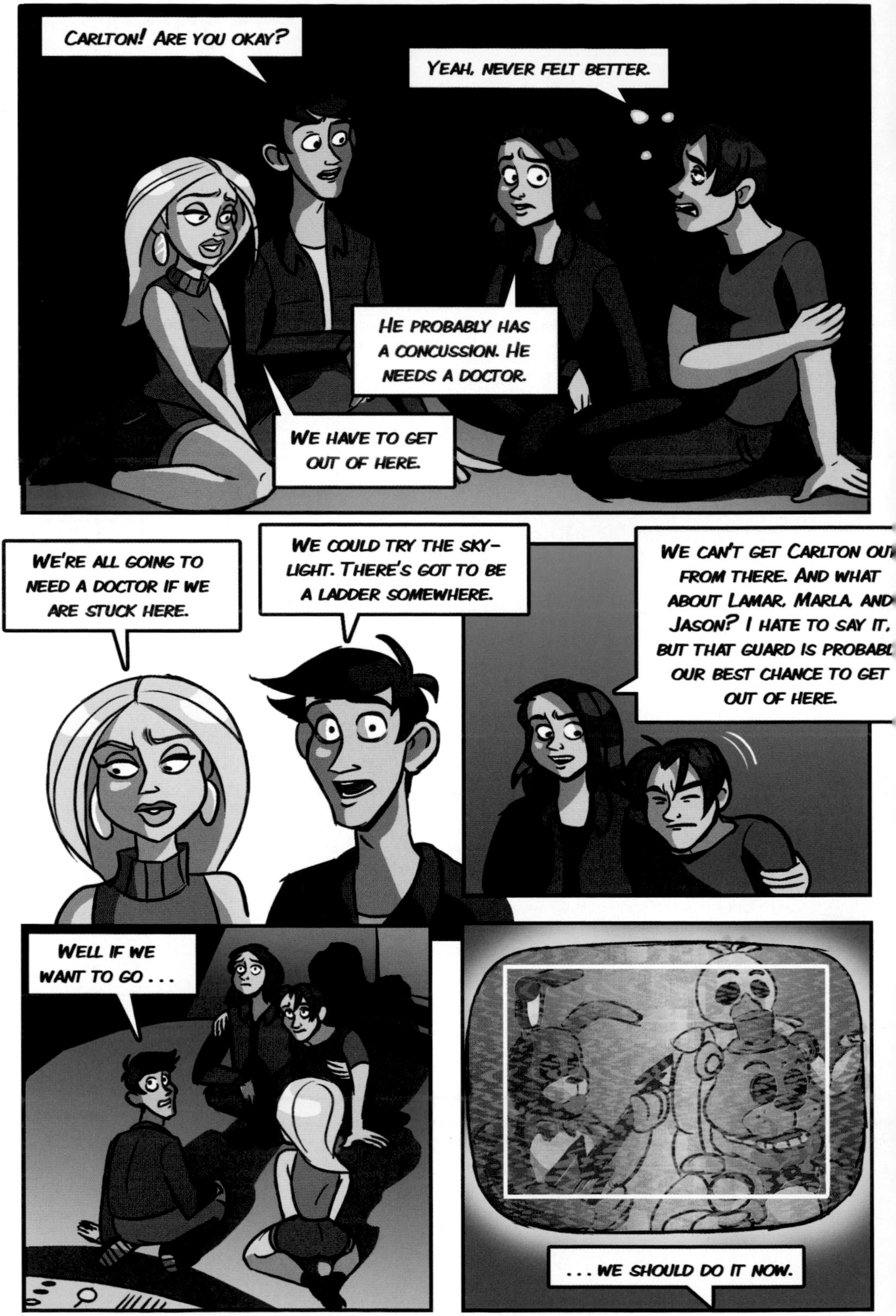
CARLTON! ARE YOU OKAY?
YEAH, NEVER FELT BETTER.
HE PROBABLY HAS A CONCUSSION. HE NEEDS A DOCTOR.
WE HAVE TO GET OUT OF HERE.
WE'RE ALL GOING TO NEED A DOCTOR IF WE ARE STUCK HERE.
WE COULD TRY THE SKY-LIGHT. THERE'S GOT TO BE A LADDER SOMEWHERE.
WE CAN'T GET CARLTON OUT FROM THERE. AND WHAT ABOUT LAMAR, MARLA, AND JASON? I HATE TO SAY IT, BUT THAT GUARD IS PROBABLY OUR BEST CHANCE TO GET OUT OF HERE.
WELL IF WE WANT TO GO . . .
. . . WE SHOULD DO IT NOW.

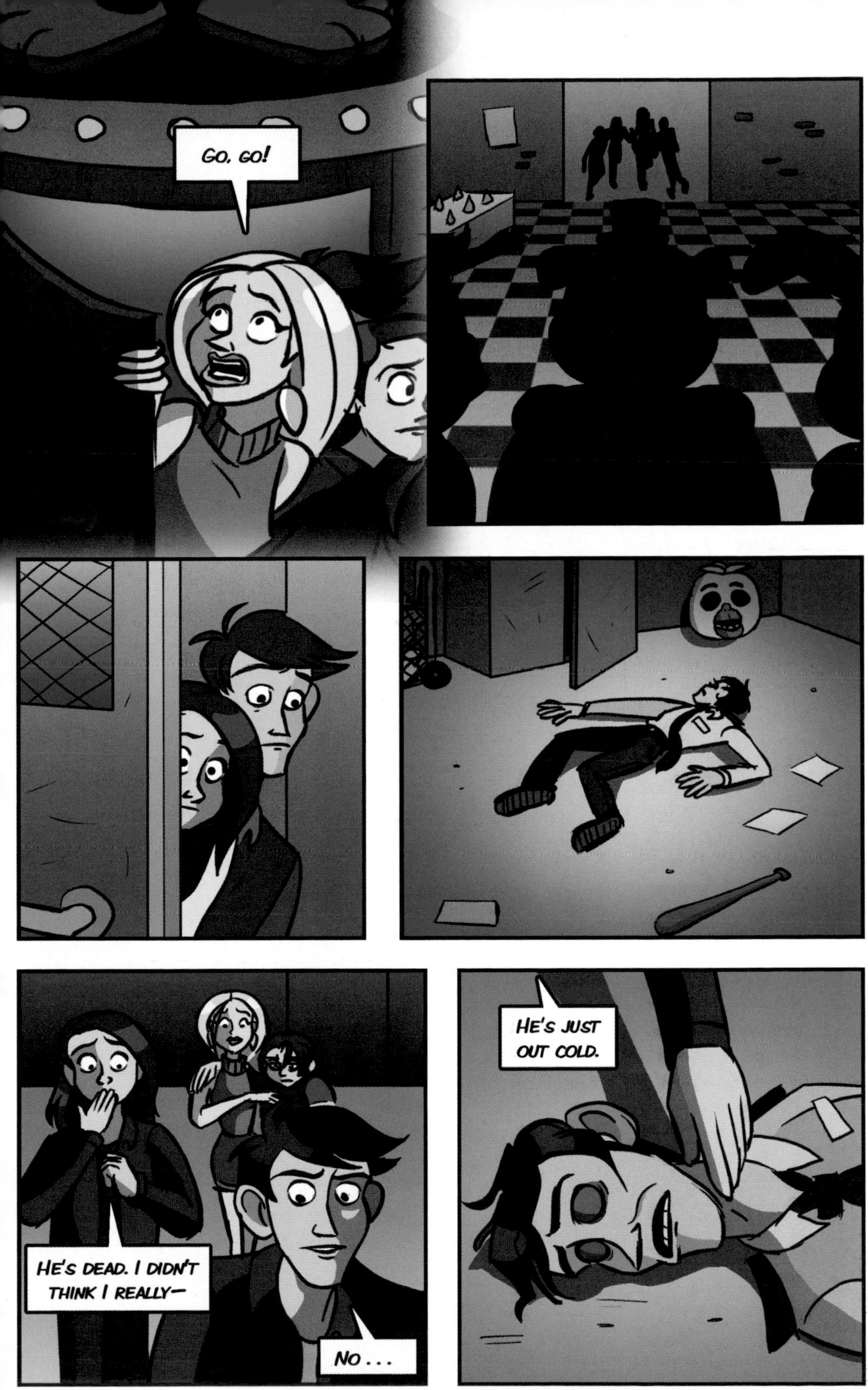
GO, GO!
HE'S DEAD. I DIDN'T THINK I REALLY—
NO . . .
HE'S JUST OUT COLD.

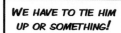

WE HAVE TO TIE HIM UP OR SOMETHING!

I AGREE. LET'S LOOK FOR A ROPE. THIS PLACE SEEMS TO HAVE EVERYTHING.

WHY DON'T WE JUST PUT HIM INTO ONE OF THE COSTUMES?

CHARLIE . . . ?

. . . WHERE IS MICHAEL?

WHAT?!

MICHAEL WAS THERE . . .

HE WAS RIGHT THERE.

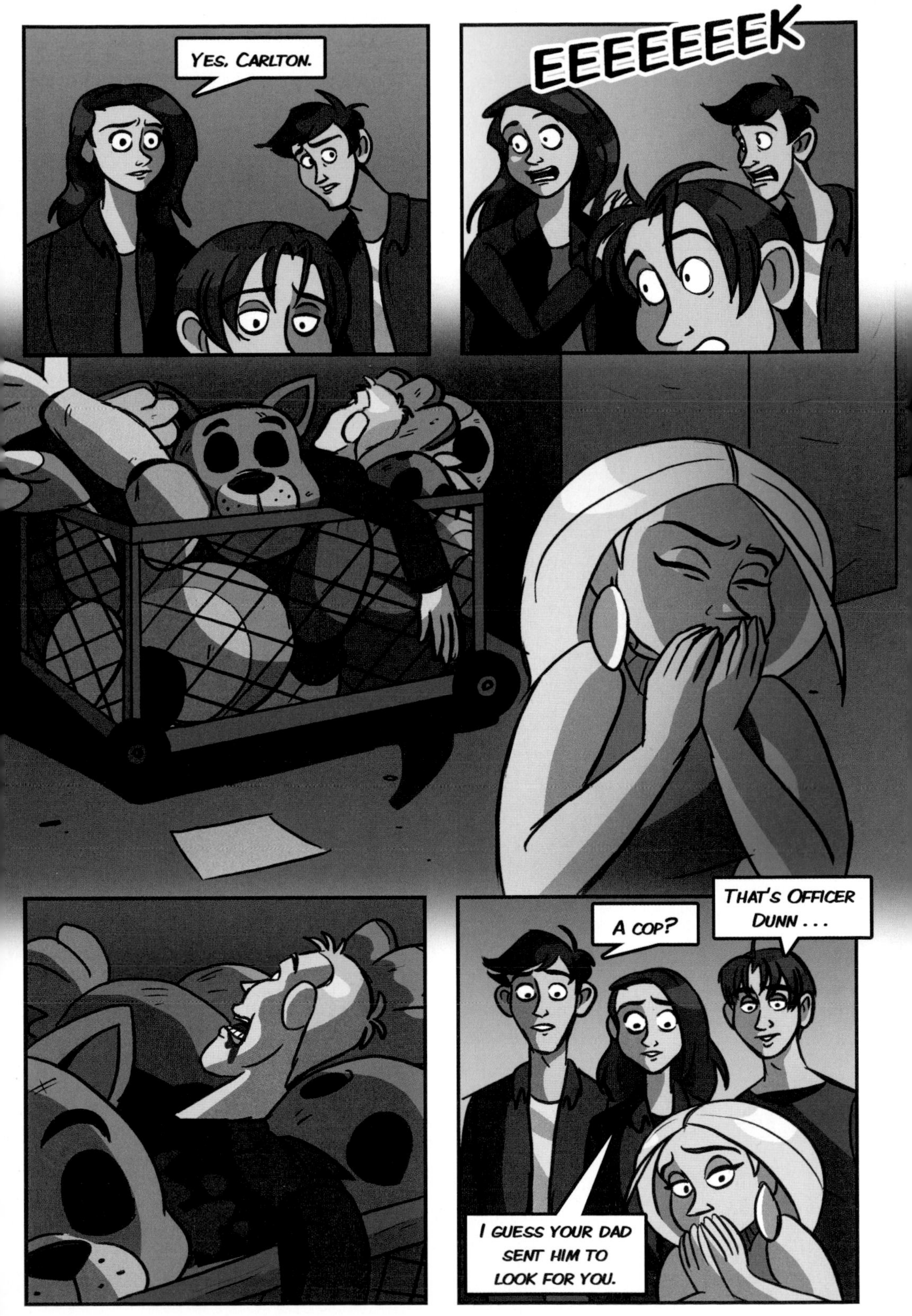
YES, CARLTON.
EEEEEEEEK
A COP?
THAT'S OFFICER DUNN . . .
I GUESS YOUR DAD SENT HIM TO LOOK FOR YOU.

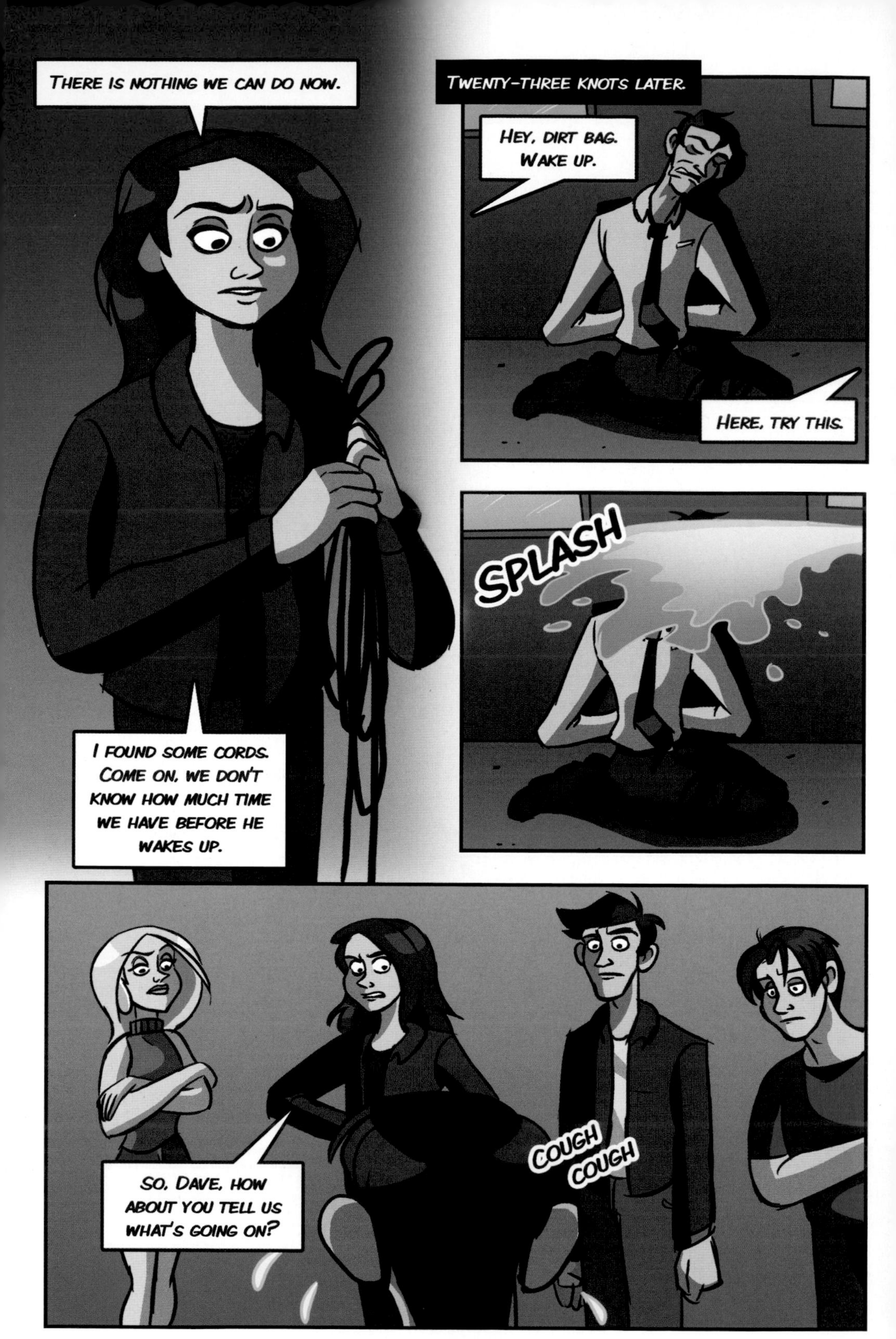
THERE IS NOTHING WE CAN DO NOW.
I FOUND SOME CORDS. COME ON, WE DON'T KNOW HOW MUCH TIME WE HAVE BEFORE HE WAKES UP.
TWENTY-THREE KNOTS LATER.
HEY, DIRT BAG. WAKE UP.
HERE, TRY THIS.
SPLASH
SO, DAVE, HOW ABOUT YOU TELL US WHAT'S GOING ON?
COUGH
COUGH

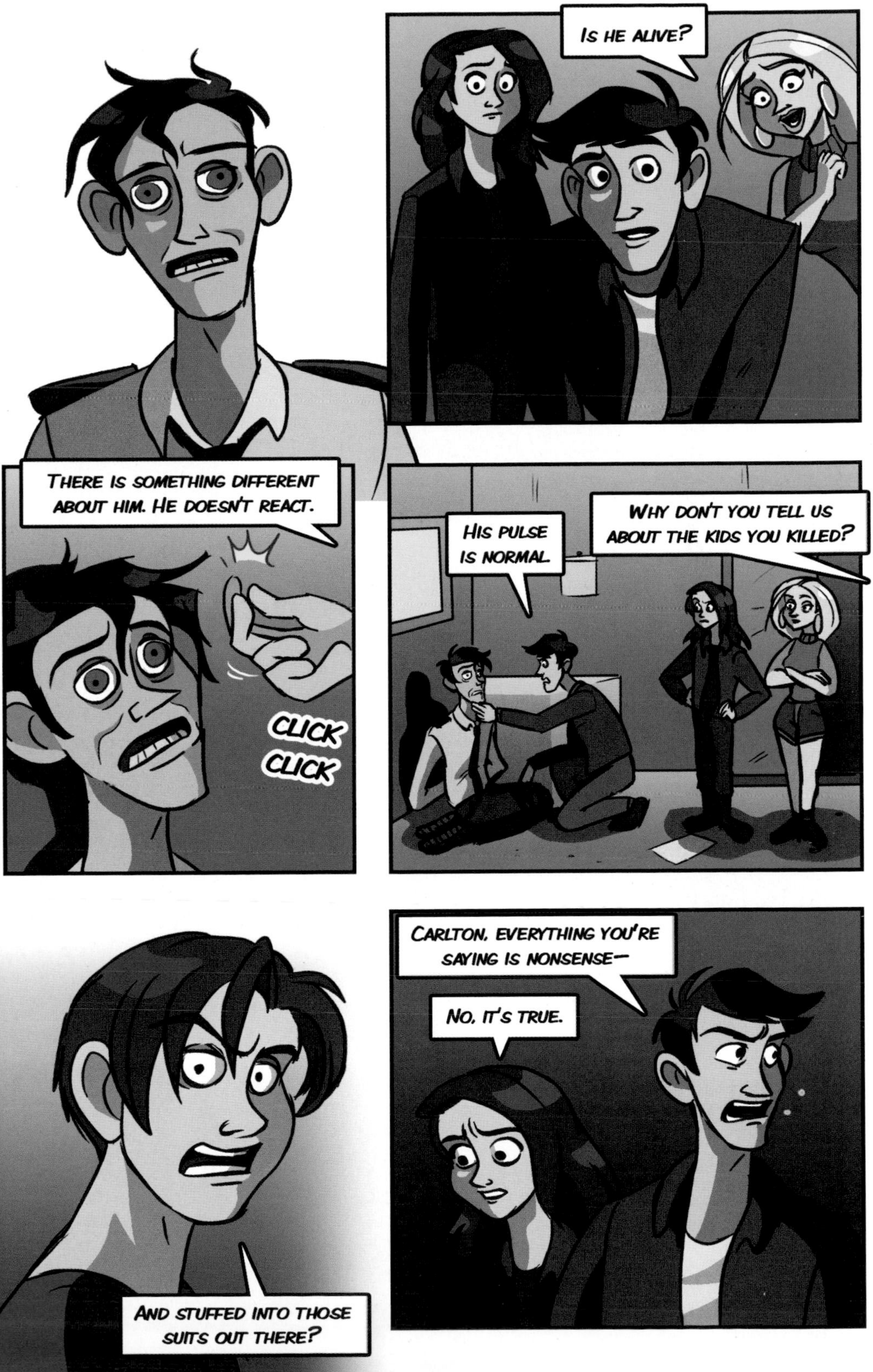

IS HE ALIVE?
THERE IS SOMETHING DIFFERENT ABOUT HIM. HE DOESN'T REACT.
CLICK CLICK
HIS PULSE IS NORMAL.
WHY DON'T YOU TELL US ABOUT THE KIDS YOU KILLED?
AND STUFFED INTO THOSE SUITS OUT THERE?
CARLTON, EVERYTHING YOU'RE SAYING IS NONSENSE—
NO, IT'S TRUE.

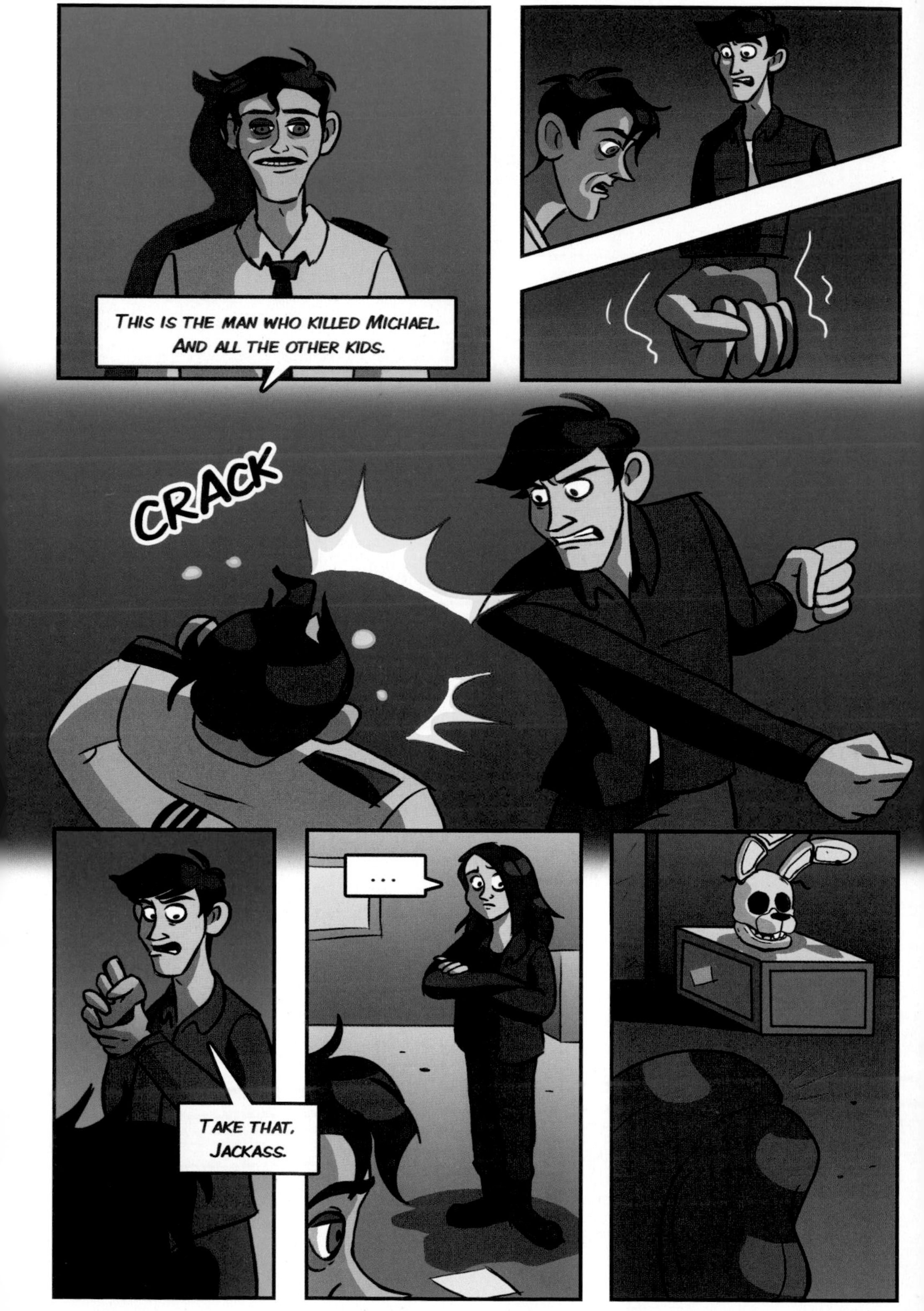

THIS IS THE MAN WHO KILLED MICHAEL.
AND ALL THE OTHER KIDS.
CRACK
TAKE THAT, JACKASS.
...

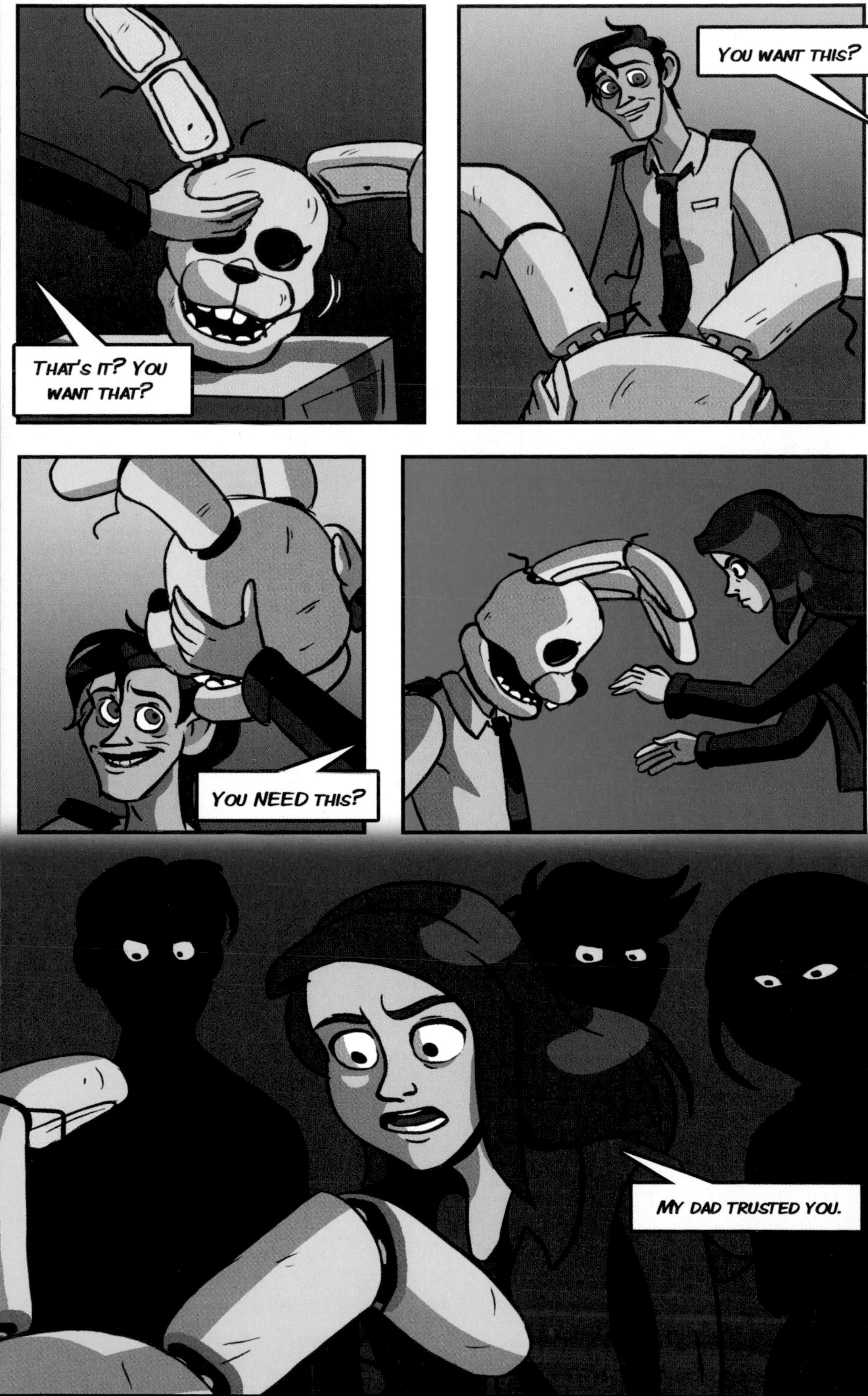
THAT'S IT? YOU WANT THAT?
YOU WANT THIS?
YOU NEED THIS?
MY DAD TRUSTED YOU.

WHAT DID YOU DO TO HIM?

I HELPED HIM CREATE.

WE BOTH WANTED LOVE. YOUR FATHER LOVED. AND NOW I HAVE LOVED.

SICK BASTARD! THE KIDS YOU KILLED ARE STILL HERE—YOU'VE IMPRISONED THOSE KIDS!

NO. THEY ARE HO. WITH ME. THEIR HAPPIEST DAY.

THEN YOU'RE TRAPPED HERE, TOO. SO YOU'RE NOT GOING TO HURT ANYONE ELSE.

HOW DO WE GET OUT?

THERE IS NO WAY OUT ANYMORE. ALL THAT IS LEFT IS FAMILY.

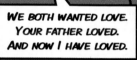

I DON'T HAVE TO

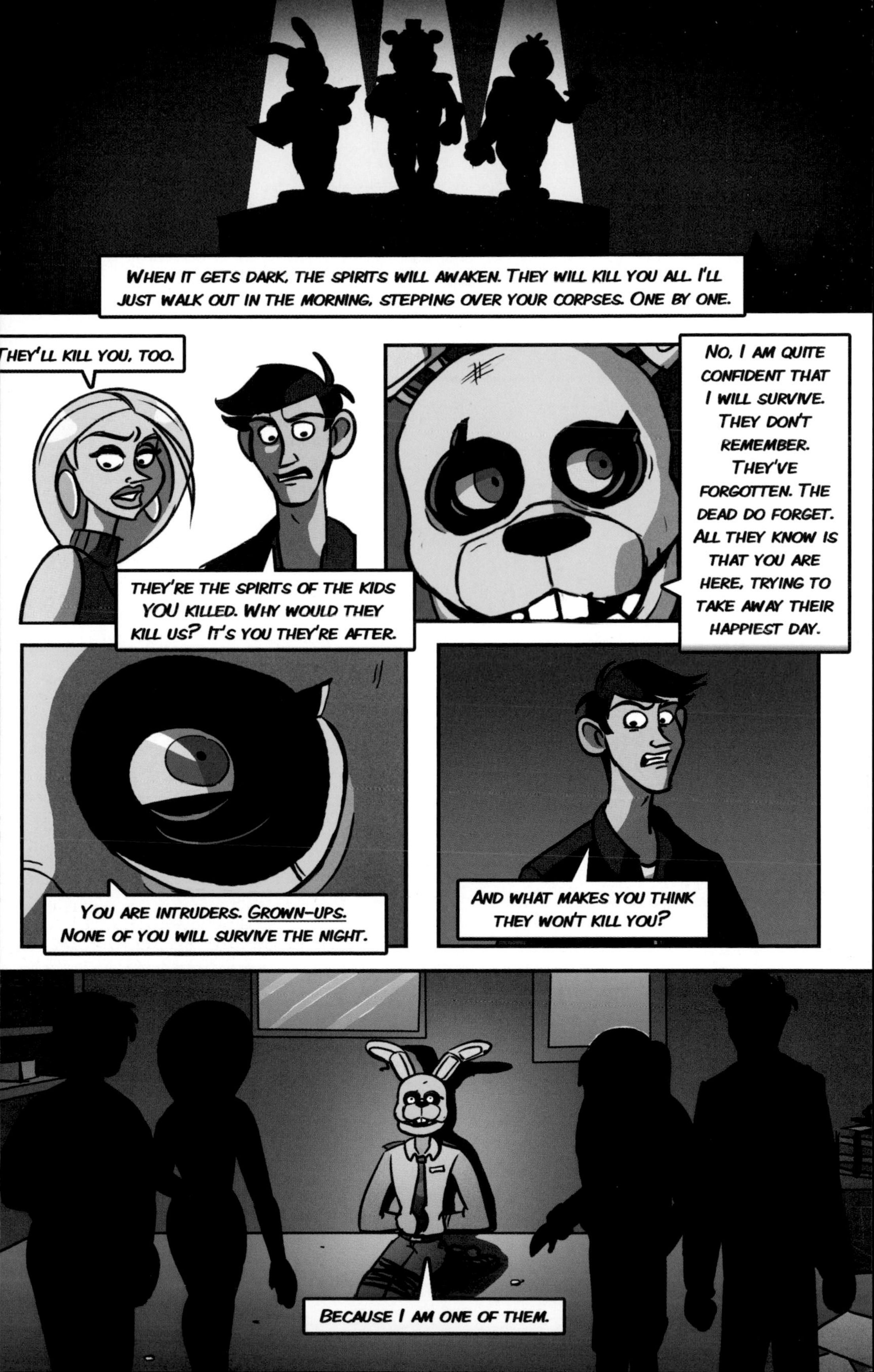

WHEN IT GETS DARK, THE SPIRITS WILL AWAKEN. THEY WILL KILL YOU ALL. I'LL JUST WALK OUT IN THE MORNING, STEPPING OVER YOUR CORPSES. ONE BY ONE.
THEY'LL KILL YOU, TOO.
THEY'RE THE SPIRITS OF THE KIDS YOU KILLED. WHY WOULD THEY KILL US? IT'S YOU THEY'RE AFTER.
NO, I AM QUITE CONFIDENT THAT I WILL SURVIVE. THEY DON'T REMEMBER. THEY'VE FORGOTTEN. THE DEAD DO FORGET. ALL THEY KNOW IS THAT YOU ARE HERE, TRYING TO TAKE AWAY THEIR HAPPIEST DAY.
YOU ARE INTRUDERS. GROWN-UPS. NONE OF YOU WILL SURVIVE THE NIGHT.
AND WHAT MAKES YOU THINK THEY WON'T KILL YOU?
BECAUSE I AM ONE OF THEM.

CHAPTER 12

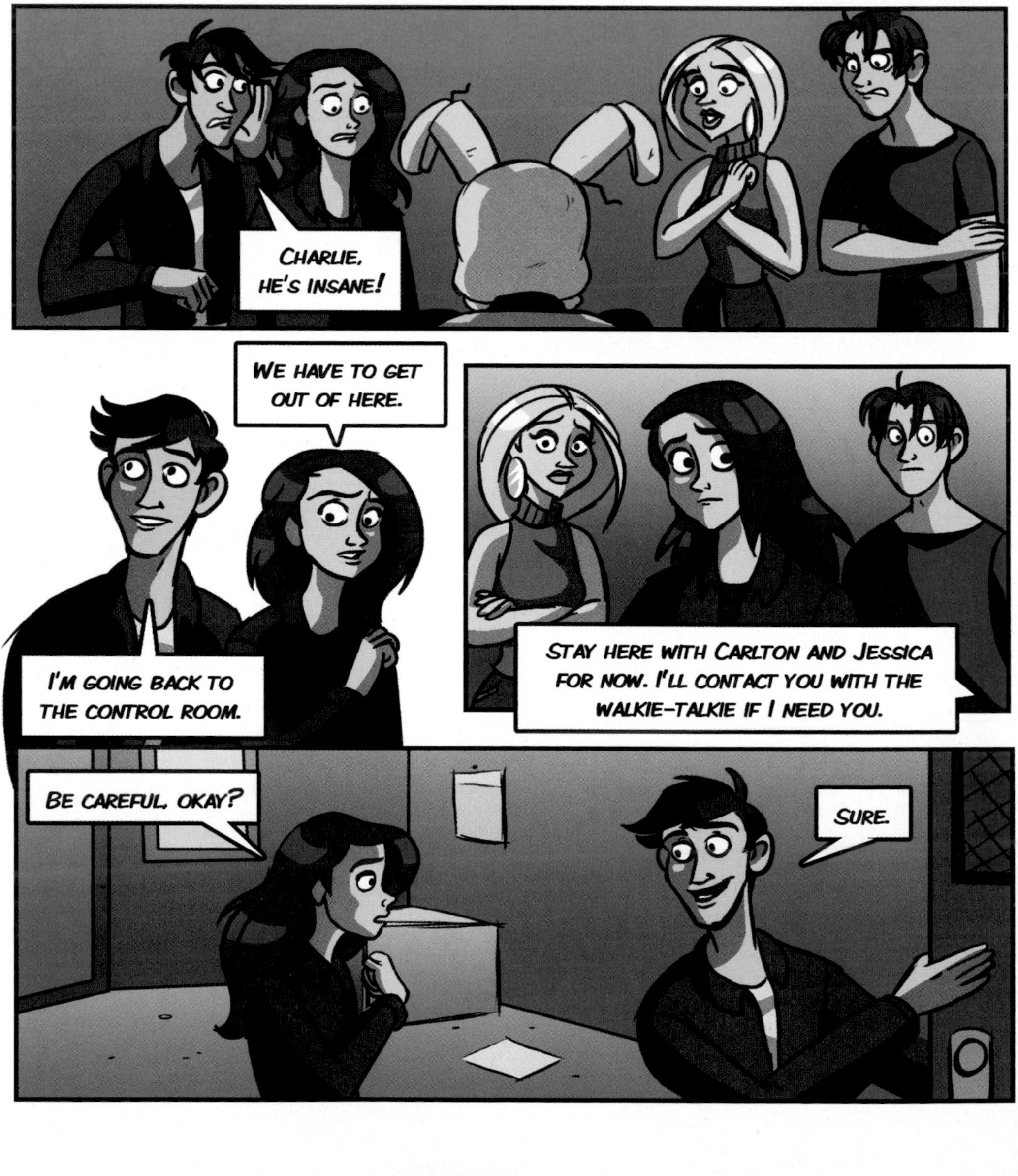
CHARLIE, HE'S INSANE!
WE HAVE TO GET OUT OF HERE.
I'M GOING BACK TO THE CONTROL ROOM.
STAY HERE WITH CARLTON AND JESSICA FOR NOW. I'LL CONTACT YOU WITH THE WALKIE-TALKIE IF I NEED YOU.
BE CAREFUL, OKAY?
SURE.

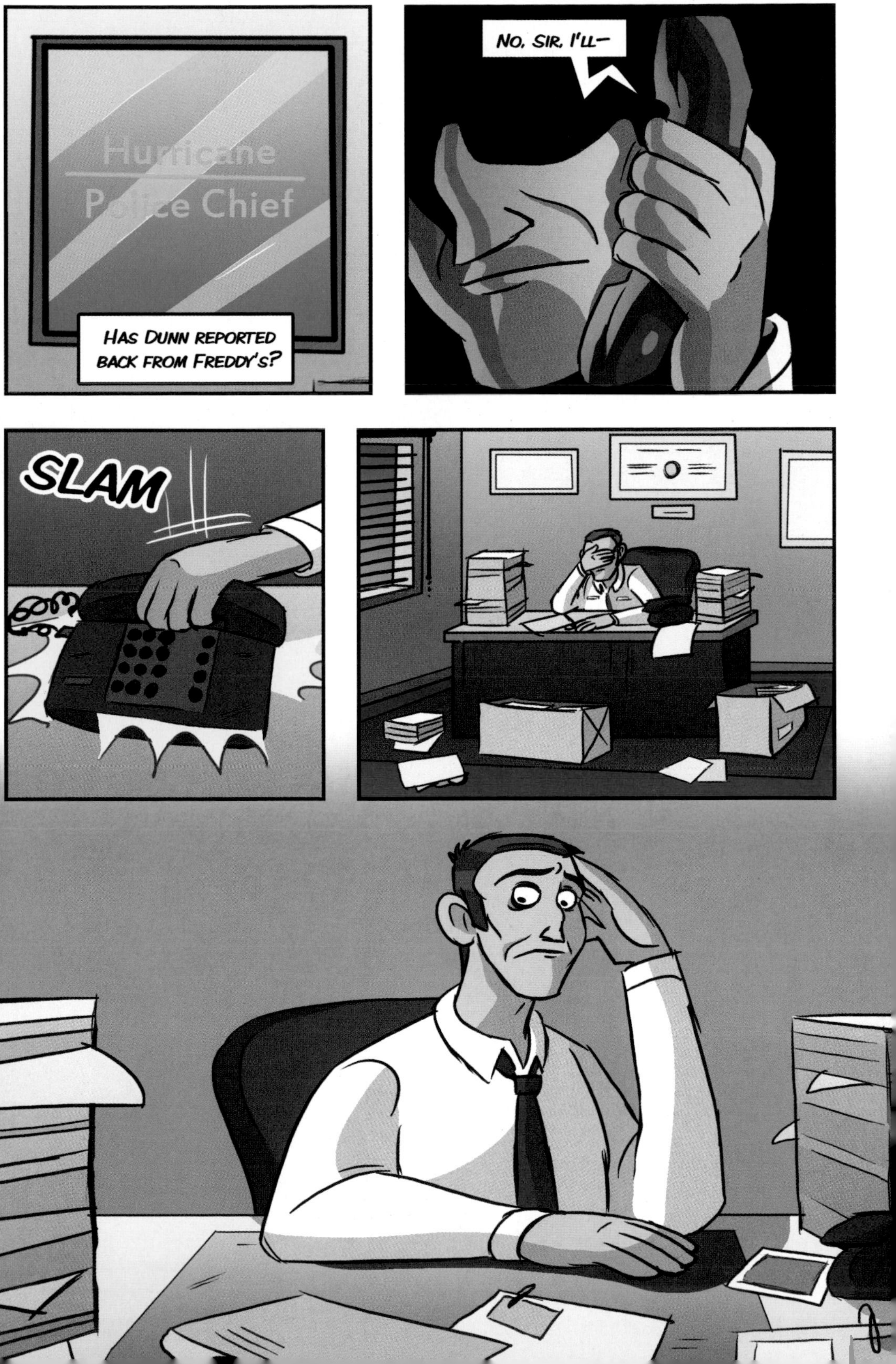
Hurricane
Police Chief
HAS DUNN REPORTED BACK FROM FREDDY'S?
NO, SIR, I'LL—
SLAM

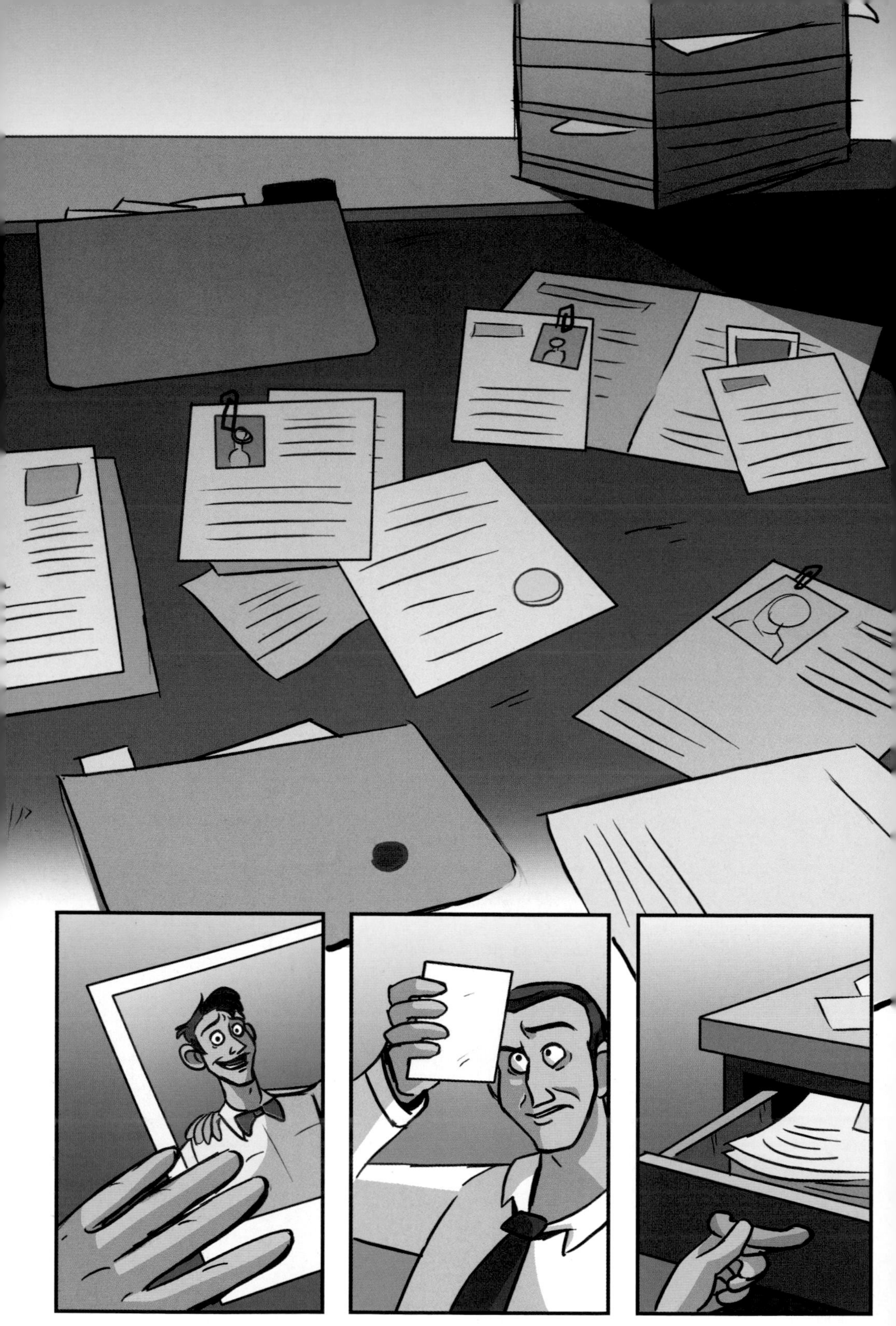

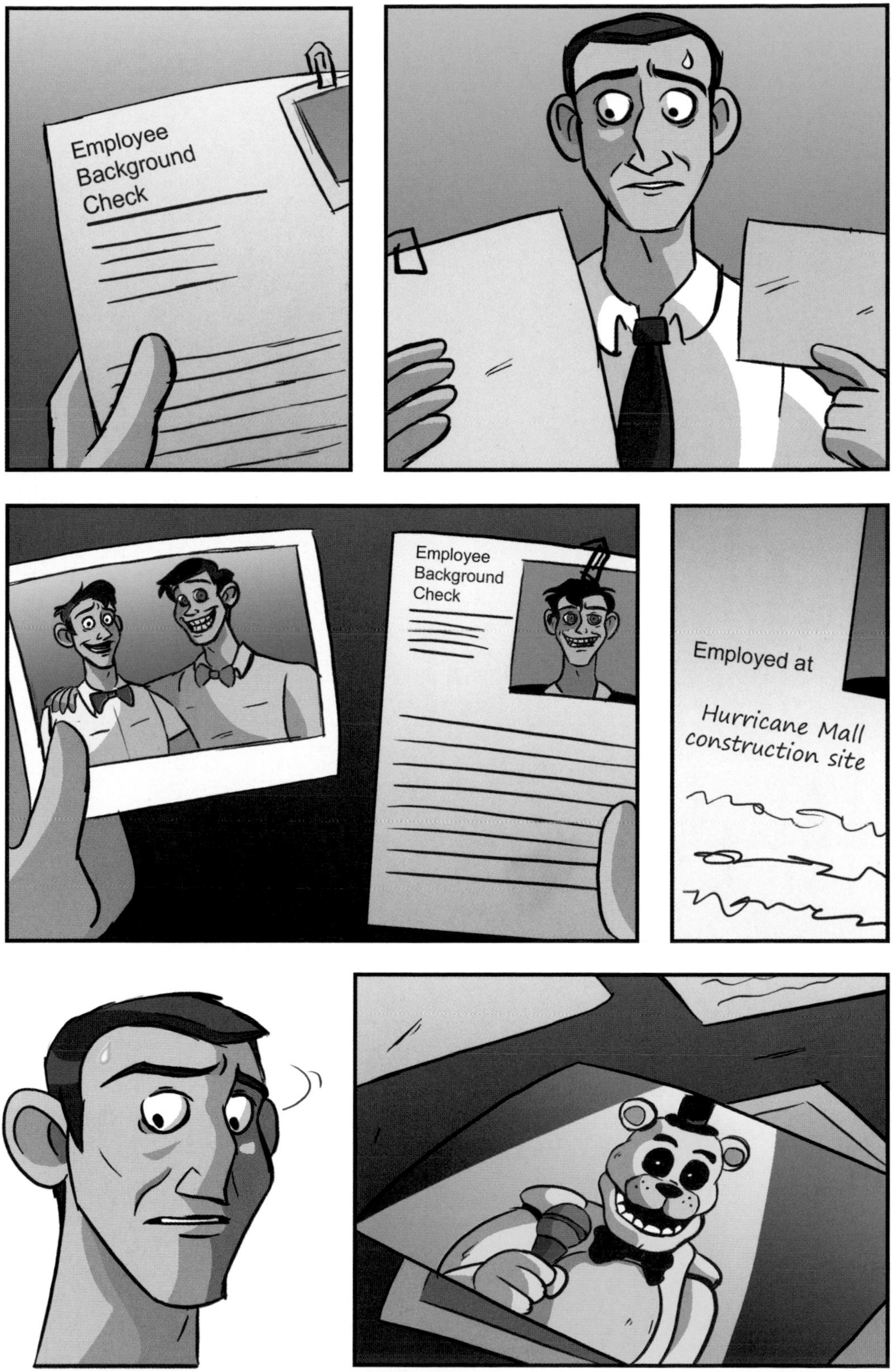
Employee
Background
Check
Employee
Background
Check
Employed at
Hurricane Mall
construction site

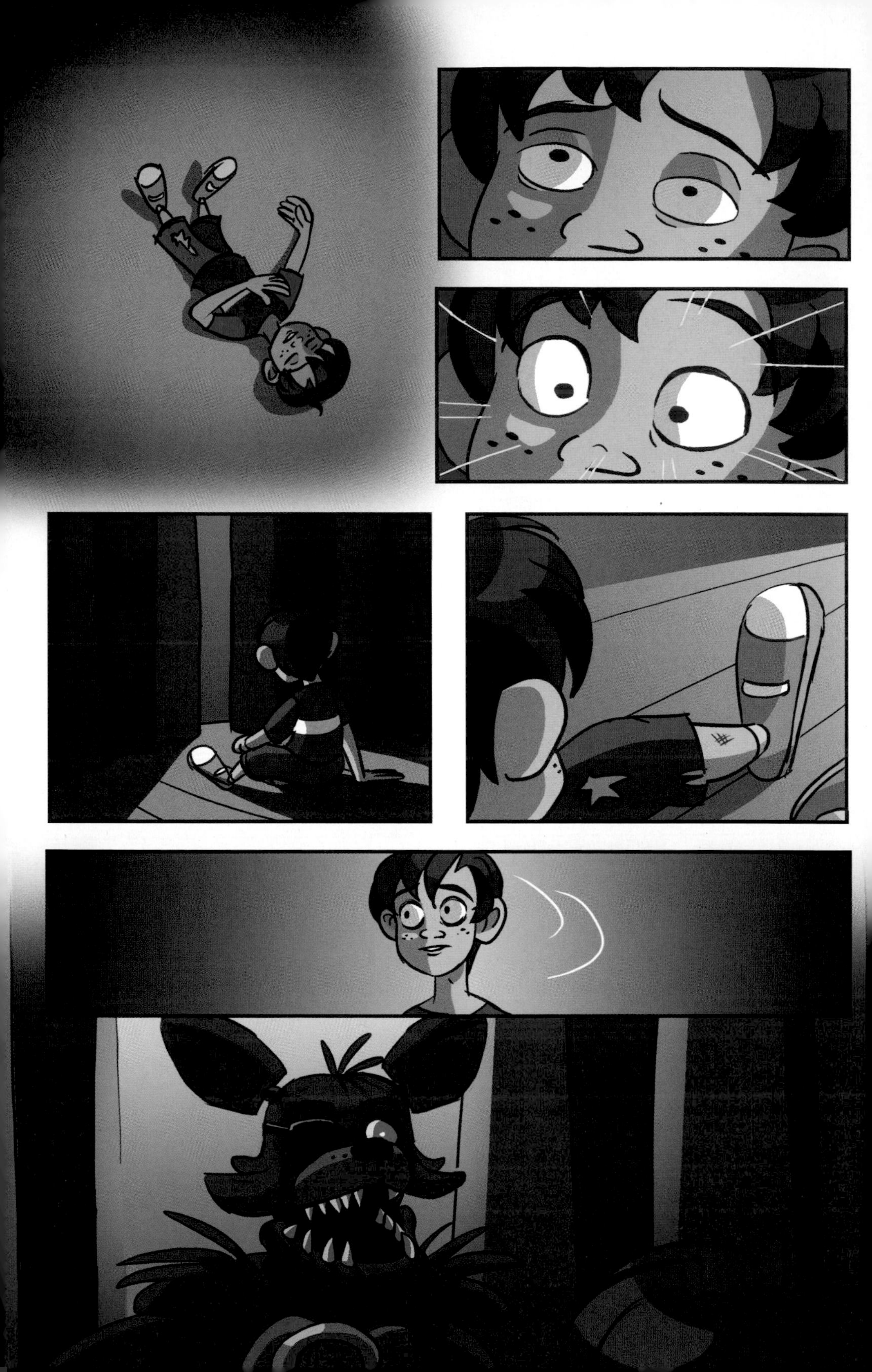

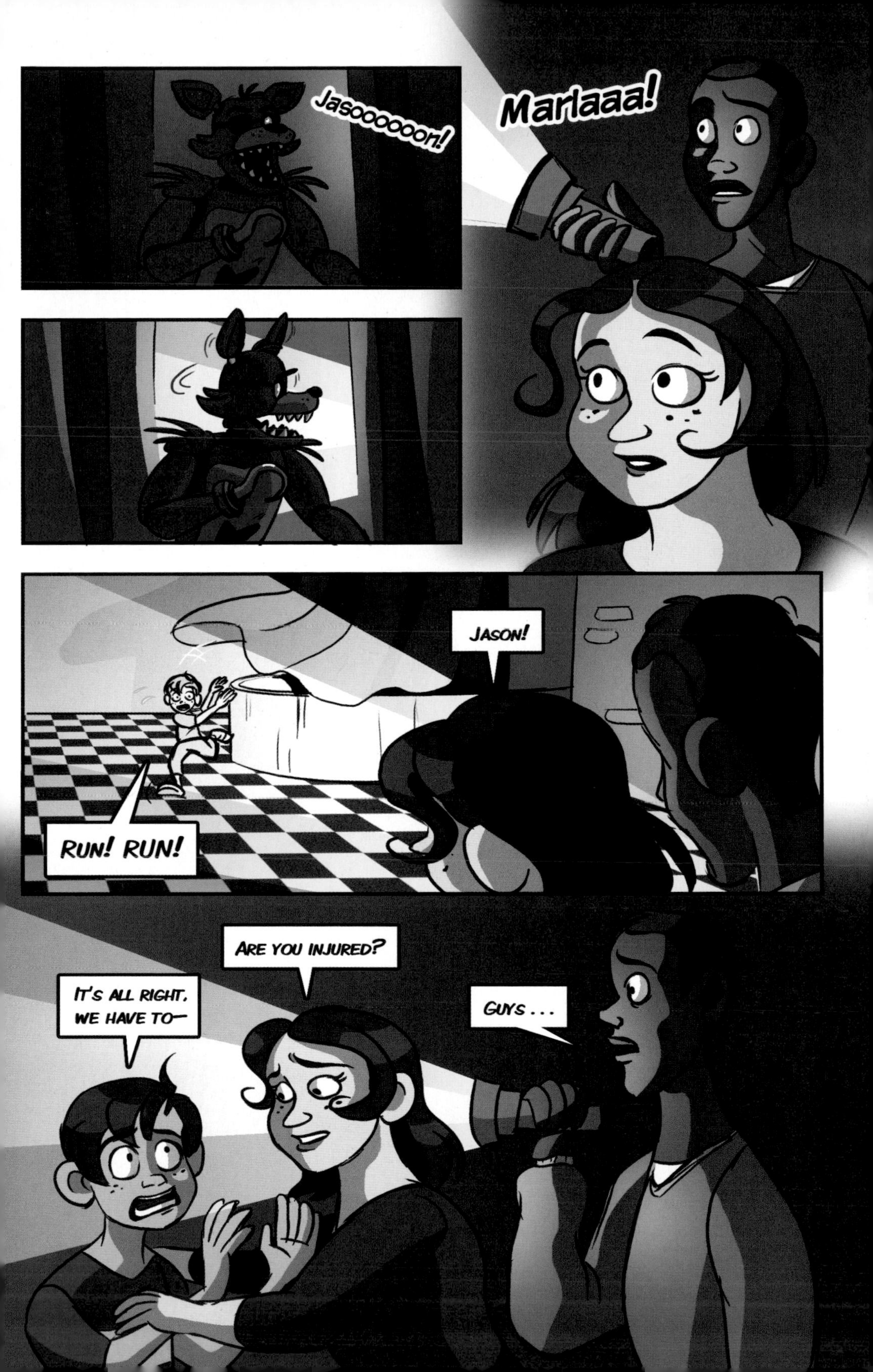
Jasoooooon!
Marlaaa!
JASON!
RUN! RUN!
ARE YOU INJURED?
IT'S ALL RIGHT, WE HAVE TO—
GUYS . . .

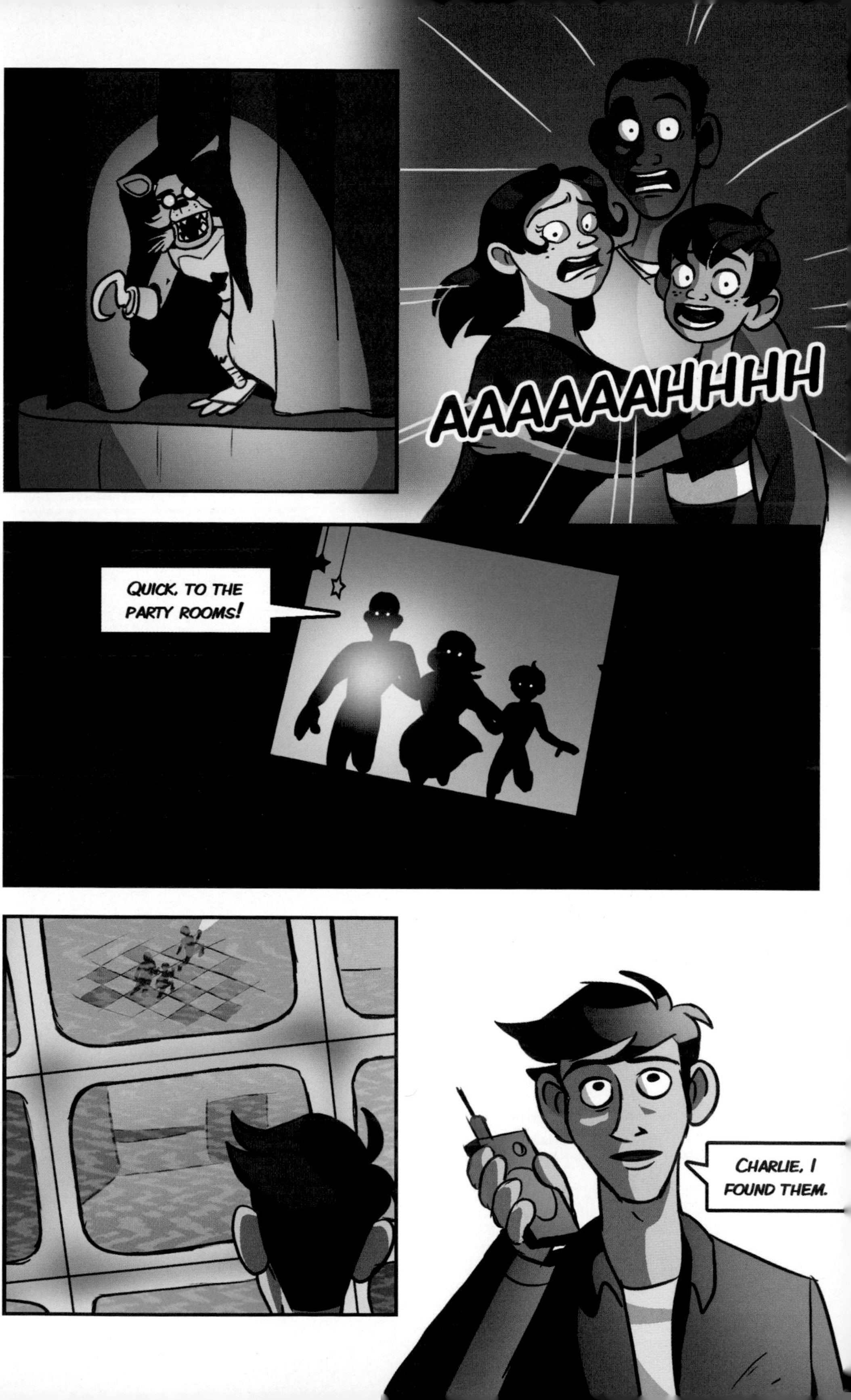
AAAAAAHHHH
QUICK, TO THE PARTY ROOMS!
CHARLIE, I FOUND THEM.

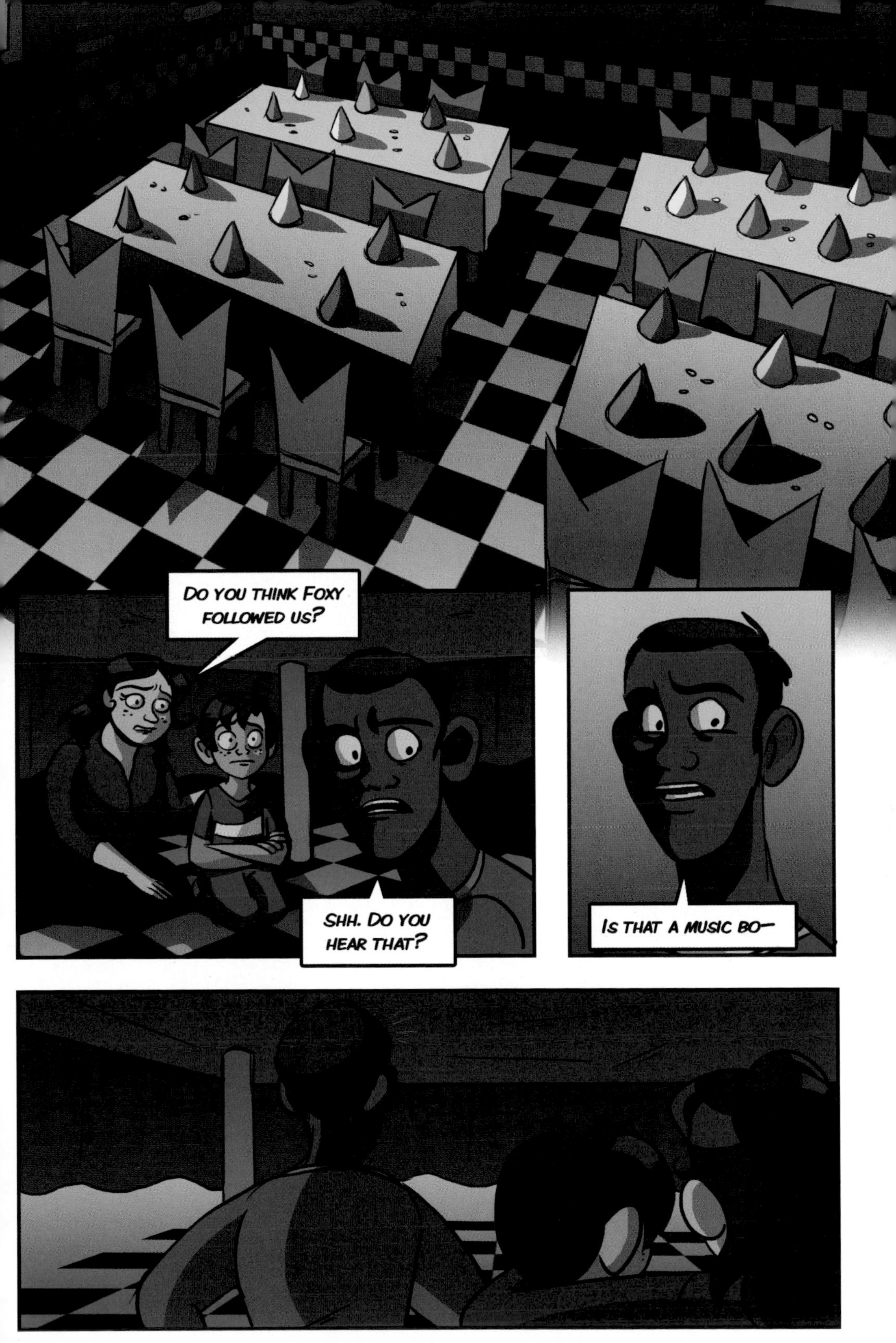
DO YOU THINK FOXY FOLLOWED US?
SHH. DO YOU HEAR THAT?
IS THAT A MUSIC BO—

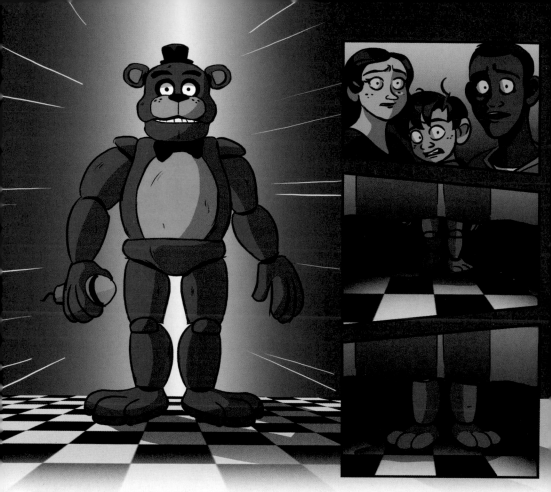

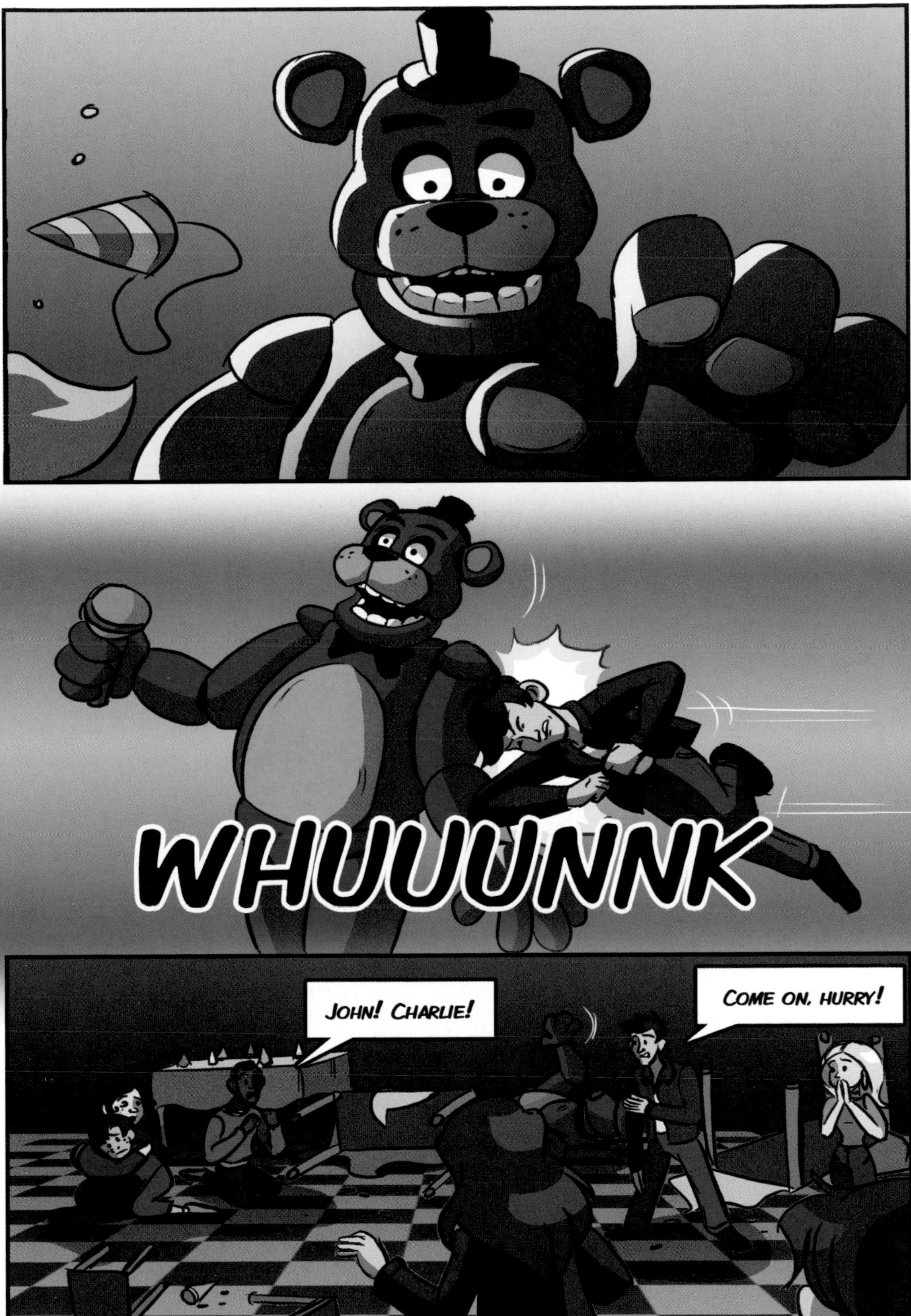
WHUUUNNK
JOHN! CHARLIE!
COME ON, HURRY!

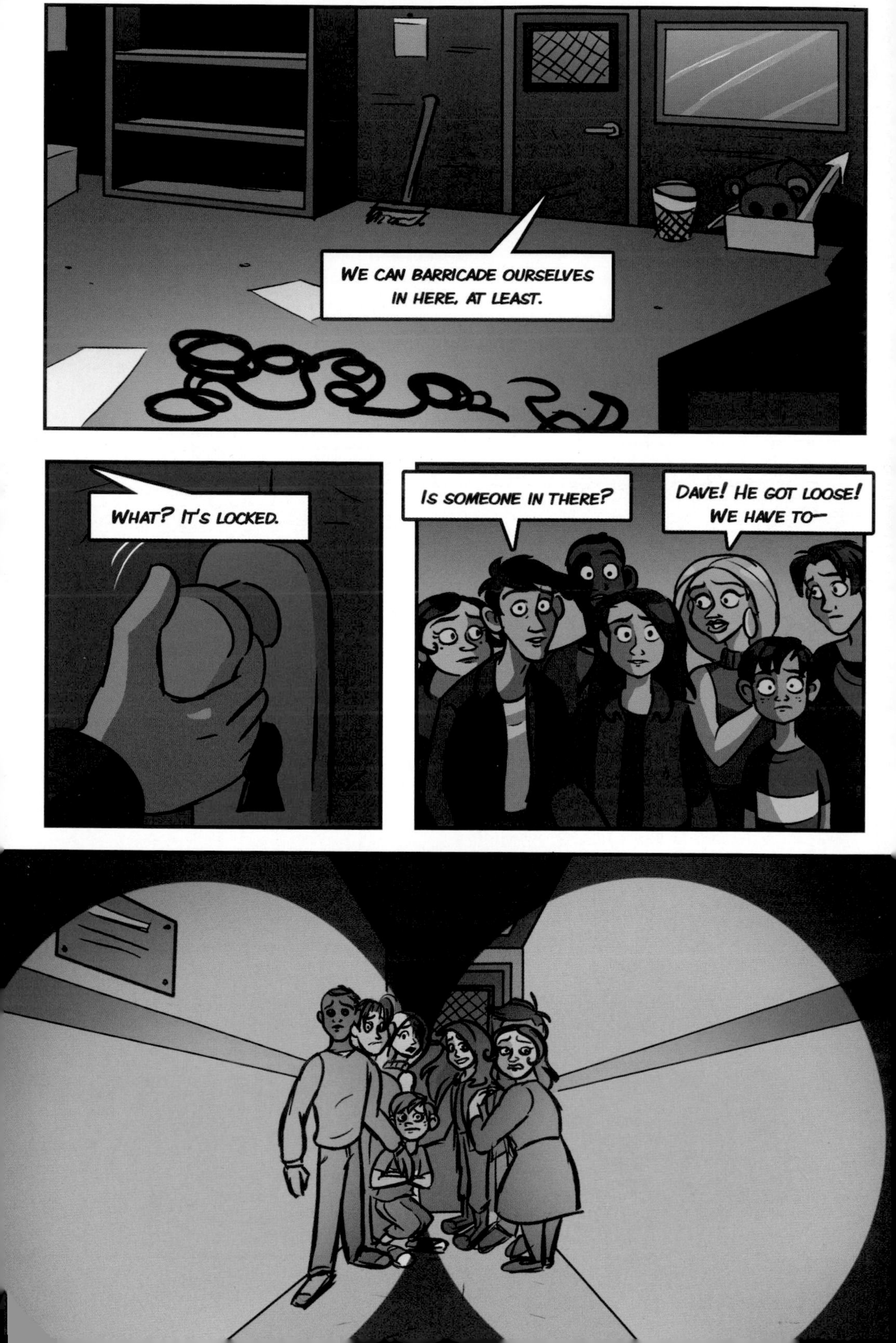
WE CAN BARRICADE OURSELVES IN HERE, AT LEAST.
WHAT? IT'S LOCKED.
IS SOMEONE IN THERE?
DAVE! HE GOT LOOSE! WE HAVE TO—

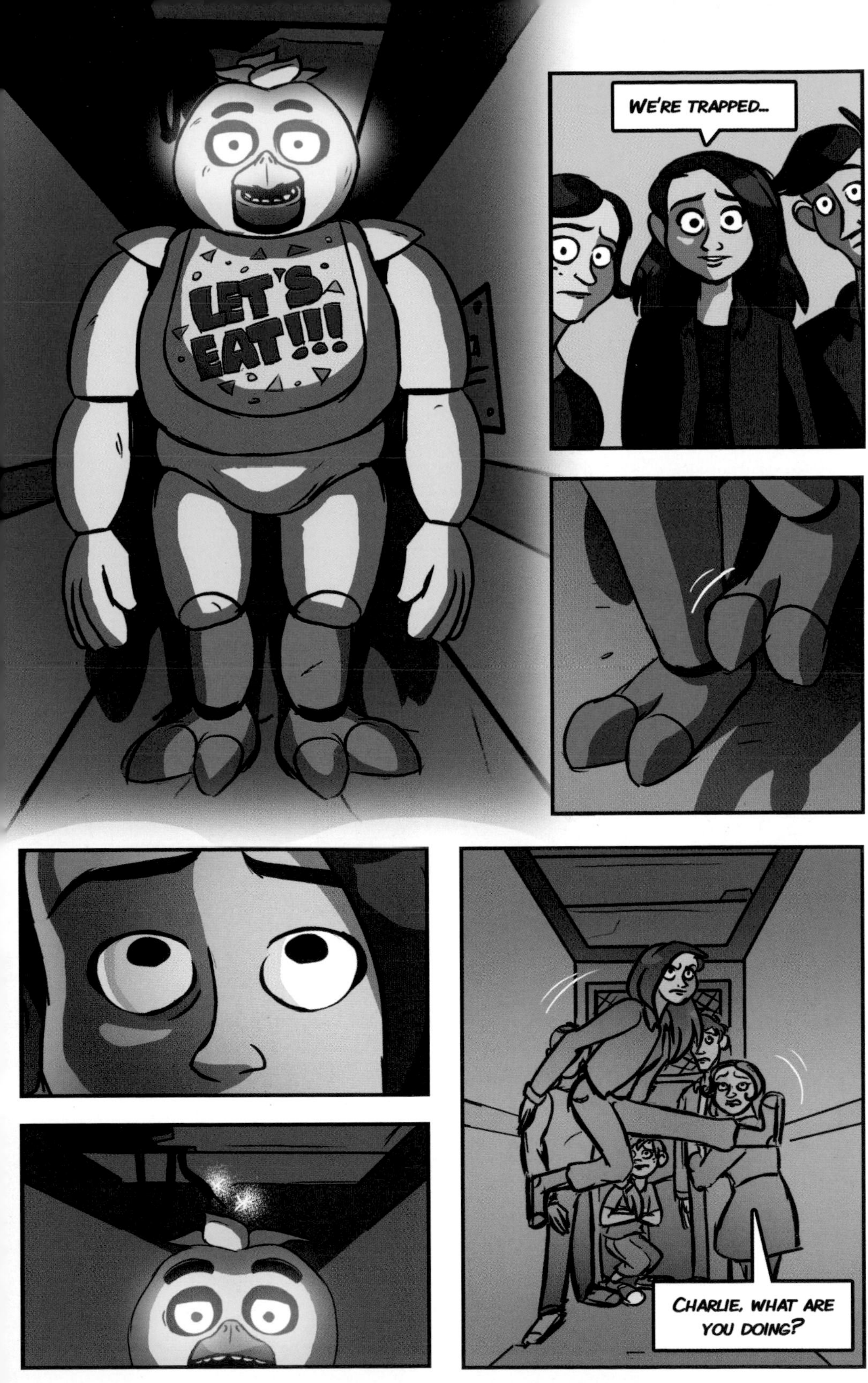
LET'S EAT!!!
WE'RE TRAPPED...
CHARLIE, WHAT ARE YOU DOING?

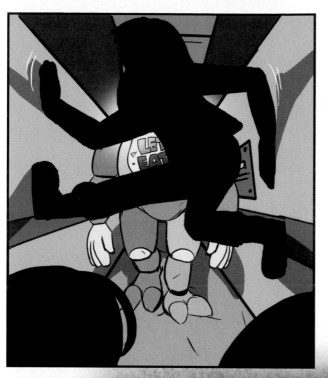

BRRRZZZZRRRRZZZ

TSCHUKK

AAAAAAAAHHHHHHHHHH

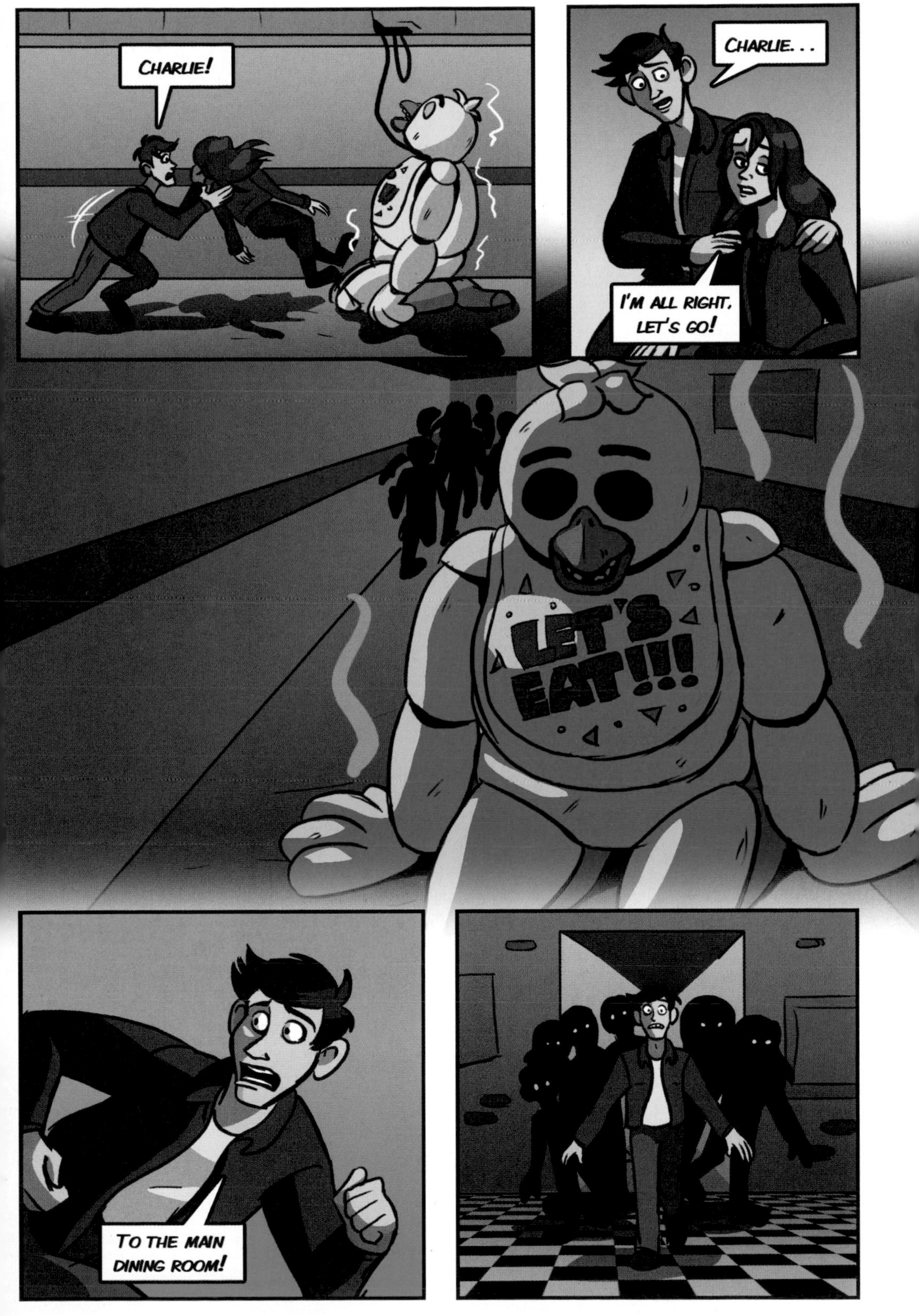
CHARLIE!
CHARLIE. . .
I'M ALL RIGHT. LET'S GO!
LET'S EAT!!!
TO THE MAIN DINING ROOM!

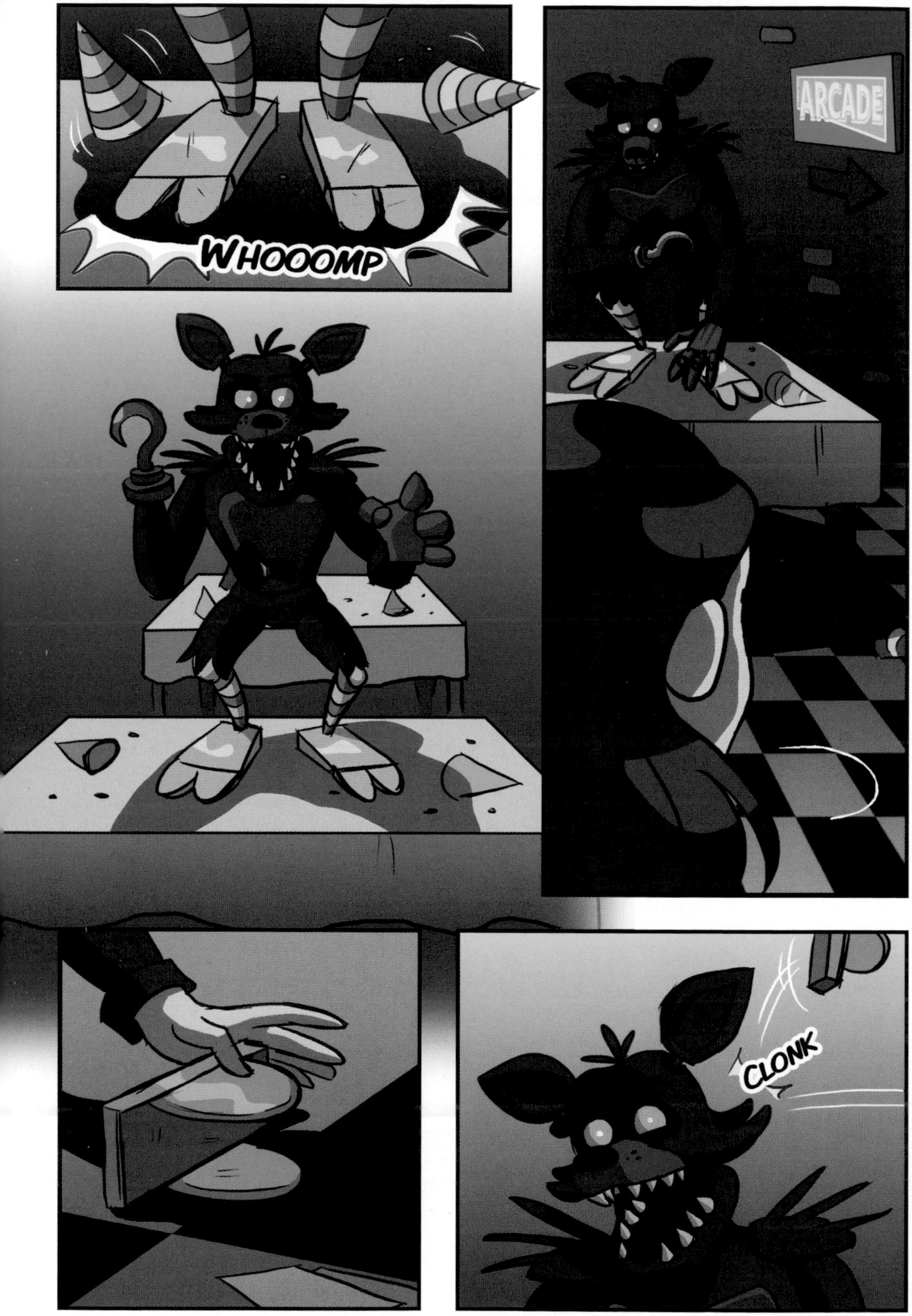
WHOOOMP
ARCADE
CLONK

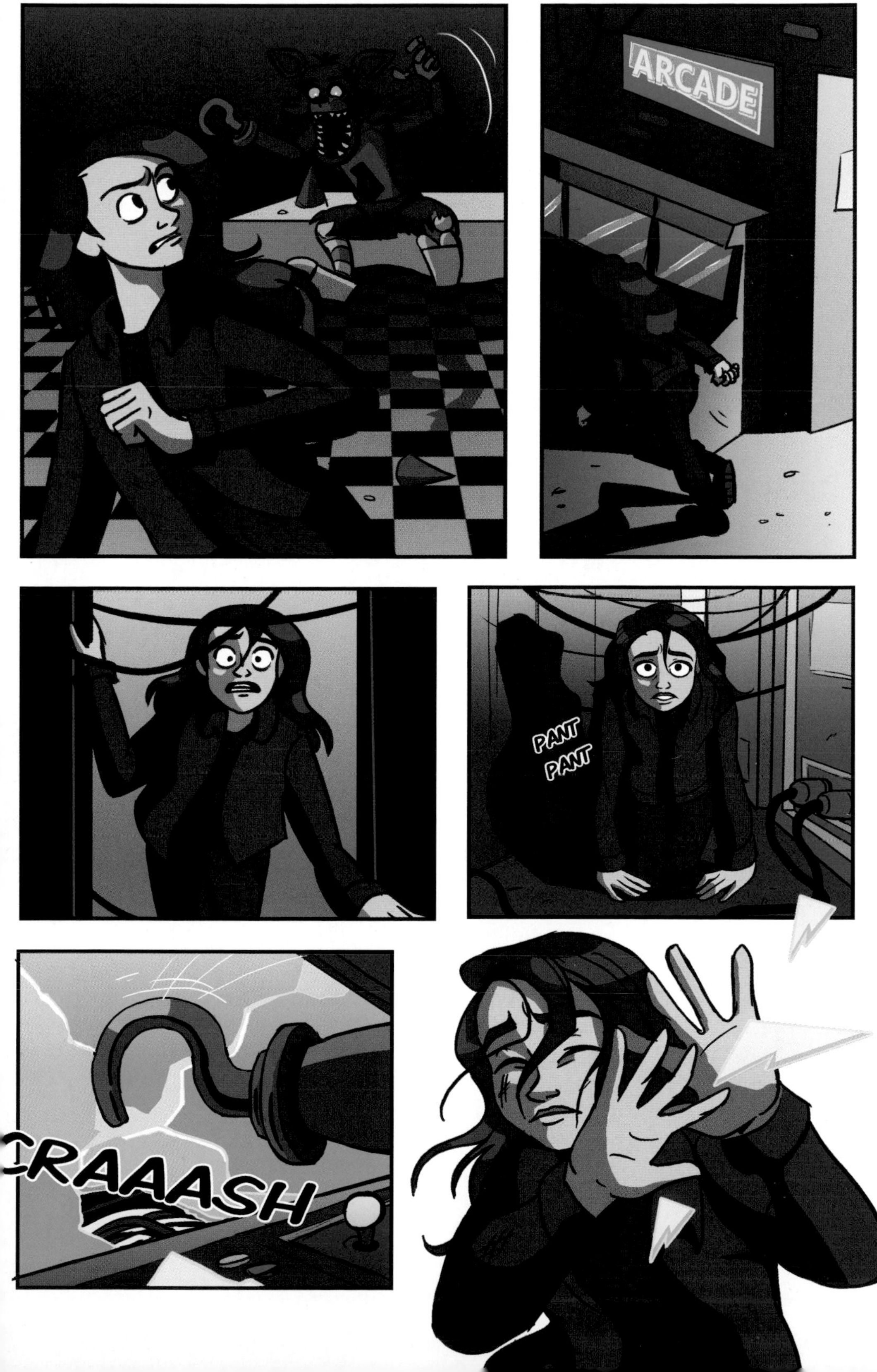
ARCADE
PANT
PANT
CRAAASH

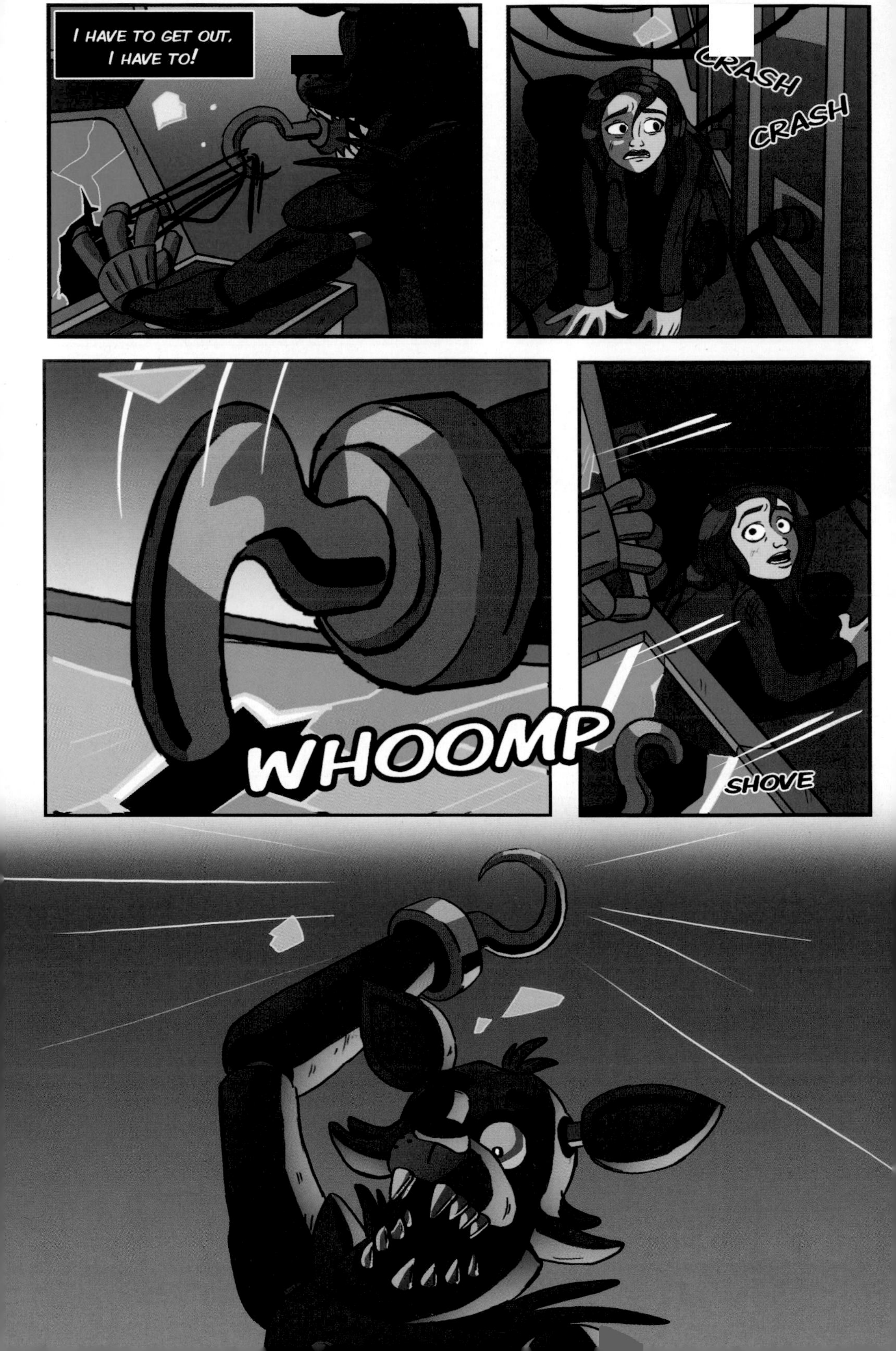
I HAVE TO GET OUT,
I HAVE TO!
CRASH
CRASH
WHOOMP
SHOVE

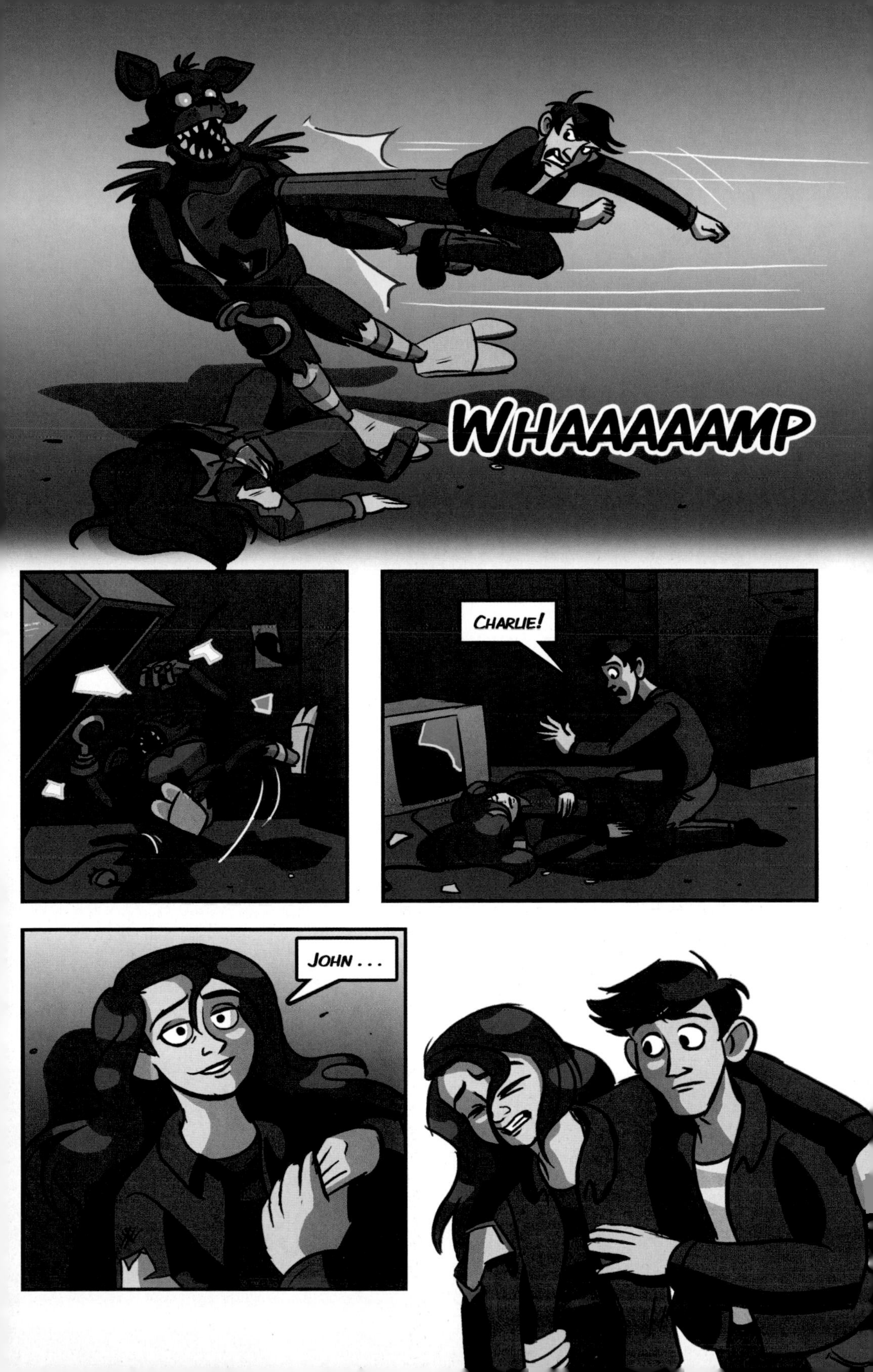
WHAAAAAAMP
CHARLIE!
JOHN . . .

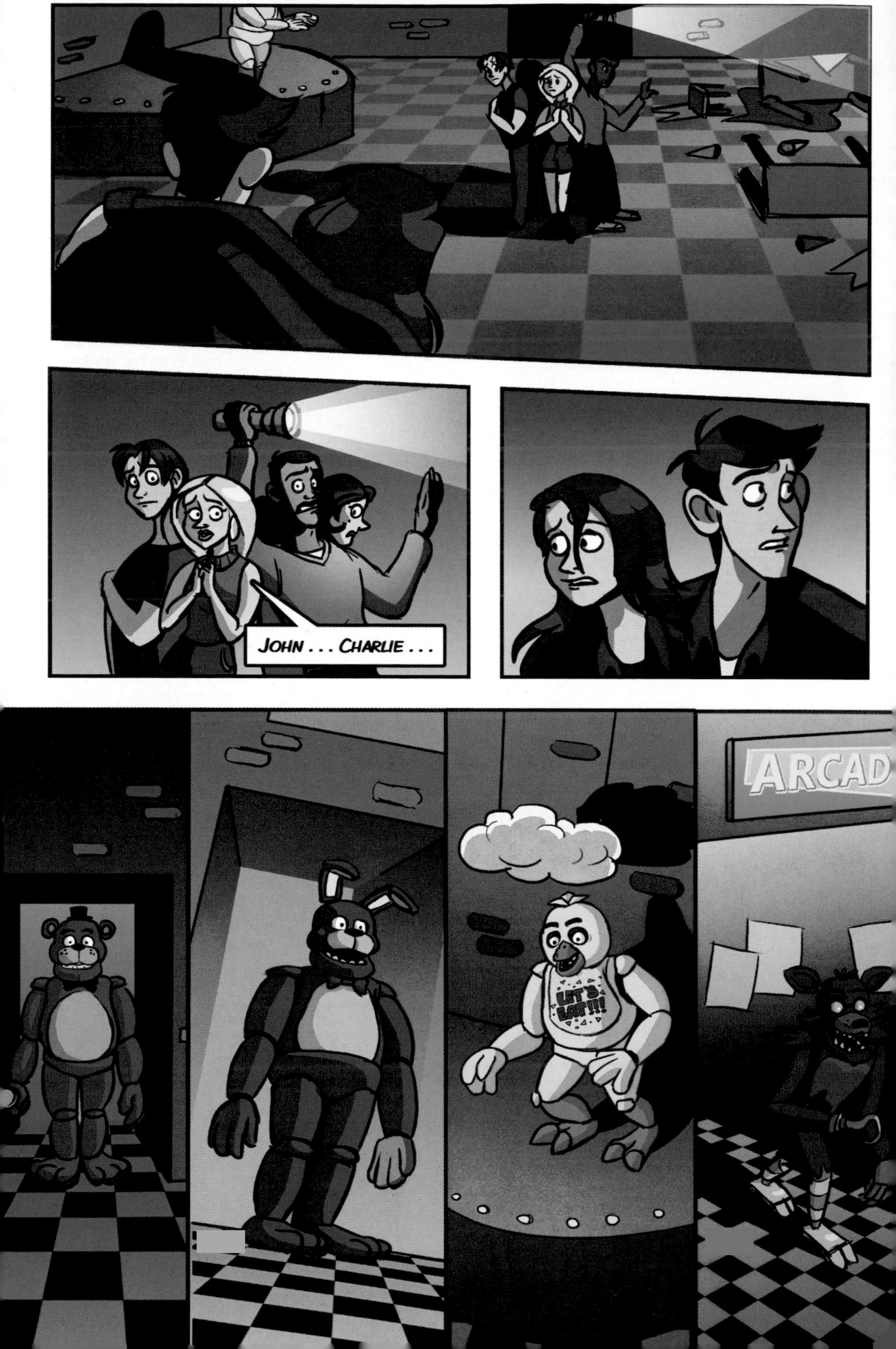
JOHN . . . CHARLIE . . .
LET'S EAT!!!
ARCAD

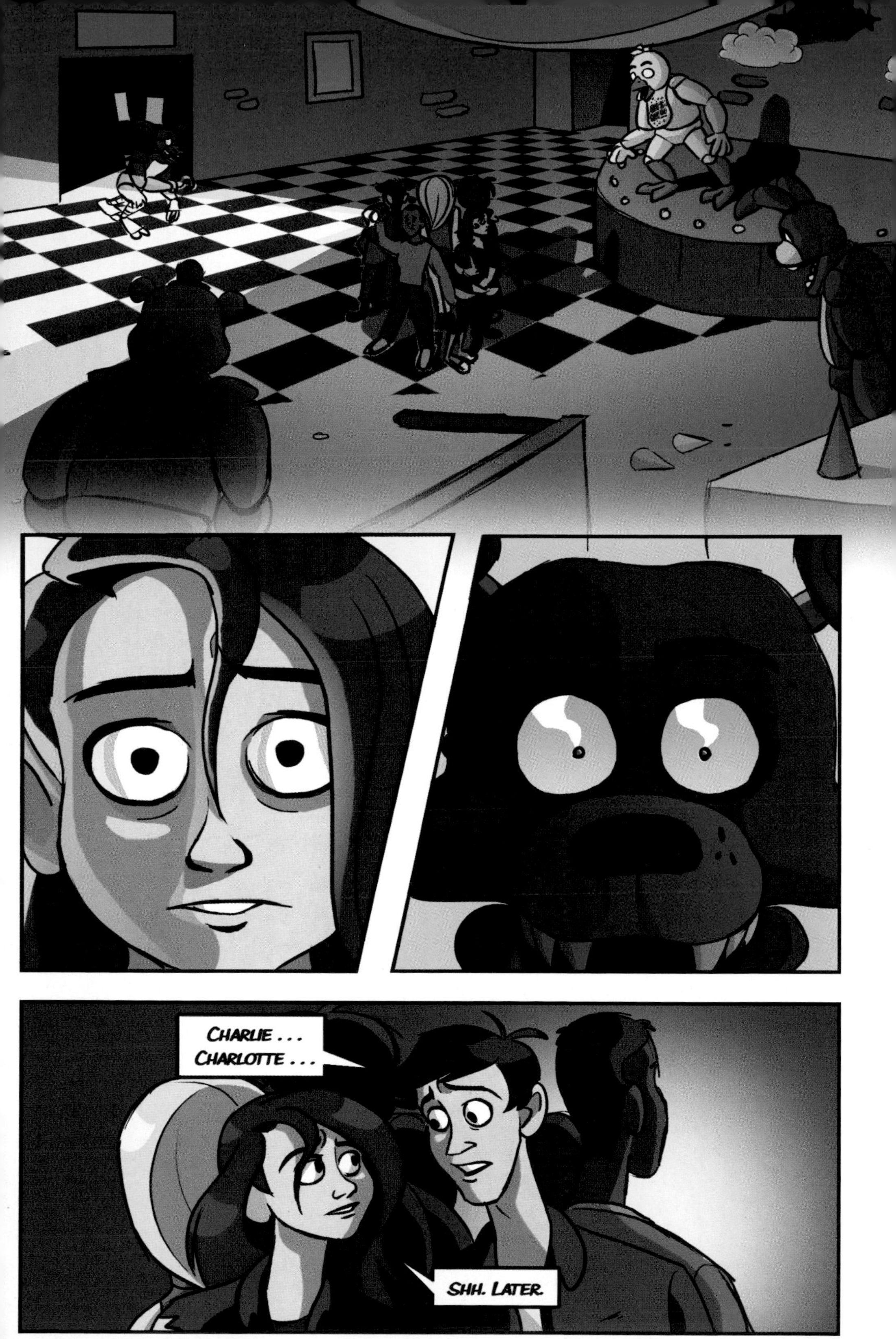
CHARLIE . . .
CHARLOTTE . . .
SHH. LATER.

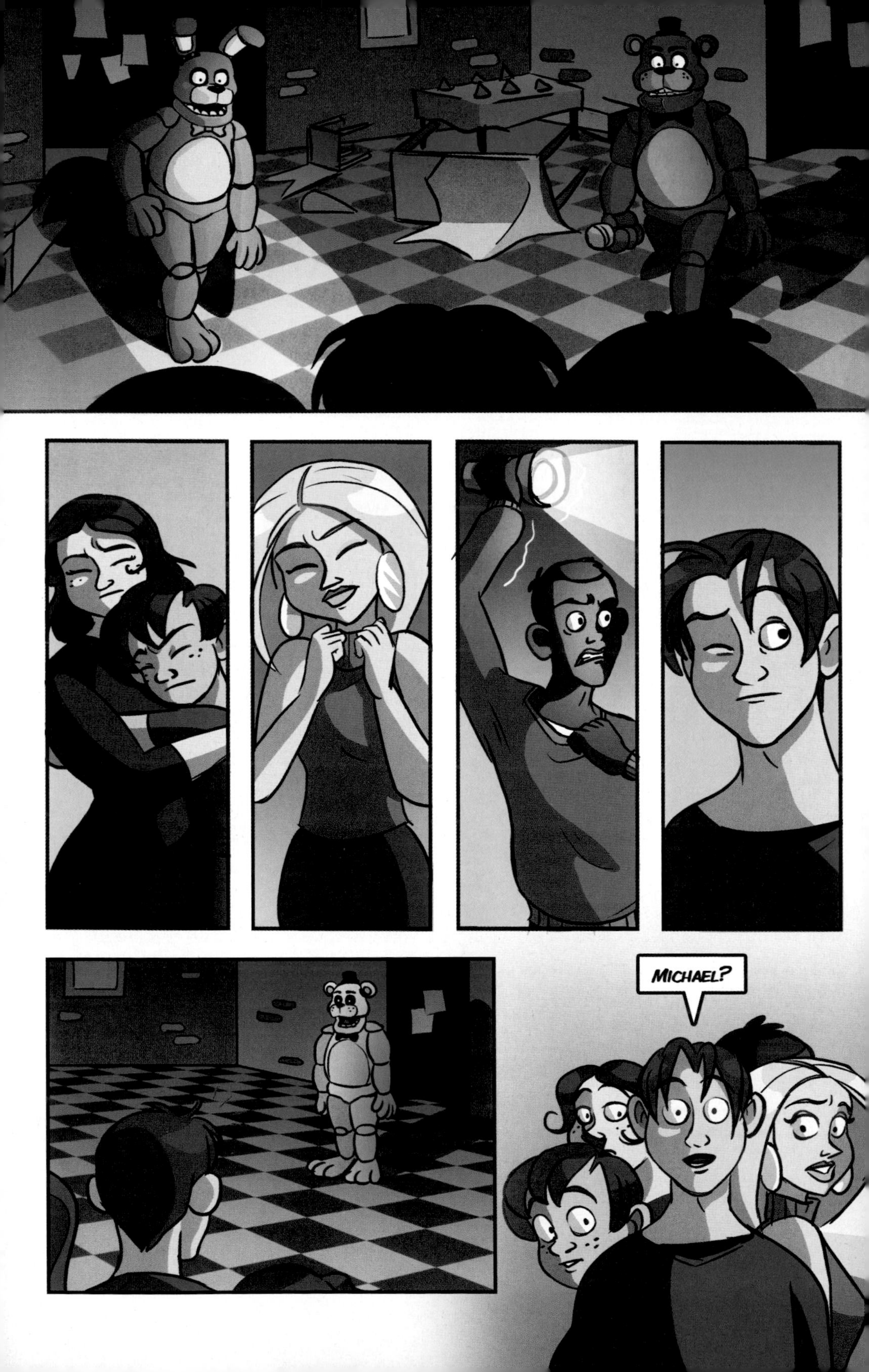
MICHAEL?

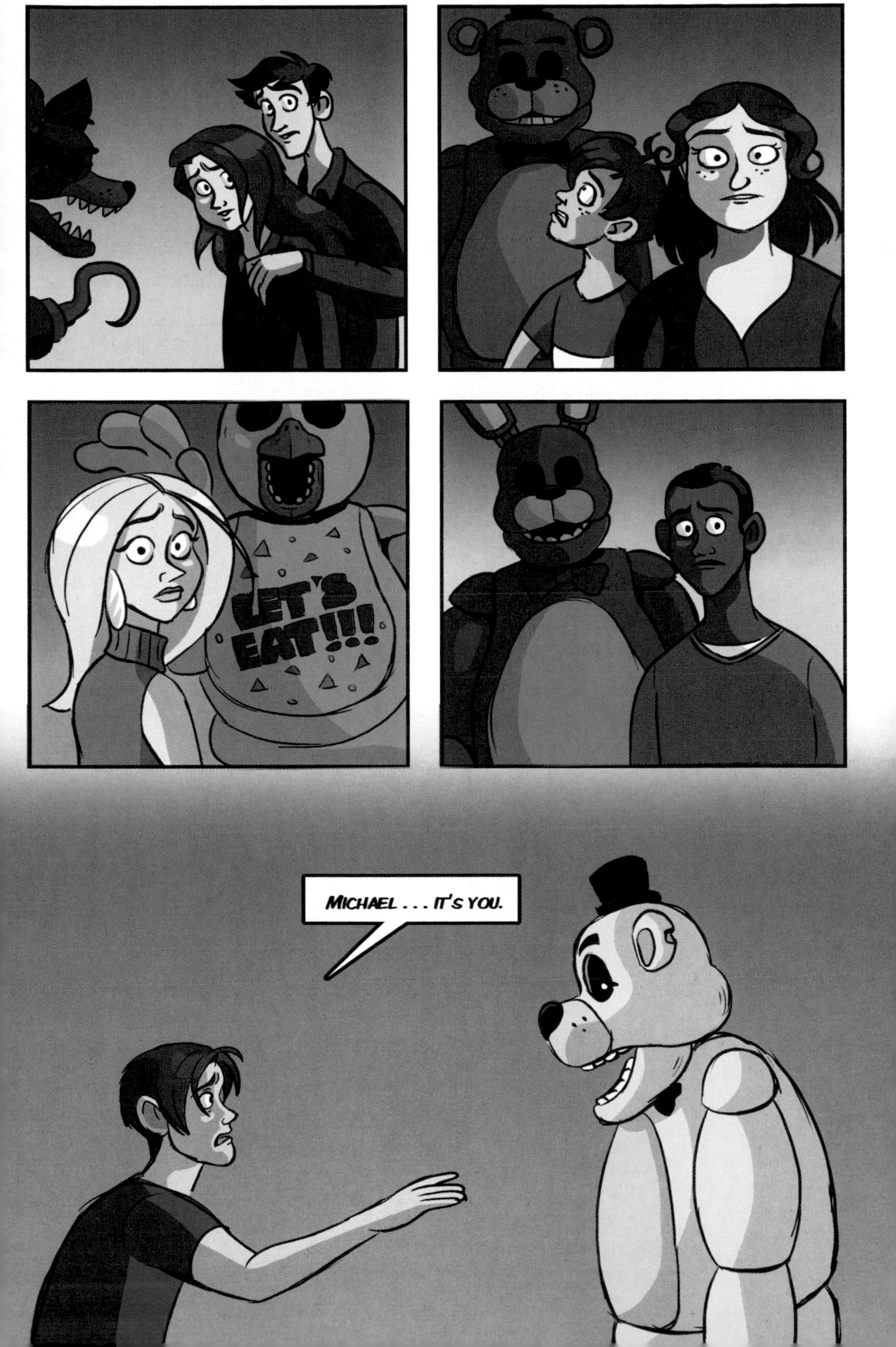
LET'S EAT!!!
MICHAEL . . . IT'S YOU.

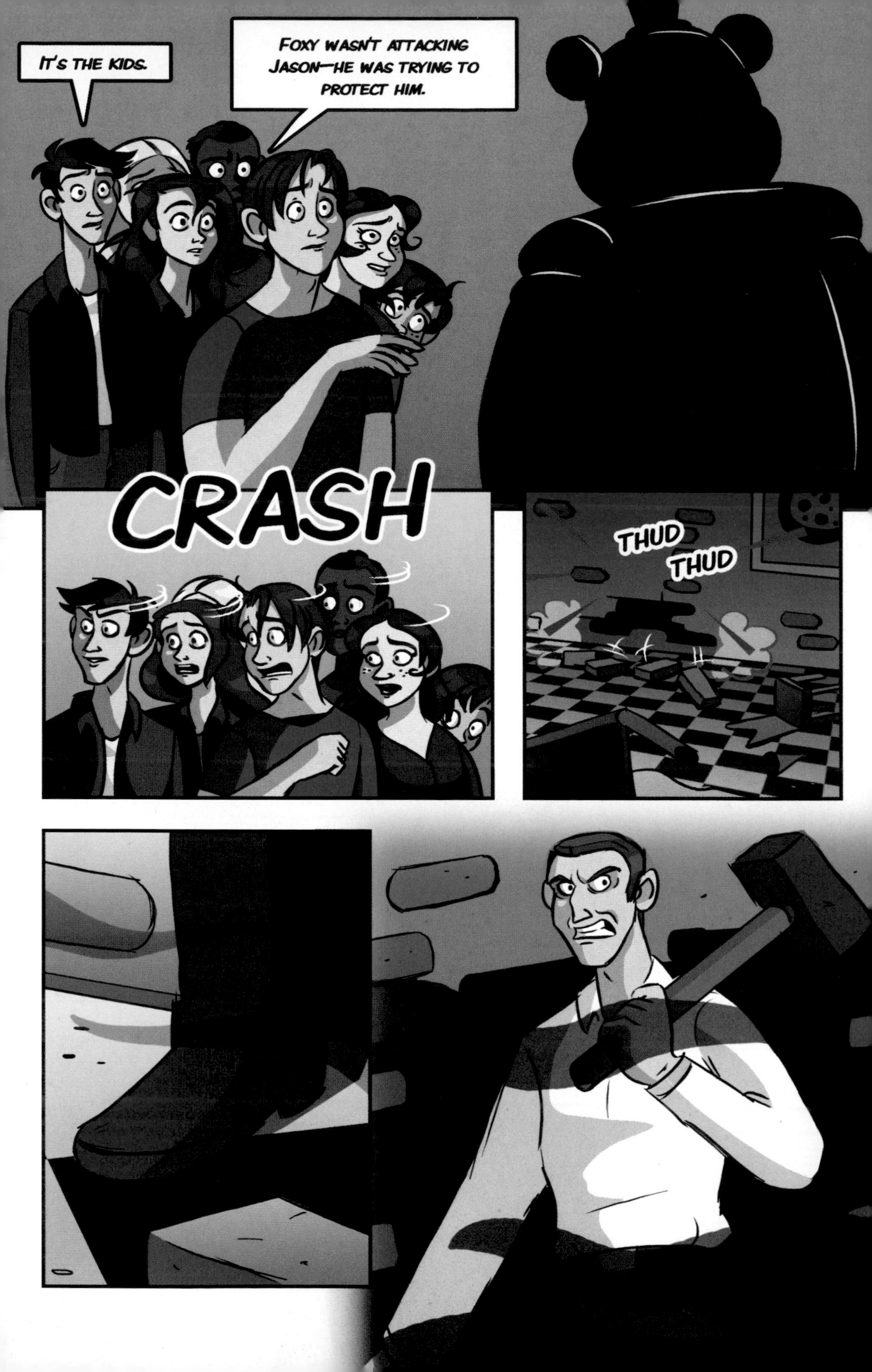
IT'S THE KIDS.
FOXY WASN'T ATTACKING JASON—HE WAS TRYING TO PROTECT HIM.
CRASH
THUD
THUD

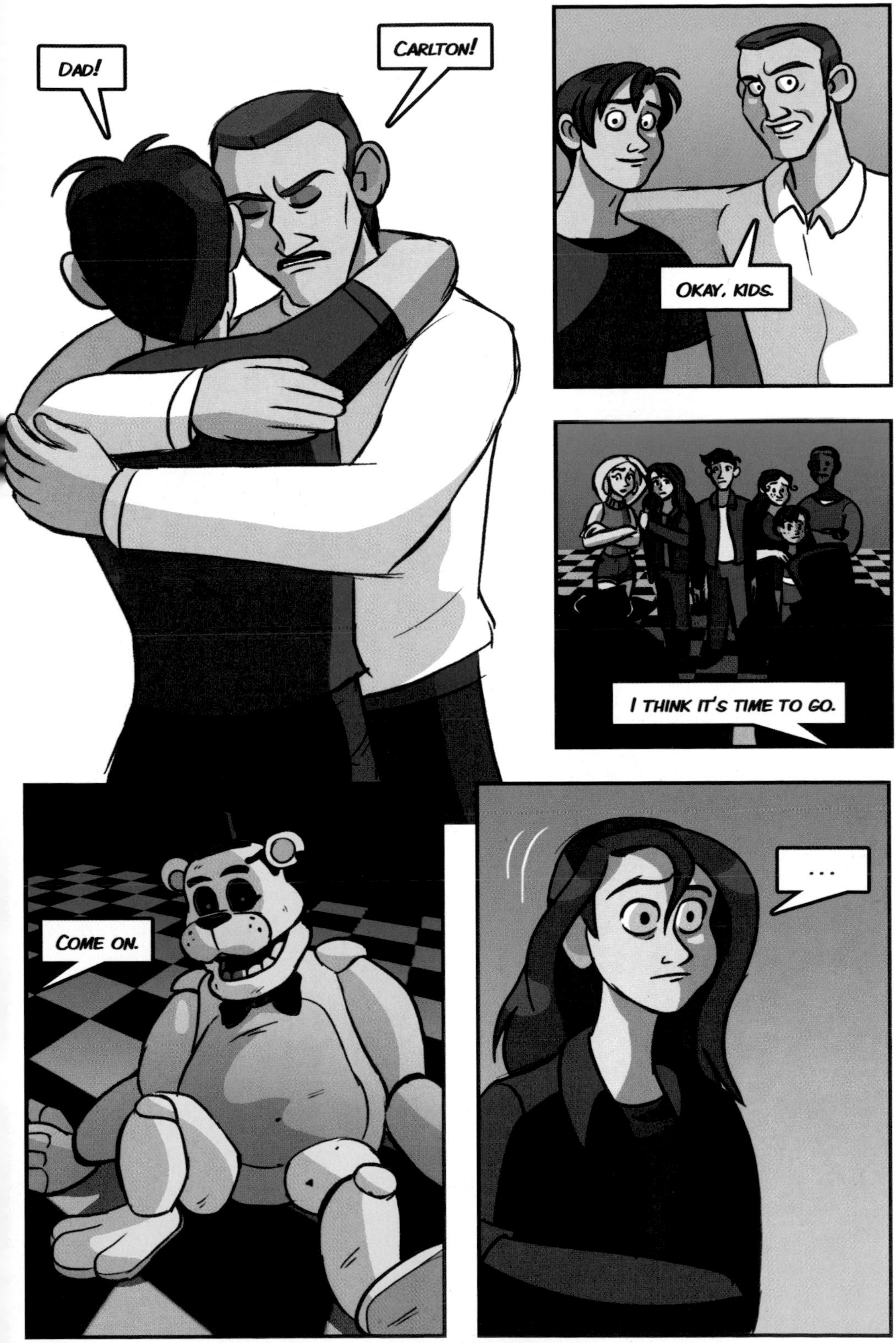
DAD!
CARLTON!
OKAY, KIDS.
I THINK IT'S TIME TO GO.
COME ON.
...

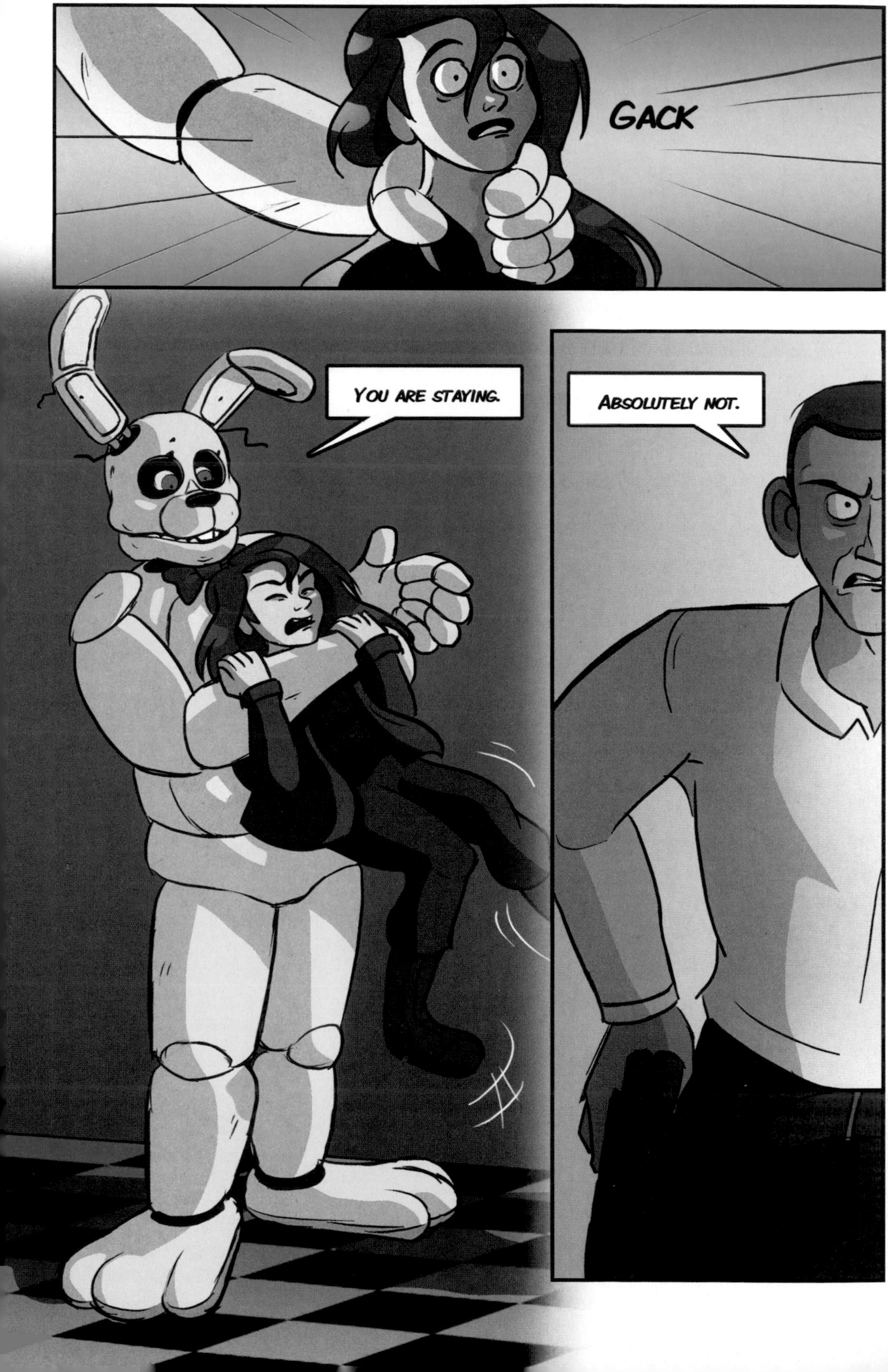
GACK
YOU ARE STAYING.
ABSOLUTELY NOT.

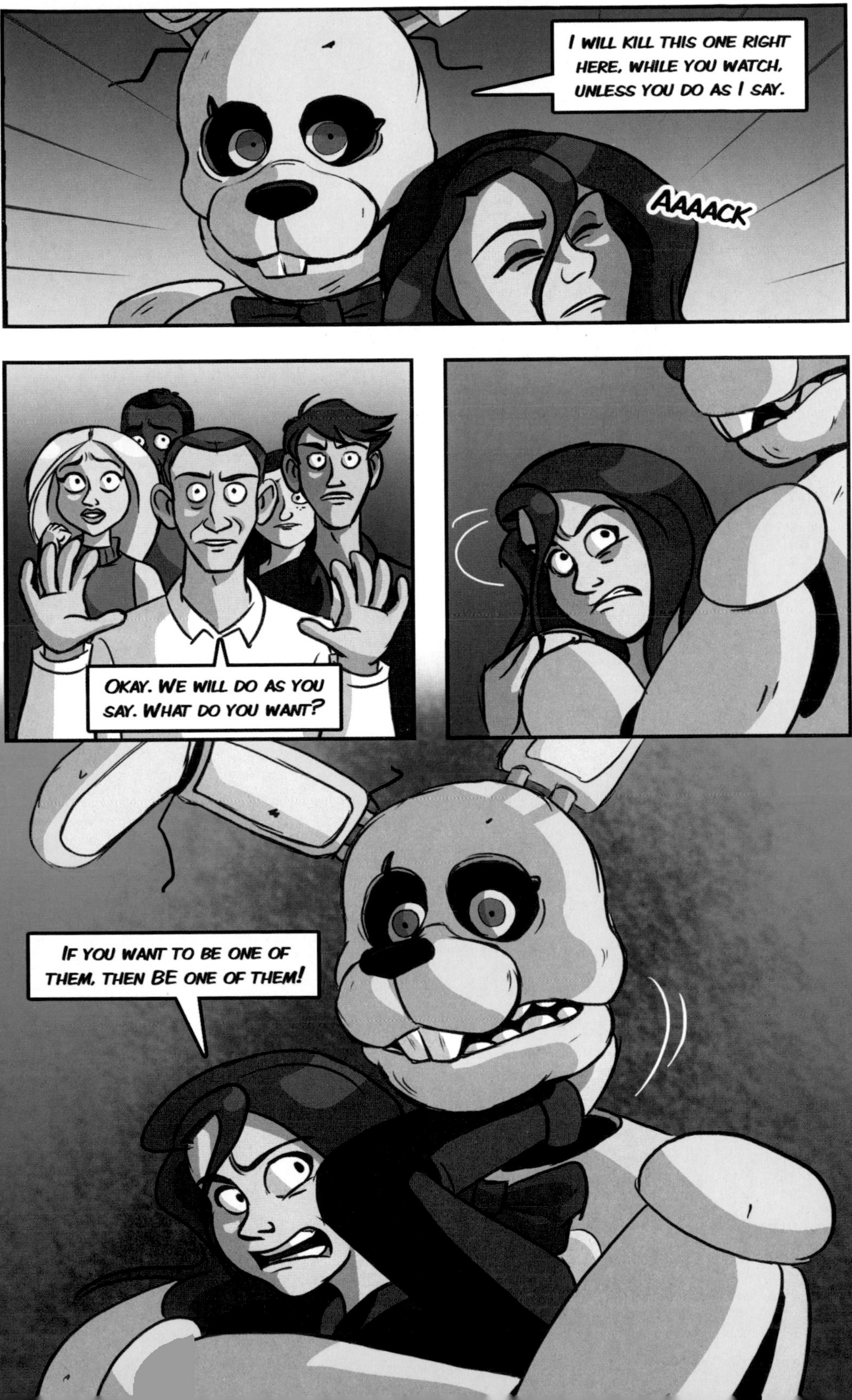

I WILL KILL THIS ONE RIGHT HERE, WHILE YOU WATCH, UNLESS YOU DO AS I SAY.
AAAACK
OKAY. WE WILL DO AS YOU SAY. WHAT DO YOU WANT?
IF YOU WANT TO BE ONE OF THEM, THEN BE ONE OF THEM!

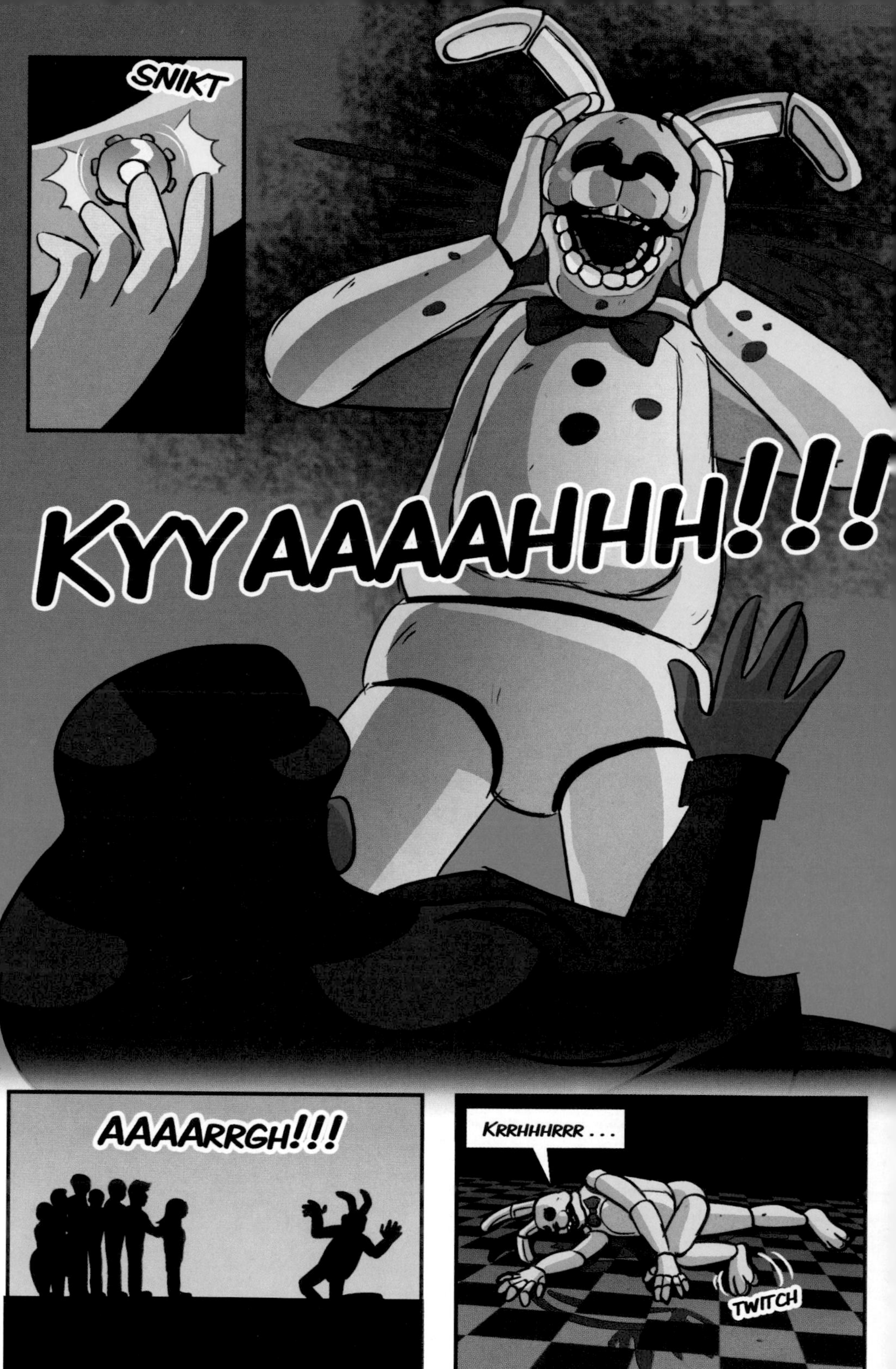
SNIKT
KYYAAAAAHHH!!!
AAAARRGH!!!
KRRHHHRRR . . .
TWITCH

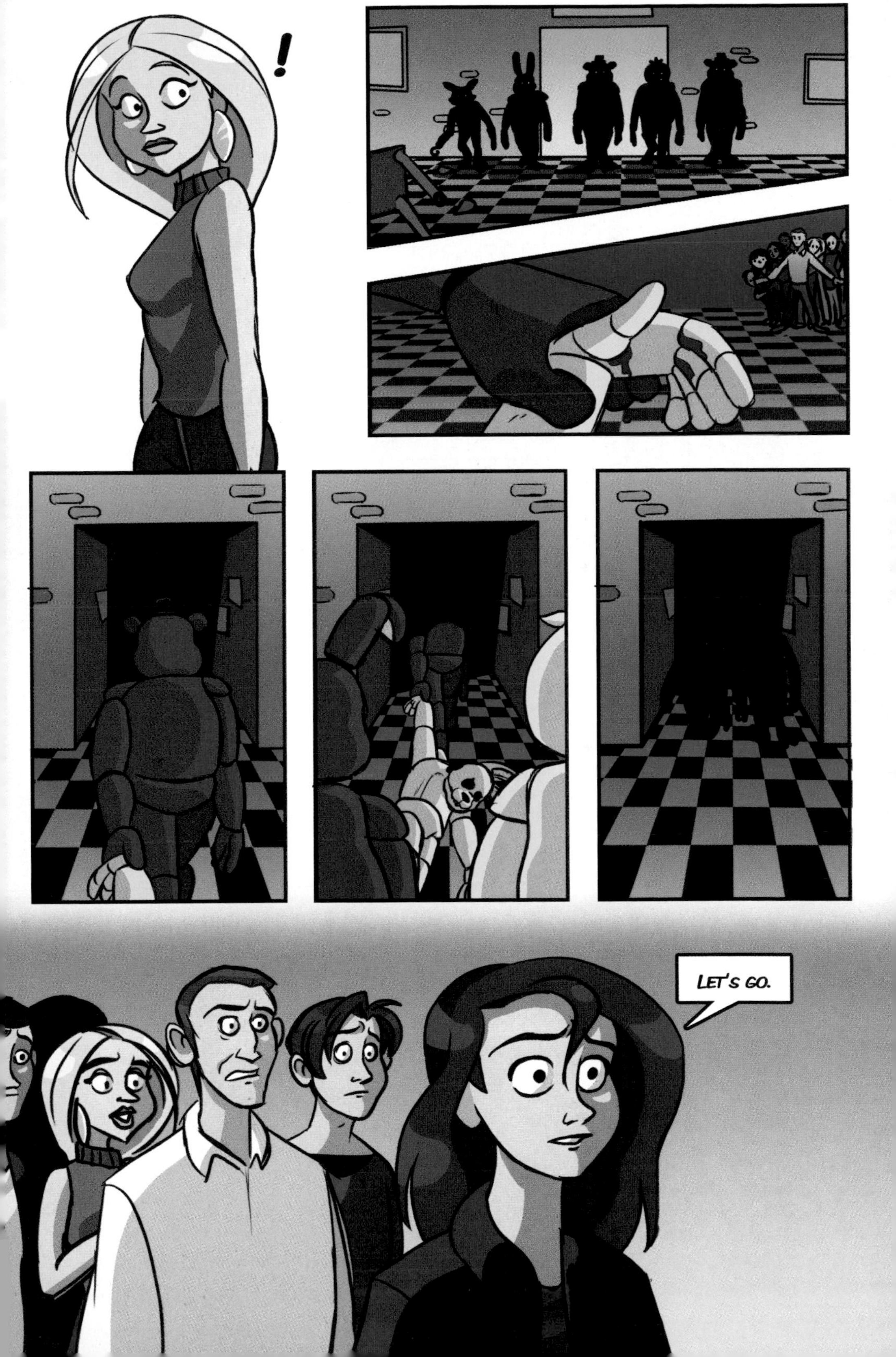
!
LET'S GO.

CHAPTER 13

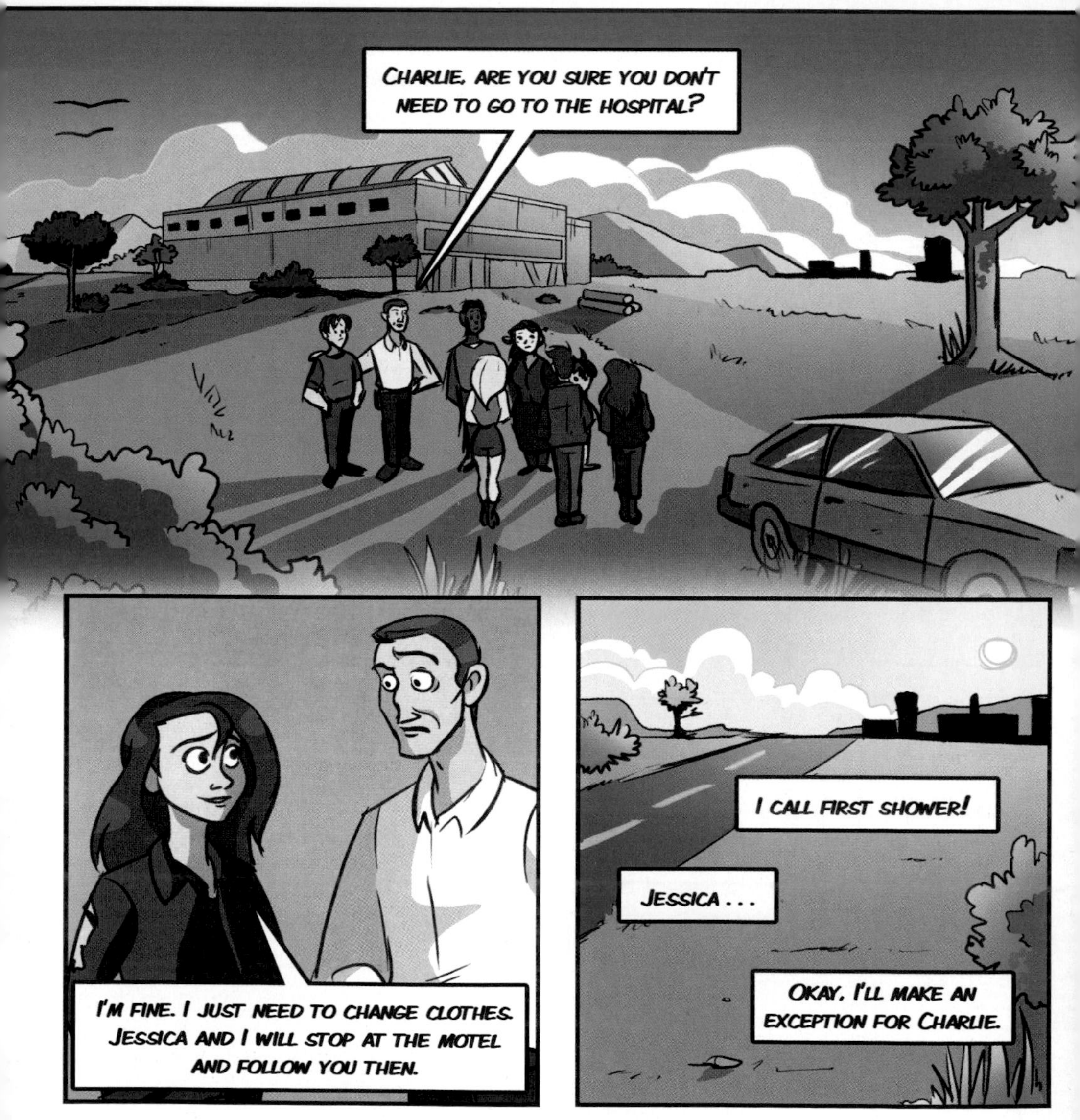
CHARLIE, ARE YOU SURE YOU DON'T NEED TO GO TO THE HOSPITAL?
I'M FINE. I JUST NEED TO CHANGE CLOTHES. JESSICA AND I WILL STOP AT THE MOTEL AND FOLLOW YOU THEN.
I CALL FIRST SHOWER!
JESSICA . . .
OKAY, I'LL MAKE AN EXCEPTION FOR CHARLIE.

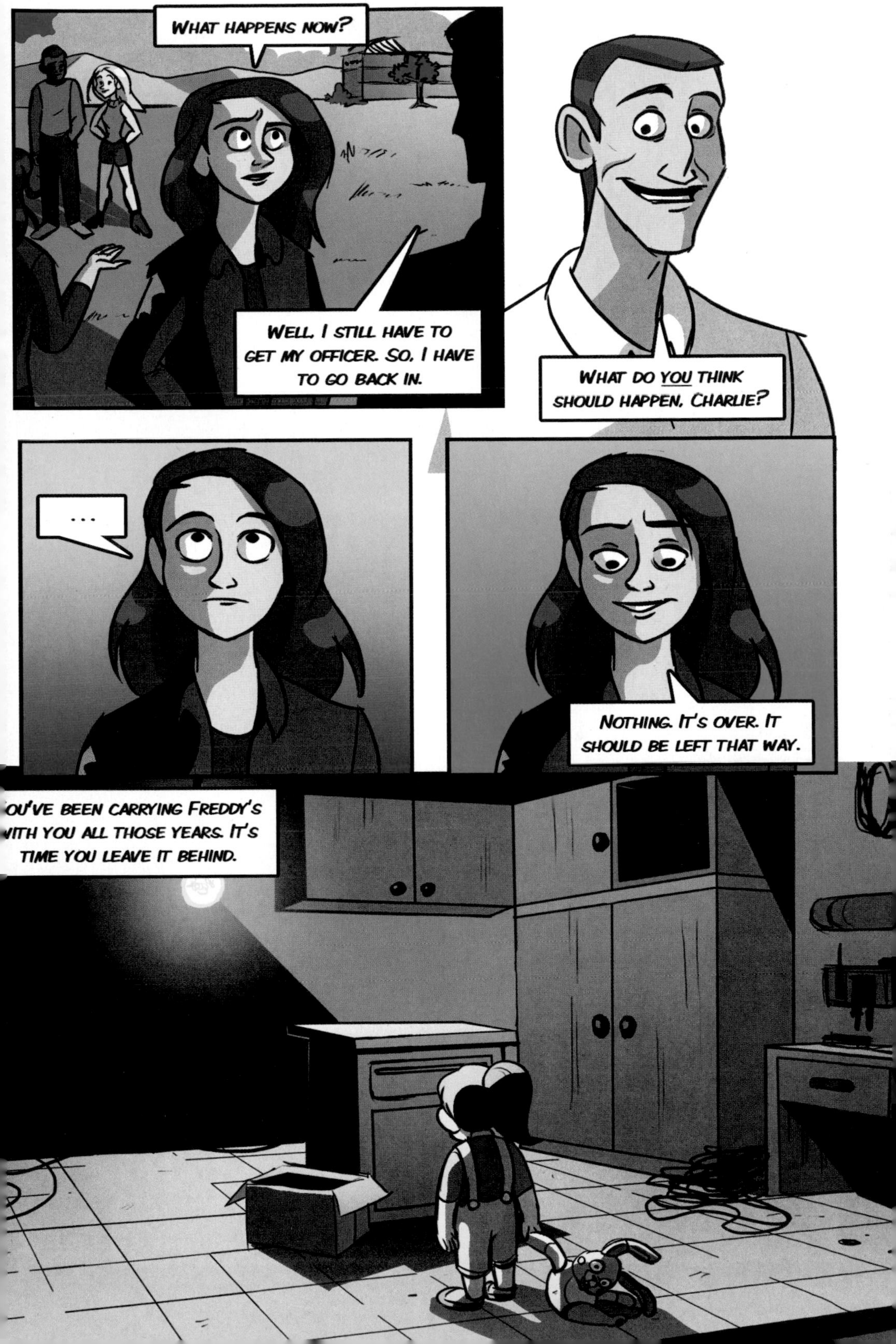
WHAT HAPPENS NOW?
WELL, I STILL HAVE TO GET MY OFFICER. SO, I HAVE TO GO BACK IN.
WHAT DO YOU THINK SHOULD HAPPEN, CHARLIE?
...
NOTHING. IT'S OVER. IT SHOULD BE LEFT THAT WAY.
OU'VE BEEN CARRYING FREDDY'S VITH YOU ALL THOSE YEARS. IT'S TIME YOU LEAVE IT BEHIND.

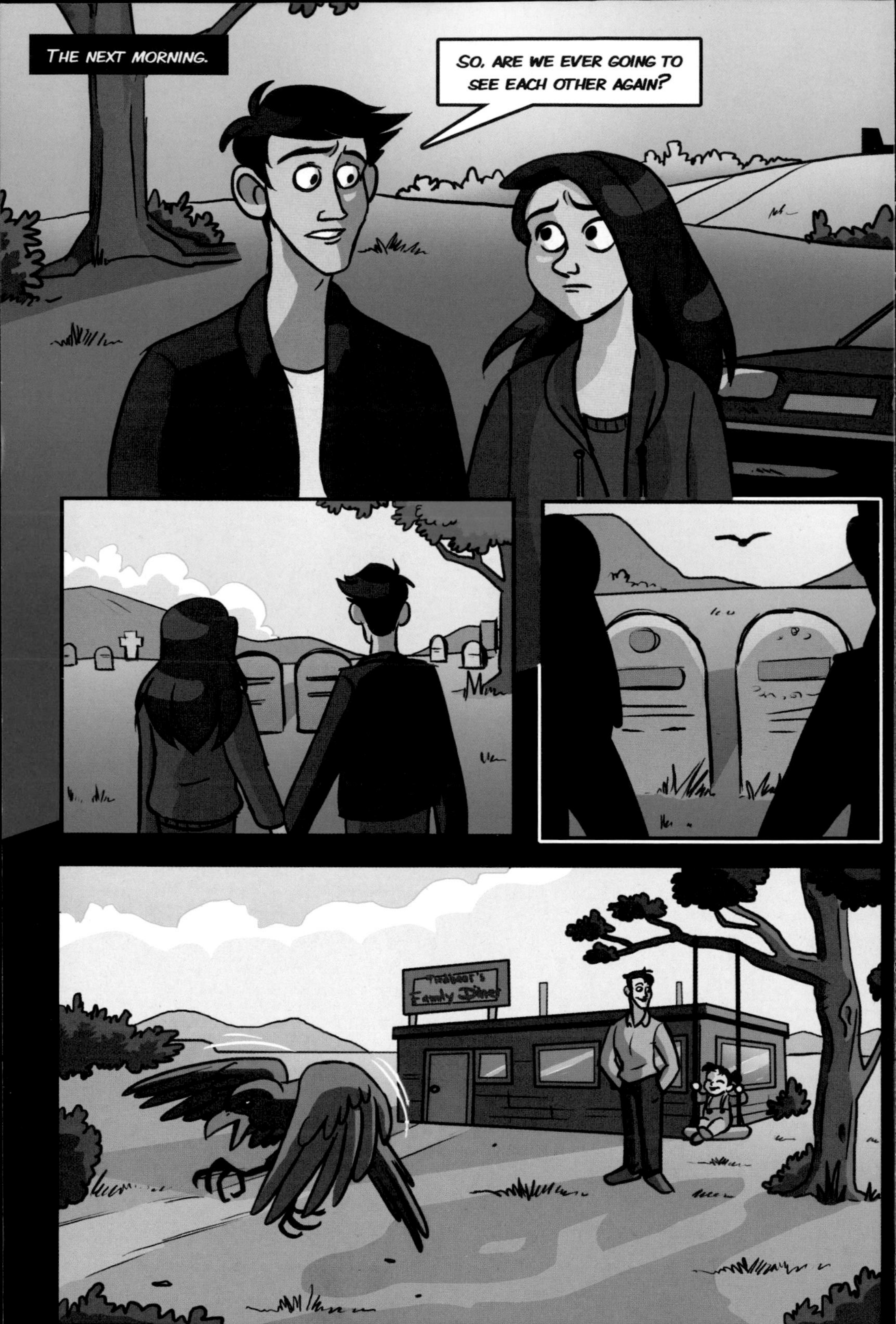
THE NEXT MORNING.
SO, ARE WE EVER GOING TO SEE EACH OTHER AGAIN?

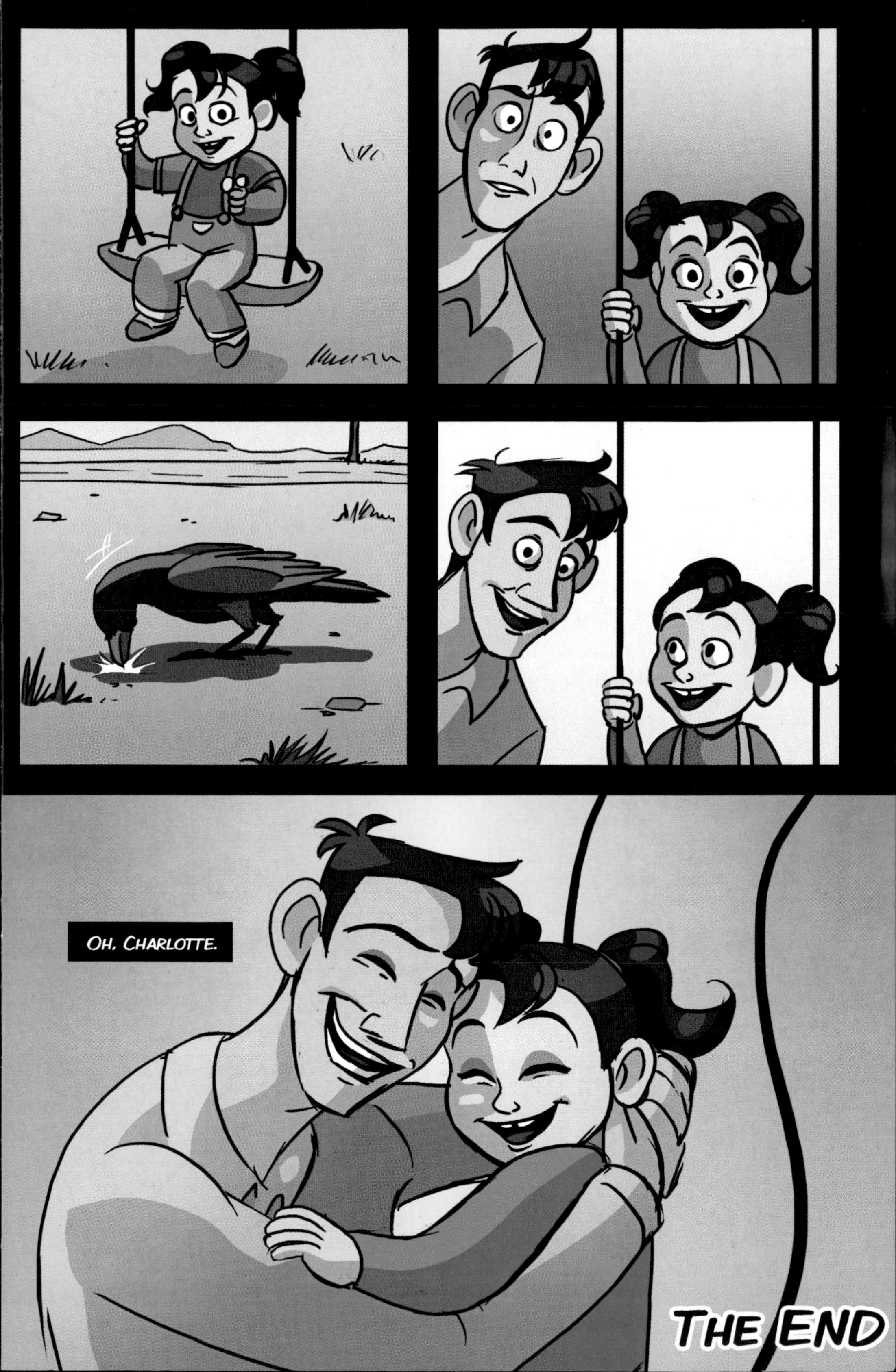
OH, CHARLOTTE.
THE END